SATAN'S ALTERNATIVE

JAMES STEVENS

First impression: 2012

Cover design: www.matthewtyson.co.uk

ISBN: 978-1-84771-482-4

Published and printed in Wales
on paper from well maintained forests by
Y Lolfa Cyf., Talybont, Ceredigion SY24 5HE
e-mail ylolfa@ylolfa.com
website www.ylolfa.com
tel 01970 832 304
fax 832 782

ABOUT THE AUTHOR

Born in 1949, Steve James (James Stevens is a pseudonym) spent his formative years in the Royal Air Force, serving mostly overseas. He began his teaching career at Rhydywaun Secondary School in Hirwaun before moving to Aberdare Boys Grammar in 1978. In 1987 he returned as head of religious studies to the school in which he was educated: Maesydderwen Comprehensive.

Retired, he holds a BE from Cardiff University and a BD in theology. This is his second novel.

AUTHOR'S COMMENT

Teaching religious education in a secular world proved a challenge at the best of times. One of the most difficult concepts to get across was the idea of a conscience. After much trial and error, I settled on an example that seemed to work for students of all ages.

"It's a little voice inside your head, the one that tells you whether something is right or wrong. Put another way, it's the voice that regulates your behaviour and dictates the actions you take throughout your life."

"Fine," said one of my more able students. "What happens if you have no little voice? What then?" she asked.

The nightmare scenario portrayed in this book might well provide the answer.

ACKNOWLEDGEMENTS

First and foremost I would like to thank Ewart Alexander, scriptwriter par excellence, and David Roberts, publishing director of BrynGold Books. Apart from setting me on the right path, they offered hope that there might be light at the end of a long, dark tunnel. And, of course, Lefi and his team from Y Lolfa for their patience and professionalism. Without them the book would never have been published.

A vote of thanks also goes to Vanessa Oloughlin and Kevin, who managed to smooth out many of the jagged edges and come up with some excellent suggestions for improving the book.

My thanks also go to Wayne and my son Ashley for their help on the computer, but in particular Howard Richards. As for proofreading, as usual, Geoff and Laurence spotted myriads of stupid mistakes.

Finally, I would like to thank all of you who helped the first time around. It may have been something as simple as a kind word of encouragement, or even a short phone call. Believe me it meant a great deal.

And, of course, a huge thank you goes to all who bought my first novel, *The Judas Codex*, in particular Mary, Paul and the family in America.

DISCLAIMER

This novel is a work of pure fiction. All characters, institutions, names, places and incidents portrayed are creations of the author's imagination. Any resemblance to actual persons, living or dead is entirely coincidental. In particular there is no secret passageway leading from the Houses of Parliament. Not that I'm aware of anyway.

Prologue

August 1945
Unit 571, human experimentation facility
Mengjiang, China

Yoshiro Immada's facial characteristics were a contradiction in terms; something created in the mind of a mad sculptor. Outwardly, he gave the impression of being a strange-looking old man. Bad tempered and vain yes, but harmless despite his faults. The reality was very different.

He almost missed the question.

"How long before we know anything positive?"

Snapping out of it, Immada glanced at his watch. "The latest results should be ready."

As always, the piercing black eyes of his young assistant were drawn to the collection of photographs covering every square inch of the office walls. Holding various poses, they showed Immada in the company of all manner of influential people. Yet, one figure appeared in almost every one, General Shiro Ishii.

He was the reason he had applied to join Unit 731. Nana-san-ichi butai, or Unit 731, had started life as a covert biological and chemical warfare research unit. It became so successful that four years later the emperor issued a decree authorising its expansion. Under the leadership of Ishii, a special project code named 'Maruta' was set up using humans for experimental purposes. Based in Harbin, a puppet state of Manchukuo, the complex covered some 6 square kilometres. Made up of more than 150 buildings, much of the work carried out was so horrific it was known locally as the Death Factory.

Like a spider's web, Unit 731 consisted of several subdivisions. Torn with indecision as to which to join, Rui had been spared an agonising dilemma when one morning Immada had appeared and offered him a post in a newly formed unit, called 571. Few people knew of its exact purpose, Immada had said, and even fewer knew of its secret location deep underground.

Immada's voice dragged Rui back to the present. "The situation in the Pacific's becoming desperate. Though pockets of resistance have dug in here and there, Japan appears doomed."

"Unless we manage to perfect the Apocalypse Virus," said Rui.

Immada was under orders to provide the emperor with an antidote for the virus. The emperor's logic was faultless: what was the point of creating something that had the capability of wiping out the whole Japanese nation as well as the enemy? The top-secret research facility was in reality nothing more than a series of underground caves. Found by accident, the military had decided to give nature a helping hand. Within a year, the subterranean complex had been converted into a huge sophisticated bio-chemical facility. Comprising four interconnected levels, the first was reached by means of an elevator from the surface. Thereafter, a series of steel staircases provided access to the lower levels, each one some twenty feet or so below the other.

The largest of the caves was situated on level four. Roofed with boxes of fragile equipment, it was used as a storage area. At the far end was a gaping chasm. On the other side of the divide stood two massive steel doors accessible by means of a narrow steel bridge. Behind the first stood a huge incinerator used for ridding the complex of failed human experiments. The second of the doors, sealed from the rest of the facility by means of numerous fail safety devices, was where the most dangerous chemical and biological agents were housed.

The primary laboratory, the one in which the two now stood was hidden from the outside world by an ingeniously camouflaged false door. Should the complex be overrun, it ensured the nest of secret laboratories would never be found. One wall was covered with steel filing cabinets; on the opposite side stood a series of tall fridges. To the left of the fridges was a row of cubicles. Inside, hanging on pegs was a selection of the latest in bio-hazard gear. The centre of the room was fitted with two rows of wooden benches, lined and edged with stainless steel. A variety of glass containers, test tubes and vials of all shapes and sizes were spread across the surfaces. The whole scene was reminiscent of a young boy's chemistry set, only hundreds of times larger and infinitely more sophisticated.

Removing a bunch of keys from a side pocket of his lab coat, Immada made his way towards the door at the back of the room. Selecting the correct key, he placed it into a large brass lock. Opening inwards, it came to rest with a loud crash on the wall behind. Entering the room was an unnerving experience. The entire right-hand side was covered with row upon row of see-through plastic booths. Sealed, each one contained a person. Neatly labelled, there were twenty in all.

The first half dozen cubicles contained the results of experiments performed with human specimens, ones which had been infected with various pandemic diseases. Live specimens were essential to the programme as previous experiments had shown the process of decomposition adversely affected results. Incredibly, a few of the pitiful creatures were still alive. Summoning reserves of energy from an unknown source, several raised their heads. A range of emotions was clearly discernible. Fear, suffering, agony, all these were apparent; the overriding one was despair. Though the cubicles were sealed, the stench of sickness and decay was everywhere. Over the months, Immada had found even the strongest disinfectants were unable to rid his body of the cloying odour of death. When he'd first started performing invasive surgery on humans, the screams had been off-putting. Since then, the tongues of each had been removed. Procuring a constant supply of healthy specimens had turned out to be problematic. Eventually, test subjects rounded up from the surrounding countryside had provided the solution. Distracted for a moment, he turned. "The experiment using plague fleas in blankets turned out to be a great success: cholera and smallpox were rampant in days. Wiped out a village of nearly 2,000 people," he chuckled.

"Survivors?" asked Rui.

"A few; the mobile team took care of them. The bodies were dumped into mass graves and covered with lime. Some of the other projects haven't fared so well. The prisoners injected with animal blood didn't last long."

Several cubicles to his right were filled with some kind of clear preservative, the contents the result of experiments gone hideously wrong. Gesturing towards number five, he said, "Take this one. Though she's alive, for some reason her skin has turned yellow."

Under their gaze, the young woman began to tremble and twitch. It was, thought Rui, like watching someone in the grip of an epileptic fit. Moments later, her eyes turned opaque, her head snapped backwards at an impossible angle, and she was gone. "Damn," cursed Immada, "we've lost another one."

While his face betrayed no emotion, his eyes told a different story. Unable to keep still, they kept darting back and forth to the other cubicles. A few moments later, nonplussed, he turned once more to Rui. "Compare her condition to number six." Tapping his teeth with the end of his pencil, he muttered, "Now what on earth could have caused those pustules?" Finally they reached the last of the cubicles. The sight was so appalling; even Immada was taken aback. Dead for some time, both corpses had bled profusely from every possible orifice. Strangely, the skin of both had turned black. A bolt of primal fear surged through the old man. Instead of providing a cure, it seemed the antidote had merely accelerated their deaths. A cold hard certainty washed over Immada. He'd given birth to something so malevolent that unless a way could be found to contain it, mankind was doomed.

About to explain his feelings to Rui, the door leading to the lab swung open. Thinking it was one of his colleagues, he was astonished to see a figure dressed in military uniform enter the room. Approaching, the old man's powerful spectacles took over and the rugged arrogant features of the stranger came into sharp relief. Used to giving orders, more importantly to having them obeyed, Immada knew instinctively that the man was a high-ranking officer. It was bad news, he was certain. His suspicions were confirmed by the bullying tone of the man's voice. "What is the situation regarding the Apocalypse Virus? The emperor demands a firm date for mass production."

A white lie at this stage of the game, was, Immada knew, neither here nor there. "The latest tests are highly promising. Another few weeks and we will have the answer. I'm sure of it."

At his reply the ghost of a reaction appeared in the officer's eyes. "Time is the one commodity we have little of. With the Red Army at our doorstep, you are to close down the facility and destroy the virus. Arrangements have been made for the more senior scientists to return home. But, you must act quickly. Am I making myself clear, little man?"

Having delivered his ultimatum, the figure bowed from the waist, turned on his heels and disappeared. Rooted to the spot, Immada eventually regained his composure. Addressing Rui, he said, "Given time I could have found an answer. Sadly, it seems fate has decreed otherwise."

Suddenly he felt an involuntary rush of affection for his young assistant. A genetic defect had left his skin almost translucent. So pale, he often appeared less healthy than the specimens they experimented on. Despite the abnormality, it was not what people remembered about him. Instead, it was his eyes. The colour of black anthracite, they were cold and piercing. Once seen they were never forgotten.

"Take this," said Immada, removing a key from around his neck, "it fits the safe in my office. Inside you will find a leather briefcase containing letters of introduction to friends of mine. Should you survive, they will prove invaluable. Besides the letter are several files describing what I regard as some of my most significant breakthroughs. One more thing, hidden in one of the side compartments is a pouch containing a handful of diamonds. Used wisely, they could make you a wealthy man. Now, off with you, get the briefcase."

Yards from the door, a troubled feeling began to gnaw at Rui. Turning he was in time to see a pistol appear from Immada's coat pocket. A second later, the back of the old man's head exploded outwards, accompanied by a fine red mist and shards of bone and brain cartilage. Stunned, the implications of what he had just witnessed struck Rui. He was no longer part of an elite group working on a project deemed priority one by the emperor. Worse, he had lost his guide and mentor. Standing over the body, he made a silent vow. Should he survive, he would continue Immada's work, whatever the cost. Retrieving the bunch of keys from the old man's pocket, he steeled himself for the task ahead. Stepping into the adjoining laboratory, he suited up. Approaching the sealed glass case, he manipulated the steel arm. Lifting the Apocalypse Virus from its resting place inside, he placed it carefully into a small aluminium cylinder. It took an age to accomplish, but when dealing with something as deadly as this, Rui knew that safety was of the essence. Moving the cylinder towards the outer edge of the case, he inserted it into a small square opening. Free of the casing, the flap closed automatically. Removing the contents gingerly, he placed the cylinder inside a large steel container which looked remarkably like a thermos flask. Finally, he screwed the top down tightly before placing it inside one of the huge fridges nearby. Only then did he allow himself to relax. Heading for the outer laboratory, he de-suited. Calmer now, he retraced his steps to Immada's office. Opening the safe, the leather briefcase was lying snugly on the bottom shelf. Undoing the clasps hurriedly, he looked inside. The files and journal were there, as were the diamonds.

Leaving the room, Rui was filled with conflicting emotions. A feeling of profound sadness was offset by wonder – wonder at how in a heartbeat his life had been altered forever. Standing outside the laboratory door, he glanced right and left. Seeing no one, he applied pressure to the hidden lever. After the slightest of delays, the spring-loaded catch came to life. Suddenly, a section of the wall moved slowly into place. The facility was now sealed from the outside world. It was then he remembered: the next batch of human specimens had been prepared for tomorrow. Trapped inside their Perspex coffins, they would die agonising deaths. Not that it mattered, thought Rui: they were no more than lab rats anyway.

ONE

THE EARLY MORNING silence was broached by the noise of an approaching vehicle. Bursting into the clearing, the tread of the Land Cruiser's tyres threw up handfuls of stones and loose chippings. Clattering against the side of the bodywork they made a loud metallic sound. Coming to a stop in a cloud of dust, the driver killed the engine and stepped out.

"Years since I've been to this neck of the woods," said Dan, turning to his new partner. "Roads seen use recently though. Not exactly the M1, but look here," he said pointing to the floor. "Fresh tracks; deep, too, whatever made them was heavy."

Approaching sixty, Dan Dempsey had spent forty years working on the railways. There was little he didn't know about the underground. It annoyed him when colleagues said they knew every inch of the tunnels in and around London. A crock of shit was his take on things. In his opinion you could spend a hundred years working the maze beneath his feet and still only scratch the surface.

Dan was feeling sorry for himself. His usual partner was off sick, again, and so he'd been landed with a young apprentice. And not a very bright one if the odd word they'd shared on the way over was anything to go by. Having two kids of his own, he knew that having any kind of meaningful conversation with the youth of today was difficult. Every other sentence seemed to be punctuated with, 'cool', 'like' or 'you know', which he assumed was the 'in' thing. Though he knew every era had its ritualised patter, he couldn't help but feel the phrases in vogue these days were more irritating than most. Whatever the reasoning behind their choice of words, one conclusion was inescapable, verbal contact was usually limited to one-word answers or grunts. Unless it came to asking for money, he thought wryly.

"What we supposed to be doing?" shot the youngster.

"Gaffer said something about late-night goings on, wants us to take a look below."

Hefting his work bag from the tail gate, Dan closed the hatch and switched on the alarm.

"How are we going to get down there? Underground, I mean?" said the bemused youngster.

"That's the interesting bit," said a smiling Dan. "Only way is through that manhole over there."

"You're bloody joking," was the astonished response.

"Before we start, I'd better call in."

Removing the mobile from the pocket of his overalls, Dan flicked open the cover and punched in the numbers with his thumb. He wasn't hopeful, past experience had shown that reception was notoriously patchy in this area. A dead zone, they called it. On cue the words 'no signal available' appeared. Staring at the offending object angrily, Dan attempted a response by willing it to work. When that failed he resorted to a more time-honoured method and swore at it. It made no difference. The signal bars stubbornly refused to cooperate. Sighing wearily, he returned the mobile to his pocket.

"Seems we're on our own, kid," said Dan.

"Not dangerous is it?"

"Course not. Hope you're not claustrophobic, though."

Seeing the lad didn't have a clue what he was on about, Dan let it go. A few yards further on, Dan stopped. Lowering the bag from his shoulder he removed two steel rods. "Here, give me a hand with these."

Inserting them into the allotted grooves of the cast iron manhole, he muttered, "Things are buggers to shift at the best of times. Hold onto your hat. Ready? Now heave."

Grunting with exhaustion they managed to move it sideways inch by inch until, finally, with one last heave it fell to the floor. Lowering themselves carefully through the mouth of the narrow opening, the pair clambered down a succession of steel ladders until a short time later they reached the bottom. Allowing a few moments for his eyes to adjust to the gloom, Dan pushed forward with vigour. Following closely behind, the youngster gazed in awe at the labyrinth of small openings dotted at each side of the narrow tunnel. In places the low-vaulted ceiling seemed mere inches above their heads. Overhead, bulbs spread at regular intervals made loud buzzing noises. Several flickered erratically while disturbingly a good many others seemed to have given up the ghost. Covered in slime and dripping in places with God knows what, none of it appeared to faze Dan.

Nervous, the youngster kept glancing over his shoulder. To his mind it was a place for rats and spiders rather than humans, and he let out an audible sigh of relief when Dan switched on his heavy duty torch. Hooking a sharp right-hand corner Dan almost collided with a huge steel door. In pristine condition it was emblazoned with the words 'Danger keep out'.

"That's new," said Dan, rubbing his hand over a two-day growth of stubble. Puzzled, he added, "We've no way of getting inside even if I had a key." Pointing to a rectangular box-like structure at roughly shoulder height he said, "that's a fancy digital code system. Why the hell they'd want such a device down here's beyond me."

About to form a reply, Dan silenced the youngster. He'd heard a noise. Diving for cover, they were just in time as the door opened and a figure wearing what looked like a bio-hazard suit appeared. In moments it had disappeared down the dark concrete walkway. Dan noticed that for some reason the door hadn't closed fully. The temptation was too much. Ignoring the warning bells ringing in his head, he made a decision.

Easing the door open an inch at a time, it was a while before he gathered the confidence to enter. Leading the way hesitantly, his curiosity quickly turned to astonishment. What he was looking at was unbelievable. One glance was enough to tell him the shelter was designed to be self-sufficient for at least six months to a year. To his right, attached to the wall, was a colour-coded map of the complex. Taking a moment to get his bearings, he made his way towards the first door. The room appeared to be some kind of dormitory. Further on was a purpose-built kitchen complete with walk-in refrigerators. Opening one he was astonished to find it contained all kinds of delicacies. Behind it was a smaller room stocked with hundreds of cases of beers, wines and spirits. Though he had seen only a little of the facility, it was enough. With a growing sense of unease, he wondered what the hell they'd stumbled across. He'd once read somewhere that successive governments had built underground shelters in the event of biological or nuclear attacks by terrorists. Was this what he was looking at here, he mused?

Until now the youngster hadn't uttered a word. Suddenly, he found his voice. "It's like the fucking Tardis."

"Tardis or not," Dan replied, "we'd better get out of here before it's too late."

Unfortunately, it was already too late. The minute they'd entered the shelter, overhead CCTV cameras had picked them up. From then on their every move had been monitored. Removing the phone from its cradle, Medusa said, "I take it you're watching?"

"Affirmative. I'll take care of it immediately," came the reply.

Andreas Lucifer ex-spetsnaz was a man of few words. A product of one of the toughest fighting units in the world, his propensity for mindless violence had eventually become too much for even them. Aware he had a strange name he'd been amazed when he found out its true meaning. In its original form Lucifer meant 'bringer of light'. However, as the 'bringer of death', as he liked to think of himself, he'd immediately seen the funny side.

The pair had almost reached the door when Lucifer materialised. For Dan, death was instantaneous. Coming to his senses, the youngster did the only thing he could. Turning on his heels, he ran towards the safety of the shelter. Shot in the back he was thrown forward violently. Finding reserves of energy he never knew he possessed, he somehow managed to roll onto his back.

Gazing up at the huge figure standing over him, he noticed that the man was smiling. Bending over, Lucifer forced the tip of the weapon into the kid's mouth. Then, in a sadistic attempt to prolong the agony, he waited a few seconds before throwing a theatrical salute and pulling the trigger.

The chopper came in low, cresting the waves which broke over the reef some two hundred yards off shore. Of American design the Sikorsky HH-60 Pave Hawk, the US Air force version of the UH-60 Black Hawk, was a modified search and rescue model.

Situated to the south of Sri Lanka, the Maldives is made up of 1,190 coral reef islands and is often referred to as the last paradise on earth. The majority of the islands are uninhabited, making it ideal for what the pilot had in mind. A seven-day exercise in survival was what the participants had been told. Though it had raised a few eyebrows, for what they were being paid, they would have been prepared to do anything.

Risking a glance over his shoulder, the pilot noted preparations were at an advanced stage. Satisfied, he concentrated on providing a stable platform for their descent. The two passengers were ex-military. Mercenaries now, they sold their services to the highest bidder. Selected for the mission on the grounds each had no family ties, strangely none had queried the oddity. Dressed identically in camouflage trousers, short-sleeved T-shirts and combat boots, vicious-looking hunting knives were strapped to their thighs.

A few minor last-minute adjustments and they were ready. Moments later they made their exit. With practised ease they rappelled the fifty or so feet to the beach. Unhitching their safety harnesses, they dumped their gear onto the sand. Knowing the pilot was on a tight schedule they raised their heads skywards and brushed the forefingers of their right hands across their cheeks in the time-honoured salute. Acknowledging their thanks with a wave of his own, the pilot banked sharply and headed out to sea. In moments, the chopper was nothing but a speck on the distant horizon. Seconds later, it had disappeared completely.

Retrieving his kit bag, the leader hefted it onto his shoulder. Gazing around the small island, he took time to savour the foreign sights and smells, allowing them to filter through his sensory organs. By now the sun was brutal, and so without further preamble he headed for the welcoming shelter of the nearest stand of coconut palms.

A month later the helicopter returned. "That's odd," said the solitary passenger, speaking through the built-in microphone of his helmet, "Place seems deserted. Must be on the other side of the island," he muttered, while buckling on his safety harness.

It took him less than two minutes to find the bodies, the rank smell of death leading him to his target. Removing his T-shirt, he wrapped it around his face and approached the doorway of the makeshift hut. Inside he was greeted by an angry black cloud. Huge blue bottles, engorged on the blood of the victims were darting everywhere. Flying into the walls of the hut, it was as if their radars had malfunctioned.

Tearing his eyes from the scene, it was then he noticed what they'd been feasting on. It was several moments before he managed to pull himself together. Close scrutiny revealed the bodies had turned black in places, in particular the area of the armpits and fingers. Faces frozen in silent screams, they bore mute testimony to the horrific way in which they'd perished. Turning on his heels, he ran back to the helicopter. Using the hand-held radio strapped to his waist he relayed a graphic description of the state of the bodies, along with a request as to what to do.

"Jesus H. Christ," came back the reply, "how the hell should I know, I'm only a fucking chopper pilot."

Several seconds of intense silence was finally broken by the exclamation, "Wait, wait, I've got an idea. I'm going to throw out a can of gasoline and some flares. When you've got them, go back to the hut, pour the fuel over the bodies and set fire to everything."

"Why the hell do you want to burn the bodies?" was the astonished response.

"From your description it looks as if they've contracted some kind of infectious disease. In that case fire is the only sure way of cleansing the site, so don't bloody argue, just get on with it."

In his confusion it never crossed the man's mind to wonder why a run-of-the-mill pilot should know so much about infectious diseases or, more importantly, why he just so happened to have the flares and gasoline handy. Instead, his first thought was for his own safety.

"What about me?" he pleaded. "If it was something like a fucking plague, I'll catch it, won't I?"

The lie rolled off the pilot's lips with practised ease. "No chance, whatever it was will be long gone. Burning the bodies is just a precaution."

Hefting the can and flares out of the window they landed on the beach in a flurry of sand. Shortly afterwards the first wisp of smoke drifted towards him over the palm trees, followed immediately by a thick black cloud. The lone figure ran along the shore as if the hounds of hell were at his heels. Waving frantically he indicated for the chopper to land. Alighting softly, M16 in hand, the pilot took careful aim. Taking a deep breath, he squeezed the trigger gently. A loud retort was followed by a look of complete bewilderment as the figure collapsed to his knees in what looked amusingly like an act of supplication. Half his head missing the man eventually toppled sideways. Within seconds, the sand was stained bright red as blood leaking from the remnants of his shattered skull settled around him like a crimson halo. His task complete, the pilot took to the air hurriedly.

Lucifer had warned him the stuff was lethal. Yet, though he had once been a military doctor, never in his wildest dreams had he guessed anything could act so quickly and efficiently. His instructions to sanitise the area now made perfect sense.

Two

Friday, 16 November 2012
9.00 a.m.
10 Downing Street

CHARLES HILLARY GAZED at his reflection in the mirror. He was looking at a stranger: the worry of the previous few months had seen the pounds drop away alarmingly. A fact even his skilfully tailored suits could no longer disguise.

On being elected prime minister, he'd resolved to reintroduce the 'Great' into Great Britain once more. And in reality he'd been successful. During his tenure, the stock markets had risen to dizzying new heights while the economy had blossomed as never before. Unemployment had been at a record low. Then, out of the blue, things had taken a downward turn. One he was at a loss to halt.

Brushing aside negative thoughts, he filled the washbasin with ice cold water. Splashing his face lightly, he felt better. Emptying the basin, he picked up a towel. Drying himself vigorously, he folded it neatly before threading it through the chrome ring holder which was its home. Recovering his suit jacket from the back of the chair, he placed it over his frail shoulders. A final look in the mirror, a minor adjustment to his tie and he was ready.

Stepping out of the bathroom housed on the second floor, he turned right and headed for his private study. Not only was it his favourite room, it was also where he did most of his thinking. Following in the footsteps of Ramsey McDonald, he had opted to furnish the house with art borrowed from national galleries. The more easily recognisable were scattered around the house, hung in places of strategic importance. Staring at the painting above the fireplace, until today it had never failed to lift his spirits. This morning, however, even Cézanne seemed unable to overthrow his mood of dejection.

Making his way towards the larger of two substantial windows, he reflected on how the quiet facade of the famous black door had guarded many a state secret. Over the decades, but in particular during the course of two world wars, it had been the setting for many a clandestine activity. Riots, passionate protests, think tanks, matters of life and death – the old building had seen them all. A loud rap on the door dragged him out of his reverie. "Enter, he shouted."

Turning from the window, he saw Matthew Denning, minister for finance, approach carrying a bundle of mail and several copies of the morning newspapers. One of his oldest and dearest friends, Matthew was the one member of the cabinet who he could talk to freely. And he needed to talk; to unburden himself.

The grim expression told the PM that there was yet more trouble looming.

"Spit it out," he said wearily.

"Before we get down to business," replied Matthew, "Stanford asked me to bring a few things to your attention. Ever heard of a village called Sanctuary?"

A shake of the head indicated that the PM hadn't.

"Neither had I, so I looked it up. Set in the heart of Wales it's in the back of beyond. Until a few years ago the only thing it had going for it was an open-cast mine. Now even that's closed. Normally it wouldn't have raised a ripple on the radar except that several years ago an eccentric billionaire called Rui Medusa built a sophisticated genetic research facility there. Set deep in the heart of the mountain, we decided to keep an eye on things. Till recently everything seemed above board. During the last twelve months or so, however, rumours have been surfacing that some very unusual work is being conducted there."

"Unusual in what way," asked the PM, raising his eyebrows.

"We've nothing concrete to go on, simply rumours and the odd report from the local police. But one thing's certain: something untoward is taking place."

"The second point?"

"Several young children have gone missing in the same village. It's as if they've disappeared into a black hole. Nigel Adkins, the Liberal Democrat representative for Powys has been making waves on their behalf for months. More recently a rally took place in Trafalgar Square. Organised by the local vicar, most of the village turned up; caused quite a stir. Anyway, the firm would like your permission to look into things."

"Granted," came the reply. "Tell Stanford to organise things. There's something else though, isn't there?" said the PM shrewdly.

"During the last few days a few strange incidents have had the media drooling. The first involves the discovery of three bodies on a remote Maldivian atoll. Two were burnt beyond recognition; the third had half his head blown away. Not the kind of thing you normally associate with the Maldives, is it? Had it not been for one of our junior ministers holidaying in Mali, the capital, the incident might never have come to our attention. Something smells and so young Thomas has volunteered to hang around until the local forensic boys have identified the corpses."

"And the other oddity?" enquired the PM.

"Concerns the disappearance of two workers conducting a routine survey of the underground near Down Street tube station. Reported missing days ago, there's been no sign of them since. Unsurprisingly, the bizarre incident hit the front page of several of the tabloids."

Pensive for a moment, the PM said, "I know something of the old stations history. Close proximity to the much larger stations at Hyde Park and Dover Street meant it was never busy. The final nail in the coffin arrived when Dover Street was refurbished. After that it was bricked up. Its location remained something of a mystery until Winston Churchill decided to use it as a secret bunker and war room. Never appeared on any map or diagram, was even given a fictitious address to make sure it's real location was kept a closely guarded secret."

"Thought the name rang a bell," said Matthew. "Site's been open to the public for the last few years, hasn't it? Conducted tours around the war room and all that?"

"Until someone decided the whole thing needed a face lift," answered the PM. "For months now the station's been undergoing extensive renovation."

"Hadn't heard about that," said Matthew.

"Seeing the cost of the operation was donated by a private benefactor, you wouldn't have," the PM replied smiling. "Whole system is a labyrinth of tunnels and corridors, couldn't the workers have simply got lost?"

"Precisely what the company thought," said Matthew, "but one of the two was highly experienced, so it hardly seems likely."

Making his way back to the window, hands clasped behind his back, the PM continued, "Let's pretend it's the good old days. Considering the present circumstances," he added, "the good old days seem a life time away, don't they?"

In reality, it was nearly three years since the credit crunch had arrived. Like an avenging angel it had effectively crippled the country. No, not the country, he thought, that analogy was wrong. It was a global problem. Still, that was no comfort to the people he had sworn to serve. They weren't really interested in what was happening on the other side of the world, only what was happening to them. He wasn't even sure if they gave a shit about their partners in Europe. A partnership was only a partnership when things were going well, wasn't it? Now that things had gone – for want of a better phrase – 'tits up', such admirable sentiments had flown out of the window.

Where had it all gone wrong? He supposed it was an easy question to answer. The previous decade of unparalleled plenty had been built on trust. Since earliest times it had been common practice for the man in the street to have trust in their elected officials. And while the wheels of big business were turning over smoothly, people were prepared to turn a blind eye to the fact that some of those officials were making huge personal profits. Gradually, however, a subtle change had taken place in the corridors of power. Drunk with wealth and self-importance, the fat cats began to elevate themselves to god-like status. Deciding laws and regulations were for mere mortals, in a single stroke, the golden rules of finance, ones established over centuries, were set aside. In their minds, they could be ignored, broken or simply bent. Depending, of course, on how it suited their purpose.

Refocusing, the PM carried on. "So, Matthew, my lack of judgement has come back to haunt me. As minister for finance, you warned the cabinet about problems in world banking years ago. Deciding the crisis was short term I foolishly gambled on riding out the storm."

But Matthew hadn't stopped there: he had explained that there were serious problems closer to home. A sudden sharp rise in unemployment allied to enormous debts piled up by people using credit cards would result in chaos. Like a moth caught in the flame, he had asked the million dollar question. What would happen if the crunch should arrive? The best case scenario, according to Matthew, was that the world's stock markets would go into free fall. People everywhere would lose fortunes. But, on the whole, mankind would survive. The worst case scenario was appalling – Armageddon. In this instance, the world's money markets would never recover. People would turn on each other, neighbour against neighbour and nation against nation. In short, people would do whatever it took to protect their families and survive.

Shuddering at the grim picture, he had never forgotten Matthew's words: words that had turned out to be chillingly prophetic. Going off at a tangent, a deeply repentant Charles Hillary said, "Was there anything I could have done that might have saved the country?"

Matthew took a minute before answering. "If you want a philosophical answer, I'd say no. As a species, we seemed to have been doomed from the beginning. Once Eve took a bite out of that bloody apple," he said. "More seriously, the foundations that once held society together have been crumbling for years. And the result? The real 'us', as Freud would say, has been allowed to surface. So, yes, I know exactly what happened. But, if it's answers you're looking for, I'm afraid I've none. If there's one consolation, Charles, the problems we're facing are worldwide."

"True," came the reply, "but you'd think that with all the brainpower available to us globally, we world leaders would be able to come up with some kind of answer. I'd give a year's salary to find someone who could offer a solution."

Looking at the PM's earnest expression, Matthew Denning knew it was no idle boast.

Listening in on the conversation, Medusa knew that he had struck gold. He'd been quietly confident that Charles Hillary would take the bait and after what he had just heard he was more confident than ever. The main problem was whether he would be prepared to come alone. Knowing how desperate the PM viewed the situation, he was willing to wager that he would see the invitation as a last throw of the dice and take a gamble. He was surprised at how quickly they had found the bodies in the Maldives. The atoll was so remote that he'd thought they might never be found. Risky, the experiment had been essential. It was the only way he could find out whether his calculations concerning the potency of the virus were correct. Not that he was worried, by the time the authorities had identified the mercenaries as being on his pay roll it would be too late. As for the underground workers, that had simply been a case of being in the wrong place at the wrong time.

Allowing himself a tinge of nostalgia, he remembered reading somewhere that, statistically, mankind's patronage of earth was nothing but a tiny fraction in relation to how long the world had been in existence. The author had taken the example of Nelson's Column as a way of getting his point across: place a postage stamp and lay it flat on his head, and the thickness of that stamp in relation to the height of the column is how long we humans have been around.

Impressive, thought Medusa, until he realised just how quickly humans had taken to destroy a once beautiful planet. Worryingly, no one was prepared to take responsibility for their actions. Like ostriches burying their heads in the sand, the world was pretending it was simply a matter of time before things took a turn for the better. Everyone was expecting a magical solution. There wasn't one.

But there was an answer. And he Medusa had it.

The shrill buzzing of the phone cut through Charles Hillary's train of thought. Puzzled, he lifted the receiver from its cradle. His bemusement increased when he realised the voice at the other end belonged to a total stranger. How the hell had he managed to get his private number?

Matthew Denning watched spellbound as the internal conflicts raging inside the PM slowly reached his face. In seconds the range of emotions went from anger, to astonishment and finally downright incredulity. Few, if any, had the power to elicit such a strong reaction from the normally unflappable Charles Hillary. And so he was left wondering who it was.

He didn't have long to wait. Replacing the telephone with a loud crash, the PM exploded into action. Gone was the guilt-ridden PM of moments ago, to be replaced by the old decisive Charles Hillary. Gesturing to Matthew, he headed for his private bathroom. Once there he turned the shower and taps onto full power. Beckoning him close, he whispered, "When we've finished discussing arrangements, I want you to get security. Tell them to bring their high-tech surveillance gadgets. Our whole conversation was bugged. Saw a film once where the hero did the same thing. Apparently the sound of running water makes it impossible to eavesdrop."

"But the building's swept nightly," said Matthew.

Struggling to keep a lid on his temper, the PM said, "I know – it was at my insistence. Yet, someone has found a way to get around our security measures. The person on the other end of that line," he said pointing at the phone, "could tell me the entire contents of our conversation."

"Blackmail?" asked Matthew quizzically.

"Oddly enough, no. Wants a meeting. He's convinced there is a way out of the present world crisis. Seems he has a sense of humour too, told me should I accept his radical proposal, he wouldn't hold me to my offer."

Seeing Matthew's expression, he elaborated, "To give up a year's wages. There's one stipulation: I have to go alone."

"Surely to God you're not contemplating it," said Matthew, in astonishment. "That would be bloody madness."

"Desperate times require desperate measures," said Charles.

Relaxing somewhat, Matthew replied, "Excellent sentiments and I applaud your reasoning, but forget it, security would never sanction it."

"They wouldn't have to know, would they," replied Charles Hillary. "On a more serious note, the alternative appears to be martial law and to prevent that I'm willing to clutch at any straw." Unknown to anyone, even Matthew, after yet another sleepless night he had come to a decision. This was to be his last term in office. He was no quitter, but he was tired both physically and mentally. The country needed fresh ideas, a new impetus – neither of which he was able to provide any more. And so, despite the obvious dangers, if there was the slightest chance this character had a solution to the country's problems, he was willing to put his body on the line. He owed his people that much.

With the ghost of a smile, the PM said, "Now go and find security."

Shortly after the PM had returned to the study, Matthew appeared with two men, one of whom was carrying what looked suspiciously like a miniature Geiger counter.

The bulkier of the two said, "Just heard sir, my immediate reaction is it's impossible. The room is swept every night. Apart from the cleaners, no one has access until you arrive."

"I know, but it's not a pleasant experience having what you thought was a private conversation recounted to you word for word. There must be some way of ensuring privacy in your own office, for God's sake?"

"Short of using a screen room, which, in layman's terms, is a space enclosed by a grounded ferromagnetic mesh gauze capable of blocking out the transmission of radio frequency signals, there isn't, I'm afraid."

"Glad you gave me the layman's version," said the PM, with a trace of his normal good humour.

Chuckling, the head of security said, "If it's here, sir, we'll find it. That's a promise."

Ten minutes later, after every square inch had been covered they were puzzled.

"I'm sorry, sir, the room is clean. Our equipment is so sensitive, if there was anything to find, it would have found it."

Waiting until the two figures had exited the room, Charles Hillary finally turned his gaze on Matthew, "If the best money can buy can't solve the problem of whose bugging us, we must be up against some very powerful people."

THREE

Saturday, 24 November 2012
7.00 p.m.
TGA Studios, London

DEATH WAS COMING. At present it was no more than a distant echo. One thing was certain, with each passing day it would get louder until finally the grim reaper would arrive in person. Considering his age, it was hardly surprising. He'd tried to visualise death, but all he had managed to create was a vision of vast emptiness. Maybe there was another world beyond this one, but he doubted it. In his opinion, the only thing waiting on the other side was darkness: a pitiless void.

Despite the assurance of his grossly overpaid specialist, that he had at least a year before the cancer claimed him, he knew differently. He could already feel the disease gnawing at his brain. Chemotherapy was out of the question: his frail body would never survive the treatment.

Receiving the news the tumour was inoperable, despair hadn't been his overriding emotion. It was relief. Relief that there was yet time to see a lifetime's work come to fruition. Time to fulfil a promise made to a dead man.

Labelled 'Genesis', the foundations had been laid decades ago. Stage one, the construction of underground facilities placed in hidden locations around the globe was complete. Stage two, adapting the virus to suit his purpose had proved to be far more difficult than he had envisaged. Retrieving a sample had been straightforward: the facility had been left untouched since the end of the war.

Struggling to find an antidote, he had been at his wits' end. It was then that he had struck lucky. Through a process of trial and error, he'd discovered the potency of the virus had a limited time span. Amazingly, after a period of roughly fourteen days, it became harmless. The experiment in the Maldives had confirmed his findings.

Stage three, genetically engineering the race of 'super beings' Immada had envisaged had been beyond one person. A brilliant young scientist called Anna Heche, allied to his old mentor's notes, seemed to have worked. According to the latest report, success was a matter of weeks away.

The biggest stumbling block had been the quantity of children required for Anna's work. In the old days all that had been taken care of. For a while it had been a real headache. Eventually, a solution was found. And it had been simple.

Thousands of youngsters left home every year without a word. The majority of parents, after spending vast sums of money on fruitless searches, finally gave up. Yes, there were always bodies to be found, providing of course you had no conscience and were willing to pay the right price. Devoid of the first, but endowed with vast amounts of the latter, he had eventually found what Anna had needed.

And, of course, there had been the village.

Cocooned in his sumptuous leather armchair, Medusa stared at the forty-two inch plasma screen. In thirty minutes, the programme would be on the lips of everyone in Britain. An hour or so later and the world would be talking about it.

Sipping vintage brandy, he studied the amber liquid as it swirled around the glass. According to medical journals, a man of his age should be drinking whiskey. Whiskey thinned the blood, brandy thickened it. But he didn't like the taste of whiskey.

The tune heralding the beginning of the popular chat show startled him. A quick pan of the audience showed the studio full to capacity. Then the camera focused on the host of the show,

Tony Morel. Smiling broadly, he slipped with oily smoothness into his well-rehearsed patter.

"Ladies and gentlemen, please welcome today's special guest, Dr Takeshi. Born in Japan, the doctor has been a resident in our country for over ten years." After the slightest of pauses, he added, "Considering the amount of immigrants residing here these days, it almost makes him a native."

A calculated gamble, the remark paid off. A round of applause was followed by a few colourful phrases. Once again, he had correctly judged the mood of an audience. Allowing the rowdy faction to settle, he was ready.

"Over the past few years, the country has been treated to an almost annual dosage of doomsday scenarios. Global warming, cosmic destruction, famine, overpopulation, war, the list seems endless."

Suitably grave, he pressed on.

"Strangely, the scaremongers failed to see a further problem looming: the meltdown of the world's economy. The financial wizards informed us it was nothing to worry about. Everything would be back to normal in a matter of months. A matter of months became six months, and then a year."

Giving a theatrical sigh, he added, "It's now almost three years since those assurances were given. Correct me if I'm wrong, but every time I switch on my television, I get the impression that things have got a good deal worse. Unfortunately, it appears the good doctor has yet more bad news for us."

The distinguished-looking figure removed his spectacles. Using a bright red handkerchief from the top pocket of his suit jacket, he began to polish them. Satisfied, he replaced the handkerchief, donned his spectacles and looked up. An almost imperceptible nod indicated that he was ready.

"The examples you mentioned, though interesting, Tony,

are not set in stone. At present there seems to be no definitive answers for any of them. Worryingly, the news I bring is not of a hypothetical nature, but concerns cold hard statistics. Disease and sickness have been a part of our lives since the dawn of civilisation. That much is indisputable. So far, we seem to have been extremely lucky. Occasionally, we have been faced with obstacles that at the time seemed insurmountable. Yet, on each occasion we either found an answer, or nature, deciding she'd had her fun pulled us back from the brink."

Choosing his examples carefully, he said, "The Black Death: the mere mention of the name evokes all kinds of horrors, doesn't it? For all the research produced on the topic, its actual origin is still in dispute. It's fair to say that most now believe it started in China, in the lungs of an animal called a marmot. Transmitted by rats and fleas to humans, it spread across Europe by trade routes and so forth. Eventually, it reached our shores around 1346. Fatalities," he said, raising his eyebrows. "The latest figures show that by the fourteenth century, 75 to 200 million died worldwide. Of that number, 20 to 25 million were Europeans. Some suggest the disease reduced the world's population from about 450 to 375 million by the year 1400. It doesn't take a rocket scientist to work out what might have happened if it hadn't died out as mysteriously as it appeared. It didn't vanish, however. The plague returned in one form or another until sometime in the 1700s."

Using his fingers to tick off the salient points, he continued.

"There were three distinct types of the disease. The first and most common was bubonic plague. Heralded by high fevers, headaches, aching joints, sickness, etc., four out of five who contracted it were dead in eight days.

"The second was the pneumonic plague. Carrying with it a 90 to 95 per cent mortality rate, its symptoms were fevers, coughing, but, in particular, blood-tinged sputum.

"Finally we have the least common, but most deadly. With an almost 100 per cent mortality rate, the septicaemia or blood-poisoning strain was the worst all. Strangely, the tell-tale symptoms were less externally severe than the others. Bouts of coughing, allied to high fevers and purple skin patching were in the main the only warning signs."

Affording the audience an opportunity to digest his words, he carried on.

"Since the 1970s, scientists have had to combat equally infectious diseases. Take haemorrhagic fever. Its fatality rate is almost 90 per cent. As I speak, there are no standard anti-viral therapies. The problem with this kind of disease is just how quickly it can replicate itself. It isn't the only one. Ebola is part of a family which includes Marburg, Lassa, River Valley and Congo fever. Again, nature seems to be toying with us. What is potentially a pandemic has so far been restricted to a few serious but isolated incidents."

Pausing a moment, he added, "I almost forgot AIDS. It's hardly surprising. Recent reports indicate that everything is under control. Inside sources assure me that far from being under control, figures in the more remote outposts of Africa are so horrendous they defy logic."

Smiling, he said, "Mother Nature doesn't seem to come out of all this terribly well. But she isn't vindictive. She doesn't hold a grudge against humanity. It's just that with the world's population now standing at over six billion, there seems to be more of us to get in her way."

An uneasy hush had settled over the audience.

Finding his voice, Tony Morel said, "If I'm reading you correctly, you're about to inform us that despite everything we've just heard, there's something even worse waiting in the wings."

"That's correct. Recent research has shown that contrary to

popular belief, there are viruses appearing now which are able to jump species."

"Surely," said the astonished host, "Such a thing's impossible."

"Until recently I'd have agreed with you. Not with the fact it was impossible, but that, theoretically, the chances of it occurring were so slim, no one gave it a second thought. Things have altered."

Getting to his feet, one member of the audience shouted, "What are you trying to say?"

About to quell the disturbance, Dr Takeshi, sensing Tony Morel's intention, stopped him.

"Wait," he said, "they have a right to know. All I ask is that any questions be asked in an orderly fashion."

This wasn't in the script, thought Tony Morel, but what the hell. If the answers were controversial, they might send the ratings through the roof.

"I'm sure you're aware of the terms bird flu and swine fever," said the doctor. "They've been in the news often enough."

Seeing the nods, he said, "Then let's take the first as an example. The establishment, by that I mean we scientists, have long felt a pandemic of bird flu is long overdue."

Seeing a few puzzled expressions, he raised his hand.

"Let me apologise. I have used the term pandemic once before. By the looks on some faces, you seem to be in the dark as to what it actually means. In simple terms, any disease that threatens the world, or becomes global, is given the term pandemic. Oddly enough, the threat of contracting bird flu has been with us for some time. Sporadic outbursts have occurred on and off for the last decade. Fortunately, to date, it hasn't developed into a global outbreak. Many types of bird or avian flu exist. The most worrying strains are those described as H5 and H7. At present there are nine different types of H5 alone. Each of these can appear in variant forms. Some are extremely deadly, others pretty harmless. The one causing concern is the Asian variety – H5N1. To further complicate matters, there are different subtypes of H5N1. But there could be even more. Each of those we isolated was deadly to birds but, alarmingly from our point of view, they were also found to be capable of causing death in humans. Until recently, we were encouraged by the fact that test results showed it was difficult for H5N1 to pass easily from human to human. Then, out of the blue, one batch H5N1 (13) provided us with graphic evidence that we had on our hands a strain capable of mutating. There was worse to come. Once it had jumped from bird to human, it adapted to its host far more quickly than ever thought possible."

A hand shot up. "Aren't you lot to blame? Scientists are dabbling with what should be the province of God alone. Gene splicing and replication is giving birth to things we can't control. And that's the problem here, isn't it?"

"What's your name?" asked the doctor.

"David," came back the shouted response.

"Well, David, I categorically refute that suggestion. However, I find it difficult to fault your logic. There are many scientists intent on fame and fortune, who think ethics are a thing of the past. I also agree with your other point. We are coming dangerously close to playing God. But it's not the case here. Our work is done with Petri dishes and slides. Besides, we haven't discovered anything new. This is something that seems to have lain dormant for decades."

Another hand appeared; the questioner far less aggressive.

"Say the worst happens, doctor, what then? Say it spreads? How many would die? Not many, surely? After all, it's only the flu."

The last remark was followed by a ripple of nervous laughter.

Tenting his fingers, Takeshi appeared to think for a moment before answering.

"Let's look at your first point. Rid yourself of the preconception that flu is simply flu. As old as time, there are many different strains. More importantly, rid yourself of the idea that it's something that leaves you with a cough, headaches and runny nose. Flu, the old-fashioned type is the one that lays you up for a week or two, sometimes more. It is the one that even in its mildest form has the capacity for killing, especially the more vulnerable in society. What you really need to keep in mind is that it's far from simple. It's a virus. As such it is capable of mutating. The AIDS virus is a classic example. What I'm trying to say, is that there is no such thing as a simple virus. Until now the strains we've encountered have been, how can I say, manageable. The one we discovered recently, the one capable of jumping species, however, is beyond anything we've encountered before."

Not allowing the man time to recover, he delivered his *coup de grâce*. "To answer your second question, at present, this particular strain seems to be flexing its muscles. Once it decides it's ready for action then God help us. I'd say a conservative estimate to its potency would be that it would be capable of wiping out somewhere in the region of between 200 and 500 million people. That's a conservative estimate. It could be much more."

"You can't be serious," shouted a female voice. "In a high-tech world like ours, scientists will be able to come up with an antidote, won't they?"

Takeshi had timed his delivery to perfection. "Fortunately there is something we can do. Over the last few months, New World Laboratories has developed what we feel is an effective method of counteracting the virus. It isn't a miracle cure. But in the main we are confident it will work. Recent test results have been encouraging. With the backing of the government, the product is being placed on the market in about a month's time. Normally, the drug would require far more testing. Legislation lays down stringent ground rules for such things. In light of the evidence put forward, however, immediate permission for mass production has been granted."

Wiping his brow, Tony Morel let out a sigh of relief. He had almost been taken in with the doomsday scenario. The man had certainly been convincing.

"Thank you for scaring the crap out of us, doctor. If that was your intention it certainly worked."

Nods from large sections of the crowd showed they were in agreement. Drawing the various threads together, he said, "At the moment the world seems to be on the brink of some pandemic. However, it just so happens your company called New World Laboratories, has developed a kind of super antibiotic which will cure it. Excuse my cynicism. Don't you think that's a tad too convenient?"

Sensing he had the upper hand, he went for the kill. "Say, thanks to the warning given in this programme, half the population of the country bought your product. The company would make hundreds of thousands overnight, correct?"

Behind him, the first grumblings of discontent were emerging. For the last ten minutes they had been in the grip of mild hysteria. They were rapidly coming out of it.

"True," said the doctor, not in the least put off by the sudden turn of events.

Facial expressions betray a wealth of emotions and if Tony was reading the doctor correctly, the bastard was enjoying himself. Warning bells started sounding in his head. Despite years of dealing with people like him, he wondered whether he had finally misjudged a situation.

Measuring his response, Takeshi said, "I see what you're getting at and I agree. If anything, your estimation of the profits might be a little low. But I fear you have badly misjudged the company and its benefactor."

"If I have," shot back Tony, "it would be the first time any multi-billion-pound conglomerate turned down the opportunity to make a fast buck."

"I hardly think a billion pounds would qualify as a fast buck, Tony."

The remark brought a gasp of astonishment from the audience.

"Forget money for the moment," continued the doctor. "Instead of trying to win points from each other, let's behave like adults. The super antibiotic, as you label it, is far from that. Clinical tests have proven it to be effective in only some 70 per cent of cases. Still, 70 per cent is pretty good, all things considered. I would guess that given those kind of odds, most of the people out there would kill for it. However, the company has no intention of making money out of other people's misery." With a glint in his eye, he added, "That would be exploitation, surely."

When no witty response was forthcoming, the doctor grew in confidence.

"The owner of New World Laboratories might best be described as a recluse. Very few people have set eyes on him, yet this whole enterprise is being funded by his private fortune."

Fascinated at the duel of words taking place between their one-time hero and the soft-spoken doctor, the audience was hanging on to every word.

"My benefactor has decided to make sufficient quantities of the drug available for every man, woman and child in Britain. The product will also be made available worldwide. For those countries deemed too primitive to organise an inoculation programme, contingency plans have been set up. Bottled water and certain food products will be treated and distributed. One final thing, the vaccine will not be forced on anyone: it is purely optional."

Recovering quickly, Tony Morel said, "Declining such an offer would be madness."

"My thinking entirely, but there will be some who will doubt the sincerity of the offer. People are always looking for conspiracies, Tony."

About to formulate a reply, he never had the opportunity.

Bursting through the studio doors, several figures carrying snub-nosed machine pistols appeared. The cameras were still rolling and so the outside world had a grandstand view of what happened next.

Of South Korean manufacture, the DAEWOO DP51 is small, but extremely effective. As the world watched, they were put to good use. In a crude attempt at coordination, the figures opened fire simultaneously.

More by luck than judgement, one spray cut Tony Morel almost in half. Another pointed his weapon at the audience and pulled the trigger. In merciless fashion, the sleek DP51 mowed down dozens of innocent people before the weapon clicked on an empty magazine. Taken completely by surprise, Takeshi stared open mouthed. He had no idea that having carried out his task, he would become surplus to requirements. Seconds later, the top of his head disintegrated in a spray of blood and brain tissue.

Their task complete, the figures turned their weapons on themselves.

FOUR

Monday, 26 November 2012
7.00 p.m.
A remote dockland area of London

FROM HIS FIRST-FLOOR vantage point, Medusa peered into the gloom. The timing might have been better. Yet, when the announcement had been made that an emergency meeting concerning global warming was to be held in London, it was an opportunity too good to miss. The chat show he had commissioned concerning bird flu had gone exactly as planned. And so the reaction of one of his invited guests would determine the timing of the next stage of Genesis.

Glancing at his watch, he noted in irritation that they were late. And then the first of the headlights appeared.

Turning on his heels, he made his way slowly towards the open stairway leading to the ground floor. Grasping the railing, he swivelled his head. To his left was a walnut drinks' cabinet. Open, it displayed a bewildering variety of alcoholic beverages. Next to it were the requirements for making tea or coffee.

In the centre of the room, black leather chairs were arranged neatly around a circular table made of solid oak. Two waiters, members of his security force, stood at either side. Acknowledging them with a nod, he made his way painfully down the staircase.

Shaking their hands as they stepped through the door, he greeted each personally.

"Glad you could make it." Pleasantries over, he gestured to the stairs. "If you would be so kind."

Charles Hillary, Jacques Rodin, Hans Grubber, Ivan Stannic and Ed Goldstein, nodding to each other, hid their distaste at the choice of venue well. A disused warehouse in a remote dockland area of London was hardly befitting people of their stature. Entering the first-floor office, they were pleasantly surprised. Shrugging their warm overcoats, they approached the table.

"Be seated, gentlemen," their host said, indicating the plush leather chairs. "But where are my manners? I'm sure you would like a drink. Dare I say it a large one."

"Max, Daniel, see to that, please."

The orders were taken and within moments the drinks were delivered. Sipping his tea, Charles Hillary studied the immaculately dressed figure. He was surprised. The voice on the phone had given no hint as to an ethnic origin. The last thing he had expected was to be addressed by an Asiatic. He would have wagered Medusa had been born in Japan. But the man was so pale his skin was almost translucent.

That he was seriously ill was obvious, nevertheless he was still an imposing character. The strength of his personality seemed to fill the room. The eyes black and piercing seemed to glow with some kind of inner conviction. For a brief moment, he felt the stirrings of unease. It was then that the rashness of accepting the invitation struck home. It had been the Devil's own task to outwit security. Under normal circumstances he would never have pulled it off. The elaborate charade had taken days to plan. Even then without the aid of Matthew he would never have pulled it off. He had taken a great deal of persuading. Their friendship had been the deciding factor. As it was, he had a limited window of opportunity, and if by midnight he hadn't returned the shit would hit the fan.

"Shall we begin proceedings?" said Medusa intruding on his thoughts.

"Incidentally, your bodyguards are being well looked after. I'm so glad you listened to reason and brought only the one. Relieved of their weapons, once our little discussion is over, they will be returned to them. Back to business. When I first had the idea of inviting you to this meeting, I wondered how to go about it. To offer you money would have been insulting. Gambling, I decided to appeal to your curiosity. And, as luck would have it, it worked."

Ticking off mentally what he wanted to say, he began.

"At one time or another every single government outside the Third World countries has issued directives designed to address the problem of violence."

Holding one finger in the air, he said, "Note the absence of the word eradicate. The truth is there is no answer."

Changing tack, he said, "Violence is a multi-faceted hydra. In order to understand it, we have to unravel the reasons why it rears its ugly head so often. The breakdown of marriages in society is a case in point. On the surface, such a thing may appear insignificant, yet, without the stability of a settled home background, youngsters are faced with a problem. From whom do they learn their values? Single parents are becoming more and more common, while gays and lesbians are adopting children. It's no wonder the youth of today are confused. Respect for authority, self-discipline, looking out for one's neighbours, all these are things of the past. According to religious authorities it is we, the present generation, who are to blame. Having touched on religion, the Bible informs us that we are the custodians of the earth. If so, we seem to have made a mess of things. To date we have recklessly squandered its natural resources. Resources, may I add, that can never be replaced. At the present rate of usage, by the year 2050, a mere forty-odd years into the future, the world's supply of both oil and gas will have dwindled to nothing. Coal too."

Shaking his head, he continued, "Every year we have the same promises regarding fossil fuel targets. And, yet, the powers that be know only too well such targets are completely unrealistic. True, strides have been made in terms of finding alternate sources of power, but all of these amount to a mere drop in the ocean. Can you imagine the two emerging giants of industry, India and China using less? I think not. And so people are blindly putting their trust in science. Let's not panic, I hear them say. Leave it to the boffins; they'll come up with the answers. Unfortunately, many scientists are openly admitting it may already be too late. All things considered, the situation facing us is grave."

Pointing to the folders, he said, "In front of you is conclusive proof that despite what the experts say, there is a way out of this mess. Extreme it may be and it will take a great deal of personal courage to implement. Nevertheless, it is a solution. To take it a step further it is not only a solution, it is the 'only' solution. At first, what you read will horrify you, but it's amazing what we humans will do in order to get what we want. In my experience, people tend to be extremely flexible when it comes to such things as the law, or what they perceive to be fair and moral. Don't misunderstand me: I'm not against having principles. All I'm saying is that, under the present circumstances, can we afford them?"

Concluding his speech, he said, "After studying the folders, what you have to decide, is into which category your principles fit. If, like me, you feel the rules pertaining to society, ones may I add that have failed us miserably, were made for other people and not us, then what I propose will make perfect sense. The first section is a detailed synopsis of what I have already outlined. The remainder is my proposal for tackling the problem."

Exhausted, he sat down.

Studying the document with practised ease, Charles Hillary's eyes darted from line to line, from paragraph to paragraph. Each page only reinforced the sickening feeling in his stomach. Glancing at the others, he was puzzled. They had barely looked at theirs. Refocusing, he paused at sentences of seeming significance while scanning the remainder quickly. Finally, he came across what he was looking for. Staring at him from the bottom of the last page, his deepest fears were confirmed.

Though he had been prepared for it, his mind could not comprehend the enormity of what the man was proposing. And so his brain, like any computer which has been fed too much information reacted in the same way. It shut down.

Allowing his gaze to settle on Charles Hillary, Medusa was reminded of a prism. In this instance, however, it was expressions and not colours on display. At first, the brows were furrowed in concentration. Moments later, when the implication of what was being proposed sunk in, surprise, disbelief and indignation gave way to amazement, loathing and horror.

From the beginning, Medusa had feared that his lack of moral courage would blind Hillary to the realisation that his suggestion was the only viable option. Still, he was disappointed.

Finally able to close his mouth, Charles Hillary smiled. Coughing nervously, he said, "If I didn't know it wasn't April the first, I'd say you were playing us for fools."

The smile Medusa had been wearing vanished. "Appears I've hit a raw nerve; surely to God you can't be serious?" The French billionaire Jacques Rodin's face held a hint of a smirk. The equally wealthy duo from Germany and Russia remained mute. Ed Goldstein, a Texas oil tycoon slammed his fist onto the table, the impact sending cups and glasses several inches into the air.

"You're mad. Don't get me wrong, I know you're serious. That's what frightens me." Lifting his head and sniffing the air theatrically, he snorted, "The stench of insanity is overpowering, so excuse me while I leave."

Pushing the chair out of his way roughly, he turned to the group, "Anyone else with me?"

Pausing only to retrieve their coats, the others followed. The march to the top of the stairs was halted by their host. Showing iron powers of self-control, he never raised his voice. In hindsight, it made what he said even more frightening.

"Gentlemen, I appreciate your frankness." Getting to his feet, he faced Ed Goldstein. "Especially you, my friend, and may I say that I respect your opinion. However, I must make one thing clear. Not a single word of what transpired in this room tonight must ever be repeated on the outside."

Looking at each in turn, he added, "Not a single word. Having cleared that little matter up, I shall arrange for you to be returned to your hotels."

Looking at Medusa, Charles Hillary saw that beneath the placid facade of a sick old man, his eyes revealed his true nature. Dragging his away, he hurried to catch up with the others as they made their way down the staircase with undignified haste. The moment the outside door closed, a voice drifted across the room. "Is everything in place?" said Medusa, staring from the window into the darkness of the car park. The query was made without turning his head.

"Yes, sir."

The arrival of the removals van was announced by the sound of squealing tyres and slamming doors. Moments later, six security men dressed in identical clothing appeared at the head of the stairs.

Within five minutes the room was stripped bare. There was still work to be done. As the last three guards moved downstairs, the others, their loads already deposited in the van, reappeared.

With military precision, they wiped the surface of everything the visitors had come into contact with. Starting with the upstairs room they made their way quickly down the stairway, finishing up with the door handles, both inside and out. At the bottom, the old man glanced at his watch. The whole operation had been completed in a shade less than five minutes. He mentally congratulated his men.

As promised, the cars were ready and waiting. On entering the building, the armed bodyguards had been relieved of their weapons. Until now they had been enjoying a cup of coffee in a small downstairs room. The meeting over, their weapons were returned to them and they followed their paymasters into the cold night air.

The passengers and bodyguards safely seated in the backs of their respective vehicles, each of the drivers closed the doors gently. In seconds, they had taken up their stations behind the wheels of their cars.

The fifth driver, looking up, saw the old man nod. The limousines pulled away smoothly, leaving a precise twenty-yard gap between each. All five sat low on their tyres.

Negotiating the roundabout at the rear of the factory, the convoy swept left onto a narrow road that bypassed two smaller warehouses. The final turn took them onto a concrete strip that skirted the jetty. Riding inside the specially adapted Jaguar XJ limousine, Charles Hillary let out a sigh of relief. Unable to decide whether the chap had been having them on, he dismissed the thought instantly.

Turning, he peered through the rear window. By now the fog had lifted somewhat and he saw the headlights of the other cars. Spaced out evenly, they looked like ducks in a shooting gallery. The idea popped into his mind before he could retract it. What the man had proposed had been nothing short of insanity, yet the warning had been no idle threat, of that he was sure. So what had he been up to? Running various scenarios through his mind, he felt the car slowing.

It came to a stop. Bemused, he turned, wondering if the other cars were stationary too.

They were.

Lifting the handle in order to step out, nothing happened. Thinking it was fitted with a child lock, he looked for the release mechanism. There wasn't one.

Overcoming his initial fear, he banged his fist on the glass partition separating him and the bodyguard from the driver. What the hell was going on? Peering over his shoulder, the chauffeur smiled.

Like a maggot, the first prickle of fear began to gnaw at Charles Hillary. Craning his neck, he saw that each of the other chauffeurs was standing outside their vehicles. Hats off, heads bowed, they looked suspiciously as if they were paying their last respects. It was almost like watching mourners at a funeral, he thought.

Moments later the chauffeurs disappeared. Sensing something was wrong, the bodyguard leapt into action. Smashing his elbow into the glass partition several times, he eventually gave up. It was a futile gesture.

"Your gun, man," said the PM, "use your bloody gun."

Sliding his weapon from beneath his jacket, he pointed it at the glass partition and fired. A muffled click was the only response. Unable to believe what was happening, he attempted several more rounds and with the same result. The truth hit him like a sledgehammer: the bastards had emptied the weapon while he was in the building.

"Surely there's something we can do?" said the PM, his voice on the edge of hysteria.

Seeing the look of resignation on his face, Charles Hilary threw himself at the nearest window. Pounding his fists against the glass in desperation, in moments the glass was streaked with blood. His hands a pulpy mess, he was oblivious to the pain. For several minutes more he kept at it, until finally accepting defeat he slid to the floor in abject despair.

Suddenly the acrid smell of urine filled the air. Looking down in horror, he saw that he had lost control of his bowels. He had often wondered about heroes, about how they reacted when death came calling. He had wondered about cowards, too, about their reaction. Now he knew.

Starring at his wallet, at photographs of his family, the bodyguard was desperately trying to absorb every last tiny detail of their faces. Sobbing, he realised belatedly that he was in the wrong profession.

The first explosion dragged Charles Hilary out of his stasis. The other explosions occurred in precise five-second intervals.

After the fourth had died away, it was the longest five seconds of his life.

And then the car disintegrated.

FIVE

Monday, 26 November 2012
9.00 p.m.

LACING HIS NIKE trainers, Jonathan Hudson searched for his iPod. Unable to find it, he let rip with a few choice expletives. Eventually he gave up and went without it. Pounding the same route for months, he realised that until today, without the distraction of music, he had never really taken in his surroundings. Beneath the tired concrete road and the wrecks littering the wharf, the old dock had a simplistic beauty which hinted at better days. Peering through gaps in the swirling mist, the jumble of derelict ships stood out starkly against the inky blackness of the London skyline. Despite their diversity they had one thing in common: there appeared to be more rust than steel on show. The surface of the water was jet black, its glossy surface hinting at all kinds of unspeakable filth. In the distance he noticed a light coming from one of the many disused warehouses that littered the surrounding area. Unusual, he thought, before dismissing the oddity.

Some ten minutes later, perspiring freely, his mind turned to the interview he had arranged between Wolfe and his brother. It seemed to have gone well. More than well, he reasoned: they appeared to have hit it off.

The first explosion took him by surprise. The others followed at precise intervals.

Some fifty yards further on, he stopped in his tracks. The scene, one of utter devastation, was reminiscent of a battlefield. One in which there appeared to be no survivors. Ahead, several deep craters were clearly visible. Approaching nervously, the air was laced with a sickly cloying odour, one he couldn't place.

Milliseconds later, the realisation jolted his brain. It was the smell of charred and burning flesh. Gagging, he covered his mouth in an attempt to block the vile stench from his nostrils. With mounting terror he inched his way forward. Suddenly, a thin wheezing sound drifted towards him on the breeze. Coming from a patch of scrub to his immediate left, he approached cautiously. Reaching it, he was horrified to discover the remains of a man. Below the waist, the only thing left was a tangled mass of flesh and bone. Incredibly, the person was still alive. And with a rush of recognition he knew who it was.

Opening his mouth, Charles Hillary tried to speak. Fighting his loathing, Jonathan leaned closer. He caught the words, Medusa Industries, Genesis and something about a research complex in Wales. About to say something else, the PM gave a racking cough, his eyes rolled in his head and he was gone.

Knowing whoever had taken out the PM might be still be around, Jonathan took off.

It was 8.00 p.m. and by now Paul Hudson was a lone figure in the office. Frustrated, he swivelled his chair to block from view what he had already produced. Away from the prying eyes of his laptop, he removed the pencil from behind his ear and hurled it across the room. A petty gesture, it still made him feel better. Hitting the wall, it performed several impressive somersaults. Landing on the carpet unscathed, it sat there smugly, as if suggesting he couldn't even get that right.

Journalism was like that, he knew. Sometimes the ideas flowed thick and fast. At others, his mind seemed to go on strike. Writers block, some authors called it. For those who earned their living juggling with words it was a nightmare scenario. Experience had taught him that when it happened, instead of giving up you simply had to plough on.

What he had written sounded contrived, artificial. Perhaps he was being too hard on himself, but it didn't wash. His father's credo had been the standard he had always strived for. 'Never sell yourself short.' Years ago he had come across a saying by Confucius: 'Be sure you know the difference between boredom and laziness.' In an oblique way it echoed his father's sentiments exactly. The phrase had left such an impression that he'd installed a foot-high printout to the outside of his work's cubicle.

Savouring the solitude, he glanced around the empty office. In the early days he had wanted to become a teacher. Wanted an occupation in which he could make a real difference to people's lives. Taken in by the recruiting commercials, the reality had been very different. He hadn't lasted long. It was then that the idea of journalism came to mind. An opportunity to be creative, to be expressive, suddenly had enormous appeal. Three years after attending Cardiff University, he'd graduated with a 2:1 in journalism and media studies. A year later he had completed his masters.

The article driving him crazy involved a politician, one who – according to his brother – was going places. Cynically, he had asked himself how often he had heard that before. Jonathan's earnest expression had been the deciding factor.

The problem was how to pitch the damn thing. The balance had to be just right. On the one hand, it had to be informative while, on the other hand, it couldn't provide too much detail. That would smack of inside information. Similar to walking a tightrope, the skill was in striking a balance between impressing his readers and making sure no one would be able to trace the story back to his brother. Alike facially, on numerous occasions they had been mistaken for twins.

And, then, out of the blue, Jonathan had contacted him offering him an interview with David Wolfe. For a moment he had thought about turning him down. The deciding factor had been Jonathan's earnest conviction that, in a short time, David Wolfe would be a genuine candidate for prime minister. Held discreetly in an out-of-town restaurant, the setting was relaxed and informal. Choosing a table by the window, Paul ordered a beer; Wolfe a small glass of red wine. When the drinks arrived, Wolfe raised his: "To a successful interview."

Moments later, Paul knew that his preconceived ideas had been way off beam. Instead of the pretentious arsehole he had been expecting, Wolfe appeared to be likeable and charming. An imposing figure, his rugged good looks would make him an instant hit with the media should he ever get to power.

"Getting straight to the point, Mr Wolfe…" he was unable to complete the sentence.

"David, call me David. I don't hold with formalities. Besides, this is an informal interview, isn't it?" smiling to make his point.

"As my private secretary, your brother is doing a fine job."

Brushing away a non-existent speck from his trousers, he added, "Before you make any rash promises, I know it's almost accepted practice these days for the press to distort, to take things out of context. It's not beyond some of them to edit interviews with the intention of making people in my line of work look foolish. Contrary to what the media believe, that all politicians keep things from the public, some of us really are different."

A half smile creased his face. "On the other hand, aren't people in your line of work often accused of bending the rules, blurring the edges between fact and fiction when necessity dictates? So you see, Paul, I can call you Paul, can't I? In that respect, politicians and journalists aren't so very different."

Waving his hand in the air, he said, "Where are my manners. I'm sorry for the rude interruption. In future I won't speak until I'm asked to."

Touché, Mr Wolfe, thought Paul. You really are an impressive son of a bitch. About to form a reply, he was never given the opportunity. Ignoring his promise of seconds ago, Wolfe waited until Paul was about to open his mouth before stepping in.

"What we also have in common is that the people out there", he said, pointing through the bay window of the restaurant, "Are extremely dangerous when starved of information. Under those circumstances, when they feel rightly or wrongly they're being left in the dark, they tend to fill in the blanks with all kinds of conspiracy theories. And that's when problems arise."

For the first time since coming into contact with the man, Paul had a glimpse of the person behind the mask. Beneath the benign, charming exterior there lay a man of fierce determination. Strike two for his brother.

Taken out of his stride, he desperately tried to gather his scattered thoughts. Finally in control, he said, "Anyway, David, when my brother speaks about you, it's in such glowing terms I find myself being wary. Surely no one can be that good?"

Clarifying his statement, he added, "Then again, I would say that as a cynical journalist, wouldn't I? It's what I'm paid for," grinning to show no malice was intended. The last thing he wanted to do was to get the man's back up. A glance at Wolfe indicated such a scenario was unlikely to happen: the man appeared to be unflappable. Besides he had a good feeling about the guy.

The longer the interview went on, the more Paul realised that Wolfe was an enigma in the true sense of the word. His background was a genuine mystery. He was a shooting star that had appeared from nowhere. Discreet checks had established virtually nothing about the man. It was almost as if a cloak of secrecy had been drawn over his former life. To date there had been no hint of any sexual indiscretions, late-night drinking binges, drugs and the like. And that was strange. If he really was squeaky clean, it was bad news. Good deeds never made headlines. Still, should Wolfe turn out to be a modern saint, there was always the possibility of the rumour mongers making up their own scandals. A colleague of his had once said "Why mess up a good story with facts?" It was something that had stuck in his mind ever since.

Time to take off the gloves, he decided.

"According to reports, your background seems to be clean. No skeletons in the cupboard, nothing out of place." Shaking his head for emphasis he said, "I can't accept that. The age of chivalry has long since passed."

Pointing an immaculately manicured finger at Paul, Wolfe chuckled. "Now, now, that was naughty. Have you never thought I might have lots of skeletons in the cupboard, but so far no one has been clever enough to find them? And, before you ask, I'm not married. And I'm certainly not gay."

Seeing Paul's startled expression, he said with a flash of wicked humour, "So you can uncross your legs and relax. Even if I had been, you wouldn't be my type."

Knowing that he had been outwitted, Paul could do nothing but join in the fun. And somehow it broke the ice.

Over the next half-hour, Wolfe showed his more serious side by outlining what he saw as the main threats to world stability.

"According to my reasoning, the problems facing mankind are centred on three key issues. The first is the price of crude oil. Once that reaches a certain level, those countries without it are going to take up arms. They will do whatever it takes to get it. Secondly, we have the Arab-Israeli conflict. Eventually the US will be forced to take sides and it doesn't take a genius to know which one it will come down on. Finally, we have the spectre of North Korea. South Korea being under Western control was, until the arrival of the credit crunch, basically booming. North Korea, however, is under the auspices of the Chinese. Because the majority of their resources are spent on military issues, much of the country is starving. The production of long-range nuclear missiles eats up money at an alarming rate. And what little remains is spent on chemical and biological research. The time is approaching and rapidly when China will be forced to back the North Koreans against Uncle Sam. And then bingo."

"World War Three," said Paul.

"Precisely, and of course, should that prove to be the case there will be no winners. It's a little-known fact, but the next great war will not be won on the battlefield."

Seeing Paul's quizzical expression, he elaborated.

"Surprisingly, the spectre of China flexing its muscles isn't what worries me. A nuclear solution would benefit no one. The next war will be won in secret laboratories hidden around the globe. From where I'm standing, bio-chemical weapons are the greatest threat to the future of mankind. Invisible to the naked eye, and measured in the trillions, diseases capable of wiping out nations can be mounted on a pin head. Worryingly, against such threats we have very little deterrent. True, treaties are in force forbidding not only their use, but their production, yet everyone knows these treaties are worthless paper exercises. The policing of such facilities are also a sham. Those complexes we know about, or are allowed to see might be a better way of putting it, have cleverly cultivated a warm and friendly facade. Designed to appear non-threatening, it works. The inspectors see scores of men and women dressed in starched white lab coats going about their business competently and efficiently. On the surface everything seems fine. And of course it is: the real work is conducted in secret underground facilities which no one knows anything about. As a result, these death factories are almost impossible to detect. Despite the appalling consequences of unleashing such weapons on mankind, there are insane dictators out there who would pay a fortune to be able to arm their long-range missiles with pandemic diseases. And once that happens, God help us."

"Do you see a way out?"

"There's always a solution to every problem, Paul, even this one. The trick is in finding it."

Paul came to a sudden conclusion. Either the man was the finest actor he had ever come across, or the best ministerial candidate. Either way, he could see why his brother had fallen under his spell. Here was a man who was going places. Thinking back on the interview made him feel better. Within half an hour, he had not only rewritten the article, he was pleased with it.

Glancing at his watch he saw it was 10.14 p.m. Time for home, he decided. Placing several sheets of A4 paper into a large brown envelope, he cleared his desk and reached for his coat. About to switch off the lights, his phone rang.

SIX

Monday, 26 November 2012
9.15 p.m.

MEDUSA WAS INTERRUPTED by one of his aides. "Sir, we have a problem."

"What do you mean 'problem'?" shot the old man.

"You'd better take a look."

Lifting the collar of his quilted parka, he made his way painfully towards the ramp of the luxury mobile home. The inside was roofed with an array of high-tech equipment: split screens showed every inch of the surrounding area.

Slipping a disk into the DVD player, the operator pointed to the top right-hand corner of the screen.

"The footage was caught on tape a few minutes ago."

The images were not of the best quality and the fog was thick in places, but the jogging suit was distinctive.

"Get in closer," came the barked order.

Immediately a badly charred body filled the screen.

"Christ," said the head of security, "It's the PM, and the bastard's still alive."

"Not for much longer," came the reply.

Using a remote control, the operator manipulated the images before freezing a particular frame. "This is what I wanted you to see, sir."

As they studied the screen, the figure leaned over the dying PM.

"Keep looking. There, see it? The PM whispers something into the man's ear, seconds later he speeds off into the mist."

Until now, Medusa's life had revolved around not taking

chances and so he came to an instant decision. Turning, he said, "Lucifer, I want him silenced."

"Finding him should be no problem, sir," answered Lucifer in a confident tone. "Besides the little matter of the distinctive track suit, he's only got a few minutes start."

"Then get on with it," came the curt reply.

Glancing over his shoulder, Jonathan was reasonably sure he hadn't been followed. For the last five miles he'd set a furious pace. Nearing the point of exhaustion, he came to a halt. Head bowed, hands on knees, he dragged in mouthfuls of air.

Filtering through the horrors it had witnessed, his brain was frantically trying to make some kind of sense of the carnage. Eyes darting back and fore, he searched for somewhere to hide. Panic had driven him far from the beaten track and the location he found himself in was an unsavoury one. But beggars can't be choosers, he thought, before the irony of the pun struck him.

Knowing his track suit would make him conspicuous, he picked up handfuls of dirt, rubbing them in thoroughly. By the time he had finished, he was satisfied he would fit in.

Head lowered, he made his way towards the brazier in the distance. Huddled around the fire, they were the dregs of humanity.

Divided into three distinct groups, the first were a surly looking lot. Unshaven and unwashed, they glared at him. One look confirmed his suspicion, they hated the world, but in particular him. Despite his attempts to cover his identity, they had seen through his disguise in an instant.

Avoiding eye contact, he hurried on. To his left, backs against a rusty chain-link fence were the alcoholics. Sipping from some kind of bottle, it would probably be a cheap red wine, he thought, or something infinitely worse depending on how the day's begging had gone. On the opposite side of the alley, scattered among the cardboard boxes sat the junkies. Beneath concrete walls covered in graffiti, many were injecting themselves openly. The brazier made out of an old oil drum barred his way. Punctured here and there, the glowing embers gazed back at him like fiery demons. Even from a distance of several feet the heat was so intense he had to cover his eyes with his sleeve.

Moments later, he was out in the open heading towards the main road. Stooping to tie his lace, the wall immediately behind erupted with a series of muffled explosions. Shards of concrete flew around his head like angry hornets. One sliver sliced his cheek like an open razor.

Ducking behind a pile of rubble, he peered out. The gunman was less than fifty yards away. Huge, his head shaved, he looked like some third-rate bouncer. And he was grinning. Fate had thrown him a lifeline, but Jonathan knew that if he didn't get out of there quickly it might only be a brief respite. Tightening his lace, he ran.

Seeing a tangle of high-rise buildings in the distance, he made directly for them.

Suddenly, he was there.

Looking both ways, he noticed a row of narrow obscure openings to his right. Taking a gamble, he headed towards the labyrinth of dark alleys. Reaching an area of relative safety, he dropped his pace to a brisk walk. Senses on high alert, he peered into the shadows. Allowing his eyes to become accustomed to the gloom, the alleyway – deserted – appeared to stretch for miles. Most of the windows were broken. Even those protected with meshing, he noted uneasily. Several of the doors were chained.

Then he found what he was looking for. A side entrance hidden from view stood behind a row of large refuse bins. Inside, the floor was dotted with pools of stagnant water and rubbish of all descriptions. It was ideal.

Watching from the safety of the shadows, he allowed several minutes to pass. Then he stepped out of hiding. Breaking into a jog once more, he gradually increased his pace. Relief flooded through his veins: he knew where he was. The next right hander would bring him alongside a row of telephone kiosks. And that was exactly what he needed.

Taking off like an Olympic sprinter, fear seemed to lend him wings. He reached his destination in record time. Satisfied that he had lost his attacker for the moment, he made one last brief 360 degree survey of the area. The luminous figures of his watch indicated it was 10.13 p.m. A workaholic, his brother would probably still be in the office. The telephone card he carried for emergencies was stashed in a Velcro-tabbed pocket in the back of his joggers. Removing it, he tried to insert it into the machine. His hands were trembling so badly it took him several attempts to find the allotted groove. Picking up the receiver from its cradle, he willed his brother to answer. Moments later his prayers were answered. Before his brother had time to realise who was on the other end, he had poured out his story.

"The PM's dead."

"Jesus, Jonathan, is that you?" came the astonished response.

"Slow down, for Christ's sake. You're not making any sense, bro. Take it from the top and give it to me word for word."

"No time, no time," was the agonised plea. "I stumbled onto something big. Now they're after me. Don't interrupt. The killer might be here any second. Just listen, okay? Before he died, the PM managed to whisper a few words. Didn't catch everything, he was in too bad a shape. Said something about Medusa Industries, Genesis, and an underground research facility in Wales and..."

He didn't finish the sentence. The killer appeared like a phantom. The first Jonathan knew of his presence was an arm like a steel band closing around his throat. Trapping Jonathan's larynx in the crook of his left elbow, Lucifer held Jonathan's head, palm flat against the side of his right temple and twisted. Lowering the inert figure to the floor, he propped him against the back of the booth.

About to replace the receiver, he heard anxious cries from the other end.

"Hello, hello Jonathan? Are you still there?"

Moments later the line went dead.

A feeling of icy coldness settled over Paul Hudson. With a sickening sense of finality, he knew that he would never see his brother alive again.

Seven

Tuesday, 27 November 2012
9.00 a.m.
London

Drinking coffee and scanning *The Times*, Wolfe was in receipt of the basics regarding yesterday's disaster. What he was interested in now was the media's take on events. The shrill tone of his telephone cut his train of thought.

"Good to hear from you, Paul. If you're enquiring about last night's tragedy, I can't tell you much. I'm not being evasive, I honestly know little more than you."

Seconds passed and instinctively he knew something was wrong. About to break the silence, Paul beat him to it, "Jonathan's dead. The police found his body early this morning. He was an eyewitness to the carnage. Before the PM died, he whispered a few words in Jonathan's ear."

Silencing him mid-stride, Wolfe said, "This is too important to discuss over the phone, meet me in Ramblers in fifteen minutes."

Pushing his way through the revolving doors, he glanced at his watch; it was exactly 9.15 a.m. Moments later, he was sipping his second cup of coffee in under twenty minutes.

"Before we get down to business, let me say that Jonathan was not only one of the nicest people I ever met," said Wolfe, "he was bloody good at his job."

Then, with a hint of steel, he added, "I'll find out who did this. You said something about a whispered message."

Paul took over. "It was a few words rather than a conversation. By then the PM had only moments to live."

"Tell me exactly what he said. The words may not be significant to you or I, but they may well be to others."

"All Jonathan caught was the word Genesis, and then something about a complex in Wales."

"Have you told the police?"

"It's the first thing I did."

"Good. Do you know who's handling the case?"

"Danny Harris and his team apparently. Ever heard of them?"

"If it's any consolation, they're good. This guy Harris is a no-frills copper, someone who does things his way. Extremely talented, he's refused god-knows-how-many promotions. And for the simple reason he doesn't want to end up behind a desk." Pensive, he looked up. "If Harris is involved, you can bet Stanford and the firm are too."

"I'm sorry, you've lost me, David."

"I'm glad. Had you known about the firm, those of us regarded as the ultimate exclusive club would be in trouble. From now on, what you'll become privy to is top secret. Do you know what I'm saying?"

"Suppose it's off the record, then," said Paul with a trace of his former humour.

Changing tack, Paul decided to ask a direct question. "Going to accept the post?"

"I was offered it this morning. Thought they would turn to someone senior. It's what I would have done. You know, it's strange, I've been dreaming about this for the last five years, yet now the time's arrived, I just don't know," he said shaking his head. "I've asked for time to think it over. Might not be the best time to ask, but how do you feel about coming to work for me? If, and I say if, I decide to accept what's on offer."

"Are you serious?"

"Deadly. Your brother was extremely good at his job. Having come to know you, it's clear you have the same kind of qualities.

Besides," he added with the hint of a smile, "you have additional skills you can bring to the post."

Holding up his hand to ward off protests, he added, "You don't have to give me your answer immediately."

"What about Thomas Adams, Charles Hillary's old private secretary?" asked Paul. "He has all the right credentials."

"Word doing the rounds is he was fiercely loyal to Hillary. Wouldn't offer him the position anyway, I want a fresh face with fresh ideas. God knows the country could do with them. To cut a long story short, I like to choose my own people."

To his amazement, Paul heard himself saying he would accept the post.

"Sure?" was Wolfe's comment. "I don't want this to be an off-the-cuff decision, one you might regret later."

"Perfectly," replied Paul, "For two reasons. The first is I want the people responsible for killing my brother. Secondly, strange as it seems, I believe in you."

"In that case I'd better make a call. Excuse me for a moment."

With that Wolfe disappeared. Five minutes later he was back. Taking immediate charge of the situation, he said, "First thing to do is to find Stanford. And, then, Paul, I want you to arrange an official visit to the site of Medusa Industries."

EIGHT

Tuesday, 27 November 2012
12. 30 a.m.
Covent Garden, London

THE RARE SUNNY day had worked its magic; the square was filled with shoppers of all nationalities. Despite the continuing downturn of the economy, the cafes and restaurants were crowded. Her first visit to London, Jodie was having the time of her life. Brought up in the country, city life had come as a shock, but it hadn't taken her long to adjust. Wanting to take her somewhere special Jared had opted for Covent Garden. Surrounded by theatres in the heart of London's West End, as the capital's premiere and leisure district, Jared hoped he had made the right choice.

Earlier that morning, like all children her age, Jodie had wanted breakfast at McDonald's. Ordering the biggest meal Jared had ever seen, he'd noted in amusement how after eating every scrap, she had licked her fingers in a determined effort to let nothing go to waste.

And now they were here. Her eyes open wide in amazement, Jodie stared at the small Italian-style piazza in awe. The large glass-covered building housed several arcades of fashionable boutiques, cafes and art and craft stores. One look at Jodie's face and Jared's fears vanished: once again Inigo Jones's creation was weaving its spell.

Spotting a street entertainer, Jodie squealed in delight. Grasping her father's sleeve, she dragged him towards the milling throng. Disappointingly the crowd was so dense that the man was blocked from view. Lifting Jodie onto his shoulders, she watched the action spellbound. Wearing a yellow and red stripped hose, a tunic festooned with bells and a huge multicoloured hat, he was reminiscent of a medieval jester. Sadly, it appeared to be the last act. Minutes later everyone drifted away.

Keeping to his earlier promise, Jared bought Jodie a new pair of headphones for her iPod. That done the next step was to find a pavement cafe so she could try them out. It was easier said than done. Everywhere they looked, the streets were crowded with visitors. Some were in a mad rush. Others took a more leisurely view of things. Though money was in short supply, many shops appeared to be doing a roaring trade. Looking more closely, Jared realised his mistake: the majority were window shopping.

Distracted for a moment, he saw that a crowd had gathered around a glass-fronted store full of televisions. In seconds he knew why. A close up of utter devastation had snagged the onlookers' attention. Instantly the deep craters in the pitted concrete road brought back unwanted memories. The flashing lights of ambulances were in evidence, while dotted around the perimeter stood several police cars. Stationary, they, too, had their lights on. Five craters were clearly visible, though one seemed smaller than the rest. Police and ambulance crews were sifting through the mess, gathering small items into clear plastic pouches. Trace evidence, Jared reasoned. Others were placing slightly larger objects into green sacks. He knew exactly what they were doing. They were collecting body parts. And by the look of it, there seemed to be very little left after the blasts.

Realistically, he knew it would be next to impossible to find any kind of real evidence when bits of cars had travelled through the air at speeds of up to 30,000 feet per second. Finding any identifiable remains of the occupants was even more remote. Working on instinct, the crews shuffled about like zombies.

Ex-SAS, Jared had long ago learned to control his feelings. In his mind war was war, pure and simple. You either came to terms with it, or it drove you mad. But this wasn't war. It was senseless slaughter. Danny Harris momentarily appeared in the far left corner of the television screen. Seconds later, Tina and Gareth came into sharp relief. Before he had time to register what they were doing, the camera moved into a close-up of a pretty blonde reporter. Standing in the middle of the road, she was fighting hard to keep a lid on her emotions.

It was clear the focus of the world was on London. The incident had reached such epic proportions, it had swept everything else aside. If Jared wasn't missing his guess, at this very minute, experts were being rushed into studios across the globe to give their opinions as to why such a thing had happened.

Frustratingly, each of the sets was silent. The scene changed again and moments later they were back in the studio. The news reader, normally so perky had on her most serious face. A few strands of conversation drifted over and it took Jared a few moments to realise that the noise was coming from inside the shop. The last customer must have left the door ajar. Straining his ears, he was able to make out a few sentences.

"The world is stunned... late last evening... five craters all of what remain of several extremely wealthy businessmen... Charles Hillary PM of Britain... one of victims... Remote place... mystery... Terrorist attack puzzling... No one yet claimed responsibility."

His concentration was broken by the ringing of his mobile. Slipping it out of his back pocket, he eased his way through the crowd and flipped open the cover. Instantly, he was greeted by a familiar voice.

Relaxing in the back seat of the taxi, Jared allowed his mind to drift. It had been almost three years since Emma's death. And yet he could remember the details as if it were yesterday. The discovery of an ancient manuscript hidden beneath the floor of an old Welsh chapel as a teenager had set in motion a train of events that had changed his life forever. The contents of the manuscript had led Jared and a group of close friends to a subterranean cave system, a mummified body and a chalice containing the ashes of Judas Iscariot.

And then the horror had started. By disturbing the seal on the chalice, they had unwittingly released a 2,000-year-old curse. Locked in a battle against evil they had come up against the Brotherhood, a sect of assassins sworn to protect both Judas and the chalice. Along with Danny, Gareth, Tina and a few others, they had eventually managed to lure the spirit of Judas back to the old chapel. Prepared to offer his life for the sake of mankind, things had gone disastrously wrong.

In Jared's mind everything beyond that point had become a jumble of disjointed images. One thing he was sure of, unaware only someone without sin would be an acceptable offering, the spirit of Judas had been inches from taking Jared's life when Emma had sacrificed herself for him. Since then he had been tortured by guilt. Without warning, the incident that had driven him from Raven's Hill all those years ago came crashing back into his mind.

Childhood sweethearts, he and Emma had been inseparable until one night he had discovered her in the arms of another boy. The betrayal coming so soon after his family had been killed in a tragic accident had affected Jared deeply. Unable to come to terms with what he had witnessed, he had decided on the spur of the moment to abandon his plans to accept a place in Oxford University. Leaving a note of explanation for his grandmother, by the following day he had taken up a career in the army.

Returning home years later, he was amazed to find Emma still living in the village. Even more surprising was that by now she had a young daughter: Jodie. Inquiries about Emma's partner had met with a brick wall. Strangely, no one seemed willing to talk about the subject. Emma's confession as she lay dying in his arms had cleared up the mystery.

There had never been any partner: she had made up the story to hide the fact that Jared was the father. The only man she had ever been with, the only person she had ever loved had been Jared. As he'd left home without telling her, he had denied her the opportunity to explain matters. The kiss on the cheek had been one of sympathy because the boy had just informed her that he'd been diagnosed with leukaemia. And so with her last breath she had informed Jared that Jodie was his daughter.

Struggling to cope with the guilt of Emma's death, the vicar of Raven's Hill had taken Jared under his wing. There were several stages of grief, Eric had informed him, each one so subtle it sometimes required a psychiatrist to define the edges. Fitting the classic profile, Jared had slipped into denial. According to Eric, that was normal. In the case of the death of a loved one, the brain steps in to help out.

"That's what denial is," he had expounded. "Nature's way of cauterising the wound."

Though an incredibly well-adjusted young girl, Jodie had recently started to experience nightmares. Asked to describe them, all she could say was that ghost-like figures, staring at her from dead soulless eyes, were begging for help. "The voices are in my head," she had explained. "Because of the horrible way they died, their spirits are trapped here on earth. There's one little girl in particular. About my age, she's called Amy. She visits me every night."

"What makes them think you can help?" Jared had asked.

The answer had taken him by surprise.

"It's your help they need, not mine. I'm only the messenger.

Everything's linked to some underground complex buried deep in the heart of the Welsh countryside."

Before seeing the shimmering ball of light at Emma's funeral, had anyone suggested to him that the dead had the ability to communicate with the living, he would have laughed. Yet, what he had seen that day had convinced him of one thing: death was not the end.

He had read somewhere that besides having a unique blueprint for our physical bodies, we also have one for our soul. When the body dies, trace evidence of it can be seen leaving at the moment of death. To Jared's mind it was something similar to the vapour trail left behind by the passing of a jet aircraft. Had it been the lingering profile of that which he and Jodie had seen?

Though he had lost touch with many of those involved in the Judas Codex affair, he still spoke regularly with Danny, Tina and Gareth. Sporting a mop of unruly black hair and blessed with dark skin, Gareth was a hit with the women. Tina, a dead ringer for Jennifer Aniston, wore her hair in a ponytail and was never seen in anything but a classy trouser suit. Professional to the core, she was also a superb shot. Danny was Danny. An ex-rugby prop and a few stone overweight, his broken nose and cauliflower ears gave the mistaken impression that he was slow witted. Nothing could be further from the truth. The outer shell hid a fierce intellect and gritty determination. Like a human Rottweiler, once he got his teeth into something he never let go. Amusingly, when Danny came across something that didn't sit right he would phone Jared. It was why he knew there was more to the proposed meeting than met the eye.

Approaching from a distance, Danny spotted them. Casting his eye over Jared, he was surprised to see that his hair was a little longer than the last time he had seen him; more fashionably cut.

And the designer stubble was something new. To hide the scar, he wondered, before dismissing the idea. The denims, checked shirt and desert boots were the same. A seriously good-looking bastard, Jared was totally unaware of the impact he had on women. The thought came unbidden, the new look, had he met someone? He dismissed it instantly. The wounds of Emma's death were still raw; besides, since leaving the firm some three years ago Jodie had become his life.

Waving them over, he shook hands with Jared, before turning his attention to Jodie.

"And how is my favourite little girl?"

Pouting, Jodie pretended to be annoyed. "I'm not a little girl anymore, Uncle Danny, I'm ten now."

"I stand corrected, young lady." He replied.

Gathering her into his arms, he threw her into the air before catching her again. "You've grown so much, I won't be able to do that for much longer, will I?" he said, putting her down breathlessly. "Would you two like a drink?"

"Coke for me and a white coffee for my father, please," Jodie replied.

Danny raised his hand, and a waiter appeared instantly; moments later, the drinks arrived.

Aware that Jodie was to become privy to some unpleasant details, Jared made a suggestion. Sitting on the table opposite, with the new headphones glued to her ears, Jodie was content.

Clamping his hands around the mug of steaming coffee, Jared blew on it, watching as a cloud of steam rose into the air. When he was ready, he took a tentative sip. Satisfied, he took a much larger one before sitting back and looking up. Giving Danny the once over, he noted how he had piled on a few more pounds since he had last seen him. Recognising the signs, Danny waited for the first question. It wasn't long in coming.

"Today's little incident isn't the only thing on your mind."

"Something smells. It might well be my devious mind. I don't think so. That's why I want your take on things. The TV programme the other day, see it?"

"If you're referring to the one that ended in bloodshed, I saw a repeat showing."

"What did you make of it?"

"Exactly what you did, you crafty old bugger," said Jared. "Amateurish, no previous skill with handling their weapons, the weapons too sophisticated for the job in hand. Want me to go on?"

"And the doctor?" asked Danny.

"The look on his face before he died, you mean? Came as a shock to him, didn't it," chuckled Jared. Changing tack, he said, "Saw you at the crime scene. Do we know who they were? The victims, I mean," enquired Jared.

"Didn't get much from the bodies, wasn't enough left of the poor sods for that. But, if they were in the company of Charles Hillary, then I'm guessing they were either seriously wealthy or influential people. Amazingly, and this is something that hasn't been released to the press, the PM lived for a few moments after the explosion."

"You're joking," said an astonished Jared.

"Seems the device didn't function properly. The others never stood a chance, they were almost vaporised. It was way and above what would normally be needed to kill the passengers. So, the question I'm left with is why?"

Thoughtful for moment, he added, "A report came in recently from the Maldives, something about a mini-massacre on one of their islands. Fifty-odd miles from one of our old bases apparently. Royal Air Force GAN, ever hear of it?"

"Vaguely, it was way before my time. Used as a stopover

between Britain and the Far East, by the 1970s, the UK was withdrawing from its commitments east of the Suez. These days Diego Garcia, a US military base some 200 miles south of the Maldives is used."

"Impressive recapping," commented Danny. "Anyway, three bodies turned up. Two of them, burnt to a crisp, were discovered in some kind of make-shift hut. The other was shot. Not locals, they're small in stature. These were big guys. So why did the killer feel the need to incinerate two of the bodies? What was he trying to hide? Nearly forgot, shortly before his death – a few days in fact – Charles Hillary received a phone call from someone who'd bugged his private conversations."

"In No. 10?" was the incredulous response.

"Won't bore you with details, only to say it involved an offer of a meeting between him and some mysterious stranger. Not difficult to put two and two together and come up with the idea the same thing happened to the others. Don't know whether what I'm going to tell you next has any bearing on the overall picture, but you know the way my mind works. In the last few months we've been hearing rumblings about some top-secret research complex in the back of beyond. According to sources, it's state of the art. It isn't what brought the place to our attention though. Recently, quite a few young children have gone missing in or around the village."

Darting a look at Jodie, she was oblivious to what had just been said.

"Anyway, questions were being asked in Whitehall. Before the PM died, it was known he was about to look into things. Might that be the reason for his death? Hardly seems likely, though," continued Danny, "otherwise why were the others taken out? We're missing something here. And for the life of me I can't get my head around it."

About to ask a question, Jared was interrupted by Danny's mobile.

"Yours or mine?" said Danny hating all things technological.

"The theme tune from a fistful of dollars isn't my thing," said Jared struggling to keep a straight face.

"See your point," said Danny. Removing the offending object from his pocket, he flipped the cover and pressed the green button. Shouting loudly – an irritating habit most people who use a mobile phone have – Jared interrupted, "If that's important, you might want to lower your voice."

Embarrassed, Danny noted how several customers had turned in his direction. Lowering his voice, he whispered, "What's up, Tina?"

Shortly after, terminating the conversation, he looked up. "Seems we have, or perhaps had might be a better way of explaining it, a witness."

"What do you mean?" said Jared.

"Tina just heard from the local police. Some guy called Paul Hudson, a reporter apparently, claims his brother Jonathan was a witness to yesterday's killings. Moments before the PM died, he managed to whisper a few words. But there's a problem, the brother knew someone was after him. Halfway through the conversation they were cut off. This guy Hudson's convinced his brother's dead. His instincts were right. Police found a body in a telephone booth a few miles from where the incident took place. His neck had been broken."

"What did he say before he died?" asked Jared.

"That's the interesting bit, something about a research centre in Wales." Rubbing his chin thoughtfully, Danny said, "Curiouser and curiouser, is what Dickens would have said."

Having become bored with the music, Jodie had removed her headphones and was making her way over to her father's table.

Overhearing the comment, she intruded on the conversation. "Think you'll find it's a direct quote from *Alice in Wonderland* rather than Charles Dickens, Uncle Danny."

The observation brought an instant burst of laughter from both men.

NINE

Bio-Slim Laboratories
Bedfordshire
Some five years previous

THE DIRECTORS OF Bio-Slim were deeply troubled. A once thriving empire was threatening to fall apart. Things had started to go wrong when a weight-loss supplement labelled 'Magi-Slim' turned out to be fundamentally flawed. Despite warnings, they had pushed the product onto the market without adequate testing.

The first fatality had been labelled a freak accident. An assumption reinforced by the fact that for months afterwards nothing untoward happened. Relieved, they had put the incident down to a one off occurrence. As with all new products there were bound to be teething problems, they'd reasoned. Now, the issue had reared its ugly head once more.

In the last six months there had been five more reported fatalities. The latest figures showed that in total, a staggering thirty-eight people had died. Still unwilling to face facts they had brushed the problem under the carpet. In terms of statistics, they'd argued, it was an insignificant number in light of the hundreds of thousands of people who had actually bought the product.

Johan Steger cut an imposing figure. And he knew it. Physical and psychological intimidation had ensured that through the years, he had always had his own way. His steel grey hair, cut short, gave the impression that he was ex-military. Nothing could be further from the truth. In fact he was a born coward.

The centre piece of the boardroom was a large walnut table. New, Richard Anthony noted it was designed to accommodate thirteen.

"Unfortunate number," he commented.

Counting, the others saw what he was alluding to. "Anyone know why thirteen's unlucky?" asked Dave Tomlinson.

Seeing the bemused faces, he explained. "Thirteen was the number which attended The Last Supper."

"Don't see the relevance," said Steger eager to begin proceedings.

"Look what happened to Jesus," came the reply.

The laughter lasted for several moments. Order restored, Steger allowed his gaze to settle on each of his fellow directors. Assessing their strengths and weaknesses, he concluded that they were caricatures of business men. Worse, incapable of thinking for themselves, they were moral cowards.

The decision to push the product onto the market early had been the correct one. In a hedonistic world like the present, he'd pointed out nothing was ever foolproof. He had been right; in no time they had made a small fortune.

Time to put them out of their misery, he thought.

"According to this file," he said, waving a manila folder in the air, "Thirty-eight people have died as a result of our product. Report says the investigation which as we know has dragged on for years is nearing its conclusion. Now for the bad news, my lawyers inform me that should we contest the findings, we'll lose."

"Then we're finished," said an incredulous Dave Tomlinson, "All those millions will be wiped out."

"And a lot more besides," said Matthew Carter, unable to believe his ears.

"If my information is correct," continued Steger, "The millions we've already made won't even be enough to cover the compensation claims."

He would never have money worries. His father would bail

him out. He always did. He had phoned a few months ago offering the use of some underground complex in Wales. At the time, he hadn't given it a thought. Last week, seeing the writing was on the wall, he'd phoned to accept the offer.

An anguished retort from Carter made him look up. "If things are as bad as you say, I suggest we cut and run."

"Exactly what do you mean by cut and run, Matthew?" asked an amused Steger.

"We go into hiding. First we sell our homes and any other disposable assets and then we withdraw whatever savings we've stashed away."

"Well done, Matthew. I didn't think you'd have the balls to come up with such a suggestion. Unfortunately it wouldn't work. However much money we'd recoup wouldn't be enough."

"Why not?" inquired an indignant Matthew.

"The kind of lifestyles we're accustomed to, the little nest egg we'd accrue wouldn't last very long. Then what? We'd be back to square one. What we need is a guaranteed income."

"Remember one thing, Johan," said Richard Anthony interrupting. "Between the three of us we have enough to hang you, so don't get any fancy ideas."

Seeing the meeting was getting away from him, Steger changed tactics. "Instead of going into hiding, why don't we relocate," he said.

"Surely there's no time?" said Tomlinson, suddenly sensing a glimmer of hope.

"Already made contingency plans. When we placed the product on the market I took the warnings about inadequate testing seriously. Also envisaged making enough profit during the first few years that should things go wrong, we'd have enough to do what I'm suggesting now."

With a self-satisfied smirk, he added, "Already got a new place lined up. Situated deep in the heart of the Welsh countryside it's so well hidden most of the locals don't know of its existence. I know, I know," he added with a wave of his hand, "It's a Third World country, but it's perfect for our needs."

The remark brought the expected burst of laughter, except from Richard Anthony, who he could tell wasn't buying any of it. Not that it mattered. All he had to do was to soft soap him until he could find a solution to the problem.

The bastard was right, of course, they had him by the balls. Unused to being compromised, he came to an immediate decision.

Dragging himself back to the present, he said, "Everything's underground."

Seeing their startled expressions, he added, "When I say underground, I don't mean one of those bunkers used during the war. This is a massive self-contained facility, state of the art. Never appeared on the market," he said tapping the side of his nose.

"Complex is ready, so I've taken the liberty of hiring several people. Heading the project's a guy called Brad Davison. Weak willed and naive, just the type we want. Made it clear from the outset those in key positions must be without family."

"Why should that be a priority, Johan?" Richard Anthony asked suspiciously.

"Should be bloody obvious," said Steger. "Remember the incident with our last project manager a few years ago?"

"Christ, yes," came the reply. "Melrose committed suicide, didn't he? Shortly after we found out he had family. Son, I think, but no one could trace him."

Having contributed very little to the conversation for the last ten minutes or so, Dave Tomlinson found his voice. "You're a ruthless bastard, Johan."

"You'd better believe it. Some of the projects though risky could make us a fortune, so what do you say?"

"What choice do we have?" said Tomlinson. "Thank God you saw what was coming."

"Then we've reason to celebrate," said Steger handing out brandy and cigars from his private stock.

Taking a pull from his hand-rolled Cuban, Steger inhaled deeply. Instantly a look of deep satisfaction creased his craggy features.

By 8.00 a.m. the following morning, all three families had died in tragic circumstances. In a strange coincidence that had the local police baffled, it seemed the husbands had killed their wives and children first, before dousing their bodies with petrol and setting fire to themselves.

TEN

Thursday, 29 November 2012
Fort Worth International Airport
Dallas, USA

KATHY SULLIVAN STUDIED her ticket. Past experience had shown that the best method of reaching her seat with the minimum of hassle was to allow others passengers to board first. Tired after two internal flights, thankfully this would be the final leg. The sixth busiest airport in the world in terms of human cargo, Kathy knew that Fort Worth International handled some 60 million passengers annually. The busiest of all Texas airports, she was prepared for a lengthy delay. Amazingly, the flight was on time.

Stuffing her hand luggage into the stowaway compartment above her head, she was surprised to see that, besides hers, there was only one other. I couldn't be that fortunate, she reasoned. But she was.

A wide-body jet, each row of the nine seats was divided into three sections. Two by the window on the portside, five down the centre, and another two by the window on the starboard side.

Petite and blonde, Kathy was an extremely attractive woman. Rather than being beautiful in a conventional way, she came across as alluring. Like Amanda Tapping of *Stargate SG-1* fame someone had once pointed out. The compliment hadn't sat well with Kathy. For some reason she was always looking for faults in her appearance. To her way of thinking, her nose was too small and her dimples too deep. Dressed in a pair of faded denims and loose-fitting shirt, a pair of tan boots completed the picture.

Lady Luck had provided her with a window seat; more

importantly the two seats next to her were empty. Blowing an audible sigh of relief, her subconscious had painted a nightmare scenario, one in which she had been sitting alongside someone who either wanted your life history or, worse, was determined to give you theirs.

A tiny television set popped out from its hiding place in the roof. Seconds later, an animated puppet-like creature set about running the passengers through the safety regulations.

From previous flights, Kathy knew that shortly the aircraft would be going through its final pre-flight routine. The noise of the engines grew in intensity; they were almost ready for take off. Buckling her seat belt, she was just in time. From nowhere, a blonde stewardess, a smile wide enough to show off a set of perfect white teeth, leaned over to check everything was in order.

Relaxed, Kathy cast her mind over the events of the last few weeks and the way that they had impacted on her life. To say everything had been thrown into turmoil was an understatement. She hadn't been back to the UK since the death of her father several years ago. Breaking up with Steve had forced her hand.

When the offer had arrived from America, how long ago had it been now? Nearly five years, if her memory served her correctly, her father had described it as an opportunity of a lifetime. "People with your unique talents are extremely rare," he had pointed out. "And these people know it." Adding, "If things don't work out, you can always come home."

Cutting her train of thought, she concentrated on the view. A hard-bitten scientist, it always amazed her how such an ungainly lump of steel, plastic and God knows what else ever managed to get off the ground. Let alone stay in the air for hours.

Never one to sit still, her brain was constantly working, always looking for fresh challenges. Unknown to her, it was what made her such a good scientist. Several magazines later and what seemed like endless trips to the toilet, she dozed off.

She woke feeling refreshed. Unbuckling her seat belt, she walked several lengths of the aircraft to ward off the symptoms of the dreaded deep vein thrombosis. Returning to her seat, she was in time to catch the drinks trolley. Not a big one for alcohol, a large coffee was ordered instead. Surprisingly, it was quite good, as was the microwave-heated dinner which arrived soon after.

With time to kill, she reflected on past mistakes. It had been a whirlwind romance. They had met at a party and fallen hard. Weeks later they had moved in together. Within months they'd tied the knot. The first year had been idyllic. Head over heels in love, they had had eyes for no one but each other.

The change, when it came, had caught her off guard.

Barely perceptible at first, things gradually deteriorated. In no time, they seemed to be arguing and quarrelling a good deal. In fairness they had both been at fault. A combination of stressful jobs and too little time together was bound to take its toll. And it did.

Eventually they came to a decision that it might be best to spend some time apart. Both knowing deep down it was to be no short-term separation. Their once glorious relationship had simply run out of steam.

From then on, coming home had always been on the cards. Even the job had become monotonous. The company had wanted to go one way, she another. Working her notice had given her the opportunity to sell the furniture and some other odds and ends. The two large suitcases sitting in the hold somewhere below her feet were the sum total of everything she owned. The legacy of her time spent in the land of the free.

According to the information she had been given at the desk, the journey would take just short of ten hours. Not long, the time still dragged by interminably. Finally, the instructions to buckle up came over the speakers.

A hard-boiled sweet was popped into her mouth to reduce the pressure on her eardrums, shortly after the noise of the engines altered. Taking advantage of the few moments left, she gazed through the window. London was a wonderful city. To her mind it was a classic example of organised chaos. The one constant was the Thames. Like a giant serpent, it wound its way through the lowlands below. The main tourist attractions were by now visible. London Bridge, St Paul's and the Big Eye jumped out at her immediately, along with the impressive bulk of the Houses of Parliament. One or two other landmarks flashed by.

Suddenly, the huge car parks servicing the busy airport loomed beneath. Seconds later, as gently as a lover's kiss, the huge plane landed on the surface of the runway.

Employing the same trick as before, she sat back and waited. What seemed like an age later, she headed for a bank of overhead television screens to check which carousel her luggage would be arriving on. On this occasion, the wait for her cases was surprisingly less than expected. Finding a trolley with which to lug them around proved to be another matter. Eventually she spotted one tucked away in a remote corner of the building. Counting her blessings for her stroke of good fortune, it wasn't long before the reason for its abandonment became apparent. Turning left or right appeared to be something the manufacturers hadn't allowed for. Finally managing to steer herself towards the exit, she joined the throng of people making their way through customs.

Since 9/11, along with most other airports in the world, security was tight. Armed police were in evidence everywhere. Dressed in black, torsos complete with body armour, each sported a vicious short-barrelled machine pistol. Not being an expert on this type of firearm, the make eluded her. All she knew was that they looked distinctly bad for your health.

The main area was full of people welcoming home families, either from long-haul holidays or, in some instances she supposed, greeting relations that had been away for years. Maybe several are like me, thought Kathy, instantly realising that, unlike them, there would be no one waiting to greet her. There would be no one to hug and kiss her, no one to help with her luggage. Fighting back the tears, she allowed her gaze to drift lazily over the myriads of holiday makers.

Scuttling around like ants, the tourists were everywhere. The Japanese were easy to pick out. Cameras hanging from their necks, they were frantically looking at maps which at times seemed larger than them. Eventually she spotted what she was looking for. Amidst a row of small glass-fronted booths offering everything from money changing to cigarettes and perfumes was a car hire firm.

Entering customs, a cursory glance from the female officer in charge was all she merited. Heading for the Avis rental sign, she hired a modest Ford Focus. A short time later, she was on her way.

In the grip of a strange dream Michael Conrad was staring at an open grave. The sky the colour of kneaded dough was split by a fierce arc of lightening. Instantly, thin slanting rain, cold and merciless, began falling in torrents. As he watched, a coffin was lowered into the gaping jaws of the pit. Shortly afterwards it was followed by two much smaller ones.

Hovering some twenty feet above the ground, Michael studied a lone figure. Spurning an umbrella, the man was drenched. Lost in some private hell, he was gazing skywards, staring through hate-filled eyes towards the heavens.

Something about the scene was achingly familiar. He almost had it, then it was gone, the notion as insubstantial as smoke. Waking, Michael was a bath of sweat.

It had been the same dream again. Haunting his sleep, the details were always the same. And he knew why.

The man had been him, the coffins, those of his wife and baby daughters. After all these years, the dream still had the power to whisper to him in the depths of the night, to mock the memory of his loved ones, forcing him to re-live those awful moments over and over again. And there was the guilt, always the guilt. Was there never to be any respite?

The funeral had turned out to be a grim soulless day. The priest had gone through the expected charade. The speech, delivered in precise and measured tones was made up of meaningless phrases. Meant to bring him comfort, it had brought him none.

A self-made man, he'd become successful by working incredibly long hours. His was the original story of rags to riches. Penniless at sixteen, by the age of forty he had become a billionaire. And yet it had all been for nothing. For some reason God had decided to abandon him.

A week after the funeral he had returned to the grave.

Placing three red roses beneath the simple headstone, he had vowed on the memory of his loved ones to find those responsible and make them suffer.

That had been some five years ago, yet despite spending a small fortune he'd had no success. He was beginning to despair of ever finding the culprits. Was that why the dream was so vivid? Did his family feel his mounting despair? Was his resolve crumbling?

The accident was still fresh in his memory.

Several miles into the journey to visit her parents, Zoe had made a few choking noises before slumping against the steering wheel of the Jaguar XF saloon. In a vain attempt to wrestle control from his unconscious wife, Michael had let go of his baby daughters and launched himself from the back seat. He had almost made it when the inevitable occurred. Out of control the car lurched sideways and clipped the flimsy barrier at the side of the road. Curiously because of the angle of deflection, instead of plunging over the side, the car flipped into the air and took off vertically.

Speaking to the police afterwards, all Michael could recall was being thrown out of the passenger door. Hitting the ground hard, he'd been saved from toppling into the steep ravine by a thicket of brambles. While this was taking place he'd been afforded a grandstand view of the car as it headed skywards. The Jaguar completely unaware of the laws of physics sailed majestically upwards, until inevitably gravity overtook inertia and the car plummeted back to earth with far less grace than it had displayed in taking off. Performing a series of spectacular summersaults it finally plunged into the ravine some fifty feet below. Hitting the rocks beneath, it burst into flames.

The inquest revealed that the accident had been anything but: Zoe had died of a heart attack brought about by a foreign substance in her blood. It was then that he had remembered the slimming pills. In a cruel twist of what he viewed as poetic justice, the directors of the company had died shortly afterwards in tragic circumstances.

The faceless man who had fronted the company had disappeared, however; no trace of him had ever been uncovered. Since then, he had spared no expense in hunting down the bastard he held responsible for killing his family.

ELEVEN

Friday, 30 November 2012
5.00 a.m.
Bournemouth, England

THE MINDLESS MONOTONY of the drive helped clear the demons crowding Kathy's thoughts. At this time of the morning the roads were quiet. Free from commuters hurrying to and from work, the traffic was mainly a flotilla of vehicles delivering goods to the myriads of supermarkets dotted around the country. Complications aside, she'd make it to Bournemouth well before the inevitable inner city snarl. The bulk of the journey over, she was glad now that she had opted for a hire car rather than travel by train.

Nearing the outskirts, the motorway suddenly took a sweeping left turn and her mind was dragged into the present. Within moments the main roundabout was in sight.

Taking the inside lane and drifting across to the right, she was now heading in the opposite direction. Many an unwary tourist had come unstuck here.

Slowly the landscape began to change its personality. Heavily populated areas of houses and industrial complexes gave way to lush green fields flanked on either side by wide open countryside. Within ten minutes the car entered a neighbourhood of impressive red and brown bricked houses, fronted by well-manicured lawns and flower gardens. Bournemouth was a decidedly middle-class area, however, the further you moved away from the confines of the town, the more you were left with the impression of real wealth.

Suddenly she was there. The dirt road leading to the beautiful old thatched cottage was pitted and worn. Here and there were several fairly deep pools of standing water.

Pulling up outside the front door of the little cottage, she killed the engine and set the handbrake. As if accepting it was the end of the line, her body decided to give up. Like sand filtering through clenched fingers, what little energy remained seeped from every pore of her being. Defences down, memories of a distant past came back to haunt her. Giving in to her fragile emotions, she slumped against the steering wheel and burst into tears.

Afterwards she felt better. It was as if she had been cleansed of something deep inside. Taking a lungful of air to control her breathing, she released the seat belt, opened the car door and made her way towards the cottage.

Realising she had no key, panic set in. How on earth was she was going to get inside? Breaking windows was not her forte. Then it came back to her. Standing on tip toe, she put her hand into one of two small flower baskets hanging either side of the door. A moment of trepidation was followed by a sigh of relief. The key was still there. Not a very original hiding place, it was one her father had been happy with.

Shortly after the funeral, she'd been asked if she would be interested in renting the cottage, but had refused. Allowing strangers into her home would have been an insult to her father's memory. She had made one concession: a cleaner had been hired to come in on a regular basis to stave off the musty smell houses tend to acquire when left empty for long periods.

Opening the door, the accumulation of letters sprawled across the mat was reminiscent of an invading army. Shuffling the bundle into some kind of order, she closed the door with her foot and headed towards the kitchen.

Everything was exactly as she remembered. Unbidden, the

story of the ghost ship *Mary Celeste* came to mind. Shaking off the disturbing image, she was convinced the rest of the house would be exactly the same. And it was.

The focal point of the cottage had always been the kitchen. The stove, originally wood burning had been converted to gas several years ago. Underneath the kitchen window stood the sink, a huge white porcelain bowl complete with old-fashioned plug.

Through the rear window, several large trees made up the backdrop to the boundary of the cottage. In the right-hand corner, next to the rockery, was the pond. Her attention focused on the lawn. Usually immaculate, it was badly in need of love and care.

Strangely, now that she had cried herself out, tiredness was no longer a problem. Deciding on a cup of tea, she filled the kettle with cold water. Waiting for it to boil, she sifted through the mass of letters. Most were junk mail. The one she was looking for was near the bottom, the solicitor's name clearly embossed in bold capitals. Scanning it, the relevant part was in the second paragraph. Now she had finally decided to come home, he would be happy to discuss her father's estate. An appointment had been pencilled in for 2.00 p.m., today. The clock told her it was just after eight. She made a decision. Once she had finished her cup of tea, she would phone; confirm the time was fine.

Rising, Gerald Harland stuck out his hand. "Thank you for coming, Kathy, it's been years since your father's death. As you requested everything's been left untouched." The formalities taken care of, he gestured with an outstretched arm at one of two comfortable chairs standing either side of his desk.

"Have a seat."

Remembering his manners he added, "Sorry, would you like a cup of something?"

"Tea would be lovely, Mr Harland."

"Milk and no sugar?" he enquired.

Pleasantries over, Kathy let her eyes wander around the room. There were so many antiques it was as if she had been transported back to Dickensian times. Three of the four walls were covered in damson and white, while several water colours of a generic nature were dotted here and there. The fourth, the one directly behind his desk was covered in photographs showing Gerald Harland with a host of local celebrities. In one he could be seen clasping hands warmly with the mayor. Smiles as big as their wallets, they radiated false sincerity. In another, he stood shoulder to shoulder with some bigwig who had just donated a small fortune to charity. Too far away to see how much the cheque was for, the way the whole thing was staged managed, arms around each other and peering into the lens of the camera, she was willing to bet it was for a goodly sum. The whole scenario left you in no doubt as to just how important they were.

A large portion of the remaining space was filled with his qualifications. And there were quite a few. Mounted and covered in glass to protect the contents, they had been placed so as to ensure maximum exposure. Her daydreams were interrupted by a knock on the door. Seconds later his secretary appeared with the tea.

Handing it over, she smiled at Kathy, swivelled on her heels and retreated. Several feet from the door she was stopped in her tracks. "And, Wendy, hold my calls for the next ten minutes or so please. Thank you."

All business now, he took a key from his pocket and walked across to a steel safe in the right-hand corner of the room.

Removing a large manila file, he returned to his desk. Undoing the knot, he opened the file and adjusted his spectacles. Several seconds passed as he pretended to scan the documents. Ready, he placed everything on the desk and looked up. Tenting his hands under his chin in a well-rehearsed gesture, he began. "I'm sure you're aware of it, but in the last few years the value of property has risen alarmingly. Besides which the little nest egg your father left for you has increased twofold. Everything considered, you've become quite a wealthy young lady. The sum after my little deductions for expenses comes to," he said fingers flying over his pocket calculator, "Exactly £550,000.87p."

The astonishment was clearly expressed on Kathy's face. Dad had been quite well off, but never in her wildest dreams did she guess he was worth that much. "That's without the value of the house. At today's prices," he rambled on, "Added to the extensive land surrounding it, you'd be looking at another cool half million. Should you want to sell, that is," he added smoothly.

Too smoothly was her thought. Next, he would be telling her it just so happened that he had someone who was interested in the house.

Determined to stop the bullshit before it got off the ground, she said quietly but firmly. "I've no intention of selling my father's home, Mr Harland. It's nice of you to put a value on it all the same."

Knowing he had been caught red-handed, he attempted to cover his embarrassment. "No, no, it's nothing like that I assure you. The value is a rough estimation, that's all. A ball-park figure I plucked out of the air, nothing more."

Knowing such a lame excuse was only too transparent to a woman of Kathy's intellect, he decided to leave it at that.

TWELVE

New World Laboratories
Genetic research facility, Wales
Some six months previous

HEADING FOR THE bank of computers, Harvey Dillinger, project manager for New World Laboratories, rescued the pen from its hiding place on the clipboard. Studying the latest information, he recorded it meticulously. Double checking his findings, he frowned.

"These results don't make sense," he said turning to his colleague. "Mind nipping downstairs – see what the lab boys have to say?"

Mark Hanson made his way towards the door. He'd almost made it when he heard Harvey's voice, "And don't forget your moon suit."

"Been working here months and he still reminds me," muttered Mark under his breath.

Tall and pencil thin, Harvey looked more like a businessman than a project manager for a research facility. Approaching his sixtieth birthday, he was strangely without family. During a quiet drink, Mark had tried to quiz him about his private life. Harvey had endured his enquiries stoically, but had told him nothing. Since then Mark had backed off.

Approaching the lift, he winked at the guard while holding up his access card.

"Morning, Trevor, and how are you today?"

Studying his pass, Trevor stepped aside without a word. Have a nice one, you miserable bastard, thought Mark.

Pressing the button for level 4, he reflected on how it had all started.

He had been working for a company called Genentech. It was no secret that he was in demand, his growing reputation made it a sure fire cert that eventually he would be headhunted by one of the larger companies. But things were going too slowly for Mark. Young and ambitious, according to his thinking there were worlds to conquer. Despite his lofty ambitions, he still had reservations about his chosen field. Advances in genetic research had taken such quantum leaps forward in recent years; the implications for mankind were frightening. Everything seemed to be geared towards breaking down the biological barriers Mother Nature had dictated. Mark was convinced that the time was approaching when humans would be able to control their own evolution. According to this hypothesis, a new species would emerge, one that transcended human boundaries. In Mark's eyes, this was dangerously close to not only playing God, but becoming God. And he wanted no part of that.

Shelving his misgivings he had applied to Phoenix. It was exactly the kind of move he was looking for. And in the end everything had turned out to be so simple. Early one morning, during one of his coffee breaks he had been called into the head of faculties office. His boss, Conrad Phelps, had informed him that a company called Phoenix had faxed him. Conrad had made it quite plain that he was disappointed that Mark had applied elsewhere, but that he had no doubt that he would be successful in obtaining the post – he had added that should things not turn out well, he would always be welcomed back. The brief meeting had ended with an amicable handshake. And that had been it.

The company had been the devil's own job to find. Surrounded by dense forest, it had been hidden from view. Approaching by car, gaps in the trees had provided evidence of floodlighting, a huge perimeter fence and the occasional armed guard. The elaborate precautions had prompted one question. What kind of projects warranted such safety measures?

Showing his pass which he'd been given at the gate, he had been allowed through. Without further preamble he'd made his way towards what was obviously the main part of the building. It was another five minutes before he arrived at the office in which he was to be interviewed. Above the receptionist's desk stood a well-crafted sign. In bold black letters almost a foot high, the mission statement was touted.

Greeted by an extremely attractive woman, she directed Mark to an outer office.

"The professor is waiting for you, Mr Hanson. Have a nice journey?"

"Very pleasant, but I'd be a lot more relaxed if I knew what to expect."

"Don't worry, you'll soon feel at home." She chuckled.

Moments later they were inside Brad Davison's office. The professor shook Mark's hand warmly. Gesturing to a leather armchair, he said, "Sit down, Mr Hanson, or may I call you Mark?"

"Mark's fine. I must admit I'm a bit thrown at the speed with which everything's taken place though."

"Appreciate that. What if I explain things first? Then you can ask questions later. How does that grab you?"

"Fine," said Mark, beginning to get a good feeling about things. Over the course of the next hour, the professor outlined what the facility was about.

"Granted you know a good deal of what I'm about to say, but bear with me, please. Recently we've considerably enhanced out knowledge of the brain. Yet, despite this, details of what actually happens when we think, remember, dream or imagine, are still vague. The activity is mainly electrical. It sends and receives currents from its own nerve cells, to and from the many millions situated in various parts of the body. These basic cell units which make up both the brain and the nervous system are called neurones."

Mark nodded.

"Neurones differ in shape and size, often considerably. They can be oval, round or even spindle like. Each, though incredibly small, approximately 0.025mm, has a tiny charge even when not in use. This electrical charge is produced by the chemical difference between the interior of the nerve cell and the tissue which surrounds it. Touching, tasting, along with other stimuli alter this chemical balance and can be recorded. It's what we're concentrating on at the moment. Electrical impulses flow like sparks along a fuse. Current initiated in one neurone often causes neighbouring neurones to undergo electro-chemical changes. In turn, they 'fire' in order to assist in the operation required. Millions of neurones are firing every second. Perceived by the brain as being coded messages, many are rejected because they're not recognised as belonging to 'priority' categories."

Sensing Mark's restlessness, the professor hurried on.

"The astounding versatility of the brain comes into focus when you consider it's in charge of an interior as well as an exterior environment. It keeps us alive by balancing the process of growth and decay. Though it does relax in sleep, as long as it lives it finds no actual rest."

"Excuse me for interrupting," said Mark, "But what is it you actually do? When I saw your security arrangements, I had visions of biological warfare and that kind of thing."

"Lord, no, it's nothing like that. We're a commercial company. Haven't a clue what goes on below – on levels 3 and 4, that is. Out of bounds to people like me, we never see any of their scientists, or very infrequently anyway. They have their own entrance, car park, canteen, living quarters, laboratories and the like. In short, they live a totally separate existence."

"What kind of projects are you working on presently?" asked Mark.

"Utilising the information I touched on earlier, we're experimenting with specific areas of the brain to find commercial applications."

"Care to give me an example?"

"Obesity is one of the biggest problems in society. Most people, apart from those living in Third World countries eat far too much. Present company included," he said patting his waistline. "If we could only find the area which controls our eating habits, we could stop it. Drugs could be produced which would put an end to those busy little neurones sending the message that we're hungry all the time. The financial rewards of producing something like that would be incalculable. It's why we're willing to pay so much in order to recruit the right people. Not all profit, mind you. Apart from our massive wage bill, there's the huge cost of the research itself. Anyway, let's pop down the hall for a moment, there's one other person I'd like you to meet."

Knocking, they waited until a loud booming voice shouted, "Enter!"

The professor's office had been small but comfy; this was palatial. Sitting, legs propped on a gargantuan desk, was a bear of a man. In one hand he held a huge cigar, while the other, perched near his mouth, sported a glass of whiskey.

"This is Mr Johan Steger," said Davison.

Oblivious to Mark's presence, Steger shouted to the professor, "No family ties, I hope?"

Seeing the nod of affirmation, he lifted his feet from the desk, swivelled in his reclining chair and turned his back on them.

All that had taken place some five months ago. Since then he had been promoted. Now he was working for New World Laboratories, a subsidiary of Medusa Industries, the company that owned levels 3 and 4. Making his way along the narrow corridor made entirely of stainless steel, Mark reached the elevator. Punching in the code, he waited. A soft ping heralded the arrival of the lift. Stepping inside, he tensed: he hated lifts. Not claustrophobic, it was simply that being entombed in such a confined space, his mind was allowed scope to conjure up all kinds of scenarios, none of which bore thinking about. He didn't have long to wait: in moments he arrived at his destination.

He was now on sacred turf: level 4. Entering the furthest of several laboratories in the vicinity, he selected a bio-hazard suit from dozens hanging on pegs. Kitting up, Harvey's words were still fresh in his ears and so he double-checked both seals and fittings. Satisfied, he entered the main body of the laboratory.

He'd taken a few steps only when he stopped dead in his tracks. Two assistants were holding an animal at arm's length. Controlling it by means of a long pole and leather collar, a third was delivering intermittent pulses of electrical current directly into its cerebral cortex. It was sickening. Never having been witness to anything like this before, he wondered what the hell they were doing.

Raising his hand to Anna Heche in silent greeting, it brought no response. And yet, it was hardly surprising, in terms of pecking order, she was the jewel in the crown. Not that it bothered him. He was perfectly content with his lowly position on the totem pole.

Around five feet in height, she weighed in at around nine stone, of which every pound was solid muscle. Blessed with subtle Asiatic features, she was truly beautiful. Considering himself attractive to the opposite sex, for some reason his boyish charm had failed miserably to penetrate her cool exterior. Casting his eyes around the cages, something didn't gel. These animals were a different species to the ones he had seen yesterday. Instead of chimps, the cages now held dozens of rhesus monkeys. In itself that wasn't surprising, normally it was this type of animal that was used. Yet, this batch was like nothing he had ever seen.

Then it struck him. The creatures had been tampered with. The evidence was in the eyes. Blood crazed, they stared at him with a combination of pain and hatred. Mouths wide open, they displayed hideous looking fangs. Hissing at him like reptiles, Mark's unease mounted by the minute. The electrical prods and tranquiliser guns he had seen earlier now made perfect sense. A mutant breed, it was the only way they could be controlled.

Suddenly, a cold hard feeling settled in the pit of his stomach, inadvertently he'd stumbled onto something he was never meant to see. And yet it didn't make sense. Security had made no attempt to stop him entering the lab. So what the fuck was happening?

The final cage held further horrors. Designed to house a pair of animals, it now contained one. Covered in blood, the solitary creature appeared to be sleeping. Of the other specimen nothing remained except bones. Every scrap of flesh had been consumed.

As though waking from a dream, the animal gave a long shudder, opened its mouth and grinned. Directing his gaze at Anna Heche, he switched on his helmet microphone. "What the hell have you done to that animal?"

Startled, she looked up. What the fuck was Mark Hanson doing here? Security had been given strict instructions that no one but her and a few chosen colleagues be allowed access to the lab today. So what had happened? Someone was going to pay for this with their job. In the meantime what the hell was she to do?

Fighting to control her emotions, she took a few deep breaths. Returning his stare, she said, "There's no need to overreact."

"Overreact," said an astonished Mark. Then in a burst of intuition he had it. This batch must have been given the notorious R90 which the rumour mongers had been banging on about for weeks. A sobering thought stuck him, what would happen if the creature should escape?

Having gone through the lengthy process of decontamination, he exited the lab. Brushing past the security guard, he headed directly for Harvey's office. Dispensing with pleasantries, he marched in. "We've got to talk."

Such was his anger he failed to notice that he'd been followed. From a discreet distance Anna saw him entering Harvey's office. Making her way over, she leaned towards the door and listened. The voices were distant, but the volume loud enough to make out some of what was being said. It was enough to piece together the gist of the conversation. Shit, she cursed: Hudson walking in on her little experiment unannounced might have serious repercussions for the future, she realised. Livid, a single vein in the side of her temple was throbbing uncontrollably. Caught in two minds, she was unsure whether to walk in and confront him, or cut her loses and leave. Mulling things over, she heard footsteps in the distance. Instantly, her choice became academic. Turning on her heels, she retraced her route, heading back the way she had come.

Mark came straight to the point. "Anna Heche is playing God."

"You've lost me, Mark," said Harvey. "I'm a project manager, not a scientist, so take it slowly."

Marshalling his thoughts, Mark answered, "Insert human

genes directly into something like chimp embryos and you create what's known as a transgenic animal. In layman's terms she's creating hybrids."

"Nonsense," said Harvey. "We don't carry out that kind of research here."

"And that's a fact, is it Harvey?"

"Well no, but I have assurances from…"

"That's your problem," said Mark, interrupting. "You take everything at face value." For the next few minutes he outlined the rumours circulating, in particular those concerning Rodaxin 90.

"What I don't understand," continued Mark, "is how, apart from her inner circle of initiates, no one else has caught on to what she's doing." And then he had it. "Of course, hidden away in the facility somewhere she has a laboratory of her own, one that only she knows about. It's the only explanation."

THIRTEEN

Saturday, 1 December 2012
10.00 a.m.

RETRIEVING THE PILE of letters she had discarded yesterday, Kathy sifted through them once more. This time more carefully. About to bin them, she noticed it. Confused, the memory came flooding back. The envelope was an expensive one. Embossed with the logo of the Palace of Westminster, she was amazed she had missed it the first time around. It had completely slipped her mind that she had applied for the post. The ad had caught her eye on-line. Something about it had captured her imagination. Not precisely what she was looking for, it was nevertheless a step in the right direction. With her CV, she had been quietly confident of being offered an interview.

Looking more closely, she noticed it was for Monday. That didn't leave much time for preparations.

Days after speaking with Danny in London, Jared's phone rang again. His mind in turmoil, he missed the opening gambit, but caught the stinging mockery of the second.

"Come now, Jared, don't be so naive. Unlike the majority of your colleagues, you were always a thinking robot. A soldier moulded into what the military wanted, true, but there the similarity with others of your profession ended. You took orders like the rest. Unlike the herd, however, you evaluated them. And so I expected better. You didn't really believe that someone with your special qualities would be allowed to disappear did you."

The voice belonged to Latham Stanford, head of station for Black Ops. Part of his remit had been to recruit promising youngsters like Jared. Like all the others in his unit, and they numbered a mere handful, none had time for politicians and theorists. Their trade required they rely on their own expertise and instincts for survival. Knowing each mission might be their last, they respected only those who had proven themselves in battle. And despite the dislike Jared felt for the man, he grudgingly admitted that unlike many of the other pen pushers in Whitehall, he had spent most of his life in the field. A departmental legend, he was one of the few he actually trusted.

"Many before you terminated their contracts, embittered and disillusioned by what they had to do," Latham continued. "Things like that eventually catch up with you, don't they? However, in your case it was different, wasn't it? You began to enjoy what you were doing. And as we in the firm know, that's a far more dangerous scenario than the one I spoke about earlier."

Jared knew he was being played like a violin. Finally, the words he had been dreading arrived.

"Take this as a compliment if you like, but only you can handle such a dangerous situation. Do this one last mission and you can walk away. Knowing how much you mistrust me, I'm prepared to put pen to paper as a guarantee."

Pondering the ironies of life, Steger took a generous hit of his malt whiskey. Several months ago, he had been staring at a long stint in prison. And then that little prick Richard Anthony had attempted to threaten him. Thanks to his father, he had landed on his feet yet again.

The facility was beyond his wildest dreams. And the name Phoenix had been inspired. Just like its namesake, his career had risen from the ashes. Yet, according to his twisted logic, he deserved it. One thing rankled. Unless invited, he was never to set foot in the lower reaches. Then he had added one other stipulation, one that baffled Johan. The fact he was his father had to be kept secret. Not that anyone would have guessed, he had inherited none of his father's Asiatic features. His genes had come from his mother's side.

For the first few months he had been curious about levels 3 and 4. Lately, that curiosity had become something of an obsession. Then, completely out of the blue his father had invited him to a conducted tour of the site. The whole thing had been a huge disappointment. Within half an hour he had become bored. For the remainder of the tour he'd switched off. There had been one moment when his lack of interest had been broached. The recipient of a voracious sexual appetite, as soon as he had set eyes on Anna Heche he wanted her. Small and athletic, she had the delicate features of someone born in the Far East. For the best part of an hour he had poured on the charm. To his amazement she had remained cool and aloof. He had been on the point of telling her just who he was, when he remembered his promise.

His father, a witness to the whole thing, had looked on with an expression he couldn't quite fathom.

FOURTEEN

Sunday, 2 December 2012
2.30 p.m.
Sanctuary, Wales

THE JOURNEY TO Sanctuary proved uneventful. At the last minute, Jared had decided to set out earlier than instructed. He couldn't explain why, somehow he had felt compelled to. Knowing that he would be away for a week or two, he'd asked Eric and his grandmother to look after Jodie at Mendel Hall.

Some fifteen miles short of his destination the fun had started. The satellite navigation system had never heard of the village. For the last twenty-odd miles the only living thing he had seen were sheep, thousands of the bloody things. And then there was the forest. Deep and dark, it seemed to stretch into infinity. Frustrated, he almost missed the turning.

Braking hard, he came to a skidding stop. Gazing out the driver's window, everything seemed artificial. It wasn't anything he could put his finger on, but things didn't sit right. Here and there, the undergrowth was dotted with oil drums, pieces of discarded machinery, old tyres and a host of other detritus. Then it clicked, the area must have been part of an open-cast site at one time.

Several hundred yards further on, the road curved steeply upwards towards a wilderness which was almost alpine in quality. The trees, a mixture of fir, pine and spruce, dotted here and there with the occasional oak, crowded in on either side. Looking for a glimpse of the village through the dense forest, he saw nothing. Ten minutes later and the road twisted through an almost 180-degree angle. Hitting a narrow tunnel of trees everything was coated in darkness. About to switch on the headlights, he was suddenly free and into bright sunlight once more.

Without warning, a sign came into view. Written in both Welsh and English it informed visitors that Sanctuary welcomed careful drivers. On the other side, some fifty yards further on, was another sign. In large blue letters, it announced the population to be 356. For some strange reason, the number had been crossed out several times. Near the bottom, the figure now read 339.

Pondering the oddity, in no time he found himself on the outskirts of the village.

The entrance was guarded by a stone-clad bridge. Dropping the Kuga into a low gear, he made his way over carefully. Reaching the other side, his inner voice went into overdrive. Disturbingly uninviting, for some inexplicable reason the twenty-third Psalm popped into his head. "Yeah thou I walk through the valley of the shadow of death..." – it was exactly the feeling this village was giving him. Suddenly, his head exploded with the sound of whispering.

Pulling the Kuga to the side of the road, he yanked the handbrake, opened the door and stumbled out of the vehicle. Jamming his hands over his ears to drown out the noise, it made no difference. Growing in intensity, he recognised the voices as belonging to children. Speaking as one, it was impossible to make out what they were saying.

Gradually the voices became visions. Insubstantial at first, slowly they began to take definitive shape. Subtly different in composition, each vision told a story. In the first he saw a young girl, covered in scales, her head seemingly too large for her frail body. In another, a boy of no more than eight years of age was covered in suppurating sores. Watching in horrified fascination, Jared saw a thick malodorous puss seeping from a gaping incision in his head. Momentarily, an image of something small and white, its body almost translucent, flashed across his retinas. But it was gone in an instant.

The ghostly figures had one thing in common. Broken skin, torn and bleeding torsos, their heads shaven and dressed in white, each had been horribly mutilated. It was obvious that they had been the recipients of some kind of human experimentation. Underlying everything was the sense of rot and decay.

And then they were gone. As swiftly as the voices had appeared, they vanished.

Some ten minutes later, in control of his emotions once more Jared made his way back to the Kuga. Switching on the engine, he shifted into first gear and drove off slowly. A few hundred yards later he noticed the posters and everything fell into place. Jodie's visions had been right. Something was dreadfully wrong. And if he wasn't mistaken, the root of the problem had its epicentre in the heart of this tiny Welsh village.

Those working in the complex tended to give the village a wide berth. Declared off limits, the majority took the warning seriously. Possessing both a stubborn streak and rebellious nature, Mark was a frequent visitor to the village inn. As the solitary pub, The Laughing Man tended to be the focal point of the community. Though money was in short supply, the same faces tended to pop up in the same seats on the same days of the week. On the surface they were a dour lot, but there was more to it than met the eye. Those parents who had lost their children had a haunted look about them. Conversely, those fortunate enough to still have theirs were constantly on the alert. It was as if they were calculating the odds as to whose would be next. Considering the circumstances, thought Mark, it was hardly surprising that many locals had decided their daily calorie intake should be provided by a glass or bottle.

Reaching the village was something of an expedition. The single road in and out was nothing but a rough track, until you hit the concrete strip leading to the complex. Though Mark had made friends with several of the locals and bought the odd round, he had been careful not to be too flash with his money. Some had been easier to befriend than others; one in particular.

Walking through the door he was greeted by the vicar. "About time too," he muttered good-naturedly. "Get the round in, shall I?"

Shedding his coat, Mark made his way over to their usual spot. Shortly after, the pints arrived.

"Sit down. She won't bite," he said pointing to an attractive young woman sitting in the corner.

Finding the vicar to be good company had been something of a surprise. At first Mark hadn't realised who he was. The way he spoke, the way he dressed, had given no clue as to his vocation. He wondered who the woman might be. In the mid-twenties' bracket, her raven hair was unfashionably short, but on her it looked stunning. Eyes the colour of a Caribbean lagoon glanced across the table at him.

"My daughter, Samantha," said the vicar, putting Mark out of his misery. "Mature student, she's just completed five years in university. Problem is, until she finds a job, I'm stuck with her."

Jared hadn't a clue where he was going and as Ian and the boys weren't arriving for a few days, he decided to look for somewhere to stay. His credo had always been, when in doubt, head for the nearest pub.

It hadn't taken long to find. Not a betting man, had he been, he would have placed a hefty wager that apart from the church, it was the oldest building in the village, and far better attended. Lifting the latch of the front door he walked in. Had it been a set from some Western, his arrival would have been greeted with a deathly hush. The reality was different. He hardly warranted a second glance.

Approaching the bar, someone called his name. Peering into the far corner, he noticed Danny, Tina and Gareth. And they were grinning like Cheshire cats.

"Seen a ghost?" said Danny, striding over.

"What gives?" came the astonished response.

"Some bigwig named Stanford called. Said you needed a helping hand. You're not due till tomorrow though. Seeing as I'm on my feet, better get you a drink."

Familiar with Mark's moods, the vicar eyed him curiously. "What's up?"

"That obvious, is it?" Mark replied "Been feeling distinctly uneasy about things lately."

"Care to explain?" said the vicar.

"You know I'm not allowed to visit the village, far less discuss the work that goes on in the complex, but I've got to talk to someone." Catching Daniel's eye, he said, "and, seeing as I trust you, I'm afraid you've drawn the short straw. Anyway, a split site: the two complexes are completely separate entities. Site one, where Phoenix is based, handles work of a purely commercial nature. New World Laboratories, the other site, is another ball game. Made up of levels 3 and 4, level 4 has its own bio-hazard facilities. Sophistication of that kind is usually only needed for dealing with viruses and other nasty bugs. The ones mankind haven't yet found a cure for. But, to get to the point, I've just been promoted. About a month ago, I quite Phoenix to join New World Laboratories."

"So, what gives?" asked the vicar. "Surely you're pleased?"

"I was initially. Guy in charge was very persuasive, said the projects would ultimately benefit mankind. Yet, a few things have happened recently that have got me wondering whether I made the right choice."

"So, what's eating you?"

"I'm convinced their working on something behind closed doors. Security is so damned tight only a select few have access to that section. Person in charge is Anna Heche."

"What's it like down there?" said Samantha, breaking in on the conversation.

"The best analogy's a rat's nest. Submarine doors provide entry to one level at a time, and security guards cover each of the elevators. Access is by means of coded passes. Much of the area contains bubble corridors fed by negative air pressure to prevent infectious micro-organisms from flowing into other parts of the building. Don't expect you to understand, but I'll describe the precautions."

"I might be able to understand some of it," said Samantha. "Studied biochemistry in university for a year, before deciding to change my course, only scratched the surface, mind you."

"Then you'll understand that special filters check the air before it enters our bodies, or the atmosphere."

"What about bio-suits?" she asked.

"My pet hate – I was coming to those. Made from vinyl, they fit the body from head to foot. Getting into them is a complicated procedure. You have to remove all your clothing, including underwear and jewellery. Then you put on surgical scrubs. After that come the boots, the gloves and hood; each of which have their own specially adapted seals. If that isn't enough, you have the quick release air hose to plug in. This is only to get in. On the way out you have to do the converse. And it takes a good deal longer."

"Why so?" asked Daniel in surprise.

"You have to shower in your suit. First with a decontamination solution and then with water on a predetermined cycle; the process takes about five minutes. The decontamination shower is simply a cubicle with spray faucets situated on the sides and ceiling. That done, you have to remove your suit and scrubs and stand under the shower naked for another five minutes. Finally, you have to clean your nails thoroughly, blow your nose, clear your throat and spit. Only when all that's done can you get dressed."

"Where's all this leading, Mark?" asked the vicar, a worrying frown creasing his face.

"Just before I was given my new post, stories began to reach us in Phoenix about some kind of research being carried out on level 4; something about a revolutionary drug, a prototype called R90. God knows if the rumours are true, but according to the grapevine it's to do with the creation of hybrids." Seeing Daniel's bemused expression he explained the process. "If you insert human genes directly into certain animal embryos, like those of a chimp for instance, you can create a transgenic animal. To cut a long story short, you can produce a hybrid. It's only rumour, I grant you, but you know what they say about rumours," he said, shrugging his shoulders, "there's no smoke without fire." He didn't have the courage to tell them what he'd stumbled across the other day, that he had witnessed first-hand a practical demonstration of what the notorious R90 was capable of. Or had he, had it all been his imagination, he wondered? And then he dismissed the thought instantly. The evidence had been there before his very eyes. There was no other explanation for what he had seen.

"Surely that kind of research is unethical," said the vicar. "Apart from that I should imagine it's illegal."

"Right on both accounts," said Mark.

Unknown to Mark, Jared and the others had been listening to every word of the conversation.

"Looks like we might have our first break," said Danny, whispering from the corner of his mouth.

FIFTEEN

Sunday, 2 December 2012
5.30 p.m.
Sanctuary, Wales

ORIGINALLY JARED HAD thought about booking into the Laughing Man. Overhearing the conversation on the next table, he revised his plans, deciding instead to enquire about bed and breakfast with the old vicar. The opportunity to pick his brains over the next week or so was too good to miss. To do that he would have to come up with some kind of cover story, and then he had it.

Nestling between mountains to the west and a vast forest to the east, the valley housing Sanctuary was both narrow and deep. According to directions, the manse was on the outskirts of the village. The old building turned out to be fairly substantial. Set back about fifty feet from the road it appeared to be in good condition. The lane on the other hand was a different story. Full of potholes, many had never been repaired. Instead, over the years they had been filled with loose rubble, dirt and the odd bucket of ashes. Both sides of the track were overgrown with weeds and rushes. Climbing ivy clung tenaciously to the front of the house, in places reaching almost bedroom height.

Approaching from the side, the back garden was divided into a lawn and a vegetable patch. He hadn't seen hide nor hair of the church. Normally, it was the focal point of most Welsh villages – that or the chapel. As he had observed earlier, however, that role appeared to have been usurped by the pub. And the funny thing was, rather than resenting the fact, the old vicar seemed to have gone with the flow. It hadn't taken a genius to work out that he was a regular.

Undoing the gravity latch of the wooden gate, he made his way up the winding footpath. Small stones crunched under his feet as he approached the door. Knocking, it was answered almost immediately by the vicar's attractive young daughter. If she recognised him from the pub she didn't let on.

"Sorry to bother you, but the inn down the road seems to be full and well..."

"You're wondering if we have any spare beds," she said, smiling.

Her smile was devastating and for a moment he was taken aback. Without knowing why, he was suddenly filled with odd and conflicting emotions about the girl. None of which he could make sense of at the moment.

"Don't stand there with your mouth open," she said, "come in. I'll ask Dad if you can have one of the spare rooms. God knows we've enough of them. He doesn't usually do this kind of thing, but seeing as you're out on a limb. Besides I'm sure the old bugger would be glad of the extra revenue."

"Less of the old, if you don't mind, young lady," said a voice breaking into the conversation.

Smiling, he beckoned Jared in. "Of course you can have one of the spare beds. Daughters," he chuckled, "who'd have them?" he said, leading the way along the corridor towards the kitchen.

"They can be a problem, can't they?" said Jared following behind.

The vicar and his daughter turned in surprise. Speaking as one, they blurted out. "You have a daughter? But you look too young."

Addressing his answer to Samantha, Jared said, "Now, whose mouth is hanging open?"

Laughing, she said, "Fifteen all in tennis parlance. How old is she?"

"Ten going on eighteen, at times," he answered.

Confused, she said, "Then, why isn't she with you?"

Immediately embarrassed, she apologised. "Sorry, I didn't mean to pry. It's none of my business."

"No offence taken. Her mother died last year and since then Jodie's been my life. If this job wasn't so important, wild horses wouldn't have dragged me from her side."

Samantha was struck by the emphasis he had put on his job. When he mentioned it, quite unintentionally a cloud had passed over his handsome features.

The interior of the house proved to be unremarkable. A dark and narrow corridor led to the kitchen at the far end. Glancing sideways, Jared saw that a mahogany staircase led upwards at a fairly steep angle to the second floor. The kitchen itself betrayed a woman's touch. The breakfast table was ancient. Made of oak, its surface was worn and smooth. Alongside it, and set at various angles, were four chairs. One glance was enough to confirm that they had been made from the same wood. Copper pots and pans, well used, hung from low wooden beams straddling the entire length of the ceiling.

Moving into the front room, Jared's first impression was that it was warm and cosy. The three-piece suite had seen better days, yet, like everything else in the house, it had been well looked after. In one corner stood a grandfather clock, next to it, hanging in pride of place, was a huge barometer. The furthest wall was filled with bookshelves. A quick glance showed Jared that the vicar had a wide variety of interests. Not a speck of dust was to be seen anywhere.

SIXTEEN

Monday, 3 December 2012
9.00 a.m.
New World Laboratories

EMERGING FROM A drug-induced sleep Medusa heard the telephone on the third ring. By the fifth, he was wide awake. A call at this hour meant bad news. In that respect he wasn't to be disappointed.

"We have a problem." Clearing his throat, the caller added, "Or, should I say, several little problems and one rather more worrying one."

"I'm all ears," said Medusa.

"Remember Hanson?"

"The one we stole from Phoenix?"

"Yes, sir, the one that cost us a fortune."

"People of that calibre don't come cheap. According to sources he was an emerging star. So what are you trying to say, we got it wrong? If he's not up to it, get rid of him."

"It's not as simple as that." Deciding to take the bull by the horns, he said, "After a period of, shall we say apprenticeship, I decided to promote him."

"To level 4, you mean?"

"Exactly. Since then he's had access to some of the more sensitive areas."

"You mean he's now in contact with Anna?"

"And that's the problem."

"What has she been up to now?" said Medusa wearily.

Paid handsomely to check on her input to Genesis, he'd prepared his speech.

"She achieved her objective – that of genetically producing

a batch of perfect specimens for the programme – quite some time ago. Somehow, she managed to keep the fact from everyone, including me. Since then, she's been doing a little moonlighting: working on things of her own design. One of those projects has produced an alarming side effect."

"Alarming in what way?"

In detail, he explained what she had been doing in her hidden laboratory.

From the first Medusa had known that she possessed a wild streak. Yet, to date, her input to the programme had been enormous.

"Sadly, it seems being part of our brave new world wasn't enough. Her stupidity has placed a lifetime's work in jeopardy. And the other matter?"

"Hanson's got wind of her sideline, accidentally walked in on one of her experiments. I know it should never have happened; security let its guard down, since then he's been sacked. But the damage has been done. Hanson saw something he was never meant to. It's partly my fault, the computer readings didn't equate so I sent him to check on things." Anticipating the outburst, he said, "I managed to defuse the situation."

"Why do I get the feeling there's a 'but' hovering on the horizon."

"He intends getting his hands on a sample of the R90 she's been experimenting with. If successful he'll take the story to the press."

"Did he give any indication of a time scale?"

"The next few weeks," came the reply.

"Hanson's also been shooting his mouth off in the village pub. Has the ears of the vicar, of all people."

"But the village is out of bounds," shouted Medusa. "The rules expressly forbid anyone mixing with the villagers. I know,

I know," he added immediately afterwards. "It's impossible to keep tabs on everyone all the time, I understand that. But there's something else, isn't there?"

"Yesterday, several strangers turned up at the inn. They're either police or military."

"Suggestions?" asked the old man.

"Hanson will have to be taken care of, and quickly. Want me to do it? Or would you prefer Lucifer to see to it?"

"Lucifer would be overkill," said Medusa. "Set a trap for our illustrious Mr Hanson and then dispose of the body. Take care of Caroline yourself."

Replacing the phone in its cradle, the man realised that his boss was a twisted genius. It had been several years now since Medusa had drafted him into the inner cadre. He had envisioned an old boy's network. Secret societies normally involved a matrix of money, influence and power. Like a gossamer thread it ran through everything, affecting everyone in a kind of 'I'll scratch your back' philosophy. In some ways there had been an element of that, but it had been secondary to the vision.

It had started with a man called Yoshiro Immada. He had propagated the theory that it was possible to develop a race of super beings. Well on the way to proving his concept, things suddenly started to go disastrously wrong for Japan. In the space of a few short months, the once mighty imperial army had been brought to its knees. And so, instead of being allowed to pursue his hypothesis, Immada had been forced to channel his energy into looking for a way to turn the tide of the war. It had all been in the great man's notes. After his tragic death, Medusa had carried on Immada's work.

Given the details of Genesis, his initial reaction had been one of incredulity. Once he had thought about his proposals logically though, he realised that it was the only answer. Eventually, he had come to recognise the seed of greatness lay within Medusa. He had often heard the expression, 'There's a fine line between genius and madness.' Medusa was living proof. He had taught him that ordinary human beings were limited as to what they could achieve by a misguided sense of loyalty to their fellow men. To a code of honour, a moral ideology that was simply unworkable. Mankind, he'd added had drawn fences around themselves with outmoded philosophies. They had even given them silly names such as, love, honour, friendship, dignity, trust and the like. Medusa had shown him that such things were nothing but hollow sentiments.

The one stumbling block had been Medusa's age. Then, in an inspired move, the old man had put his faith in Anna Heche. Despite her many flaws, she had come up with the goods. Genesis was now ready. Like a giant crossword, the final piece of the puzzle was now in place. Medusa would be remembered for all time. All of them in varying degrees would go down in the history books as having a greater contribution to mankind than, struggling to find superlatives with which to compare their achievement, he was lost for words.

Suddenly, he had an inspiration – The Beatles. With that he burst out laughing.

Medusa had hardly placed the telephone in its cradle when it rang again. Unlike the first phone call, this was an external line.

"Anything important?" he enquired.

"Though Lucifer took care of the little matter concerning the jogger, he was able to pass a message to his brother Paul before he visited the pearly gates. The name Genesis and the location of the facility cropped up. Some very skilled and tenacious people are now involved."

"Names?" said Medusa, his voice like a whiplash.

"Danny Harris and his team for one, but there's more. A character called Jared Hunter has been thrown into the mix. Retired after what's known in the trade as the Judas Codex affair, he now looks after his young daughter. Worth a fortune, they live in a mansion left to him by some ancient sect called the guardians."

"Hunter, was he the one who took out the western arm of the Brotherhood?"

"The very one," came the reply.

"Impressive. Is he as good as they say?"

"Better. Apart from me, I'd say he's the best."

"Self-praise is no recommendation," said the old man.

"Depends on how good you are," came the retort, "but there's more."

"What now?" Medusa said, barely able to conceal his frustration.

"Heard the news?"

"Putting the final touches to Genesis, I've had no time. Still, everything is almost ready," said Medusa. "The first shipment will be in place by December the 16th. The first wave of inoculations will begin on the 18th."

"How deliciously appropriate. Just in time for Christmas," was the caller's witty comment.

"And the other matter?"

"David Wolfe's been announced the new PM for Great Britain."

"Breaking with protocol, isn't it? Rushing something like this through without the usual formalities I mean. Would have thought they would have invited a senior figure to take the reins for a while. Tide them over during such a traumatic time."

"Desperate times call for desperate methods, I'm afraid."

"Foresee any problems?"

"The chap comes from the same mould as Charles Hilary."

"Not another politician with a conscience? Two in such a short time, it almost restores you faith in human nature, doesn't it?" said Medusa dryly.

"Almost, but not quite." came the reply. "From what you've just described, by the time he gets his feet under the table, Genesis will be up and running."

"True," said Medusa. "It's the damage he might do in the interim that worries me."

"Sources indicate he intends visiting your little empire. And if my information is correct, it will be soon."

"How soon is soon?" asked Medusa, for the first time a trace of worry in his voice.

"Several days tops."

"Then it will be no problem," said Medusa. "The fool will be allowed access to everything but the one thing that could incriminate us. What did you say his name was?"

"David Wolfe, Wolfe is his second name."

"As in big bad?" chuckled Medusa in a rare flash of humour.

"There is an 'e' on the end of this one," was the reply.

"Then, Mr Wolfe with an 'e' will be shown every courtesy when he arrives. He will leave here perfectly content. About the team of detectives you mentioned earlier, any idea of their whereabouts?"

"By now they'll be in the village of Sanctuary, desperately trying to fathom out what's going on in the bowels of Medusa Industries."

"Do they know about me?"

"Only that you're some eccentric multi-billionaire throwing money around like confetti. And for the benefit of mankind, may I add."

"Ah, the inoculation programme," chuckled Medusa.

"Knowing Harris as I do, he already has an idea there's something wrong. They're a formidable combination. But this chap Hunter is particularly good. Still, like all of us, he's human. As the saying goes, if we are cut, do we not bleed?"

"Any suggestions?" said the old man.

Often, killing someone wasn't always the best way of dealing with a situation: it drew too much unwanted attention. In this instance, however, there appeared to be no viable alternative. And so the answer was automatic.

"Take them out."

SEVENTEEN

Monday, 3 December 2012
9.00 p.m.

After their latest bout of love making, Mark was fast asleep. Strangely, instead of dreaming about Caroline, his thoughts were centred on the conversation in the pub. Mark hadn't been entirely truthful with Samantha and Daniel because what he'd witnessed had shaken him. The discovery had been so horrific that he had been unable to take them into his confidence.

Caroline studied the naked figure of Mark Hudson. He was good-looking true, but the attraction went deeper. He had an air about him of a little boy lost. A combination of that and a mop of unruly blond hair meant he was irresistible to most women.

Knowing he was sleeping, Caroline pondered the frown. So out of character, she wondered what was bothering him. Sensing he was being watched, Mark, opening one eye reached up, snaked an arm around her neck and pulled her towards him.

"Thought you were sleeping," said Caroline.

"Some sixth sense warned me I was being studied. So, why are you watching me?" asked Mark, smiling.

In an instant, his face was transformed, leaving Caroline to wonder at how such things as facial gestures could so accurately reveal a person's inner feelings.

"You were frowning. And lately you haven't been yourself. So, what gives, buster?"

"It's the complex," said Mark. "Since my promotion, I've been granted access to level 4."

"Why should that bother you? It's what you've wanted since you got here."

“Something’s wrong with the whole set up. Had the feeling for weeks. My gut feeling is that Anna’s experimenting with R90.”

“The one we’ve been hearing rumours about,” said Caroline. “So it exists?”

“It exists all right. What it did to that poor creature was beyond belief.”

About to open her mouth, Mark beat her to it. “You don’t want to know, believe me.”

“And you went off at the deep end, I suppose?”

“Confronted Harvey, but I’m not sure he believed my story.”

“What do you intend doing?” asked Caroline.

“Get the evidence to back up my theory. Going to request a week’s holiday; after my little discussion with Harvey I’m sure he’ll grant it. That way I’ll have time to do a little snooping around. If things work out, you won’t hear from me until I manage to get hold of a sample of R90. It’s highly unlikely she would leave any of it lying around, she’s not that stupid. But, if I can get a blood sample of what she injected the creature with, I’ll have my proof. Once it’s analysed the shit will hit the fan big time; then the authorities can get the place closed down.”

“You’re joking?” came the incredulous reply. “What if they catch you?”

“Nothing’s going to happen,” countered Mark, feeling less confident than he sounded.

“When do you intend to get the sample?”

“If I give myself too much time to think about, I’ll bottle it, so it’ll have to be soon.”

Reaching for his mobile, he punched in the number and waited. Recognising the voice, the vicar said, “Something up?”

Mark filled him in on his intentions.

"Won't that be dangerous?" said Daniel. "Things might get sticky if they catch you."

"You sound exactly like Caroline; minutes ago she gave me the same lecture. I know the risks, but it's something I have to do."

"Anything I can do to help?" asked the old man.

"Pray for me," said Mark.

Despite his brave words, it was several days before Mark plucked up the courage to make good on his word. Hitting the switch to his right he waited. With a delayed crackle, the first of the fluorescent lights sprang to life. A scene of bustling activity during the day, at night, the room seemed ominously quiet. A faint hum from numerous fridges was the only sound. The only smell, that of air, air laced with disinfectant and chemicals.

About to push forward, he froze. He was having second thoughts. Regrouping, he headed for the door at the far end of the laboratory. Heart pounding, he checked the pockets of his coat. Satisfied, he grasped the handle and entered. The rows of cages housing the animals reached almost to the ceiling. But these were a different batch. Docile, they took no notice of his presence. What the hell was going on? Had she found out what he intended to do and replaced the others with these? If so, he would never get the evidence he needed. For a second he wasn't sure whether he felt disappointment or relief. Retracing his steps, he almost made it to the door when he heard a noise. Hitting the lights, he dived for cover.

From the safety of his hiding place, he saw a large section of the furthest wall swing back slowly. His curiosity turned to amazement as the partition fully open, clicked to a standstill and the diminutive figure of Anna Heche appeared. Reaching to her left, she pressed a hidden lever and the wall closed with a faint humming sound. Though dark, he had the distinct impression that the room had housed more cages.

Was this her secret laboratory, the one he had speculated about? Thinking about it rationally, it was the only way she would have been able to keep her assistants in the dark. If so, his suspicions had been proven correct. Once she had gone, Mark removed the torch from his pocket. It took a while before he found the hidden lever. And then he was inside. Hooding the beam with one hand, he peered into the gloom.

Locating the animals, there were roughly two dozen specimens. Neatly labelled in cages of various sizes, two of the rows ran along the side of the room, the third wound its way down the centre of the isle. Scanning the cages, the creatures made no sound. Instead they watched his every move. A sense of unease surged deep inside. On an unfathomable level, he felt as if he was standing in the presence of evil. It was as if the animals were reaching out to him on a subconscious level. As a scientist, he knew that what he was feeling was simply a subjective sensation based on the fact that he was nervous. Yet, the eyes of the creatures told a different story.

The last specimen, asleep, was the result of one of her latest experiments. One side of the poor creature appeared normal while the opposite side was covered in scales. Its head, completely out of proportion to the rest of its body, gave the creature a look that was more reptilian than monkey.

Removing a clip file from one of the cages, he scanned it. The more he read, the more horrified he became. Dotted among the findings were constant references to R90. Despite being a more than capable geneticist, what he was reading was so far above his expertise as to be almost incomprehensible. Part of the process involved retroviruses. Bio-genetically engineered, they were implanted directly into the nervous system.

Stage one had been complete for quite some time. The next step was to apply the process to humans. Surely she wouldn't be so bloody stupid, was his immediate thought, one that died instantly. The truth exploded in his brain like a hand grenade. Dear Christ in heaven, he now knew what had happened to all those young children from the village. Taking a small tranquiliser gun from an inside pocket of his overall, he hit the animal with a dart. Instantly, it became alert. Startled, Mark stepped back. Hurling itself at the door of the cage the creature attempted to pry the bars open. It tried several times more, until eventually its eyes rolled into its head and it hit the floor with a thud.

Not prepared to take the slightest risk, Mark prodded the animal with a telescopic rod. Satisfied it was unconscious he unlocked the cage and opened it. Removing a pair of thick rubber gloves from a shelf nearby, he slipped them on. That done, he reached into the cage, grabbed the creature by the scruff of the neck and hefted it onto the table. Moments later, he had acquired his blood sample.

It was while putting the animal back in the cage that the accident happened. Coming instantly awake, the creature looked directly at him. In a blur of movement almost too quick for the eye to follow, it reared its head and bit deeply into Mark's forearm. He was so astonished, the pain so exquisite, that he almost dropped the creature. Finding a sense of determination he never knew he possessed, he threw the animal into the cage and locked it securely.

Given enough sleeping draught to knock out an elephant, he was unable to believe how quickly the thing had recovered. Heading for one of the stainless steel sinks, he switched on the tap. Inspecting the wound he saw it was deep, but not serious enough to require stitches. Rummaging through an overhead cupboard, he found what he was looking for. Bathing his forearm in hot water, he applied a liberal amount of antiseptic. Finally, he covered the wound with gauze and bandage. Happy with his handiwork, he retrieved the vial of blood. Gazing around the remainder of the laboratory, he saw it was much larger than he had first thought. At the far end was a walk-in refrigerator, its door constructed of hermetically sealed Plexiglas. Peering in, he noticed row upon row of drawers, inside which were scores of vials made of tempered glass. Instinctively, he knew it was where Anna stored the ampoules of R90. Seeing the digital lock, he knew he would never be able to get inside. Beyond that was another laboratory, access to which could be gained by means of a code. Looking through the reinforced glass frontage, he gazed in horror at the sight that greeted him. As far as the eye could see were a series of transparent cubicles. As his eyes grew accustomed to the gloom he could make out what they contained. Each one housed a young child and from their appearances they had been the recipients of some kind of inhuman experimentation. Rooted to the spot, he finally came to his senses. This was no time for self-recriminations. It was his duty to provide the vicar with the blood sample so the authorities might expose Anna Heche and her activities to the outside world.

Making one final check that he had left behind no trace evidence, he made his way back to his quarters. Shaken by the incident, he decided to delay studying the sample until the morning.

That night he woke from a disturbed sleep. Burning with fever, he kicked the duvet to the floor and stepped out of bed. On unsteady feet he made his way to the bathroom. Washing his face in cold water, he felt a little better. His arm was badly swollen. Undoing the bandage, he examined the wound. The bite was inflamed. A wild thought struck him. Might the creature's saliva have been contaminated with R90? If so, was he infected?

A cold hard fear took root. Gazing in the mirror, he gasped in amazement. The eyes staring back at him were not his: they belonged to another person, or something infinitely worse. Wild and ferocious, they were similar in appearance to the creature he had taken the blood sample from. Suddenly he felt a terrible pounding in his head and for no logical reason he smashed his fist into the mirror. Jesus Christ, he thought, it couldn't be. Nothing acted that quickly.

He was wrong. Rodaxin 90 did.

EIGHTEEN

Friday, 7 December 2012
2.00 p.m.
London

TAKEN ABACK BY the rapturous applause, Wolfe wondered at the reason. He knew he was a popular choice, but this was something else. Then it dawned on him, with the country in turmoil, he was seen as the last throw of the dice.

One of his greatest assets was adaptability under pressure. And so, deciding to speak from the heart, he threw his carefully prepared speech out of the window. Holding his arms in the air for calm, he waited until he had their full attention. Gripping the podium lightly with both hands, he began:

"Ladies and gentlemen of the press, thank you for the reception. But, why do I feel like a lamb being led to the slaughter?" The remark brought the expected ripple of laughter.

Without further preamble he went for the jugular.

"Make no bones about it, we, and by we, I mean every nation under the sun, are faced with a host of problems that are so serious that unless we do something and quickly, it will be too late. From where I'm standing, I don't see that as a negative."

Seeing a few bemused faces, he continued:

"Over the decades, Britain has become an increasingly divided country. Black people are pitted against whites, while immigrants, illegal or otherwise, find themselves in direct opposition to those who regard themselves as home-grown Brits. Christian versus Muslim, rich versus poor, diminishing energy supplies, global warming, overpopulation, burgeoning unemployment and the credit crunch. The list seems endless. On top of that, violence is increasing daily. As a result, our prisons are full to capacity. To be blunt, there simply isn't room for any more. And the answer: those already in the system are being given increasingly more lenient sentences or, in some cases, given cautions and released back into society. It's little wonder that to the person in the street the law appears to be geared towards protecting the interests of the guilty rather than the innocent. Everything I have touched on so far adds up to one thing, morale is at an all-time low. So what can we do about it? It's simple, either we rip up the script and start again, or we fall by the wayside."

Breaking in rudely, one reporter shouted:

"Fancy rhetoric isn't the answer, that's for sure. Care to elaborate on how you'd go about finding a solution?"

Unruffled, Wolfe said, "Despite our grandiose speeches about equality and brotherly love, the words have been nothing but trite phrases. Each world leader, while professing loyalty and devotion to the others, has cared only about their own country. Take the oil crisis. Is it fair that several small nations should hold the world to ransom? I think not. The US, under the guise of the world's protectorate, has hidden behind a veil of hypocrisy for years. The invasion of Iraq, was it really to take down Saddam Hussein?"

Once again, the room echoed with the sound of laughter.

"It was done to protect their interests in black gold rather than to take any moral high ground. Now, our American allies listening to this might think that this is an attack on them. I can assure them it is not. I'm merely illustrating a point. It's time we took a long hard look at ourselves. By that I mean not only we as world leaders, but the ordinary man in the street."

Catching his breath, he continued:

"Religion, what an evocative word, apart from politics, sex and sport to a lesser degree, it's probably the most discussed subject on the planet. Not being an overly devout man, I find it amazing that several of the world's largest religions fight against each other in the name of the same God. There is only one God, yet, somehow, over the centuries he's been given a different name. It might upset some of our esteemed leaders, but it's about time they faced the truth. Religion has been responsible for more deaths over the centuries than all the world wars put together. Muslim versus Christian is the latest flash point of global proportions. Had the credit crunch not arrived when it did, I'm convinced it would have eventually been the catalyst for a third world war."

Allowing the import of his words to sink in, he said:

"We have to stand up and be counted. We face difficult times. Together we stand a chance of surviving; divided we will fail. That is a certainty. Somehow, we have to find a way to bury the past and look towards the future. Regardless of race, creed or colour, we have to face the sobering truth, we either live together, or we die together. There is no alternative."

Those who had been privileged to witness his speech said afterwards that they felt as if he was addressing them personally. His final words drifted across the hall to an atmosphere of stunned silence.

"And so, ladies and gentleman, the choice is ours."

With that, the PM walked off stage. For what seemed like ages, no one moved. Then a single clap rang out. Seconds later it was followed by others. Finally, the whole of the audience was on its feet, shouting and cheering.

Wolfe's whisper carried to Paul who, for the duration of the speech, had been hidden behind the huge black curtain.

"Seems my message got across. Now it's your turn."

Paul's first press conference was interesting to say the least. With so little time for preparation, it turned into an exercise of thinking on his feet. For the first few minutes, Paul was hesitant, inhibited by the fact that the whole spectrum of the media was present. TV, radio, journalists and the like, they had all managed to cram into the hall. Though he knew from experience most of those staring up at him were only doing their job, he was in for a hard time. The biggest problem would be that regardless of what he said, many would edit his words and alter them to suit their own viewpoint. Meanwhile, others would be more blatant. They would simply misrepresent what he said. As long as it suited their purpose, they saw nothing wrong in it. But, then, hadn't he done exactly the same thing?

By the third question, Paul was surprised at how easily he had slipped into his new role. It was almost, he thought, as if he was anticipating the questions, before realising that was exactly what he was doing. Having been a journalist himself, he knew what to expect. More importantly, he knew how to answer the difficult questions. At times, the same enquiry was made by a dozen different reporters all in a short space of time. Sipping coffee regularly from a styrofoam mug, the artificial stimulation the caffeine gave him kept him on his toes. The longer the routine went on, the more comfortable he felt. Wolfe had been right. Without a trace of arrogance, he knew deep down that he was perfect for the role.

Nineteen

Saturday, 8 December 2012
9.00 p.m.
Sanctuary, Wales

Sam Parsons gazed across the ravine. Hidden by a combination of rugged terrain and thick pine forest, the complex was nigh on invisible. The location was perfect, especially if you had something to hide. And by now he was sure Medusa Industries had plenty.

Its electrified fences, allied to several other more subtle defence mechanisms, told Sam one thing, whatever the buggers were doing wasn't kosher. Finding what he was looking for, he lowered the binoculars. Convinced he knew where the deer was hiding, he made the decision to return later. Old Sam was content with his lot. The village poacher for the last forty-odd years, he had roamed the forest at will. Since the completion of the facility though, there were certain areas he now regarded as unproductive. During the course of the last week or so things had become decidedly worse. Setting traps within a radius of several miles of the complex had become a waste of time. Strangely, even the birds and animals gave the area a wide berth. It was almost as if they sensed something; as if they were aware of some danger humans couldn't detect.

He had spotted the spoor days ago. The first he'd seen for a while. Convinced the tracks had come from this neck of the woods – no-go area or not – he was determined to investigate.

Forcing his way through a particularly dense patch of undergrowth he was upbeat: the sale of the venison would keep him in beer for weeks. Stopping suddenly, he swivelled his head. He was sure that he had heard movement. Convinced it was the deer, he attempted to rationalise his thoughts. Yet, whichever way he looked at it, things didn't add up. He was still a good way from its haunt, so what had made the noise? Spooked, he switched on his flashlight. Despite the comfort of the light, he started to feel as if he wasn't alone. No matter how much he tried to convince himself that there was no one following him, he was sure there was.

Deep in the forest a cry split the air. Beyond anything he had ever heard before, it died out as swiftly as it had appeared. And then everything was quiet once more. Over the years, he had built hides at opposite sides of the forest. The floors were simple wooden boards made into small platforms, the sides and roofs tarpaulin he'd stolen from the open cast mine. Covered with branches they were invisible to anyone, unless they happened to stumble on them by accident. To reach the hides he'd devised pull-down rope ladders. Getting older, he was finding them increasingly difficult to negotiate.

He had often watched people, completely unaware that they were being observed, from the safety of his hideaways. One of his targets had been the vicar. An ardent birdwatcher, people like him were a mystery. Birds were good for one thing only: eating.

He froze. This time he was certain he had heard something. For the first time in his life he tasted fear. As a poacher, he had never once given the slightest thought to his prey. Pity was a word that hadn't featured in his vocabulary. Disturbingly, until now, neither had fear. Icy tendrils of apprehension began to slide down his spine. He was getting the distinct impression that somehow the tables had been turned, that he was no longer the hunter, but the hunted.

A memory stirred. He remembered how weeks ago a few sheep had been killed on a local farm. It had been the talk of the village. Selling his story, he'd invented all manner of grizzly details, knowing it was the kind of thing people wanted to read. Alone in the pitch black, the story didn't sound so amusing.

His nerves shot, the safety of his little cottage suddenly had enormous appeal. It was then that the creature struck. Pinning Sam to the ground, it toyed with him the way a cat would with a mouse. It looked almost human, thought Sam, until you looked into the yellow feral eyes, until you took note of the head. A head that was much too large for the body.

That it had once been human was not in doubt, yet Sam knew there was nothing left now. Not a single trace of humanity remained. Not even an echo. The impression of an impossibly large mouth was brutally re-enforced when it suddenly opened its jaws. Instantly Sam was afforded a glimpse of what looked far more like fangs than teeth. A high-pitched scream was followed by a pitiful wail as Sam realised he was experiencing the last few moments of his life. Oddly, his final thoughts were about his dog. Who would look after Ben when he was gone?

Twenty

Sunday, 9 December 2012
9.00 a.m.
Sanctuary, Wales

No fool, Daniel Jenkins knew his daughter was impressed with the good-looking stranger. But it was more than a mere physical attraction. Like him, she sensed something unusual about Jared.

He was also shrewd enough to realise that, despite his cover story, he had been part of a group sitting next to them in the pub last week. That he had overheard their conversation with Mark was obvious. An intelligent man, Daniel knew they were no ordinary people. His guess was they'd been chosen to look into the strange goings on in Sanctuary. If so, it meant the lobbying of Nigel Adkins had eventually paid off. Finally, someone in Whitehall had woken up and taken notice. He had a sudden thought: might the rally he had organised in Trafalgar Square have contributed as well?

Daniel had harboured concerns about Medusa Industries long before Mark had expressed fears about the legality of the research being conducted there. The disappearance of the first few children had been more than mere coincidence. When the number had increased, he'd been confused. Despite the best efforts of the local police, none of them had ever been seen again. Thereafter, the atmosphere in the village had altered dramatically.

A once happy, vibrant community became introspective, fearful. And no wonder. The blame had been laid at his door, indirectly anyway. The question on everyone's lips was how could a caring God allow such a thing to happen? Try as he may he had been unable to come up with an answer.

Only this week, a few tourists brave enough to hike into the dense forest above the village had disappeared. Yes, there was something badly wrong. At times, it felt as if an evil entity had descended on the village. Worryingly, he hadn't seen Old Sam since yesterday. Should it work out the complex really was the catalyst for what was taking place, then it was time to do something about it. A firm believer in divine providence, he felt the strangers had been sent for a purpose.

Breakfast over, Danny had a surprise for Jared. Shepherding him out of the back door of the pub, he made his way to the car park. Nestling snugly in the far right corner, protected by a row of thick conifers, was a brand new Winnebago.

"What do you think?"

Jared's response wasn't the one he had expected. "How the hell did you manage to get it over the bridge?"

"With great bloody difficulty, it was a tight fit and it gave us a few hairy moments."

Making sure she wasn't in hearing distance, he whispered, "Tina did brilliantly."

"Take it I wasn't supposed to hear that," chirped up a little voice. Adding, "If it was a compliment, then it's a first." She continued to turn the screw. "Don't tell me you've changed your opinion about women drivers. That would be too much to ask."

"Time for a tour," mouthed Danny in an effort to change the subject.

A thirty-six foot monster, the Monaco Knight, painted in blue and white, boasted a triple slide-out facility. Inside, and to the left was a fully fitted kitchen. Further in, hidden from view was a separate shower and toilet.

"There's even a large bedroom at the rear," said Danny.

"Don't suppose you want to see that. This is something you will be interested in," he said pointing to his right.

One of the slide-outs had been converted into what could only be described as a systems control room. Packed with all manner of communications equipment, it included a fax machine, two laptops, a personal PC and a host of other items. The opposite wall boasted a medium-size plasma TV. Feet propped up on one of the chairs, was Gareth. The funeral of Ed Goldstein, the American oil tycoon, was in process. Apart from Charles Hillary's coffin, the others were empty, so little had been retrieved of the bodies.

Jared had seen glimpses of the other funerals over the last few days. The pomp and splendour of the occasions had left him cold. Moments later, the channel altered, affording him a glimpse of a simple graveyard in rural England. Coincidentally, the funeral of Charles Hillary was taking place at almost exactly the same time. Over quickly, in contrast to the razzmatazz of the American spectacle, the quiet dignity of the occasion seemed far more appropriate.

"What's on the agenda?" asked Gareth swivelling in his chair.

"Giving the complex the once over," replied Jared.

Exiting the Winnebago, Jared was astonished to see Ian walking towards him. "Thought you weren't arriving until tomorrow," he said in confusion.

"I wasn't. For some strange reason I felt compelled to. Must be getting psychic or something," he said grinning.

"Glad you're here, anyway. The others will be here tomorrow. By then I should have a better idea of what we're up against. Ask Danny to get you a room in the Laughing Man. Catch you later."

With that he was gone.

TWENTY-ONE

Sunday, 9 December 2012
12.00 p.m.

SETTING OFF AT a brisk pace, the first few miles were relatively easy. During one of his breathers, Jared spotted a red kite. Circling lazily in the warm thermals above his head, it reminded him of a satellite in geostationary orbit. A few years ago the species had been threatened with extinction. They had recovered so well, the bird was now a fairly common sight in this part of the world.

Hours later, easing past the sign informing him that he was now entering the property of Medusa Industries, there was an immediate change in the scenery. Not only did the forest appear more daunting, it had a different feel to it. The friendly chattering of birds and animals had disappeared, to be replaced by an oppressive silence.

The surroundings brought to mind an episode from Sir Arthur Conan Doyle's *Lost World*. Tangled lichen and moss reached up from the forest floor as if they were an alien species. Rich earth and leaf mould combined to produce a wealth of diverse plant life. Dark and shadowy, everywhere was filled with the scents of Mother Nature. And something else he couldn't quite place.

Negotiating two huge walls of silent vegetation, he found himself in a tiny glade. Peering into the gloom, he noticed a large flat stone. Resting on top was something he couldn't quite make out. His first thought was animal skulls. Wheels started turning behind his eyes and in a blinding flash it came to him: these weren't animal skulls, they were human. Five in all, they had been picked clean. Thinking that these might be the skulls of the missing children, he was wrong. Close inspection revealed that the skulls were those of adults. A little to his left, his keen eyes picked up a series of strange tracks. Made by bare feet, they were unlike anything he had ever come across. Warning bells were now clamouring loudly, but the intensity of his feelings had one distinct advantage: it helped sharpen his focus.

Thirty minutes later he stumbled across the site. Emerging into bright sunlight he shielded his eyes. Allowing them time to adjust, he moved forward cautiously. Pausing every few yards, he listened for alien sounds. But there was nothing. For once Lady Luck appeared to be on his side. Finding what he was looking for, he flattened himself against a stand of tall grass. What he saw worried him, whoever was running the show seemed obsessed with keeping people out. Given its isolated position he couldn't understand the need for such obsessive safety precautions. A single glance at the complex told him one thing: only a military facility, or one funded by the military, would have the finances to subsidise something on this scale. There was an alternative scenario, of course: an eccentric multi-billionaire with a hidden agenda.

Hooding his eyes, he saw a perimeter fence running along the edge of a steep ravine. The complex itself was situated on the other side of the gorge. The 12-foot high chain link fence was topped with vicious-looking razor wire. And if he wasn't mistaken, it was electrified. A nice touch, he thought grudgingly. Lifting the binoculars, he adjusted the setting. The trip wire was exactly where he expected it to be. Extremely fine, it was barely visible. Normally, they were set for about 8 to 10 lbs of pressure. Any less, and birds and small animals would set them off.

On the other side of the electric fence the security measures appeared even more daunting. Several cameras set at strategic intervals were in evidence. Housed on aluminium poles, they provided an excellent overview of the surrounding area. Sighing wearily, he knew one thing. Gaining entry to the compound was going to be next to impossible. Refocusing, he noted that to his right was a single rolling gate. Beyond it and at fifty yard intervals were tall towers holding aloft a nest of powerful-looking halogen lights. Similar to those found at football grounds was the analogy that sprang to mind.

The whole set-up reminded Jared of a macabre theme park. There the similarity ended. This one was dedicated more to death and destruction than fun and laughter. Either side of the main entrance stood armed guards equipped with machine pistols of the latest design. Wearing immaculately pressed uniforms, they were thugs dressed in decent clothes. On his stomach, covered by tall grass and overhanging branches he was invisible. But he was taking no chances. With that, a guard came into view. Leaning his rifle against the bole of a tree he unzipped his fly. Keeping perfectly still, Jared watched as a flow of bright yellow urine landed some ten feet from his hiding place. Breathing a sigh of relief, the guard shook himself vigorously before tucking his penis back in his trousers. And then he was gone.

The chopper came from the west. The sound clearly audible in the solitude of the mountain air, he heard it before he saw it. Instinctively, he knew that it was a helicopter; more importantly that it was civilian. The thumping noise of the rotor blades was far too quiet for it to be military.

For Jared, choppers meant one of two things, approaching death or, evacuation. The third scenario – which he was witnessing now – was a new experience. Seconds later, the helicopter appeared over the tops of the huge pine trees. A Bell 429, it was the most advanced light twin IFR ever created, according to some. Incredibly fast, it had seating capacity for eight people. At present, it was carrying two passengers and a single pilot.

From the safety of his position, Jared followed its flight. With the grace of a humming bird it headed low over the fence towards its designated landing spot. As power to its turbine engines was shut down, it gradually began to lose momentum. Its struts seemingly far too fragile to hold the weight of such a substantial lump of metal, it eventually came to rest with the slightest of quivers. Seconds later, the blades dropped like the wings of a giant pterodactyl. The logo on the side was impressive.

Festooned with serpents, the golden-haired Medusa contrasted sharply with the royal blue of the chopper itself. Two men appeared. Carrying snub-nosed machine pistols, they vaulted lightly from the door.

One was a bear of man, the other of modest build. Moments later they were out of sight.

TWENTY-TWO

Monday, 10 December 2012
2.00 p.m.

DETERMINED TO HAVE a serious conversation with Jared, the old vicar wracked his brain for some kind of pretext. With time on his hands, he decided to visit Sam's cottage. About to set off, a lone figure appeared from the edge of the forest. Waving, Jared's profile came into focus. Knowing it was the opportunity he had been waiting for, Daniel made his move.

Trudging across the lawn, he looked heavenwards; the magpies were out in force. Hopping from branch to branch, they called to each other with shrill raucous cries. In time-honoured fashion, he raised his right hand to salute them, before remembering it was only a single magpie that brought bad luck. Feeling foolish he lowered his hand.

"Superstitious, Vicar?" said Jared with a mischievous grin. "Thought men of the cloth didn't believe in such things as magpies and bad luck."

"Daniel, Mr Hunter, call me Daniel. Everyone calls me vicar: to be truthful I don't like it, sounds pretentious. I'm much happier when people address me as Daniel."

"In that case, Daniel, it is. Incidentally, I'm more at home with people who call me Jared."

Rubbing his chin, Daniel said, "An unusual name, biblical in origin, it means descendant."

"You're kidding?" said Jared.

"Seems I've taken you by surprise, hope I haven't said anything wrong."

"Ironic, that's all," said Jared.

Dying to ask why, the vicar was too polite to enquire. A fit man for his age, Daniel had a full head of grey hair and bright intelligent eyes. Dressed in a thick sweater and corduroy trousers, his feet sported a pair of stout hiking boots. "On my way to check on old Sam Parsons," said Daniel, "no one's seen him for days."

"That unusual?" asked Jared.

"Very, especially as people are waiting for the venison he promised. Care to join me?"

"Be a pleasure," said Jared.

"Mind if I pop in to the church and change the hymn numbers first? It won't take a minute. Morning service only these days, had to cancel the evening one ages ago. People want to stay in on Sunday evenings, feet up, TV – that kind of thing."

Winking, he said, "Has its advantages though, means I can spend an hour or two in the Laughing Man."

"Wondered where it was – the church, I mean," said Jared.

"Do I detect an interest?" said Daniel.

Shaking his head, Jared replied. "My interest in religion is purely academic. Years ago I was accepted into Oxford University to do Semitic languages. But that was another time, another place."

They had gone a few more yards when Jared stopped. "Mind if I ask you a question?"

"Fire away."

"What's with the population check?"

Seeing Daniel's frown, he elaborated, "The sign at the entrance to the village."

"Ah, that would be someone's idea of a sick joke. Takes all sorts, I suppose."

For a while he seemed lost in his own thoughts. Snapping out of it, he explained. "The village isn't a happy place."

"But it's more than that, isn't it?" broke in Jared. "It's a feeling I"ve had since I entered the valley. It's almost as if..."

He tailed off, unable to put his feeling into words, ones that wouldn't confuse the vicar.

"And there's the look on people's faces. It's in the eyes. What gives, Daniel?"

For a while Jared thought the vicar wasn't going to answer. Looking at some point in the distance, the story finally came out.

"It started some eighteen months ago, when several children went missing. When I say missing, I mean exactly that. They simply disappeared off the face of the earth. Didn't take things lying down, though. Don't think that for a moment."

With that he explained the efforts made by Nigel Adkins and the rally in Trafalgar Square.

"Lately it seems to be the odd tourist."

Jared remembered the statistics concerning child abduction. Most predictions were that if they were dead, their bodies would usually be found relatively near their homes. In most cases no more than a five-mile radius, certainly less than 30 yards from the nearest footpath. Somehow, Jared doubted that the children would ever be seen again.

"The police tried their best," continued Daniel, "brought in dogs to comb the area. All they found were tattered bits of clothing, the odd shoe or trainer. And blood, there was always plenty of that."

Recalling a snippet of conversation between two of the police dog handlers, he related the story to Jared.

"Was the strangest thing: a few miles from the facility the dogs stopped dead in their tracks. The handlers had never seen anything like it."

"How so?" asked Jared, intrigued.

"Refused to move; seconds later they began to shake

uncontrollably. Almost as if they were terrified of something or someone no one else could see."

Wrapped up in the story, Daniel failed to see the expression that appeared on Jared's face. He knew exactly what the dogs had experienced. And it hadn't been in the least bit pleasant.

"When was the last time anyone vanished?"

Thinking hard, Daniel said, "several days ago. A group of youngsters on a camping expedition called in for supplies at the village shop. They were warned to be careful, to keep clear of the area we mentioned earlier. Course, when you tell the youth of today not to do something they do the opposite, don't they? Drew them like a magnet. It was old Sam Parsons who found the camp site, or what was left of it. Place was a shambles. Like all the other instances, there was no sign of any bodies; they'd vanished without a trace."

Jared's tongue-in-cheek comment was, "Aliens, you think?"

Wise enough to know he was being wound up, the vicar took it in the spirit it was intended and laughed heartily.

Serious again, he said, "Now Sam's missing. I hope he's all right. Somehow I doubt it though."

Secretly Jared was of the same opinion.

"Whatever's out there must be nigh on invisible," said Daniel.

"Invisible?" said Jared quizzically.

"Old Sam knew these forests like the back of his hand, yet it didn't do him any good."

It hadn't escaped Jared's attention that Daniel had started to talk about Sam in the past tense.

"You keep referring to this thing as 'it'. Care to elaborate?"

"My guess would be a bear and a big one. Escaped from some private zoo no doubt," said Daniel.

"Suppose that's feasible," countered Jared, "After all, how

many times has a phantom panther been spotted in Britain? Played havoc with the wild life as I recall."

"Yes, yes." said the vicar with enthusiasm. "And no trace of that was ever found, was it? We might well have hit on the solution, my boy."

Jared was pleased the old man had convinced himself an escaped animal was the answer. As for him, he had a very different take on things.

The church was bigger than expected. A four-foot wall made of rough quarry stone separated it from the main thoroughfare. On the other side, a sprinkling of firs and yews protected the graveyard from prying eyes.

The most striking feature was a small tower which housed a single bell. Inside it smelt like any other village church, a subtle combination of polish, candle wax, disinfectant and dust. The worn wooden pews amused Jared. Few, if any parishioners, knew that they had been designed to be deliberately uncomfortable. Keeping the worshippers awake during the often long and boring sermons was essential. For him, churches and chapels differed only in size to cathedrals. In essence their purpose was one and the same. Built on the backs of the sweat and toil of worshippers, many of which were penniless peasants, they were edifices to God. Supposed to glorify his existence on earth, Jared couldn't help but think that from a pragmatic perspective, the greed and ostentation of the church leaders contrasted sharply with the fact that over half of the world's population was starving.

Dotted here and there were metal plaques commemorating individual members of the community or families who had long since died. He spent a few minutes gazing idly over the names of a few, while Daniel got on with the task of changing the hymn numbers. He didn't have long to wait. True to his word, the vicar was ready in less than five minutes.

The next port of call was an unscheduled stop at the village shop. Pleasantly surprised, Jared noted it sold a variety of things. While the vicar was ordering, Jared was aware he was being scrutinised. The look wasn't hostile. Having been brought up in a similar village, he knew that until the locals got to know you, everyone was suspect. The residents weren't being deliberately malicious or petty; it was simply that in such a close-knit community it was the way they were. Exiting the shop the old woman smiled, leaving Jared with the impression that he had just passed some kind of test.

Arriving at the cottage on the outskirts of town, Jared noted that though it was small, it was well looked after. A little rockery stood at the front, while to the side was a vegetable garden.

Knocking on the door, Daniel turned the latch and stepped inside. The cottage was furnished with a few shabby chairs and a table. In the grate, Jared noticed the remains of a long dead fire. Neat and tidy, the room was free of clutter. Sam may have been old and had lived an almost hermitic existence, but he had been proud of his cottage. With that, Jared realised that he had slipped into the same trap as the vicar. He was thinking about the old poacher in the past tense.

The yelping of a dog startled him for a second. "That's disturbing," said Daniel, "Sam would never have left Ben unless he intended coming back the same day."

Closing the door, they made their way to the rear of the cottage. Hearing footsteps, the dog scratched weakly on the door of the outhouse in a vain attempt at freedom. In a bad way, it was obvious the poor animal had been without food and water for several days. Untying the leash, Daniel carried Ben outside.

With a cold, hard certainty both Daniel and Jared knew that Sam would never be seen again.

Twenty-three

Monday, 10 December 2012
10.00 p.m.

After the visit to Sam's cottage, Daniel became convinced that Mark was right: the complex was the focal point of the evil cloaking the village. If so, as its conscience it was time that he did something about it. Letting Jared in on his little secret had made him feel a good deal better.

Pulling back the heavy drapes, it was a beautifully clear night. Donning a black polo knit sweater and long dark coat, he felt like some third-rate James Bond. Yet, they were sensible precautions. Studying himself in the mirror, he hadn't felt so alive for ages. Sliding a heavy-duty torch into his pocket, he was ready. Knocking softly on Jared's door, it was opened immediately. Like him, Jared was dressed from head to foot in black, but Daniel had to admit that on him the whole package looked a good deal better. Fortunately, Samantha wasn't home. She was babysitting for someone in the village; rather than walk home, she would stay the night. Gazing towards the heavens, Daniel saw the sky was full of stars. They shone so brightly, it was almost as if they were in competition with each other.

The whispered "Ready?" startled him. A nod and they were heading into the mountains. Daniel knew the area well, yet a large section of the forest was unchartered territory. Before the completion of the complex, he had done a good deal of bird watching. Apart from Sam, he thought modestly, he probably knew these forests as well as anyone. Above his head, the evening breeze rustled the leaves. At that moment it seemed as if they were alive, that secret messages were being transmitted from leaf to leaf. Messages only they could understand. Though he loved the forest, at this time of night it seemed distinctly uninviting.

Several hours later and they were almost there. He wondered if over the years someone else had managed to discover what he had. It had never dawned on the architects that, despite all their elaborate security measures, nature would have the last laugh.

The cave had been found by accident, on one of his bird-watching forays. Falling over the edge of the ravine, he had been saved from serious injury by a thicket growing out of the side. Scrambling back up the slope, he'd noticed a small entrance. During the rest of that particular morning, he'd explored the whole warren from top to bottom.

Fifty yards further on, Daniel leaned over the void.

"There," he whispered pointing. "It's behind that thicket about a third of the way down."

Aware of the unease he had felt the last time he was in the vicinity, Jared was loath to leave Daniel. But there was no alternative.

"Armed thugs dressed as guards patrol the perimeter during the day," Jared whispered. "As for the night, they probably don't, but, you never know. Get yourself over to the tree line and lay flat on your stomach."

The ledge leading to the bottom of the ravine was no more than a foot wide. Angling steeply downwards, the descent was hazardous. The main danger was from dozens of small rocks which littered the track. One careless step and it was curtains.

Blanking out negative thoughts, he allowed his training to take over. Feeling with his feet more than his eyes, he took one step at a time. The track ended at a dry river bed. From there, a line of bulrushes separated the woods from what he was looking for. Finding the entrance without prior knowledge would have been impossible. Even though he knew it was there, it still took him a while to locate the exact spot.

Negotiating his way blindly through the narrow passage for a distance of several hundred yards, it was then the stench hit him. His nostrils caught the first whiff of corruption. Disease, pestilence, death – it was all there, along with the coppery tang of blood.

Then he saw the cave. Entering, he rubbed both his hands against his lower spine. Feeling better, he stood to his full height. A small cluster of skeletons sat in one corner. A glance was enough to confirm his thinking: the heads were missing. Ten minutes later and he was inside the compound. Daniel had been right, the tunnel burrowed underneath all the elaborate security precautions. It took less than twenty minutes to retrace his steps. The old vicar had seen no once since Jared had left, though he was only too ready to admit he'd been terrified left on his own. Deciding against telling him what he had found in the cave, Jared knew one thing: those who had disappeared over the last few months would never be seen alive again.

TWENTY-FOUR

Tuesday, 11 December 2012
12.00 p.m.

"PLACE GIVES ME the bloody creeps," said a voice from the back of the SUV. Brought up in a less savoury district of Glasgow, Conner Travis was fearless, but studying the landscape outside the window he knew exactly what Troy was getting at. A feeling of dread washed over him. Stronger than an ordinary hunch, perhaps the best way to describe it was a premonition. And at this precise moment it was telling him that he was not going to get out of this alive. As it turned out he was wrong. None of them were going to get out alive. They had only moments to live.

"Looks like fucking Transylvania," said Kyle, reading Conner's mind. "Vampires I can handle; an ambush in this neck of the woods would be another matter."

The retort brought the expected burst of laughter, before Loki, who was driving, reminded them of the seriousness of the situation.

"Keep your eyes peeled."

"Advice works both ways," shot Connor. "That's a bloody steep drop down there," he said, pointing outside the passenger window. "One wrong move and... well, as they say in the movies, death can be fatal."

Chuckling, they turned the corner and saw a lone figure standing in the middle of the road. Jamming on the brakes, Loki brought the car to a skidding halt. The others were instantly alert, the muzzles of their weapons trained on the windscreen. With a sigh of relief, Loki said, "Stand easy lads."

By now the others too had recognised who it was.

"Jesus, that was close," said Troy. "What's the stupid bastard playing at?"

"Testing us perhaps?" was the retort.

Opening the doors, the four made their way towards the figure. Annoyed, Conner opened his mouth to let rip. He was cut almost in half by a fusillade of bullets from his right. Though the others reacted in lightning fashion, two were mown down where they stood. The third, taking advantage of the fact that one of the assassins was less accurate than his colleagues, darted for the safety of the tree line. He almost made it, but not quite.

Smiling, the lone figure lifted a snub-nosed machine pistol until now hidden beneath his coat, and with impressive precision, shot him in the back, twice. Reaching the first of the inert figures, he wedged a foot beneath the body before flipping it over. Satisfied, he did the same with the other three. Collecting the weapons, he handed them over to Lucifer. Even though there was no chance any had survived, he double tapped each in the head before barking out orders.

"Gather the bodies and dispose of them."

Seconds later, several figures in combat fatigues appeared like wraiths from among the trees. Despite the fact that each of the assassins disliked the arrogant bastard, they had been impressed with his professionalism, especially Lucifer who had had a grandstand view of just how good he was.

He had come with a glowing reputation. From what he had just witnessed, it was well deserved.

Jared was worried: the others should have arrived hours ago. Something was wrong. More than that, he was sure that he was missing something, something important. Taking the keys of the Kuga from his pocket, he motioned to Ian and headed for the door.

Ian's arrival had been a bonus. Like Jared, he had decided to ignore orders and travel alone, arriving early. Comparable to a coiled spring, Ian weighed in at a shade over eleven stone. Physically unassuming in clothes, stripped off he was raw sinew. Immensely strong, he had been known to bench press almost double his body weight, statistically something even Jared was incapable of. And his reflexes were lightening. On more than one occasion Jared had watched in amusement as new recruits, far bigger and heavier than Ian had been mercilessly taken apart. Given the choice, Ian would always be the man Jared would choose to cover his back in a life-or-death situation. Besides, without his help in procuring the specialist weaponry he would never have been able to take down the Brotherhood. His best friend had gone out on a limb for him during the Judas Codex affair. Had the powers that be found out, Ian's military career would have been over. Or so Jared had thought. The recent telephone conversation with Stanford had shattered the illusion that they had managed to fool the firm. Jared's true intentions had been known from the beginning. It begged the question why Stanford hadn't stepped in and closed down the operation. Not that it mattered, by turning a blind eye, Jared would forever be in Stanford's debt.

Within twenty minutes they found the abandoned vehicle. Puzzled, they approached cautiously, guns outstretched. It hadn't taken long to find the blood and spent shell casings. Having the hallmarks of an ambush, it didn't add up. Knowing his men as he did, there was no way they would have allowed themselves to be caught off guard. Whatever had happened had taken place swiftly but, more importantly, because none of them had felt threatened.

The blood and spent ammunition told a different story. Struggling to come to terms with his grief, he knew one thing, if they had been killed he would avenge their deaths, whatever it took. If there had been a massacre, it stood to reason that there would be bodies. So where were they? None of what he was seeing was making any sense. The doors were open, but no one was inside. It was as if they had vanished into thin air.

It struck him that he was already beginning to think of his friends in the past tense. His imagination threatening to spin out of control, Jared began to compartmentalise his ideas, to put them into some kind of perspective. Working backwards, he constructed a rough scenario of what he thought had happened. But whichever way he looked at the situation, it was impossible. There had to be another solution. The problem was, he was at a loss to see what it was.

Evening was approaching, outside the window the shadows grew longer. Apart from those spots illuminated by the lamp posts, the remainder of the lane disappeared into the gathering gloom. Behind the conifers of the garden hedge, the huge pines seemed to crowd together in conspiratorial fashion. It was as if they felt the presence of an approaching evil. Casting aside her macabre thoughts, Samantha returned to the task in hand. Turning the gas flame down a little, she watched the water as it settled into a slow boil. Satisfied, she walked over to the sink and carried on cleaning the potatoes.

"Anything wrong?" said a voice from behind.

Startled, she turned to see her father standing in the doorway.

"You seemed miles away, love."

"I'm worried Dad. Something's wrong. Do you feel it?"

Nodding his head, the old vicar replied, "And there's no doubt in my mind what's happening is linked to the complex."

"And Jared?" asked Samantha. "What do you know about him?"

"No more than you, love, but, like you I feel he's unusual."

"Unusual?" said Samantha raising an eyebrow. "Care to elaborate?"

"When I use the term, I mean 'special' in some kind of way."

"That's just the kind of feeling I get," she said in surprise. "It's almost as if he has some kind of invisible aura."

"Well put, Sam, it's what I was trying to say. I'm not psychic or anything, God forbid. I do believe, however, that if anyone can stop what's about to happen he can."

Sitting in his black leather recliner, Medusa pressed a button to his right. Instantly, the huge screen mounted on the wall came to life. With the onset of the cancer, working the keyboard had become increasingly difficult. His fingers, gnarled and painful, often refused to obey even the simplest of commands.

Today was one of his better days. After a few clumsy attempts, a map of the world flashed up. Moments later, dots appeared in several places across the globe. Five in all, each one highlighted the location of a secret underground shelter. It was time to make a few phone calls. Punching in the first of the codes, he winced. Though his body was beginning to betray him, his mind was still razor sharp. Selecting the candidates for the arks had been a difficult task. Apart from the need for possessing the requisite skills, the ratio between male and female had been of paramount importance. Each of the five shelters were capable of housing 100 people: the occupants being self-sufficient for up to three months. Unknown to them they had been chosen not only for their specialist skills, but because of their specific genetic make-up. In order to keep them in the dark about the true nature of Genesis, they had been informed that the whole thing was a feasibility study run by the government. In the event of a chemical or biological attack, how people would react to a period of self-imposed exile would prove invaluable.

An hour later everyone had been contacted. There had been no last-minute glitches. Before he could relax, there was one last call to make.

"So what are you saying? Are they out the picture? Are you sure? One mistake at this juncture and…"

"I'm sure. All that remains is to get rid of the other two, Hunter and Wilson."

"And how do you propose to do that? From what I gather these are a different proposition, especially this Hunter character. Besides, this time you won't have the element of surprise."

"Leave that to me."

"I intend to, it's what I pay you for. Incidentally, you'd better not fail."

"I won't," came back the reply, before adding, "is everything in place?"

"By this time next week, the first of the inoculation programmes will be up and running. Success is within our grasp, my friend. I can almost taste it."

Waking in the middle of the night, Samantha was shivering. At the height of her nightmare she had kicked the duvet to the floor. She remembered little, only that it had centred on Jared.

In the nightmare, he appeared as a man whose soul was filled with sadness. Though she had known him only a few days, he was beginning to dominate her thoughts – day and, now it seemed, night. Confused about her emotions, she made her way to the bathroom. Guided by a thin swathe of moonlight which filtered through an opening in the curtains, she turned on the tap and splashed her face with ice cold water. Convinced that she would get no more sleep tonight, she moved soundlessly downstairs.

Picking up a magazine from the wooden rack, she switched on the reading lamp. Lowering herself into her father's favourite armchair, she began to read. Despite her early reservations she soon dozed off.

Waking up refreshed, she headed for the kitchen and switched on the kettle. By now the first rays of the early morning sun had started to peep over the tops of the trees. Soon it would flood the valley with soft radiant light.

TWENTY-FIVE

Thursday, 13 December 2012
12.00 p.m.
10 Downing Street

KATHY MENTALLY REHEARSED her speech. In the hour leading up to the interview she had thought of scores of clever things to say. Now the time had arrived she was a bag of nerves. Past experience had shown that the two most important parts of an interview were watching and listening. Talking came last. Too many applicants failed by becoming excited and jumping in. Fearful of falling into the same trap, she was determined to take things one step at a time.

Calming herself, she looked around in bewilderment. For some reason there appeared to be no one else waiting. Baffled, she approached the secretary who was busy working on her computer.

"Excuse me," said Kathy.

Adjusting her spectacles with the forefinger of her right hand, the woman peered over the screen. "How may I help?"

"I'm here for an interview and seem to be the only one." She had a thought. "Don't tell me I have the wrong day?"

"No, my dear," the old lady said chuckling, "You're the only one."

Leaning towards Kathy, she dropped her voice. "The selection process for such a high-profile post is extremely thorough. That's why there's no one else. Out of twenty-eight applicants you ticked all the right boxes," before adding, "I think that's the right phrase isn't it? It's so difficult to keep up with the jargon of today, don't you think?"

All a stunned Kathy could manage was a vigorous nod.

Into her stride, the old lady carried on. "Processed the applications myself, so I assure you there's no one else. For some reason the PM wants a personal interview. Don't know why, usually that's left to other people; perhaps a new broom and all that. Must say he's very nice, and so handsome," she said wistfully, leaving Kathy with the impression that she was quite a character. About to elaborate, the door flew open and an impressive figure walked in. Instantly, Kathy knew the old woman had been right, he was extremely handsome.

"Is this her?"

"Yes, PM, this is Mrs Sullivan."

Kathy bridled. The way he had referred to her in such a demeaning manner rankled. About to say something, she was never afforded the opportunity.

"Do you want the post?"

Things seemed to be happening with the speed of light. This isn't how it's supposed to be, she thought.

"Well," said the voice with an edge of impatience, "do you want the job or not?"

Finally coming round, she stammered, "Yes."

Wolfe's face broke into a smile. "Then follow me. We've work to do."

Looking across at the secretary, the old lady raised her hands in a gesture of don't ask me I only work here. Reaching the bottom of the stairs, Kathy finally managed to blurt out. "Would it be too much to ask where we're going?"

"My apologies, there's no time now. We've a helicopter to catch. I'll fill you in on the details later."

Exiting the building, Kathy saw the official Jaguar saloon waiting at the pavement. The driver had the door open. Normally the PM would have had several special branch officers in attendance. On this occasion, he had decided against taking them. In seconds they were seated safely in the back of the vehicle. The whole thing from start to finish had taken less than three minutes. Some interview, she mused, as the car pulled away smoothly into the traffic.

Stepping out of the caravan, Danny noted that the temperature had dropped. Crossing to the other side of the car park, a gust of wind plucked an old newspaper from its resting place among the flower beds. One page, freeing itself from the remainder of the tangled mess, flew across the park. Lodged against the grill of a car, the headline reminded him that the inoculation process would shortly be up and running.

Turning on his heels, he headed back to the mobile home. Trudging up the walkway, he stepped into the room that housed the high-tech nonsense, as he thought of it. Oblivious to Danny's presence, Gareth was focused on the screen. Scrolling through the masses of information, what he was looking for was in there. The machine knew everyone's life history, however enigmatic. Being Big Brother multiplied by ten, it was simply a matter of being patient. A voice cut through his train of thought.

"Found anything?"

"Not so far, guv. Don't worry, we'll get there in the end."

About to walk away, Danny was halted mid-stride.

"Gotcha," shouted Gareth in triumph.

Staring at the computer, they finally knew who they were up against. Not only was his identity exposed, but his main sources of income. Speechless, they realised that the man was so immensely wealthy, just how much he was worth might never been known.

"No wonder he was able to bankroll the immunisation programme," muttered Gareth in disbelief. "According to these figures, the several billion it cost was no more than pin money."

Most of the income was hidden behind a complex facade of financial records. In this case, obscure trust funds, false bank accounts and dummy companies. Several of which stretched right across the globe.

Scanning everything, Gareth inhaled sharply. "Shit, the old man was part of the notorious 'Togo Unit'." Reading from the screen, he filled the others in on what he was reading.

"It began in 1932 with the establishment of something called the Japanese Armies Expedition Prevention Laboratory. Shortly after, General Shiro Ishii took control and put together a secret research group called 731. Based in the district of Harbin Heilongjiang, a province of Japanese-occupied China, the complex was huge. Covering some 6 square miles, the sprawling metropolis contained over 150 different buildings. Originally envisaged as a covert biological and chemical research unit, it became so successful, depending on your definition of success, that is," added Gareth, "Hirohito ordered its expansion in 1936."

Continuing, he said, "Here's an interesting bit. Under the leadership of Ishii, a special project code-named 'Maruta' was set up using human guinea pigs to test their theories. Some of the experiments conducted under the guise of science were so horrific they beggared belief. In the main though, much of the work involved deliberately infecting specimens with diseases in order to study the effects on the human body. A variety of methods were used. One of the favourites was to hand out flea-infected blankets. Carrying cholera, anthrax, bubonic plague and the like, the effects would be seen in days. Often contaminated supplies were handed out at the same time. A more subtle method was to inject the diseases directly into the bloodstream under the guise of vaccines."

Something tugged at Danny's memory, but it was gone in an instant.

"My God," said Gareth. "According to these findings, the use of biological and chemical weapons might have resulted in as many as 200,000 deaths."

"They were never short of test subjects," chipped in Tina, peering over his shoulder. "Once they ran out of prisoners, they simply rounded up sections of the local population."

"Pandemic diseases in particular seemed to have been studied," added Danny. Suddenly there it was again, that nagging at the back of his memory.

"Anyway," said Gareth, "It came to an end in August 1945 when the soviets invaded Manchuko and Mengjiang. Even they were horrified by what they discovered in the 'death factories', as they dubbed them. The clear-up took months and dozens of soldiers were killed in the process. The location of the infamous Unit 731 was never pin-pointed. A subterranean cave complex was investigated thoroughly, but no trace of the secret laboratories that claimed so many innocent lives was ever found. Rumours circulating at the time hinted that the majority of experiments carried out by Unit 731 were conducted on young children. Something about creating hybrids was mentioned, but nothing was ever proven. One thing we do know, the characters charged with overseeing the experiments were Yoshiro Immada and his young assistant, some kind of teenage prodigy."

"And the youngster's name?" asked Danny.

"Doesn't give it. Typically nothing was heard of them after 1945."

"Strange," said Tina, "we know a fair bit about the others, so why not them?"

"Good question," said Gareth. "The story doesn't end there. Both scientists and physicians were warned in advance about the Russian invasion; appears they returned home safely."

"Only after being ordered to take their secrets to the grave," said Danny.

"The older guy has long since gone to meet his maker," commented Gareth, "but the teenage assistant might still be alive. Say he was sixteen or seventeen in 1945, that would make him about eighty-three or eighty-four now."

"Think it could be Medusa?" said Tina.

"Anything about his personal appearance," added Danny.

"The file isn't that detailed," answered Gareth. "But we know he's Asian. And the age fits, so I'd say it's a distinct possibility."

"And you say there's nothing in the files about what they were working on?" said Tina.

"Nothing, but taking into consideration Japan was on its knees, I'd lay odds they were attempting to produce some kind of super weapon to turn the tide of the war."

Coming to the end of the file, Gareth said, "Good God. Seems the secrets relating to Unit 731 didn't disappear. When Japan surrendered to the allies, Douglas McArthur granted immunity to the physicians in exchange for providing the USA with their files on biological warfare. In the same vein, after the Second World War the Soviet Union built a biological weapons facility in Sverdlovsk using documentation captured from Unit 731 in Manchuria."

Leaving the best to last he added, "Incredibly, and this is hard to believe, some former members of 731 became part of the Japanese medical establishment. Dr Masaji Kitano became head of the Green Cross, Japan's largest pharmaceutical company. Meanwhile, General Shiro Ishii, the big cheese, moved to Maryland, Virginia to work on a bio-weapons research project."

TWENTY-SIX

Thursday, 13 December 2012
1.00 p.m.
New World Laboratories

DURING THE JOURNEY Wolfe found time to scan Kathy's CV in more detail. He was impressed. Parted from her husband recently, it appeared that the split was terminal. Though a brilliant microbiologist, he had one reservation: would the post be challenging enough? Not that it mattered. For the moment what was important was that she was familiar with the kind of complex that they were visiting.

Greeted immediately the chopper landed, they were escorted to the main door by two uniformed guards. Wolfe's immediate take was that, despite being immaculately dressed, their demeanour proved their trappings of civility to be a sham. He would have wagered a month's salary had their job applications been scrutinised, they would have proved to be a complete fabrication.

Declining the proffered tea or coffee, Wolfe wanted to begin the tour post haste.

"In that case, sir, if you would follow me," said the secretary.

The inspection of the first two levels was brief. Even to his untrained eye, everything seemed above board. Security on levels 3 and 4 was incredibly tight, the complex best described as a maze. Wolfe's immediate impression was that in a place as large as this, it might be possible to hide anything. Approaching a large elevator, from the outside it looked like any other. It was anything but.

Access was granted by use of a complex digital code and a magnetic swipe card. Exiting the lift, they were greeted by someone called Hiram who, it turned out, was to be their guide for level 3. Knowing he would be denied access to any of the more sophisticated laboratories on the grounds he hadn't the requisite training, he was confident that Kathy would be able to sniff out any problems.

Ambling along corridors of uniform white, he paused every so often to peer into rooms. The workers seemed happy enough, going about their business with quiet efficiency. Access to level 4 was once again by elevator. The same process with the codes was repeated. Here, Hiram bid them good day and another guide introduced himself. An extremely tall man: his name was Harvey.

While the PM was busy asking questions, Kathy's eyes missed nothing. With professional curiosity, she noted how each opening in the seemingly never-ending corridor had reinforced doors. Many sported locks that would require an electronic pass to gain entry. The whole thing was beyond her wildest expectations. The microbiology section was something from another planet. Peering through the Perspex partition, she saw that airtight submarine doors led from changing rooms into the biohazard zones. One thing was strange. The atmosphere on level 3 had been relaxed and informal. The moment that they arrived on level 4, there had been a distinct change of mood. Despite the fact it was where the dangerous materials were stored, she felt it was something more.

Between laboratories, dozens of people passed every minute. Oddly, no one said a word. Harvey, pointing through a large Perspex frontage, indicated the section beyond.

"This is where the more sensitive work is carried out. Each door is electronically linked to the other. The next one won't open until the last one has shut. Air pressure is reduced in stages to prevent the escape of any dangerous agents."

Approaching yet another door, Kathy and Wolfe were informed politely, but firmly, that access beyond this point was restricted to only those carrying the highest security clearance. Shrugging his shoulders and spreading his hands, Harvey explained even he had no idea what lay beyond that door.

"It's no coincidence the people who work in that section are the most skilful," he added.

"And the most highly paid," chipped in Kathy, a remark which elicited a smile.

Wolfe had the sudden feeling he was being studied. Turning quickly, he was in time to see someone disappear at the end of the corridor. It had been for a moment only, but he had the distinct impression that it had been a woman. Refocusing, he caught the end of what their guide was explaining.

"Much of the work conducted here can often be very dangerous. In the case of an emergency, we have a system of fail-safe devices dotted around the corridors."

Before deciding to visit the complex Wolfe had done his homework. He knew that politicians in Britain, as in the US, tended to be told only what the military thought was fit and proper. Was there anything going on down here that was military driven he wondered?

Towards the end of the tour, they were shown around a series of small laboratories, where several assistants were in the process of plating bacterial cultures. Kathy was impressed, what she was looking at was the cutting edge of technology.

Several times she had waited for the expected pressure on her elbow, the one which conveyed the message that they should move on. It never came. Even during the tour of the sensitive areas. And that had been the clincher.

Everyone had been cooperative, because they really didn't have anything to hide. If that was the case, it could mean one thing.

The real work, the one they wanted to see was being conducted elsewhere. She cast her mind back to the other laboratory, the one they had been denied access to. No, she reasoned, it was too obvious, besides the old man knew should the PM care to flex his muscles he could have forced him to grant them access. What they were looking for was hidden, hidden in some place known only to a chosen few.

"Might I be allowed two questions?" asked Kathy.

"Fire away," said Harvey.

"The anti-virus, was this where it was produced? The one mentioned in the TV programme by the Japanese doctor?"

"Dr Takeshi, you mean? Yes, it was produced here. As a matter of fact it was in the laboratory you were denied access to."

Convenient, thought Kathy, before continuing. "It's just I vaguely remember him saying the virus they'd isolated had the capability of jumping species. Isn't there a chance it might escape the laboratory?"

"That's perfectly true. However, due to the sensitive nature of the materials handled here, the safety procedures are almost foolproof."

Breaking into the conversation, Wolfe said, "Why does the word 'almost', not inspire me with confidence."

Seeing that the PM was serious, Harvey added hastily. "Just a figure of speech, sir, though I suppose you're right. Nothing in this world is ever foolproof."

"And the second question?"

"The vaccine, is it stored here?"

"Some, though not all. Even a facility as large as this would have been unable to cope with the amount the government wanted. To speed the process up, the formula was sent to several of our other laboratories sited around the country. As for global production, the same thing applies. Across the world selected laboratories have been working flat out for months to meet the deadline."

Smiling, he added, "All the hard work has been worth it. To borrow a phrase from our American friends, as from tomorrow we have lift off."

"So the actual product is ready and waiting?" said Kathy.

"All that remains is the logistics. By that I mean transportation of the vaccine to the designated areas."

"And that's where you come in?"

"Yes, I'm a businessman rather than a scientist. I'm not as important as the people who came up with the product. Still, I like to think I have my uses."

Some twenty minutes later, the tour complete, they were ushered into a huge office. They were greeted by an old man who was seriously ill, if Wolfe wasn't mistaken. That he had some genetic defect was obvious. Gaunt and pale his skin was almost transparent. It was like staring at a cadaver. This time the proffered coffee was accepted.

Rising unsteadily to his feet, the figure moved forward to shake hands. Careful to grip the old man's hand lightly, Wolfe notice that his veins stood out like small tributaries in a river. The liver spots were many and varied. Despite his illness, he seemed to project an image larger than life. While Wolfe was scrutinising the man, trying to gauge his mindset, Medusa spoke.

"May I say how honoured I am to meet the new PM. Word on the grapevine is you are a man of high integrity and brilliance, and those are your worst points," he said, laughing at his own joke. "I don't envy you your task: it seems you've taken over at an extremely inopportune time. According to several well-placed sources, Charles Hillary was so worried about social unrest he was on the verge of declaring martial law. Unfortunately, Britain is not alone in this respect. What's happening here is being mirrored worldwide. Globally, things appear to be deteriorating so rapidly most of the world's leaders can see no way out of the present predicament."

Changing tack, he said, "Incidentally, I was very sorry to hear of Hillary's sad demise."

Wolfe wasn't fooled for one minute by Medusa's ready charm. There was no hint of any genuine sadness in his voice. The look of sympathy was a sham too. Having been a businessman himself before entering politics, he knew such a look could be cultivated; that's what he was seeing here. It told Wolfe one thing, the man was not only a dangerous adversary but a consummate actor.

"If I might be permitted a question, PM, I'd like to know how you hope to succeed. Where your predecessor failed, I mean?"

Unwilling to be baited, Wolfe said, "It's a little too early for talk like that, Mr Medusa."

Stopping him mid-stride, Medusa said, "Rui, Prime Minster, call me Rui."

Waving his hand in the kind of dismissive gesture only the truly wealthy are capable of, he carried on. "People of our standing should be on first name terms, don't you think?"

Reopening the conversation, Wolfe said, "So, Rui, it seems there's money to be made in the commercial aspects of genetics."

"Certainly, but it isn't all profit. The upkeep of this place and the wages to pay all these clever people is nothing short of a king's ransom. And one has to be careful. Everyone with the relevant qualifications has jumped on the band wagon. In the entrepreneurial sense, I mean."

"I suppose such a situation has created the opportunity for all kinds of unethical practices?"

"Precisely," said Medusa. "Many of these bogus companies push products onto the market without adequate testing, sometimes with tragic consequences."

Medusa caught something in Wolfe's eyes. It had been so fleeting, for a moment he thought he'd been mistaken. Experienced at reading people, it was a combination of pain and hatred.

Wolfe stepped in, "It's one of the things I want this government to clamp down on."

Turning to Kathy, he said, "This young lady is the first pin on the map in that direction."

"Exactly what kind of role do you envisage for her, David?"

"A roving inspector might be the best way to put it," answered Wolfe. "I want Mrs Sullivan to visit companies that, in the eyes of the government, are producing pharmaceuticals of a dubious nature."

"There are so many out there, it might prove impossible to target them all," explained Medusa. "Incidentally, have you been satisfied with everything you've seen this morning?"

"Without doubt," said Wolfe entering into the spirit of the game. "By the way, who is your director? Of the upper levels, I mean."

"That would be Johan Steger. Besides him there is Professor Davison, my general manager. As to levels 3 and 4, I'm afraid I'm the sole director."

Pre-empting the next question, he said, "I would have asked Steger to show you around. Unfortunately, he is away touting for business. I have no real knowledge of what he does. Since my illness, most of my time is spent down here. Speaking of illnesses, at this time of day my old body is crying out for a nap. Would you mind if we called a halt to proceedings?"

Knowing that he had been politely dismissed, Wolfe finished

his coffee, which by now was tepid. About to exit the room, he was stopped in his tracks.

"I forgot to mention, the anti-virus is ready. In fact, the first consignments have already been shipped out to key centres around the globe. I hope Harvey explained the details to you."

Seeing Wolfe's nod, he turned to leave. This time it was he who was halted yards from his destination.

"On behalf of the country, no, the world," said Wolfe after a slight pause, "I would like to thank you for your incredibly generous gesture. It must have cost a fortune."

"It did," was the reply. "But look at me. I haven't long to live. What would I do with all my riches? Unlike many wealthy people, my story is one of rags to riches. I don't suppose you would know anything about that."

A ghost of a smile played on Wolfe's face.

"It's fortunate you aren't a betting man, Rui, if you were, you would just have lost the whole of your empire in a single throw of the dice."

TWENTY-SEVEN

FREE OF THE confines of the complex, Wolfe turned to Kathy. "So, what did you think?"

"The same as you," she replied.

"How do you know what I was thinking?"

"It was in your face."

Startled, he said, "I hope everyone isn't able to read my face as easily, or my tenure as PM isn't going to last long."

"Why would you say that?" said a puzzled Kathy.

"All politicians are supposed to be consummate liars, aren't they? If I can't lie with a straight face I'm in the wrong profession."

"It's not that you're in the wrong profession," said Kathy, "it's that you're in the company of someone who can tell the difference."

"I can keep my job, then" said Wolfe, chuckling. "Incidentally, you're my second appointment. My first was Paul Hudson. Having been in America for the last few years, you won't have heard of him. He's a reporter."

Holding his hand up, he said, "One of the good guys."

Taking a more serious tone, he added, "I owe him. His brother Jonathan was my personal assistant, helped launch my campaign."

"So why hire Paul?" said a bemused Kathy.

"Jonathan was killed last week."

"I'm sorry to hear that," said Kathy, and Wolfe knew instinctively that she meant it.

"He was out jogging the night the delegates were massacred.

The incident wasn't released to the press for obvious reasons. It was Jonathan who found Charles Hillary. Amazingly, he was still alive when he got to him. Before he died he whispered a few words. This isn't common knowledge, so I'd appreciate you keeping it to yourself."

"Of course," said Kathy. "Official Secrets Act and all that."

"By the way you're going to have to sign that," said Wolfe.

"I know, I was only teasing."

An extremely pretty girl, when Kathy smiled she was beautiful. For a moment their eyes held each other and it was Kathy who broke off first. Cynical since the break-up of her marriage, she found her instant attraction to the man unsettling.

"Where was I?" said Wolfe. "Ah yes, he whispered something about Genesis, Medusa and a complex in Wales."

A light came on in Kathy's head. "So that's the reason for the visit."

"Fancy a spot of pub lunch?" said Wolfe.

"You asking as an employer, sir, or because I'm female?"

"You can forget the sir, or I'll have to relieve you of your duties."

"Need seven days' notice, even if you are the PM," said Kathy with a straight face.

Startled, Wolfe realised that he was enjoying a woman's company for the first time since... Instantly he cut his train of thought, stopped it before it could do any damage. "In answer to your question, it's a combination of factors. The main reason is I want to meet a group of people in a village not far from here." Glancing at his watch, he added, "In about ten minutes' time."

"What about this?" she said gesturing to the helicopter.

"Taken care of, Danny Harris informs me there's ample room in the car park to dump it. Are you still open to offers?"

"As it's in the line of duty, I can't see a way out. Besides, you were going with or without me, weren't you?"

"I'm afraid so. Joking aside, I'd value your input. I wasn't teasing when I said your dossier was impressive."

"Your secretary said it was her decision."

Caught out, he raised his hands in mock surrender. "True, but I did make one suggestion. Go for the youngest and prettiest. Incidentally, you fell into neither category. However, as I said before, your credentials were the most impressive so I decided to give you the post."

Though she had been in his company for a short while, it was blindingly obvious why the man was such a good politician. He had the knack of putting you at ease, yes, but one of his biggest assets was that he made you feel as if only you mattered.

Despite Danny's assurances about the chopper, it turned out to be a tight squeeze. Exiting, Wolfe tapped on the window.

"Excuse me, young man, what's your name?"

"It's Kinsey, sir."

"Well, Kinsey, if I'm buying lunch for this young lady, I might as well buy for you too, so hop out."

Shaking his head in astonishment, the young pilot looked over at Kathy in wonder. They both knew that they were in the presence of someone whose people management skills were unlike anything they had come across previously. No, thought Kathy, that was too trite. There was nothing contrived about him. Asking the pilot to lunch had been a completely spontaneous gesture. Hard as it was to believe, especially as he was a politician, he seemed an incredibly nice guy.

As none of them had met before, the first thing on the agenda was introductions. That concluded, they moved on to more important matters: ordering food. Wolfe summed up the feelings of everyone by declaring no decision of any importance should ever be taken on an empty stomach. Afterwards, knowing that what they were about to discuss was of a delicate nature, the pilot thanked the PM and excused himself.

Danny got the ball rolling. Unsure of the protocol involved, he said, "Sir, Mr Wolfe, PM, what do we call you?"

"Don't know about you, Danny, but I tend not to stand on ceremony. How about sticking to first names?"

"David it is then," said Danny, secretly relived. "Right, sir – sorry," he said, before carrying on. "How did things go?"

"Know what impression I was left with, but I think I'll leave it to Kathy to answer."

Taking up where the PM had finished, she began.

"Something about the set up doesn't equate. Everything seemed above board and that was the problem. I don't know how to put this but, for me, the whole place seemed devoid of any buzz. Most research is boring, tedious and a grind, nevertheless, there's still that air of expectancy about the place. And that was missing."

"Any theories?" asked Jared.

Explaining how she believed that the real research was taking place somewhere hidden away, Jared interrupted.

"Like a secret laboratory?" he said, before adding, "It all fits."

"Don't get carried away," said Kathy. "I haven't any proof. At present it's nothing more than an educated guess."

"But I know someone who can. Get the proof, I mean," was Jared's response. "And talk of the devil, he's just walked in."

Kathy was in time to see a distinguished old man on the arms of a striking young woman. His daughter was her immediate thought.

Spotting Jared, he waved and made his way over.

"Saved us a good deal of trouble," said Danny.

"Why?" asked Wolfe.

"You can get the story from the horse's mouth. And believe me, it's a story worth listening to."

At first, Daniel thought the others were joking; eventually, however, he became convinced that the person he was shaking hands with was actually David Wolfe. For the next thirty minutes or so, he and Kathy sat transfixed as he recounted Mark's story. Finally he told them about the telephone call.

"How does he propose to get the proof?" asked Wolfe.

"It's going to be difficult; I think he can pull it off though. I've every confidence in the young man. The odd thing is, since the phone call I've heard nothing from him. I do hope he's all right." Frowning, he failed to see the look that passed between the others.

"Daniel's been a great help in other ways," said Jared.

"How so?" asked Wolfe.

Listening to the account of their early morning visit, Wolfe exploded with laughter. "You mean, despite the small fortune Medusa spent on fortifying his little empire, there's a way of short circuiting his security measures?"

"That's exactly what I mean," said Jared. He was careful not to mention the cave, the cluster of skulls in the clearing or the death of his colleagues. It wasn't the time or place.

At the end of the story, everyone felt in need of a fresh drink. While the others made their way to the bar, Wolfe and Kathy were left alone. Feeling slightly nervous and both wanting to keep the conversation going, the inevitable occurred. They both started talking at the same time. Lifting her hand to her mouth to stifle a giggle, Kathy spluttered once or twice, before giving in and laughing out loud. Contrite, she apologised. Wolfe, seeing the funny side, started laughing too. In seconds, tears were streaming down their faces. It was infectious. In no time, several people on other tables began to join in.

One old couple smiled across, the joy on their faces transparent. At their age, they were glad to see young people having a good time, especially since the recent goings on in the village. It didn't last, moments later they returned to staring at the bottom of their glasses. Their thoughts once more shaped by the events of the past.

Eventually, when they had stopped laughing, Wolfe lifted the bottle of wine from the table and offered Kathy a top up. Smiling shyly, she covered her glass with her hand. "I've had enough, but don't let me stop you."

"I'm not much of a drinker," confessed Wolfe, "But I've been operating at such a breathless pace recently, I think I'll have another small one."

TWENTY-EIGHT

Sunday, 16 December 2012
1.05 a.m.

COVERED IN PERSPIRATION, Jared tumbled out of bed. Another of those dreams, the details had been much the same. Children, hands held in supplication, had begged him to release their souls from torment. Unable to go back to sleep, his watch told him it was 1.05 a.m. Now that Daniel knew the score, the sensible thing to do was to join the others in the Laughing Man. But for some reason he couldn't fathom he was loathe to leave the vicarage. Who was he kidding? He knew exactly why he wanted to remain. And the reason was Samantha. He had a stab of conscience, was feeling this way a betrayal of Emma's memory?

Shrugging such thoughts aside, he donned his black clothes, strapped the twin knives to his neck and removed the handgun from his holdall. Making as little noise as possible, he made his way downstairs. Seeing the place in darkness, he was relieved. Had Samantha or the old vicar spotted him, he would have had some awkward questions to answer.

Slipping through the back door, he closed it softly. Easing through the gate, he notched the gravity latch and made his way along the rutted lane towards the village. Moments later, hugging the tree line that ran the length of the car park, he was in position. Scanning the area for signs that he might be too late, the hoot of a night owl drifted across on the breeze. He allowed himself a smile. Mimicry was one of Ian's specialities, one that had come in handy on many an occasion in the past. He knew exactly where he was. The tall conifers that made up the backdrop to the furthest corner of the car park provided perfect cover.

Dropping flat, he edged his way forward using his elbows and knees. Stopping every few feet, he studied every inch of ground, careful not to disturb anything that might give his position away. Ian was waiting.

"Couldn't sleep?" he asked in a whisper.

"Something's been nagging at me since I returned from the ambush. Have an idea. If I'm right, it explains how Connor, Troy and the others allowed themselves to be caught off guard. Solution was under my nose all the time."

"Care to let me in on the secret?" said Ian.

"Not yet, I haven't proof. Just a hunch, that's all."

"Suppose they knew about us from the moment we walked into the village," said Ian. "Surprising what a few hundred quid in the right place will do."

"There's another explanation to consider. Perhaps our special talents have flagged up on someone's radar? If so, it was only a matter of time before Medusa decided to take us out. What made you come tonight?"

"A process of simple deduction, as Sherlock Holmes would have said. After eliminating Connor and the boys, the next logical step was us. By that I mean all of us, Danny, Gareth and Tina as well. Knew you wouldn't want to involve them. Good as they are, what we're up against might be a little out of their league."

The luminous dial of Jared's watch showed that it was 2.00 a.m. The optimum time for an attack was between 2.00 and 3.00 a.m. Traditionally, this was when people were most tired; more importantly, when even the most well-disciplined of soldiers tended to drop their guard.

"What's the plan?" asked Ian.

"According to their information, we're staying in the pub. My guess is they'll try and nail us here. Apart from the old lady who runs the shop, no one knows I'm staying at the manse."

"My bet is they'll approach from the safety of the forest over there," said Ian pointing to the furthest corner of the car park. And Jared agreed.

Despite the cold, Ian's palms were sweating inside his fingerless gloves. Pulling them off, he blew on his hands before replacing them. He wished he'd had time to put on a Kevlar jacket, but he hadn't. Would Jared be wearing one, he wondered? Of one thing he was certain he would be using his old faithful. Like Ian, Jared preferred the satisfaction of a well-placed round to the crude spraying of lead thrown out by a machine pistol. Jared's weapon of choice was a Sig-Sauer P228, one of very few guns which would function when wet. His was a Heckler and Koch HK4.

Splitting up, they decided to take opposite sides of the car park. That way they could cover an almost 180° arc. Crouching in the shallow ditch, Jared was thankful that it was dry. Raising his head cautiously, he looked across the tarmac surface; it was empty.

Lying flat on his stomach, weapon outstretched, he made his way forward slowly. He was fairly certain of the direction they would be coming from. It was what he would have done had he been in their shoes. Their weapons would be silenced. A bloodbath at this hour was to be avoided at all cost. Medusa had drawn enough attention to himself lately so he would want things resolved quickly and quietly.

Whatever the bastard had been up to was almost complete, Jared was convinced of it. Releasing the safety on his weapon, the plan was simple. Jared would create a diversion while Ian fixed their position. After that things would have to take care of themselves. Seeing movement, he made an instant decision.

Standing up, he offered himself as a target. A fraction of a second later, a splinter of wood the size of a piece of shrapnel, and at this range just as deadly, flew past his ear. Close, too bloody close he thought, startled. Waiting until they had discharged a few more rounds, he made his move. Breaking cover, he bent double and weaved from side to side. According to the training manuals it was almost impossible to hit a man when he was doing this. Unless you were extremely unlucky. Or at least the chances against were remote. At the moment, with lead flying around his head like angry bees, he felt like recalculating the odds. He was sure the person who had written the book had erred on the side of caution.

Hitting the floor a few yards from the tree line, he rolled several times. Coming to his feet, he let loose a few well-placed shots in the direction of the muzzle flashes. Although he was sure he hadn't hit anyone it had been enough to force them to keep their heads down.

Ejecting the empty clip, he put in a fresh one. Then he moved again. Seconds later they appeared. There were four of them. Dressed in identical fashion, they emerged from the deep shadows. Spreading out, they came in pairs. Approaching, they advanced in a fanning movement. From their body language, it was obvious that they regarded this as nothing more than a routine task. That suited Jared. Confident people often made mistakes.

The first two mercenaries fell within a dozen yards of the tree line. Twitching spasmodically, they slid to the floor like marionettes in some kind of silent movie. For a moment the other two failed to react. Taken by surprise, it took them precious seconds to realise they'd been outsmarted.

It was all the time that Jared and Ian needed. Seconds later, the two remaining killers joined their colleagues in a crumpled heap. From start to finish the whole thing had taken less than five minutes. It had been easy. Too easy, thought Jared. Something didn't feel right. Easing his way through a copse of dense trees, Jared was some fifty yards away from Ian's position, when an arm like a steel vice snaked around his neck. "Disappointing, Mr Hunter," a voice whispered. "After all I'd heard about you, I expected better. A novice wouldn't have allowed himself to be taken so easily."

With a sinking feeling in the pit of his stomach, Jared knew he was doomed. He'd had many a lucky escape during his short career in the military, but it appeared that Lady Luck had finally run out of patience. Strangely, his first thought was not for himself, but for Jodie. What was to become of her? A second before Lucifer emptied the magazine of his silenced Glock into the back of Jared's head he felt the kiss of cold steel against his temple. Unwittingly he had broken the golden rule of engagement. If you want to kill someone don't talk: act. While he'd been mentally congratulating himself on taking down Jared so easily, it had afforded Ian the opportunity to steal up behind him. Despite having the upper hand, Ian was unprepared for the lightening quick reactions of his adversary. In a blur of movement Lucifer lashed out backwards with his foot. Connecting solidly with Ian's shin it was the split second distraction Lucifer needed. Pushing Jared to one side he dropped to his knees and fired in one fluid motion. And then he was gone. Taking advantage of the confusion, Lucifer had decided to beat a hasty retreat. For a fleeting second Jared thought about following before realising that his first priority was Ian.

Suddenly, the mocking voice of Lucifer drifted to him on the breeze. "You were lucky, Hunter; next time will be different. That's a promise."

The stinging rebuke cut through Jared's facade of invincibility.

With a jolt he realised but for Ian's timely intervention he would be dead. Once again he had come through a seemingly impossible situation. Yet, deep down he knew that it was only a matter of time. Even a cat has only nine lives.

Leaning over Ian, Jared's heart sank. The copious amount of blood meant it was bad. Fearing the worst, he checked for a pulse and was relieved to find one. Thought faint it was strong. Moments later, Ian opened his eyes.

"Time I repaid the compliment, you've saved my life so many times. Feels good to redress the balance a little."

And then he passed out again. Lifting Ian onto his shoulder gently, Jared made his way out of the tree line towards the back door of the pub. Propping him against the wall he made a cursory examination of the wound. What he saw was encouraging. The bullet had gone through the fleshy part of the shoulder, and exited the back. Fortunately, it had been a low calibre bullet, had it been soft tipped it would have taken half his shoulder away. As long as no sinews or tendons had been severed, he would make a complete recovery.

Bullets kill by destroying the vital organs, those necessary for keeping us alive or the essential blood vessels supplying those organs. Miss these, and you always have a chance of surviving, however bad the wound. The only other problem is shock. By now Ian was conscious again.

"Looks like you're going to make it," said Jared, his relief all too evident. "Wound's nasty, but it's not fatal. The problem is you're bleeding like a pig. Unless we can stop it, you're either going to die from loss of blood, or shock. At the moment I think the former is the most problematic. And there's no way we can get you to a hospital in time. Danny has a basic medical kit in the Winnebago, but something has to be done now."

"What's the answer then?"

"What they do in the movies," said Jared. "Going to hurt, but look on the bright side – if it works it'll save your life."

Ian hadn't a clue what the hell Jared was talking about until he saw the bullet in his hand. "You malicious bastard, you've been dying to try this out for years, haven't you?"

Before Jared could reply, the side door of the inn popped open and a torch beam fell squarely onto the figures. It was Danny. Grasping the urgency of the situation, he rushed over.

"Help me get him inside," whispered Jared.

By now Tina and Gareth had arrived. Between them they carried Ian into the bar. Laying him on a table, Jared took one of his knives from its sheath and stripped Ian of his parka and vest. Taking control of the situation he turned to Tina. "Get me some clean cloths and a jug of boiling water and Gareth, nip to the bar for a bottle of whiskey."

Seconds later, the cloths and the whiskey arrived.

"Take a few swigs," said Jared, "this is going to hurt."

"And aren't you going to love it," said Ian.

Taking a generous hit of the alcohol, Ian grimaced as the fiery liquid exploded in his mouth before slowly making its way from his throat to his gullet. Lifting the bottle to his mouth again, Jared snatched it away. "Not all of it, you bloody idiot."

Holding Ian down with one hand, he poured a good measure into the open wound with the other. Ian nearly jumped off the table. It was then the others saw the bullet. An old-fashioned round, it was one Jared carried for luck. One thing was certain: he never thought he would ever have to use it. Prising off the casing, he tipped the powder onto the wound.

"Oh no," said Tina. "You're not, are you?"

"He is," said a half-pissed Ian.

Guessing what was coming, Gareth handed Jared a lighter. Flipping it open, he lit it and held it to the powder. An instant flash was followed by a scream and the smell of burning flesh. Unconscious, Ian was blissfully unaware of anything more.

Satisfied, Jared turned to Tina. "Do me a favour, pour the rest of the whiskey over the wound and then bandage it. I've something else to attend to."

"Want a hand with the bodies?" said Gareth.

"Be grateful," said Jared.

Some twenty minutes later, job complete, they returned to check on Ian. Tina had taken charge.

Seeing the concern on Jared's face, she said, "We've antibiotics and a fresh supply of bandages in the Winnebago. They'll make sure the wound stays free of infection. Unforeseen complications aside, he'll be up and about in a few days' time."

He didn't like to contradict Tina, but he was willing to put odds that rather than a few days, Ian would be up and walking in twenty-four hours. And he was right.

TWENTY-NINE

Monday, 17 December 2012
9.30 a.m.

IT WAS THE phone call that he had dreaded making. Swallowing, he punched in Medusa's number.

"I take it all did not go to plan?" said Medusa.

"Affirmative, and I'm afraid they'll be on the alert now, might be a few days before we get another opportunity."

A few moments silence was followed by, "You had your chance and you blew it. Appears you're not as good as you think you are."

Refusing to be intimidated, the voice said, "Perhaps you have a suggestion?"

"There's a simple way of getting Mr Hunter to do exactly what we want. I'm surprised with your famous intellect, the one you never tire of telling me about, you hadn't thought of it first."

"I'm all ears," was the reply.

"We snatch Hunter's daughter. Then the rest, as they say, is history."

As much as he hated to admit it, the answer was stunningly simple. The old man had called the shot correctly. It was Hunter's one weak spot, and like a bloody novice he had overlooked it. About to say something to cover his embarrassment, he never had the opportunity. Medusa had hung up without another word.

Casting his eye over the kitchen clock, Eric saw it was a few minutes after 7.00 p.m. With that the front bell rang. For the last week he and Edna, Jared's grandmother, had been looking after Jodie. An emergency was how Jared had put it.

The morning he had left, both he and Jodie had acted strangely. Something was up, of that Eric was sure. The incessant ringing of the bell brought him out of his momentary stasis, for a moment he'd completely lost his train of thought. Lately his mind had started to wander. The onset of old age, he decided wryly. Wondering who it could be at this time of evening, he lifted his tired old frame from the couch and made his way slowly to the front door. Compared to his modest little terraced house, the walk seemed miles. Switching on the porch light, he opened the door. Squinting, he lifted one hand to his eyes. The man was certainly a giant. Yet, he was sure that he had never set eyes on the character before. The only visitors to Mendel Hall were people who got lost in the maze of country lanes surrounding the estate. Occasionally some of those, seeing the house, would stop and ask for directions. About to enquire how he might help, the words never left his lips.

The blow was so swift he had no warning. One minute he was wracking his brain trying to think who the giant might be, the next he was hitting the floor with a sickening thud. Replacing the weapon in its holder, Lucifer bent down and, grasping Eric by the ankles, dragged him towards the lounge. Dumping him onto the carpet, his body lay at an angle in front of the huge French windows.

The first little matter taken care of, he moved through the hallway towards the kitchen at the rear of the house. He was almost there when a door to his right opened and he came face to face with an astonished old lady. Despite his considerable bulk, Lucifer was exceptionally quick on his feet. Stepping forward, he put one hand over her mouth; with the other he pinched the carotid artery at the side of her neck. In moments she was unconscious. Like Eric she would be out for hours.

Reasoning that the little girl would be a more difficult target, he made his way forward cautiously. There were doors to his right and left. He opened several before striking lucky. Sitting in a huge leather armchair, her back to him, Jodie was playing some computer game. Concentrating on the screen, a pair of headphones was glued to her ears. Removing a tiny bottle from his pocket, he tipped a measured dose of the chemical onto a clean handkerchief. Considering her age, it was essential the correct dosage be administered.

Moving on the balls of his feet, his rubber-soled shoes made no sound on the luxurious carpet. He was within a few feet of Jodie when something triggered her alarm system. Throwing caution to the wind Lucifer leapt forward, closing the gap in a fraction of a second. Pinning her to the chair with one immense hand, he placed the other holding the handkerchief onto her face. For several moments Jodie fought like a wildcat. In a short while, her struggles became less and less frantic. Finally, she was unconscious. Removing the headphones, he hefted her onto his shoulder.

He had a sudden thought: he was getting good at this.

At first the ice maiden's requests had seemed demeaning. Gradually, however, the challenge had grown on him. Surprisingly, it had been far more difficult than he had first anticipated. Spiriting youngsters from their beds in the middle of the night had required both skill and finesse. The first few attempts had been crude. On two occasions he had nearly been discovered. Over the course of the last twelve months though he had become quite adept.

A thought was nagging at him. How the hell had she known he was there? It should have been impossible, unless of course she was psychic. Laughing at the thought, he dismissed the idea instantly. To him the paranormal was nothing but a series of old wives' tales and superstitious nonsense. He wasn't to know that his initial guess was correct. Jodie was a very special young girl. One with powers he couldn't even dream of. Powers she was only just becoming aware of herself. Carrying her through the door, he levered it closed with his foot, before taking the few steps leading to the gravel drive.

Placing Jodie into the passenger seat of the Range Rover, Lucifer returned to the house. Carrying Edna into the lounge he dumped her next to the inert figure of Eric. Removing a roll of duct tape from the pocket of his jacket, he lifted both into sitting positions. Satisfied, he placed the unconscious duo into comfortable armchairs and taped their feet and arms firmly into place.

His instructions had been specific: they were not to be harmed. That way they would be able to confirm Jodie's kidnapping. He made his way back to the car. Opening the door, he turned his head and made a final sweep of the estate. Seeing nothing, he levered himself into the driver's seat. Strapping himself in, he started the engine and was immediately greeted by the throaty roar of the powerful 2.6 litre engine. Depressing the clutch, he shifted into first gear, floored the accelerator and disappeared in a flurry of gravel.

THIRTY

Tuesday, 18 December 2012

Dr Chandra was on the road by 5.00 a.m. to pick up the supply of vaccine from the central depot in Cardiff. His intention had been to get there early to avoid the chaos. He had been disappointed. Everyone had been thinking along the same lines. And so, some three hours later, the car safely loaded with the precious liquid, he'd arrived home.

After that, there had been the inoculation programme to implement. He'd managed a ten-minute break for a cup of tea and a chocolate biscuit in some eight hours. His blood sugar had dropped alarmingly and he was almost out on his feet. According to the medical grapevine, a pandemic was inevitable. It was a matter of when and not if. Should that prove to be the case, it had been worth all the hard work. The village now had a fighting chance.

He remembered the first few months. The locals had viewed him with suspicion: seeing him as an outsider, a foreigner. Gradually, he had earned their trust and eventually they had come to see that beneath the colour of his skin he was a kindly old man, one who had their welfare at heart.

Then, it had been such a happy community, until the disappearances that is. What had started as a trickle had got out of hand. Despite the best efforts of the police, no one had managed to get to the bottom of the mystery.

"Doctor, Mr and Mrs Price and their little daughter are here," said his secretary, poking her head around the door. "And they're the last ones."

Struggling to his feet he shook their hands. Time had not been kind to the Price family. The dark rings around the eyes, the puffy skin, the sickly parlour: the tell-tale signs were all there. They had never recovered from the loss of their little daughter. Amy had been one of the first to disappear. Put to bed at exactly the same time as every other night, by the following morning she had simply vanished. As with all the others, there had been no sign of any struggle. The police had been baffled. Though they had another daughter, a year younger, it had failed to compensate for the loss of Amy. In many ways it had been harder for Stacey: she couldn't understand why her sister wouldn't come home.

Both adults were injected in a matter of minutes. Seeing the needles, however, Stacey had been terrified. Retreating behind her mother's back, she stubbornly refused to cooperate. Chiding himself for his lack of foresight, Dr Chandra knew fatigue had dulled his senses. But he had a trick up his sleeve. Removing a flavoured lollipop from a stash he kept for just such emergencies, he eventually managed to turn her round.

His work complete, he saw the family to the door before collapsing into his favourite chair. Listening to the words of the medical council, he had given himself the first shot. The government had been adamant that all essential services should be vaccinated first. It made sense, of course. If things were to reach pandemic proportions, it was imperative that the front-line troops be prepared. It was the reason in-flight instructions on board aircrafts insisted that in the case of emergency decompression, you had to take care of yourself first before administering help to others.

Thinking along those lines, his head fell onto his shoulder and he drifted into a dreamless sleep.

The television was on in the lounge of the Winnebago, and Gareth, in his by-now familiar pose, feet propped up on the leather armchair, was watching the morning news.

"What gives?" asked Jared.

"One thing on the mind of the media today, everything else has been relegated to the back page."

Watching, Jared saw a roving camera crew filming a clinic somewhere in the heart of London. The queue seemed to stretch for miles. Waiting for something, the penny dropped. It was the beginning of the inoculation process.

"Happening all over Britain," said Gareth. "Took a while for the health authorities to get up to speed, but today, December 18th is D Day."

"Must have cost Medusa a fortune," said Jared.

"And more, what we're seeing is just the tip of the iceberg. Still, considering what he's worth, it's a drop in the ocean. There'll be some who won't bother. Either they'll be afraid of the needle, or too lazy to queue. Which category do you come under?"

"The second," said Jared laughing. "Too busy worrying about other things to even think about it. If your name's on the bullet, as the saying goes. And you?"

"Till we get to the bottom of what's going on here, can't see any of us having the jab."

Jared's mind turned to Ravens Hill. He wondered if stocks of the anti-virus had arrived there yet.

By now Caroline was convinced something had happened to Mark. Since they had last slept together, he seemed to have dropped off the face of the earth. Knowing his intentions, he should have been in touch by now. But she hadn't heard anything. Had he been caught? She dismissed the idea quickly.

If that was the case, news of it would have spread around the complex like wildfire.

Discreet enquiries had produced nothing. Everyone was as much in the dark as her. As Harvey's private secretary, she was often privy to confidential information. But she hadn't heard anything on the jungle grapevine which was even stranger.

Looking at her watch, it was 11.00 a.m., time for a coffee break. Turning the computer chair through a 180 degree loop, she got to her feet and headed for the machine. About to pour a cup, she heard muted conversation drifting through the door from Harvey's office. Normally, she wouldn't be able to hear anything. Puzzled she headed for the door and the mystery was solved. The door was open several inches.

"And you say you haven't seen a trace of him since he threatened to get the evidence to expose me?" Doing the mental calculations in her head, Anna said, "That's well over a week. I didn't come into contact with him that often, so until a few days ago it never struck me that I hadn't seen him about. Thinking it odd, I decided to check his room."

My god, thought Caroline, so Harvey had known all along. More than that, he seemed to be an integral part of what was going on. His mock sincerity and charming nature had fooled everyone, particularly her. All his talk about helping Mark had been bullshit. She knew that Mark had decided to take a week's holiday in order to get to the bottom of what was going on, but not keeping in contact with her, especially when he had promised to steal a sample of the R90 was puzzling. Worryingly, if neither Anna nor Harvey knew anything about Mark's whereabouts, then what the hell had happened to him?

"Not a sign," replied Harvey. "Mark may have had his faults, being unreliable wasn't one of them. Course I knew he was popping into the village on his days off, and it didn't worry me.

It was company he craved not alcohol. So I turned a blind eye. After his week's holiday was up and he didn't report in, alarm bells started ringing. Not turning up for work is totally out of character." Biting the inside of his lip, he added, "Think he got wind we were on to him and decided not to return."

"Doubtful," was Anna's reply. "He had balls. From what you say, he was determined to get a sample of the R90. Besides, if he'd done a runner, he would have taken his car and belongings. A quick look round his dormitory showed everything still in its place. The only oddity was a phial of blood sitting on his desk and his bathroom mirror had been smashed."

"The blood, anything incriminating?" asked Harvey

"I didn't feel the need to analyse it, anything of a delicate nature is stored in my hidden lab," said Anna, "and no one but me has access to that." The remark wasn't strictly true: Lucifer had the code. Needing to deliver the abductees at night she had given it to him. But he used it very infrequently. And then, only when she was in attendance. "What are we going to do?" asked Harvey.

"Nothing, he'll turn up eventually. And then I'll take care of him personally."

Listening to the conversation Caroline made a decision. She would phone the vicar the first opportunity she got.

THIRTY-ONE

Tuesday, 18 December 2012
5.30 p.m.

AN EMERGENCY MEETING, everyone of importance was in attendance. Informed earlier about the situation, Wolfe and Kathy had arrived by helicopter. Paul had been left to look after the fort in Westminster. Scattered around the Winnebago's lounge it was a tight squeeze. Judging the moment was right, Danny got the ball rolling.

"Several hours ago, Daniel received a phone call from Harvey's private secretary." Seeing a few puzzled faces, he explained. "Seems she and Mark are an item. From a conversation she overheard between her boss and Anna Heche, appears they're as much in the dark about his whereabouts as we are. One thing we do know, he managed to get the blood sample before he disappeared. Now he's out of the equation, it's down to us to. Somebody has to get inside the facility and steal another one. Even though level 4 is unmanned during the night, without the elevator codes it would be a no go. Fortunately, that's where Caroline comes in. Convinced Mark's dead, she's prepared to put her body on the line to help us."

"And the elevator passes?" asked Tina. A light came on in her head. "Of course, as Harvey's private secretary she'd be able to steal one."

"Solution's far simpler," said Jared. "If my guess is correct she took Mark's. Thinking he might eventually return, security would have had no reason to confiscate his possessions."

"Go to the top of the class," said Danny.

"So you're not just a pretty face," said Tina maliciously.

"What about a frontal assault?" asked Wolfe. "Say the word and I'll have the necessary in place in under an hour."

"Don't even think of going down that road," said Jared. "It would be a bloodbath."

Leaning against the window of the mobile, water in hand, Jared broke the uneasy silence. "I've an idea."

At the suggestion, the room exploded.

"That's no plan," said Danny, "it's a bloody suicide mission."

Once everyone had said their piece, Jared opened his mouth to counter the arguments. He never had the opportunity. In the close confines of the lounge, the theme tune of Danny's mobile came across as unnaturally loud. Holding up his finger in a wait-a-minute gesture, he took out a leather notebook from his inside pocket and flipped it open. Adjusting the phone between his ear and neck, his brow furrowed in concentration. Scribbling down a few notes, his face drained of colour. "That was the south Wales branch of the CID, Eric and your grandmother have been found in Mendel Hall."

"Are they okay?" he asked startled.

"Battered and bruised, they'll survive. Appears strangers looking for directions heard some kind of commotion and found them. Another day or so and things might have been different."

"And Jodie?"

"When questioned, they were obviously a little vague. Piecing together the bits they did remember, it seems Jodie was taken."

So, that was it, thought Ian. Now all bets were off. He had noticed a change in Jared since the last time they'd met. Subtle – unless you knew him you might never notice – but it was still there, a softening around the eyes. He had no doubt it was because he was now a father. His arm in a sling, Jared was right to refuse his help. Yet, by allowing him to go it alone, he felt as if he was betraying him. And Danny was right: it was a suicide mission.

Jared allowed his gaze to flicker over the others.

"Nothing's impossible. It's a matter of how much you're prepared to risk," he said. "With Jodie's life at stake, mine is now unimportant." Smiling at the downcast faces, he added,"There's always a chance. The skill is in judging exactly how far to go. It's a balancing act between being reckless and taking risks."

His little speech sounded false, even to him.

"Suppose we should give in gracefully," said Danny. "You've always been stubborn and insolent, and those are your good points. If this is a one-man mission, what are the rest of us supposed to do? While you're away playing Rambo, I mean."

"Being the most tactful, I thought it would be obvious."

"Cut the bullshit and spit it out," said Danny.

"You can handle the press. If things go according to plan, we're going to need someone with his finger on the pulse."

Danny could feel the laughter bubbling up from inside. "I knew it. Something warned me I was going to draw the short straw. You've stitched me up like a bloody kipper. And with such subtlety, may I add."

"Amen to that," said Jared.

Exiting the trailer Jared approached Daniel. "Any chance of a word with Samantha? I wouldn't want to leave without explaining things."

"She's outside," said Daniel. "I asked her to stay at home, but she was worried about you. Her instincts warned her trouble was brewing and that you might do something stupid. As things turned out she was right. That was before Jodie was factored into the equation though. She doesn't know about the kidnapping, so go easy on her, please."

Listening to Jared's update Samantha's eyes widened in fear. "From the little I know about the complex you'll be signing your death warrant."

Looking into her eyes he said, "What choice do I have? If you had a daughter you'd do the same thing."

Opening her mouth to argue, she immediately closed it. Jared was right. Resigned to the outcome, she placed her hand on his arm. "If anyone can get her back you can. Be careful, that's all I ask."

Suddenly, her eyes softened. "Dear God, I don't want anything to happen to you."

Since getting to know him, she had become frustrated by the wall he had built around himself. All her adult life, she'd prided herself on seeing through male charm. Mark was a classic example: confident, cocky, yet pretending to be anything but. Jared was different. And because of it, he affected her in a way no one ever had. Affected her in a way she couldn't explain, even to herself. In his presence she felt like a schoolgirl with a silly crush. Yet, he didn't seem interested.

Had Samantha only known, she had misread the situation completely. Since Emma's death, Jared had been lonely. Never good with women, he normally shunned their company. Meeting Samantha had thrown him into confusion. He'd found himself in a situation in which he was hopelessly out of his depth. The intensity of Samantha's gaze was disconcerting. It was almost as if she was trying to memorise every little feature. Then, in a completely spontaneous gesture, she touched her fingers to her mouth. Placing them gently onto Jared's lips, she whispered, "Come back safely."

THIRTY-TWO

Tuesday, 18 December 2012
8.00 p.m.

IT WAS DARK; the last of the sun had disappeared hours ago. At least his night-vision goggles would afford him a fighting chance, he realised. Built-in infra-red sensors meant he was able to detect heat sources even in the darkest areas; segregated into quarters, the screen enabled him to monitor a 380 degree arc in a single glance.

Reaching the cave he breathed a sigh of relief: it was empty. Twenty torturous minutes later he found himself inside the grounds of the complex. The lack of activity bothered him. Something was wrong. On his first visit, heavily armed guards had been stationed either side of the entrance. Now there was no one. And the place was in complete darkness. Had they anticipated his time of arrival; made things deliberately easy? No, that was too obvious. Kicking into overdrive, his mind entered the killing zone, a state in which his body reached an icy calmness. Despite being skilled at what he did, Jared was also a realist. So many things could go wrong, unquantifiable things, ones he might not have accounted for. The only way around it was to accept it, and then trust in his skill and judgement to get him through.

Over the years he had instilled in himself a simple credo: there was always a solution. No matter how bad things looked, there was always an answer; the skill was in finding it. Retaining that thought, he pushed forward. Before entering the complex, he had something to take care of.

Five minutes later and he was ready. Suddenly, a bulky outline appeared in the periphery of his vision. About a hundred yards away, it was just at the edge of the tree line. Bringing his gun to bear, he was in time to see something bolt out of a thicket. Glimpsed for a second only, it was a blurred image. Whatever it had been was big and had moved with surprising rapidity for something so large. Refocusing, he opened the sealed door and entered the building. Inside was a lobby; opposite was a fireproof door. Briefed as to the layout of level 4, he knew he would be able to find his way around at a push. The problem was, without the access codes to the elevator he would be unable to get there.

Caroline's instructions had been specific; she would meet him at the front desk. And the front desk was deserted. With time at a premium, he decided he couldn't wait any longer. Some five minutes later he entered a long corridor leading directly to the main elevator.

According to Caroline it was always guarded, but the guard was missing. Yet, the lift doors were open. Something was definitely wrong. Sig-Sauer pointing ahead, he swept the corridor. Seeing no one, he stepped into the lift. Moments later he reached the ground floor. Exiting, he stumbled across the first of the bodies. Kneeling, he placed the first two fingers of his right hand against the neck of the nearest. There was no pulse. It was the same with the others, they were all dead.

Puzzlingly, each of the bodies seemed to be free of any wound. It was almost as if they had fallen asleep. He was struck by a sobering thought, might the cause of death be some kind of biological agent? If so, he too would now be infected. Forcing defeatist thoughts aside, he opened several other doors. The result was the same. Corpses were strewn everywhere; it seemed that there was no one left alive. But why had the old man killed everyone? It didn't make sense. Wanton slaughter was pointless, unless…

And then he had it. Not only had they outgrown their

usefulness, they were potential witnesses. Having achieved his objective, the lives of everyone had become meaningless. What had the crazy bastard been up to?

Retracing his steps to level 3, some ten minutes later he found the office.

Obeying the golden rule, Jared held the pistol close to his side. Often in films they get it wrong, entering an open doorway with arms and gun outstretched is an invitation to have it knocked away. For obvious reasons it was a mistake that once made, was never repeated.

Stepping into the room, he was greeted by a bear of man holding a pistol to Jodie's head. There was a time to fight and a time to take stock; Jared knew he was facing the latter option. Seated behind a sheet of bullet-proof glass, speakers placed at strategic points around the room meant Medusa's voice was as clear as a bell.

"Would you be kind enough to relieve Mr Hunter of his gun, Lucifer? And make sure you remove the knives from the leather pouch at the base of his neck."

Very few men alive knew about those. Finally, the last piece of the jigsaw fell into place. Lucifer studied Jared through eyes that were dead. Jared had seen eyes like that before and he knew what to expect. Surprisingly, the blow never came. Scanning the room, he noticed three leather sofas. Mint green, they were positioned in a semi-circle around a huge artificial log fire. On the walls were dozens of black and white photographs. Military in composition, several were of an odd-looking character in various poses with two people he recognised. The Emperor Hirohito and a monster called Shiro Ishii. The decor had a 1930s' feel to it and he knew why. Medusa was reliving past glories. Jared's eyes turned to Jodie. Unruffled, she sat perfectly still, her knees tucked under her chin. Winking and smiling at her, she responded in kind. Desperately wanting to take Lucifer out, he forced himself to remain calm. One wrong move and he would kill Jodie. Suddenly, a saying flashed into Jared's mind. Of Chinese origin, its philosophy was simple. However bad things appear, somewhere along the line you have encountered worse. Until now he had always believed it.

The adrenaline rush which had fuelled him earlier was ebbing, to be replaced by a growing frustration as he wracked his brain to think of a way out of the mess.

Returning his gaze to Medusa, something about the old man bothered him. He looked oddly at peace. Meanwhile, Medusa was impressed with Jared. Though the situation was hopeless, the man could still afford a smile.

Pinching the bridge of his nose between thumb and forefinger he prepared himself.

"Before we get down to business, Mr Hunter, there are some people I'd like you to meet. Without such influential figures, Genesis might never have been launched."

A figure walked into the room, one with which Jared was instantly familiar.

"Good to see you again, Jared," he said. Lowering himself into one of the mint green armchairs, he crossed his legs in a manner Jared had always found rather effeminate. So, he had been right. It had been the only answer, the ambush, his knives and so much more. The problem was he'd managed to get there too late.

"I guessed you had friends in low places," said Jared, "but this low…" He left the remainder of the sentence unspoken.

Unfazed, Medusa quipped, "Stanford and his counterparts have been responsible for setting up my arks across the globe. In fact, Stanford organised my most important, the one here in Britain. Another hour or so," he said glancing at his watch, "and we shall be safely tucked away inside our new home. Whether I live to see my dream turn into a reality is in the lap of God. Still, we all have to pay for our sins in the end. Even me it seems."

By now Johan and Anna had joined the party.

Turning, he said, "This is my son and daughter."

Staring at each other, both faces were a mask of horror.

Lost for words, Anna recovered quickly. "I thought mother died at childbirth and the brat she was carrying stillborn."

"Technically, you're correct," came her father's reply, "your mother did die giving birth to Johan, but as you can see he survived. A failure all his life, his one talent lies in squandering vast amounts of cash. Giving Johan money is akin to throwing it into a black hole. Still, what are fathers for? My darling daughter, until recently you were my pride and joy. A chip off the old block, I think the saying goes. Entrusted to developing what Immada and Ishii envisaged – a genetically perfect race – you completed the task some time ago. Had you informed me, Genesis might have been launched sooner. Worryingly, your attempt to play God almost cost me decades of careful planning. Fortunately, David Wolfe's visit came to nothing."

Drawing a painful breath, he continued, "Genesis, I take it you're familiar with the name, Mr Hunter?"

In a desperate gamble to buy time, Jared played along.

"Comes from the Hebrew Bereshit or, to give it its full title, Bereshit Bara Elohim: in the beginning God created."

"Ah yes, your background is impressive. Accepted into Oxford University to read Semitic languages, you were set for a glittering academic career, were you not? That is, until fate decreed otherwise. The rendering is perfectly correct. However, Genesis is more than a book: it is an epic, a drama on a grand scale. The words it contains are so evocative. God made the world, a world that was good. And then on the sixth day he made man, the apex of creation. For that reason it sets us apart from the animal kingdom, affords us a special relationship with him. And how did we repay God? By betraying him. The further we progress through the chapters, the more evidence we are given of how this once beautiful relationship soured. Eventually, mankind's attempt to usurp God left him with no alternative. And so, in an act of divine retribution everything was swept away in the great Flood."

Glancing at Lucifer, Medusa said, "Before I continue the story, I think a few safety procedures are necessary."

Forcing Jared's arms behind his back Lucifer tied his hands together, before injecting him with something that was a sickly green colour. A lime green slush puppy came to mind, but Jared doubted it was as friendly a substance.

"If you're wondering whether it's something as mundane as poison, then I'll enlighten you. It's the inoculation billions of people are queuing up for world wide. The television please, Lucifer, Mr Hunter will want to see this."

The screen came to life.

"What you're seeing," said Medusa "is a recording of something that took place in an inner city area of London earlier today."

In seconds the scene changed. Over the course of the next few minutes, Jared witnessed the same endless line of people in selected cities across the globe. Paris, Berlin, Jerusalem and New York were highlighted.

"The logistics behind such an undertaking is breathtaking," explained the newsreader. "Besides which, the cost of setting up such a venture must have run into billions."

"Any wiser, Mr Hunter?" asked Medusa.

"I'm baffled," said Jared.

"Then let me recount a tale. It begins with the final months of the war. With Germany and Japan on their knees, Hitler and the emperor were forced to abandon a shared vision. Historically, the term 'master race' was grossly misunderstood. Far from engineering a race of pure Aryan blood, Hitler's scientists were attempting to genetically manufacture a race of 'super beings'. Research was at an advanced stage, yet, thanks to the genius of Immada and Ishii, we were always one step ahead. According to Immada's notes, he was almost there. But for the sad demise of the Imperial Japanese army he would have pulled it off. Several months before the Red Army invaded Manchuko, Immada was ordered to shelve the project and concentrate instead on producing a weapon that could turn the tide of the war. How do I know all this, it's quite simple, I was Immada's assistant."

With a wave of his hand, Medusa said, "Anyway, Immada produced the weapon. Labelled the Apocalypse Virus, it was never used."

Seeing Jared's puzzled expression, he explained.

"Unable to find an effective antidote, the weapon was useless. What would have been the point of unleashing something that would kill indiscriminately? The virus would have wiped out everything in its path, friend or foe. We were in despair and then in August 1945, with the Red Army at our door we were ordered to destroy everything and relocate to Japan. Unable to face the humiliation, Immada killed himself. The secret underground laboratories were never found, I saw to that. Standing over the old man's body, I made him a promise, a promise that should the opportunity arise, I would complete his work."

Gasping for breath, he was silent for a moment. Seconds later, he continued.

"Armageddon, what a wonderfully expressive word, yet due to the film industry, it has become much maligned. Simply put, it means the end of the world. It doesn't have to be the end of the world, however, Genesis will see to that."

"The bodies littered throughout the complex," said Jared interrupting, "some kind of biological agent?"

"Dear me, no, nothing so dramatic," said Medusa. "A dose of carbon monoxide poisoning, that's all. They died feeling nothing. Shortly after their sad demise, the noxious fumes were flushed out with purified air."

Listening to the old man in disbelief, Jared knew with a sickening certainty that Medusa was insane.

Thirty-Three

Interpreting Jared's expression correctly, Medusa sighed. "Whatever you think of me is immaterial. Chosen by God, I am the instrument of his retribution. Surely you can see that a once beautiful world, one made by the hands of a loving, caring God has sunk into the depths of degradation. So I say to you, Jared, it's time once more to rid the earth of filth and wickedness."

Amazed that the old man had failed to see the irony behind his thinking, Jared broke across Medusa's carefully rehearsed speech. "May I be permitted an observation?"

"Certainly," was the old man's reply.

"If God isn't happy, why doesn't he take matters into his own hands? More importantly, why has it taken him so long to do something about it?"

"It is one of God's strengths, not weaknesses, that he's tolerated mankind's blasphemies for so long," replied Medusa. Oddly, the same thought had occurred to him. He was at a loss to explain how the God of the Old and New Testaments differed so greatly. He much preferred the one portrayed in the Old. A God whose philosophy was an eye for an eye was far more to his taste than the kind, loving one talked about by that charlatan Jesus. It was beyond him how an omnipotent God should have tolerated such deceit for so long.

Refocusing, he said, "It is not for me to question God's motives. As his servant, it is my duty to obey. Evil shall be wiped from the face of the earth. Read the Book of Revelation, Mr Hunter, properly I mean. It's all there."

It was the early hours of the morning. Medusa hadn't realised that things would take so long to finalise. So much talk had taken a great deal out of him. Breathless, he stared into space. Reaching into a side drawer of his desk, he removed a syringe. Taking a huge hit of morphine, he grimaced. The drug was no longer a luxury, it was a necessity. Over the last few days his condition had deteriorated rapidly. It was almost as if something was sucking the very life out of his body. And it was. Ironically, despite his enormous wealth he was powerless to do anything about it. Approaching the final hurdle, he needed to be strong for the next few hours. Recently he had been consuming a double dose; now, even that was taking longer and longer to kick in. Suddenly, the drug hit his blood stream.

"Regardless of everything you've seen and heard, you still have no idea what Genesis is. Let me join the dots together. What you saw earlier was nothing to do with compassion; it was the culmination of decades of painstaking planning. At this precise moment, billions of unsuspecting fools are being injected with Genesis."

The truth burst into Jared's brain like a firecracker. Over the last few minutes he had mentally followed the trail of evidence he'd been drip fed. Until now he had been unable to see it. Spellbound, he listened as the old man completed his tale.

"By now over three-quarters of the world's population will be infected. And there is no antidote. For roughly two days nothing will happen. The virus lays dormant in the body of its host. As a result, for a limited time period, those in the company of someone who has already become infected are safe. Once that incubation period is over, however, they become a biological time bomb. Shortly afterwards, the first symptoms will appear. Its potency is limited, however, after a certain period of time it becomes harmless. A mere handful of the world's population will escape the purge. Ideally, to survive you need specially adapted facilities, such as this complex."

Staving off comment, he continued.

"The world will recover, Mr Hunter, I have seen to that. The arks contain the chosen ones. Selected for their specialist skills and genetic make-ups, each of the survivors will be essential for rebuilding the world. And their children will become the manufactured race of super beings I alluded to earlier. Rest assured, our present technology will not become extinct. What would be the point of turning the survivors into a group of itinerant farmers?"

Turning his attention to Lucifer, he said, "When I leave, you can turn Mr Hunter and his daughter loose. Don't take your eyes off him for a moment. A word of warning, I don't want him harmed. I want him to suffer. Once you have taken care of that you can follow the rest of us to the helicopter."

Watching Lucifer, Jared saw something in the man's eyes. He was sure that it was disappointment. But it was mixed with something else, something he couldn't quite fathom. Lucifer was thinking about death, in particular Jared's. Wanting no part of Medusa's new world, he had come to a decision. He would take care of Hunter personally.

To his way of thinking, the greatest pleasure in killing was looking into the eyes of his victims prior to death. To see the dawning realisation that there was no way back. No one person ever reacted in the same way. He'd seen all the scenarios. Horror, acceptance, reluctance – each one had been mirrored in the eyes. Some accepted their fate with dignity, others fell apart. The most interesting reaction was always the religious one. This type behaved as if they had been cheated. And no wonder, he thought in amusement.

The first time he'd killed someone had been an accident.

After that he had found that he liked it. By now he was addicted to killing – a death junkie was the description that popped into his mind. Since then he'd managed to devise ever more original ways of sending his victims to meet their maker.

"You have forty-eight hours to live, Mr Hunter," said Medusa, "unless of course you can come up with an antidote. Considering I failed after sixty-odd years of trying, I'd say that was a tall order. A word of advice, I'd spend my last days with my daughter if I were you. Time with one's family is precious, don't you agree? Oh yes, before I forget," he said turning to his children. "There will be no room in the ark for fools and liars. What would you do after this was over Johan? Devoid of any skills it would be a waste of resources. However," he said looking directly at his daughter, "You nearly cost me the Genesis programme. I'm sorry my dear, you're on your own. If you want to survive, stay in the facility. There are more than enough provisions to ride out the storm. And then afterwards, well that will be up to you."

Pretending confusion, he continued, "But I forgot, our friend Jared will be on the loose, won't he? For a day or two anyway, and I don't fancy your chances against him."

Turning to the others, his gaze came to rest on Stanford. "I'm afraid Hunter will come for you first. You sold his friends down the river. Despite your boasting, you would be no match for him and so I've decided to do you a favour."

Shot in the head, for a moment Stanford stood upright, then, as if suddenly recognising he was dead he toppled sideways. Stunned by the swiftness of the attack, it took the cold calculated voice of Medusa to bring everyone back to the present.

"Before I take my leave, there are one or two others I'd like you to meet."

On cue, four supposedly dead men strode into the room. "By

embracing my vision," said Medusa, gesturing towards Jacques Rodin, Hans Gruber, Ivan Stannic and Ed Goldstein, "these gentlemen made it possible for Genesis to become a reality."

Jared was unable to believe his eyes. Of all the scenarios he had run through, this one had never occurred to him.

"Talk of their sad demise was greatly exaggerated," said Medusa chuckling. "Questions were being asked at the highest level and so it became necessary to stage-manage their deaths. Without such influential figures Genesis could never have been launched. Vast amounts of money can only achieve so much."

"But the remains, those pitiful few scraps of flesh left over after the cars were vaporised?" asked Jared.

"Ah, those would have been the bodyguards. It's why I insisted each of the dignitaries bring one. The amount of C4 attached to the vehicles meant none of them would ever have been identified. They served their purpose admirably, don't you think?"

The conversation over, Jared calculated the odds. Knowing Lucifer was anticipating his next move, he felt he had no alternative but to act. All he could hope for was that he would be able to inflict enough damage before the weapon cut him to pieces.

Suddenly, the door flew open.

THIRTY-FOUR

JARED GAZED IN amazement as Wolfe and Kathy blundered into the room. And Wolfe was armed. Summing up the situation in a fraction of a second, Jared shouted a warning, "Don't try it, David! That thing he's holding will cut you in half in the time it'll take you to finger your trigger."

A look of dismay crossed Wolfe's face. A smile creased Lucifer's. Holding the smile, Lucifer said, "Take your friend's advice. Put the gun on the floor. Carefully. That's it. Now, nudge it over with your foot."

Wolfe slid the weapon over as instructed. Bending, at the same time not taking his eyes off either of the men, Lucifer lifted the weapon. Flicking on the safety catch, he placed it in on a small table near the furthest wall. It was then Wolfe spotted the dead men.

"Good God," he said in astonishment. And then everything clicked into place. "Of course, that's why Charles Hillary had to be taken out, wasn't it? He refused to accept your vision of a brave new world."

"Things didn't exactly go to plan though, did they Medusa?" said Jared, taking up the story. "In one of life's little ironies, Hillary didn't die instantly. And from then on things became tricky. By removing the PM you thought the danger was over. You hadn't counted on David taking over. Not that it mattered in the long run. All you had to do was stall a day or two longer and the investigation would count for nothing."

"A masterful summation and you're correct. Anyway, let's return to matters in hand. From an early age you have been nothing but an arrogant bully, Johan. I had thought of allowing Mr Hunter to have his way with you, just to prove my theory that all bullies have soft centres. But in the last few days my backroom staff uncovered something very interesting. Instead, I will allow Michael Conrad and Miss Melrose, or should I say David Wolfe and Mrs Sullivan to decide your fate. Not that you would have recognised Michael in his previous life. Some five years ago, David had a fairly extensive face make over, since that time he's been active in politics."

Enjoying their astonishment, he turned to Jared. "I fear your new-found friends have been less than truthful with you. Anyway, time is short," he said, glancing at his watch, "and so I think I'll allow Lucifer to fill you in on the rest."

His chest heaving with exhaustion, Medusa activated the lock of the hidden laboratory and the panel slid open. "The lab is a replica of the original, the one in which Immada and I developed the Apocalypse Virus, or Genesis to give it its new title. A parting gift," he said pointing to a glass container, "a sample of Genesis."

Allowing himself one last lingering look, Medusa turned to Lucifer. "The helicopter will wait precisely five minutes."

And then he was gone.

As soon as Medusa and his entourage had disappeared, Lucifer headed for Jared. Producing a knife from the waist band of his combat fatigues, the razor-sharp blade made short work of Jared's bindings. Shedding the remains of the rope, Jared rubbed his wrists in an attempt to restore circulation to hands that had become numb. Moments later he was able to flex his fingers.

Anticipating Jared's next move, Lucifer smiling, shook his head.

His weapon trained on the centre of Jared's forehead, he gestured him towards the others. Satisfied he was no longer a threat he said, "Seeing as we're the only ones left, I believe introductions are in order. Prime minister, Kathy, meet the old man's children." Pointing, to Johan and Anna, he said, "A short while ago neither knew of each other's existence. Amusing, don't you think?"

Focusing on Anna, he continued.

"You enjoy inflicting pain and kill for fun. In the eyes of the world, that makes you one seriously disturbed bitch."

Laughing, he continued, "I've no quarrel with you, Anna, get out of here."

Needing no second invitation, she disappeared. About to follow, Steger was stopped in his tracks.

"Not so fast, Johan. I haven't introduced you properly. I'm sure both our distinguished guests, in particular Wolfe, will be delighted to find his long and expensive quest is finally over. For some considerable time now the man who entered this world as Michael Conrad has been searching for the person responsible for the death of his wife and twin baby daughters."

Steger's face drained of colour.

"PM, meet the director of Bio-Slim, Mr Johan Steger. Responsible for the deaths of thirty-eight innocent people, he also took care of his board of directors when they had the audacity to threaten him. Oddly, it was the only time he ever made his father proud."

Allowing his gaze to drift over the others, he said, "Johan is a coward, aren't you, Steger?" Afraid to make eye contact, Steger dropped his gaze.

Directing his attention to Kathy, he said, "By now, Mrs Sullivan, or should I refer to you by your maiden name of Melrose, you've worked out precisely where you fit into all of this."

Kathy's astonished look told him she had no clue what he was on about.

"Seems I'm mistaken. In that case, let me put you in the picture. This piece of shit over here," referring to Steger, "was your father's boss."

A light dawned in Kathy's eyes.

"Your father was a rare breed of scientist, one with a conscience. He warned Johan and his fellow directors about the dangers of pushing the drug onto the market without adequate testing. And they ignored him. When your father realised what was going on, he couldn't live with himself and so he committed suicide."

Jared held Jodie's hand tightly, his every movement covered by Lucifer's machine pistol. Pushing her behind his back for protection, he knew it was a futile gesture. He wondered whether he intended killing her once he was finished with him. One look at those cold dead eyes convinced him there would be no mercy.

And then Lucifer surprised him. Beckoning Jodie over, he said, "Be a shame for your daughter to see you torn to pieces, might leave a psychological scar. A dead body, that's different. she'll soon learn to get over that."

Needing no second invitation, Anna had stopped long enough to pack a few belongings before fleeing the complex. Mulling over her options, she headed for the forest. Her plan was to spend the night there. The following morning, when things had died down, she would retrace her steps.

Hidden in her secret laboratory no one would find her. Keeping one step ahead of the others would be no problem. As for food and water, her father had been right: there were more than enough provisions to ride out the storm. In no time she was scampering down the bank of the ravine. Thirty minutes later, making light of the steep slope and tangled undergrowth she skirted the top. The forest was fascinating in its diversity. Magnificent pine and conifers vied with each other for pride of place. Ferns and brambles lay everywhere, some of which grew to a staggering ten or twelve feet. It was then that she noticed the absence of noise. Instead of the ever present sounds of nature, there was an ominous silence. Something cold and hard danced along her spine and she felt the first prickling of unease.

Stepping inside the tree line, the moonlight disappeared, and in an instant everything was as black as tar.

THIRTY-FIVE

HERDING THE OTHERS into a side office, Lucifer led Jared into the centre of the room. He'd looked forward to this for days. The feeling of hurting and maiming a fellow human was exquisite. In this instance it would be even better as he knew he would be pitting his skills against someone equally adept.

Resolved to the fact that he could never outpace a bullet from a snub-nosed machine pistol, Jared blocked out negative thoughts.

Staring into his adversary's eyes, Lucifer smiled. Lowering his weapon, he discarded it. Jared couldn't believe his luck. The odds on his surviving were soaring. Before he could react, Lucifer flew across the room hands outstretched. For a man of his bulk, he was exceptionally agile. Against anyone less than Jared, the move might have been successful. Inches from Jared's throat, Lucifer was left clutching thin air. Believing Jared had got lucky, that no one was that quick, he tried the same manoeuvre. The result was the same.

With a growing sense of unease, Lucifer came to the understanding that he'd drastically misjudged his opponent. His next move was more cautious. Allowing him to get within an arm's length, Jared exploded into action. In a blur of motion, he turned on his left foot and kicked his opponent in the face with his right. Stunned, Lucifer stood his ground. Shaking his head, a shower of blood and spittle flew from his open mouth. Dragging air into his lungs in short sharp breaths, he attempted a grin. But it didn't sit right. Not allowing Lucifer a respite, Jared took the initiative. He threw two more kicks. The first landed on the side of Lucifer's head and was instantly followed up by another to the throat. Had it landed properly, it would have crushed his larynx. Fortunately for Lucifer, he turned his head slightly in anticipation of the blow. Before Jared could react, Lucifer managed to get his hands around his throat. Squeezing, Jared could hardly believe the man's strength. Unable to break free, he refused to panic. Instead, he slowed his breathing at the same time wracking his brains for a solution.

Under the pressure of Lucifer's brute strength, Jared felt a pounding in his ears and his vision begin to blur. He knew that his larynx, already on fire, was slowly being crushed. Soon he would pass out. All his instincts were screaming at him that he had moments to act. For a fraction of a second longer he kept perfectly still, then channelling all his power into his hands he slammed his open palms against Lucifer's ears. The concussive force of the trapped air exploded in Lucifer's cavities like a stick of dynamite. Despite the shock and pain Lucifer still hung on, but his grip on Jared's throat relaxed a fraction and it was enough. Butting him in the face, Jared connected solidly. The sound of breaking bone was followed instantly by the gushing of bright red blood and snot. Snarling like a wounded animal, Lucifer let go. Throwing his hands to his face, he tried desperately to clear his vision. It was the opening Jared had been hoping for. Resorting to a more time-honoured move than anything he had been taught in training, Jared stepped back before kicking Lucifer in the testicles. A look of pure surprise appeared on his face, before he dropped to his knees. His agony was short lived. Pirouetting on the balls of his feet, Jared delivered a vicious kick to the head. Staring at Jared, Lucifer's eyes slipped out of focus and a thin wheeze escaped his lips. Suddenly his head fell to one side. He was unconscious before he hit the floor. There was no time to gloat. Reaching the door he unlocked it. Rushing forward in relief, Kathy hugged him before bursting into tears. Astonishingly, Jodie was far more dignified. Making her way over to her father, she took his hand and squeezed. Taking advantage of the confusion, Steger bolted for the furthest door.

About to turn the handle, Wolfe dragged him backwards, before hitting him with a straight right to the jaw. Backing off, Wolfe allowed Steger an opportunity to get up. Pretending to be hurt, he stumbled. Instead of getting to his feet, he sprang forward from a half prone position. The move caught Wolfe unprepared. Hit in the midriff he landed on his back. Winded, he looked up. He was in time to see Steger aim a vicious kick at his head. Quick for a man of his age, Wolfe rolled sideways as Steger's foot landed on an empty floor.

By now Wolfe was back on his feet. Tired of the game he stepped in smartly. Two vicious jabs snaked out and Steger's head snapped back. A third was followed by an uppercut. Stunned, Steger slid to his knees. Retrieving his weapon Wolfe leaned over the defeated figure. Taking a handful of hair he placed the gun against Steger's temple. Looking over his shoulder, he shook his head. "I can't do it. I can't kill someone in cold blood."

"Even though he was responsible for killing your family?" asked Jared.

Seeing Wolfe's nod, he added, "Good. It might have given you a moment's pleasure, but you would have lived with the consequences for the rest of your life. After the first it gets easier; eventually it becomes second nature. And you don't want to go down that road, believe me."

Coming around slowly, Steger shook his head. Thread by thread, he managed to piece together what had happened. Suddenly, Wolfe's voice filtered through his muddled brain. "Join your sister, you're free to go."

Unable to move, Steger was rooted to the spot.

"Get out of here before I change my mind." Dropping his head in shame, Wolfe explained. "I made a solemn vow over the graves of my family that I would avenge their deaths. And I've failed them."

Jared's reply was devastatingly simple. "Letting him live took far more courage than killing him. You might not feel that way at the moment – in time you will. Wherever your family are they know that. Rather than being disappointed, they'll be proud of you."

Steger had all but disappeared, when a single shot rang out. Clutching his back, he slid to the floor. Two more shots followed in quick succession. Jared and Wolfe looked at each other in amazement. Turning in unison, they saw Kathy holding Lucifer's discarded gun. That she was familiar with weapons was obvious. Killing Steger triggered a range of emotions deep inside Kathy. She had imagined finding the person responsible for her father's suicide for so long. More importantly, she had always wondered how she would react should they ever come face to face. From day one she knew something had been wrong: her dad hadn't been the type to take his own life. And so in her mind she had envisaged herself as an avenging angel, as someone who would be eradicating something evil. The reality was far different. In moments her adrenaline-fuelled rage disappeared and the enormity of her actions flooded her brain. Instead of elation, she was filled with moral repugnance. Shaking uncontrollably, the gun dropped to the floor. A fraction of a second later, she followed it. Kneeling over the prone figure, Wolfe took her in his arms. Hugging her tightly, he whispered words of comfort in her ear. Instinctively Jared knew better than to interfere, instead he made his way over to his daughter who through it all had not said a word. Worried about the effect such violence might have had, he was amazed at her reaction. She seemed to have taken everything in her stride. Later they would have a serious talk; at the moment it was enough to know that she was safe.

A short while afterwards Kathy came around. Sobbing soundlessly, she seemed to have recovered some of her composure. It was Wolfe who grasped the futility of the situation. "By now the old man will be long gone."

Glancing at his watch, Jared saw barely ten minutes had elapsed since Medusa and his little circus troop had performed their disappearing act. Making a few mental calculations, he shook his head. Smiling, he explained to Wolfe the contingency plans that he had made.

When Wolfe had finished laughing, Jared said, "Life is full of little ironies, isn't it? The grim reaper was cheated the first time around. The empty coffins at the funerals, I mean. Yet in the end, they were only delaying the inevitable."

Screaming, Jodie put her head in her hands. Rushing to her side, Jared wondered whether the strain of the last few days had finally taken its toll. Clutching her tightly, the close contact triggered the emotions Jodie was feeling in his mind as well. Though the noises were in his head, they were nevertheless real. And so was the pain. The loudest screams seemed to be those of children. Those who had died in agony, in fear, in soul-searching despair.

Eventually there was one final high-pitched wail, that of a young girl in unimaginable suffering. Rising to a crescendo, it ended with a heart-rendering sigh. Then there was silence, an explosive silence, the like of which Jared had never experienced before. He waited until Jodie had stopped shaking. Recovered, she leaned towards her father. "It's all right, Dad, I'm not hurt or anything. It's over, that's all. Amy says to tell you we won't be having any more bad dreams."

Seeing Jared's nod, she said, "Now the old man is dead, she and the rest of the children can cross over."

Like a shimmering ball of light, a child's face appeared in Jared's mind. As he took time to absorb what was happening, something in her eyes seemed to reach out in gratitude, to be followed instantly by a little voice. It was the sweetest sound he had ever heard. One so quiet, that ever after Jared would wonder whether there had actually been a voice, or whether it had been a figment of his imagination.

Before she disappeared, she uttered two simple words, "Thank you", and then she was gone.

Making their way back into the main body of the office Jared stopped in his tracks. Lucifer's body was missing. But it was impossible. The blow had been powerful enough to render a normal person unconscious for hours. The man's strength was beyond comprehension. There was no point in worrying about it, however, either Lucifer had decided to flee the complex or had found somewhere to hole up. Knowing the facility as well as he did, finding somewhere to hide would be no problem. Eventually he would have to be flushed out, but for the moment there were more pressing things to attend to.

Jared looked at his watch: the luminous display showed that it was 5.00 a.m. He had been on the go for almost nine hours. Once glance at Wolfe and Jared knew what he was thinking.

Contact with leaders of other nations was a must. At the moment the world was blissfully unaware of the catastrophe hanging over their heads like the sword of Damocles. And then a live feed announcement would have to be made to the nation. But what difference would it make? The warning regarding the potency of the virus would come far too late. Especially for those who had received the inoculations. And that included him, he thought wryly.

THIRTY-SIX

MEDUSA KNEW HIS instincts had been right. Lucifer had wanted Hunter so badly he'd never had any intention of joining them. Regardless of his many faults, he was a man after his own heart. More than that, he had been loyal, which was more than could be said of his family.

Until now he hadn't realised how much he disliked Johan. Not because he was a weak-willed coward, but in his eyes he had been responsible for the death of his beloved wife. She was the only human being apart from Immada whom he had ever cared for. As for Anna, she was insane.

While such thoughts were filtering through his mind the explosion occurred. Jared had made sure there was enough explosive attached to the underside of the helicopter that no one would survive.

An eyewitness might have speculated that it was a curious phenomenon. It was raining, but only over a specific area of the forest. And, oddly, rather than water it was raining metal.

Though the explosion was a fair distance away, it sounded to Anna as if it were almost directly overhead. A mile or so distant a whole section of forest was alight. In a burst of understanding, she knew Hunter had been one step ahead from the beginning. Seeing his task as a suicide mission, he had been determined to take the old man with him. Instead of remorse, she felt a savage elation. The bastard had received his just reward.

At the scene of the carnage, the tangled remains of the helicopter lay everywhere. The body of the main fuselage hung from the stumps of several torn pines, while the intense heat had fused many of the larger parts together. Fifty yards either side of the wreckage, the earth had been scorched by the heat of the igniting fuel. Such was the intensity of the blaze, the glass of the cockpit and surrounding cabin had dissolved. One thing puzzled her: there was no sign of any bodies.

The harnesses of the pilot and her father had been ripped away, but of the bodies there was no sign. And it was the same for the passengers. It didn't make sense. What was left of the burnt and charred corpses should have been lying around somewhere. Unless they had been thrown clear in the blast. That made no sense either. So what had happened?

Switching on the torch, she scanned either side of the trail. But nothing stirred. Moments later she heard a noise. Turning quickly, she stumbled and the flashlight spilled from her hand. Striking the forest floor it bounced into the air. Spinning wildly it cast shadows on the walls of the undergrowth. Coming to rest against the bole of a gigantic conifer, the force of the impact shattered the lens into hundreds of tiny fragments. And then everything was plunged into darkness.

Without the torch, the trail was virtually pitch black. The ensuing silence was so deafening it poured like viscous fluid through the narrow tunnel. Terrified, stories from the village came back to haunt her. Recently, several tourists had disappeared around the facility and she began to wonder… Her nerves shot, she turned and ran.

Sometime later, stopping for breath, she heard the noise again. Afraid to turn around, she strained her ears to listen. The strange sound was unlike anything she had ever heard before. A hundred or so yards further on, moonlight streamed in through the end of the tunnel. She was going to make it. Then her luck ran out.

A vine hidden under the leafy coating of the animal path snagged her foot and she fell heavily. Winded, she tried to get to her feet. Instantly she fell back. Attempting to clear her scrambled thoughts she looked up. Standing in front of her was something that belonged to a different galaxy. Having the bone structure of a man, it was larger than any human she had ever come across. The texture of the torso was different too. Rather than skin it seemed to be covered in scales.

At first glance, the eyes looked cloudy. Clearing, they revealed black elongated pupils which stared at Anna with malicious intent. Its mouth sprang open. On display were a row of vicious-looking fangs. A second later the stench of its fetid breath reached her nostrils. Her first instinct was to run, until the truth dawned. There was no point in trying to escape. The thing would hunt her down mercilessly. Suddenly a flood of urine spread across the front of her joggers. Seconds from claiming its trophy, the creature stopped. Leaning over, it began sniffing the air. Immediately, a faint echo from the past registered in the beast's brain. At almost the same instant, Anna felt a faint stirring of recognition. A distant memory, one that had been nagging at her for minutes finally settled in her mind like a butterfly. The scales, the grotesque shape of the head, it all fitted. Unwittingly she had become part of one of her own failed experiments. Before passing out, the mystery of what had happened to Mark Hudson was finally solved.

Waking, the creature was standing over her. Somewhere deep underground, she was lying on her back amidst a thick layer of straw. Then she saw the skeletons. What remained were bones, everything else had been picked clean. Naked, she was cold. Willing herself to keep calm, she attempted to communicate with the creature.

"Mark, Mark Hudson? It's Anna, Anna Heche. Remember me?"

Something about Anna's voice triggered a response deep inside. Ripping the few tattered remnants of clothing from its body, Anna gasped at the size of its manhood. With a sickening certainty she knew what the creature intended.

Scuttling backwards on hands and knees, she came to rest against the side of the cave wall. Closing her eyes in despair, she was trapped. Unable to go any further she mouthed a prayer. She prayed to a God she had never before acknowledged.

The rape was short and brutal. Satiated, it gazed at her. Thinking it would now kill her, she was astonished when it handed over her clothing. Dressing quickly, she stood up and made her way towards the cave entrance. A few yards from freedom, she was lifted off her feet by her ankles and dragged back into the belly of the cave. Huddled in the corner, her mind was in turmoil.

What was it the creature wanted? Was she to be its plaything? Perhaps that was what it intended. It would kill others for food and use her for sex.

THIRTY-SEVEN

Wednesday, 19 December 2012
9.00 a.m.

DANNY HAD FINALLY managed to piece things together. One of his most valuable assets had always been his ability to focus on the tinniest details, while at the same time not lose sight of the bigger picture. During the last few hours he had started to see a disturbing pattern, one so cleverly camouflaged that unless you knew what you were looking for it was impossible to spot. But there had been a problem with his thinking. It was the reason it had taken him so long to figure things out.

Now he had it. "Where the hell's Gareth?" he shouted, "he was here a moment ago."

A head popped around the corner. "What's the problem? Can't a bloke go for a piss without asking permission?"

Danny's expression told Tina one thing. "You've worked things out, haven't you?"

Holding up a hand for silence, he said, "Be right with you. First I have to make a call."

Punching in Wolfe's private number, he let it ring for almost a minute, but there was no reply. He tried his mobile but received a 'no signal available' message. Shoulders slumped, he hung up. Flicking the mobile closed, he stuffed it in his pocket. "Not one to make lengthy speeches, I haven't a choice. Even if Jared's successful, it's already too late."

Seeing the bemused faces he outlined his explanation. "It all started in August, with the death of three people on an isolated Maldivian island. Forensics eventually managed to identify the bodies. They were mercenaries in the employ of Medusa Industries. Of course, when Medusa Industries was brought into the equation, it set off warning bells in Whitehall. Immediately afterwards, Stanford was asked to delve into things with a fine tooth comb."

"And?" asked Gareth.

"First, a few other points of interest, at roughly the same time as the incident in the Maldives, two maintenance workers doing some routine checking on a remote section of the London underground disappeared."

"How do you mean 'disappeared'?" asked Tina.

"Just that," said Danny, "the bodies were never recovered. If that wasn't enough, shortly afterwards we had the slaughter in London. Finally, but not in the correct order, we had that TV programme on bird flu. Caught the imagination of the public due to its dramatic finale. Anyone see a common link?"

"Medusa Industries," said Tina, pulling a frown. "One piece doesn't add up."

"The one with the missing workers, you mean? Threw me too until a few minutes ago, then the penny dropped."

"What about the death of that character Jonathan? David Wolfe's private secretary," said Gareth. "Wasn't for him, the complex wouldn't have come to our attention."

"Overlooked that," said Danny. "Anyway, we've a common denominator: Medusa Industries. Moments ago, I was looking at a series of disturbing but unrelated events. Then something clicked. No definitive proof, only a gut feeling. See what you think. The TV programme – from the first things didn't sit right. Until recently, the killings in the Maldives had me baffled too. In the employ of Medusa, there had to be some reason why the bodies had been cremated. It wasn't to erase their identities – too obvious. Then it came to me. Medusa's been developing some kind of biological weapon. Once I accepted that, everything else fell into place. At first my mind refused to accept what my subconscious was telling me. When it did, the incident in the Maldives made perfect sense. It was a controlled experiment on human test subjects. Medusa wanted to find out how quickly his brain child killed. Once he had the confirmation, the bodies had to be burned. The disease, virus – call it what you will – was so deadly every trace of its existence had to be eradicated."

"Say your theory's correct," said Gareth. "What's the connection between that and the missing workers in the underground?"

"Medusa needed a bolt-hole. After unleashing the virus, he would need somewhere to sit tight."

"That's why they were killed," said Tina, beginning to get the picture. "They stumbled across his bolt-hole. Sounds plausible, the underground is riddled with shelters left over after the war."

"You're on the right track," said Danny. "But, the kind of place I'm talking about would be far more sophisticated. The government has developed safe havens for themselves over the years. State-of-the-art hideaways I mean, ones adapted to sit out a nuclear or biological attack."

"It all fits," said Tina. "You mentioned there was something about the TV programme you weren't happy with, care to explain?"

"Everything about the set up was wrong. Before the terrorists killed themselves they made no claim on whose behalf they were committing the massacre. Terrorists never do that. There's always some misguided faction claiming responsibility for some cause or another. When no claim was made, I knew something was fishy. Nothing made sense. Take the gunmen, rank amateurs they had no real clue as to how to handle their weapons. And yet the machine pistols they used were highly sophisticated. Every terrorist I've ever come across may well have been crazy, but they had one thing in common, they were consummate professionals. The gunmen left the camera crew unscathed. Why? They were ordered to. Whoever paid for the programme wanted everything on tape. The look on that doctor's face before he was shot told me one thing: his death wasn't in the script. In hindsight, everything makes perfect sense. Everyone who took a leading role in the programme had to die. Medusa wanted no one left behind who could explain the real purpose for the programme."

"If Medusa's behind all this, why spend billions on inoculating the world against a pandemic of bird flu?" said Tina.

"Look at it from a different angle," answered Danny. "What if Medusa paid the doctor to scare the hell out of the nation?"

"Still doesn't add up," said Tina in frustration. "If he was doing it in order to boost sales, I'd buy that. But he's giving the bloody drug away. Where's the logic behind that?"

"What if the old man had a hidden agenda? What if he'd deliberately developed a virus with which he intended to wipe out most of the population of the world?"

"Jesus Christ," said Gareth, "what would be the point of that?"

"Convinced he's doing what's best for mankind, he would see it as a righteous quest. Probably thinks he's chosen by God or something. It was you who suggested he and Immada were working on a weapon that would the turn the tide of the war. What if they'd succeeded?"

"In that case they'd have used the bloody thing, wouldn't they?" said Gareth.

"Not necessarily. What if they were unable to find an antidote? In that case there would have been no point in unleashing something on the world that had the capability of wiping out the whole of mankind? Killing friend and enemy alike would have been counterproductive."

"Surely we're looking at the same scenario here, though," said Tina.

"You're missing the point, Tina, love, it doesn't matter now. Wiping out mankind is his intention. The underground facility he's built in London isn't the only one – I'd bet my pension on it. If I'm right the crazy bastard's developed several in different countries across the world. Seeing himself as the modern Noah, he intends ridding the world of the problems mankind has brought on itself. And then he'll start over again. Fresh start, new beginning, the philosophy is biblical."

"Hence the name Genesis," said Gareth.

"Forget his twisted agenda for the moment and accept he has the product. Now put yourself in his shoes. How would you release the virus to maximise its potential. It's not easy. Contaminate the water supplies of every major city in the world and people will still survive. Many of us drink only bottled water. It would be the same scenario with food. As individuals we have different tastes, meaning we wouldn't all eat the same thing. Don't get me wrong, millions would die, but in terms of global population it would be a drop in the ocean."

"My God," exclaimed Tina, the truth dawning. "It's the vaccination programme. By now over half the world will be infected."

"And it's too late to do anything about it," said Danny. "That call to the PM earlier was to try and get the remainder of the programme halted. Worryingly, I was speaking to a dead line."

The shocking silence was broken by Danny's mobile. Above the crackle of static a voice burst into life, "Danny, you there?"

"Made it then," answered Danny, unable to hide his relief. "And Jodie? She safe?" he enquired.

"Safe and unharmed, it's not all good news, though," said Jared.

"Nor this end," came the reply. With that he brought Jared up to speed. Alerted by the lack of response, he said, "Something tells me it hasn't come as a surprise."

"True, unlike you I didn't work it out, though. The old man explained everything before he disappeared."

"They got away, then."

"Not exactly, the amount of C4 attached to the underside of the helicopter was enough to send the bastards to the pearly gates sooner than they expected."

Sensing there was something more, he said, "You're not telling me everything?"

"Always were a perceptive bugger," said Jared, before explaining his little problem.

"The residents of Raven's Hill," said Danny in a whisper, "everyone received the jab this morning, including Jodie's grandparents."

"Anyone you'd like to bring to the facility?" asked Jared.

"I'm a loner, no family ties. Gareth and Tina are in the same boat. One of the prerequisites of the job. Ironically, the reasoning behind the screening was in case of a scenario such as this." After a brief pause he blurted out, "The whole of Sanctuary was vaccinated this morning, including Daniel."

"And Samantha?" asked Jared breathlessly.

"She refused it. Don't ask me why. All I know is that she's inoculation free."

"Then the sooner you get your arses up here the better. At least you'll survive."

"By the way," added Danny, "your grandmother and Eric are here. After what they went through though you might like them near you. And, before you ask, they haven't been infected. What with the questioning and… well, what I'm trying to say is there wasn't time. As luck happened it turned out for the best."

For a moment the line went silent. Finally gaining his composure, Danny said, "So that bloody madman was right. When the dust settles, everyone will be so intent on rebuilding what's left of a decimated world, hatred will become a thing of the past."

"Call me naive, if you like," interrupted Jared, "I think that's far too simple a way of looking at things."

"Then all this will have been for nothing," said Danny, knowing in his heart Jared's reasoning was sound.

THIRTY-EIGHT

Wednesday, 19 December 2012
2.00 p.m.

THE WEIGHT OF the world was on Danny's shoulders. Knocking on the door of the manse, Samantha opened it. Her eyes puffy and swollen, it was obvious that she had been crying. For a second he wondered how she knew. Then it clicked, she had been waiting for the news that Jared was dead.

"Jared's alive," explained Danny.

Throwing herself into his arms, she broke down. "I thought I'd never see him again. And Jodie?" asked Samantha.

"She's fine."

Embarrassed, she stepped away. "There's something else, isn't there?"

Uncomfortable, Danny was unable to make eye contact. Finally, he managed, "It's your father, love."

"My father's fine," she said, perplexed.

"Mind if I come inside?"

"Of course," she replied, her face a mask of confusion.

"Dad, it's Danny," she shouted. "And he has some bad news. No, not Jared, he's all right. And so are Jodie and the others."

"Morning, Danny. Cup of coffee?" asked the vicar.

"No, thank you, Daniel. Think it's best you and Samantha sit down."

On being told the news, neither could believe what they had just heard. For long moments Daniel was unable to move. Frozen by the implications, his brain refused to function. He blurted out, "Dear God. You're not kidding, are you? Surely the PM can go live, explain the situation?"

"He already has, half an hour ago. The announcement was

made from the complex: possessing live-feed capabilities it made the perfect choice. He's been in touch with leaders from other nations and they coordinated the announcements so that it went out globally at 1.00 p.m. BST. Whether or not people will believe the broadcast is another thing. The truth won't sink in until the first of those infected start showing symptoms of the virus, the bleeding from the nose, the boils, that kind of thing," said Danny. "And there's the other problem to consider, when people realise how serious the situation is, all hell will break loose. Soon afterwards the law of the jungle will prevail. Even though I'm privy to the inside story, I still find it difficult to get my head around the enormity of what's happening."

"The children," Daniel stammered, "what about them?"

Danny shook his head in resignation.

"Then we'd better prepare everyone." Jumping to his feet, he said, "What about Samantha, you know she didn't have the inoculation?"

"Taken care of, there are eleven of us, should Jared survive, that is."

Explaining the situation, her resolve crumbled and she broke down. Wiping her tears with his finger, Daniel took her into his arms. "Jared will be alright, love, believe me, but I'm afraid my life is over."

Throwing herself at her father, she hugged him tightly. "Then I want to die with you."

Lifting her head, he looked into her eyes, "If the world's population is to be decimated, the Lord will need every able bodied person to begin again. Your duty is to live, mine is to die, and with a little dignity. Allow your father that at least."

"May I ask a favour?" he said turning to Danny.

"Anything," was the reply.

"Arrange for a vehicle to trawl the streets of the village with a loud hailer. Explain to them there's an emergency meeting to take place at the church." Glancing at his watch, he said, "In, say, an hour?"

THIRTY-NINE

Wednesday, 19 December 2012
Palace of Westminster, Paul Hudson's office
3.00 p.m.

After what seemed like hours, Wolfe eventually managed to get hold of Paul. Annoyed at first, he had come around when it had been explained to him that his mobile phone had been stolen. He had missed the broadcast and, as a result, Wolfe was faced with one of the most heart-wrenching problems he had ever encountered: how on earth to explain the situation to Paul. Small talk out of the way, he mustered the courage to ask the question he'd been dreading. "And the inoculation, have you received it yet?"

"Yesterday afternoon," answered Paul. "Along with everyone else in the Palace of Westminster, those deemed essential personnel, that is. Shame you and Kathy missed it. Better not leave it too late, if the bug's as bad as the experts are predicting, God knows how many people will be affected."

The prolonged silence warned Paul something was wrong. "What's the problem?"

On hearing Wolfe's words, the response was instantaneous. "Jesus Christ, you're kidding, aren't you?"

The silence that greeted the remark was answer enough. Recovering his composure, Paul said, "Can't anything be done?"

"Nothing, from what I gather the virus is unstoppable."

"How long do I have?" asked Paul.

"Forty-eight hours tops. But it's not set in stone. Some might be showing evidence of the disease already."

"And the symptoms?" asked Paul.

"Bleeding from the nose and ears, followed immediately by boils and sores," explained Wolfe. "Once they appear there's no hope."

"What about those who weren't inoculated, what chance do they have?"

"If they find a safe haven in time, they'll have a squeak. Even then there are two essentials: they must have had no contact with anyone on the outside and remain indoors for something like three or four months."

"'Least you and Kathy are safe. How many are you, in the complex, I mean?"

"Eleven in all, but Jared's infected, so he'll have to be quarantined and quickly. Need anything?" asked Wolfe.

"No," was the sobering reply. "Along with most of the world I'm a ticking time bomb." With that the line went dead.

Laurence Rix stood on the first tee of his local golf club, his head pounding from last night's alcohol. A Christmas do, the pain killers he had taken earlier had been a waste of time. When his hangovers were this bad, fresh air was the only remedy. For some strange reason he felt far worse than normal and it was odd, he hadn't drunk that much. The inoculation hadn't helped. Scratching his arm he noticed the site was inflamed.

Removing the cover from his new driver, he studied it. Technically, it wasn't new, but the thing was in mint condition. And he had picked it up for a song. It felt good, yet wasn't that exactly what he had said about every other driver he'd bought? And those had numbered in their dozens.

But this was the one. This was the perfect club. The one he had been searching for all his life. His mates had warned him years ago that he was wasting his money. He was looking for a club that didn't exist. Why not spend a few quid on lessons instead, they had suggested. It was sound advice, but he had ignored it. He was convinced that somewhere out there was the holy grail of drivers.

Gripping it lightly, he took a few practice swings. One more and he was ready. Then he let rip. It was a crisp shot and for the first fifty yards it went as straight as an arrow, until suddenly, like all the others he had ever tried it began to develop a mind of its own. In despair, he watched as the ball sailed majestically out of bounds. Ah well, he thought, replacing the head cover, back to the drawing board.

By the time he'd reached the ninth hole he had reverted to his trusty three wood and things improved. Due mainly to some inspired chipping and putting, he was only two over his handicap at the start of the outward half. The day was getting better.

Standing on the tenth it happened. Without warning he bent over and vomited. His partners looked in astonishment at the pool of stinking black blood which lay at their feet. In moments blisters formed on his face. Seconds later huge boils began to break out. Before their very eyes they burst leaving a trail of thick yellow pus trickling down his face. In stunned fascination, the others watched as the same black blood began to pour from his nose and ears.

"Jesus Christ," shouted Cameron Davies in terror. "I'm out of here."

Turning on his heels, he disappeared through the trees heading for the safety of the clubhouse. The others followed in hot pursuit. By then, the unfortunate Laurence Rix had dropped to his knees in agony, his trousers soiled with blood, blood which was pouring from every single orifice. Ten minutes later he was dead. Within the hour, all three friends were dead too, along with the majority of the others on the course. For the survivors, it would turn out to be a case of merely delaying the inevitable.

The trolley was full. Stacked at crazy angles, several boxes threatened to drop to the floor amidst a jumble of choice goodies. Thank God this would be last trip before the festive season. But for the need for some last-minute stocking fillers, he wouldn't have volunteered to help. The bulk of the shopping had been done last week. His wife was like that, a fussy woman she left nothing to chance. Strangely, the supermarket was less busy than normal.

Arnold hated shopping. A shy, retiring man, he had come to accept that supermarkets had the effect of turning ordinary people into aggressive morons. Thankfully, he was almost done. A visit to the wine section for the latest three for ten-pound offer and that was it.

This morning he had woken up feeling awful, and his wife Betty had said the same. Almost like a giant hangover, she'd commented. And then he remembered the inoculations. He'd heard somewhere about flu vaccines, that you were supposed to be given a mild dose, to allow your body's immune system to develop. The first time he had received the jab was about two years ago, the week after his sixty-fifth birthday. He had asked the doctor about it. Apparently it was a myth. And the doctor had been right, he had felt fine. So why were he and Betty feeling like this? Perhaps the stuff they had been given acted differently to the ordinary flu jabs.

Lifting a bottle from one of the top shelves, a loud crash heralded the fact that someone had been clumsy. Glad it wasn't him, he turned to offer his help. An elderly woman was kneeling on the floor, red wine and broken glass surrounding her like a halo. Moving to her aid, he noticed something odd. The labels on the smashed bottles said white. Yet, the ever widening pool was red. Taking a step further, he stopped in his tracks. His first impression had been wrong. The pool of spreading liquid wasn't red, it was black. And it smelt foul. Trawling his memory to come up with a match, he was convinced it was nothing he had ever experienced before. Lifting the old lady to her feet gently, she raised her head. Blood was seeping from sightless eyes, while her nose and ears were dribbling. Arnold felt an urge to pinch himself. Was he in the middle of some nightmare? By now, several yellow boils had appeared on her face. As he watched, one or two burst open. But it couldn't be, he thought. Things like this only happened in horror films.

He was brought out of his stasis by the sound of more breaking glass as several other people collapsed amidst pools of stinking black blood. To hell with this, he told himself, he was out of here. Shouting for his wife, she came running. Dumping the trolley, they headed for the end of the aisle. They were greeted by a scene of utter chaos. Bodies lay everywhere. The only way to get to the door was to step over corpses.

They had almost reached the safety of the outside when Betty collapsed with a loud groan. Dear God, what the hell was happening? It was then that he noticed the car park. There were bodies lying everywhere. And, frighteningly, the number seemed to be growing by the minute. Spread out as if crucified, several people were lying on the tarmac floor. Others were draped over bonnets of cars. Many more were hanging out of doors. To add to the confusion, several had collapsed onto the steering wheels of their vehicles, activating the horns. The whole scene was a mixture of carnage and bedlam. The question was: what the hell should he do about it?

His mind in total confusion, he hadn't long to ponder the situation. Seconds later, he opened his mouth and vomited. Shortly afterwards, he joined his unconscious wife, who by this time had become just another meaningless statistic.

FORTY

IN THE HEART of the complex, the enormity of the situation was beginning to hit home. The little band of survivors numbered eleven: Jared and Jodie, Edna, Jared's grandmother, and old Eric, the vicar of Raven's Hill, Kinsey the helicopter pilot, Samantha and Wolfe, Kathy, Danny, Tina and Gareth. Prioritising, the survivors decided to concentrate on practical matters. Disposal of the bodies littered throughout the facility was deemed priority one, including the animals stored in cages. And hanging over everything was the spectre of Lucifer. Jared doubted whether he would stay in the complex: the odds were too heavily stacked against him. Yet, there was always the off chance. Sometime in the near future he would have to organise a detailed search, until then most of them would have to carry weapons at all times.

Removal of the bodies turned out to be a problem, within minutes there was a heated debate. One idea was to store them in the massive fridge-freezers dotted around the facility. The logistics of such an idea eventually proved insurmountable. Human nature being what it is, one thing led to another and everyone started talking at once. When it seemed every angle had been exhausted, Jared put forward his suggestion. At first, the solution seemed callous, unfeeling. Once the storm had died down, Jared explained that it was a waste of time worrying about people that were already dead.

"Like it or not," he said, "that's the scenario here. Nothing can be done for them, they're gone. The converse applies though."

With no viable alternatives available, the protests gradually died away. Wolfe, arms folded, broke the awkward silence.

“Okay,” he said quietly, “You’ve convinced me.”

“And the animals?” asked Samantha.

“Same applies.”

Placing the bodies into the huge incinerator was a time-consuming task. Disposing of Stanford’s corpse, Jared wondered why such a legend had decided to turn his back on his country, to become a willing party to such wanton slaughter. Had Stanford been able to, he would have told Jared why. There had been a time when money hadn’t bothered him. But, the older he had grown, the more he came face to face with his own mortality. And so when Medusa had made his offer he hadn’t thought twice.

While the others were taking care of the bodies, Jared’s grandmother, along with Jodie and Eric, spent time sorting through the provisions. A cursory glance at the kitchens had shown Medusa to be correct. There was enough food to feed a small army.

Kinsey had volunteered to locate the weapons. Kathy and Samantha’s role was to find a cure for the virus. Duties organised, it was Kathy who took charge. “Medusa offered the use of his lab. I suggest we take advantage of his kind offer,” she said, sarcastically. “And I’m not giving up on you, Jared. First thing is to get you quarantined. The rest of you know what to do.”

Wolfe had a sudden idea. Taking his cue from Kathy, he got to his feet. “Before we go our separate ways, how about taking a peek at his com room?”

The overhead video display of the workstation showed maps, enhanced satellite photos, flow charts, bar graphs and much, much more. Settling into the leather armchair, Gareth tapped the keyboard and the wall mounted monitor came to life. Seconds later the impressive logo of Medusa Industries appeared.

Instantly, it was replaced by an overview of the complex, one which included all four levels. Gareth had the ability to make computers tell him anything. Flexing his fingers, he said, "Your wish is my command."

"Might be worth a quick tour of the place," said Danny.

The layout included two dining rooms, one of which they had recently vacated. Besides the laboratories, of which there were scores, the facility boasted two libraries and a huge gymnasium. And there were countless dormitories.

"Interesting," said Gareth pointing the cursor, "An arsenal. That'll make your task easier," he said to Kinsey.

Standing directly behind, Danny was in awe of the kind of money it must have taken to build such a facility.

"Seen enough? In that case, let's find out what other goodies this little beauty has in store."

Manipulating the cursor, he touched another logo. In a flash, a completely different schematic came to life. Heads spinning, they stared wide eyed as the monitor now depicted the earth in a three-dimensional form. Five red dots began to flicker. Danny was puzzled, until it struck him. What he was looking at were the positions of the arks. The significance of what they were seeing prompted a comment from Wolfe, "At least there are others survivors."

Leaning over Gareth's shoulder Kinsey said, "The London ark is housed at the site of the old Down Street underground station. But it makes sense," seeing the blank expressions, he explained. "Two major types of tunnels can be found on the London underground, deep level tube lines and cut and cover."

"How come you know so much about such things?" said Gareth interrupting. "Piloting a chopper and train spotting isn't my idea of a match made in heaven."

"I was crazy on the underground when I was a kid, read

just about everything I could get my hands on, and I've kept abreast of things ever since. In the nineteenth century digging deep level tunnels, especially under water, was both tricky and bloody dangerous. Several attempts to cross the Thames ended in disaster. Brunel's Thames tunnel was the first successful one. Still used today by the East London line. Anyway, Down Street was closed after the refurbishment of Dover Street. Renamed Green Park afterwards, because the new entrance no longer opened onto Dover Street."

"Name sounds familiar," said Wolfe.

"I'm not surprised," said Kinsey. "During the war Churchill used it as a cabinet room and safe haven. Good deal of the wartime equipment's been removed, though bits and pieces of the communication centre as well as the bathroom facilities remain. Popular as a tourist attraction, the majority of the place is in complete darkness. Not for the faint hearted believe me. During the last year or so the place has been declared off limits. Massive refurbishment from what I gather. And now we know why. Medusa's chosen well, it's ideal for what he had in mind. Anyone taken a ride between Hyde Park corner and Green Park?" he asked. Seeing a few nods he added, "Probably wouldn't have noticed, but the walls change from cast iron tubing to bricks. The brighter colour of the brick indicates the walled up area of the platform. That's what we'll be looking for."

"How do we get there?" asked Tina. "When the time comes, I mean."

"We make our way through Green Park, and head for Down Street tube station." Chuckling, he said, "Unless you know where to look, you'll never find it. Front is very distinctive though."

"Distinctive in what way?" said Danny.

"You'll see. Ground floor is occupied by a small newsagent's, to the left is the entrance. Through there and the fun starts."

Kinsey's story complete, Wolfe changed tack.

"How do you think the arks will react to having no natural hierarchy? They'll be expecting someone to take charge remember."

"Now Jared has taken care of the main players," said Danny following his reasoning.

"These people are innocent," continued Wolfe. "Their only crime was in volunteering for some kind of survival exercise."

"Thanks to the warning by world leaders via television they'll already be aware of the gravity of the situation facing them on the outside, but they've no idea as to why they were chosen to populate the arks. In particular what Medusa had in store for them, I mean," Tina said.

"Think we should get in touch with them, explain the situation?"

The suggestion brought a unanimous response. During the next few hours, each ark was contacted individually by Gareth and brought up to speed regarding how they had been duped. Not surprisingly, every one reacted in the same way. First with incredulity, and then when they'd had time to digest the enormity of the picture, with hostility. Hostility at how they had been set up. The language barrier proved something of a stumbling block initially but, eventually, a solution was found. In the case of the Russian ark, it was discovered that one of the group spoke fairly fluent English. Tina and Gareth, being able to speak French and German respectively, took care of the other problem. Over the coming months, contact with the arks would prove to be their only link to the outside world.

During supper, Tina voiced the obvious. "Might there be others left alive? Genuine survivors, I mean."

"Unless like us, they had some kind of prior warning, or they simply got lucky, there will be very few," said Kathy. "Only way to avoid the virus will be to live at a high altitude; permanently. On the other hand, a mountaineering expedition isolated at the time of the outbreak might have a chance. Even so, no contact with society for long periods afterwards will be essential. If anyone, and I mean anyone, becomes infected, within days everyone will die."

Kathy's theory about how swiftly the virus would strike turned out to be only partially correct. Rushed into production, much of the serum had become contaminated. The impurities meant some would be affected more quickly than others. In some cases the virus would take hold within hours. Overall, however, the scenario she painted turned out to be eerily prophetic.

Led by Dr Lee Xiang, a group of Chinese speleologists were on a fact-finding mission to authenticate the world's deepest underground shaft. Discovered in a mountainous area known as Tian Xing, it was connected by two cave systems: Qikeng and Dong Ba. Their combined depth measured an incredible 1,026 metres. To explore the matter further, the government had belatedly funded Lee's present expedition. Enthusiastic, he was sure that the team's work would generate enough new information to produce a host of articles for magazines and newspapers. Perhaps even a TV interview, he concluded. Whatever the outcome, the publicity would only add kudos to the institution.

An old hand, he knew full well that such was the unpredictability of caving you never knew what was waiting around the next corner. True to form, things weren't going to plan. Until a few minutes ago communication with the BBC in Britain, on whose behalf they were filming a documentary for the Discovery Channel, had been fine. Then, mysteriously, everything had gone blank. The fault was obviously of a non-mechanical nature, as the equipment had been tested several times.

It was infuriating, Jed Hawkins, their link to the outside world, was there one minute and gone the next. Undeterred, they had left one member of the team behind to monitor the equipment. The others had pushed forward. That had been five days ago. Since then they had amassed an amazing amount of footage on the hand-held recorder. At a depth of 850 metres, the team had come across what in their minds were some incredible firsts. As demanded by protocol, each new specimen had been carefully catalogued and stored. During that time, Lee had cast his mind back to his first expedition. A rookie, he had approached the experience with trepidation. Studying the maze of underground chutes and crawl spaces he had almost bottled it. Some of the narrow openings he'd been forced to negotiate had terrified him. However, he knew such fear was normal. Several of his colleagues had openly admitted their greatest worry was being trapped inside a tiny tunnel. With neither the room to go forward or back, it was a case of being buried in a million-ton coffin. He was assured that all good cavers applied a simple but effective method of conquering their fear. The trick, they had explained, was to focus on what lay ahead rather than dwelling on the dangers. To allow your mind to go off on a tangent was to invite disaster. And they had been right.

On the sixth day, with provisions running short they decided to head back. Returning to the surface, they found that communication with the BBC in London was still a no go. It was a further week before they found signs of life or, as it turned out, the absence of life. A small village of some 150-odd people had been turned into a morgue. According to the doctor who accompanied the mission, every single one of the villagers had died of some kind of infectious disease, the origin of which was way beyond his expertise.

The further towards civilisation they got, the more the bodies piled up. Being away for so long, none of the expedition's members had been given the vaccine. Not that it would have mattered. As the virus was airborne, they had already become infected. Within the next few hours, the first of the party showed signs of contracting the disease. A day later every single person was dead. Before the last one passed away, the realisation of why there had been such an abrupt end to communications from the outside world became apparent. There was no outside world.

FORTY-ONE

AT ROUGHLY THE same time as the first symptoms of the plague was making its appearance among the party of cavers deep in the heart of China, a group of climbers led by an American with the endearing name of Chuck Carlson was attempting an ascent on K2.

At 28,253 feet or, 8,612 metres, K2 is situated on the borders of Pakistan and China. Given many names through the centuries, locals call it Chogri, which in the Balti language means, 'king of mountains'. The name K2 was given to it by the British surveyor T.G. Montgomerie. The 'K' designated the Karakorum Range, while the '2' was added for the simple reason that it was the second peak listed. Pyramidal in shape, it is considered unanimously by mountaineers to be by far the hardest of the fourteen summits over 8,000 metres to climb.

Stepping out of the tent, Chuck was almost blown off his feet. Deciding he was going nowhere for the moment, he retreated inside and ruminated. Perhaps he had got things wrong after all. Maybe his target of reaching the summit on Christmas Day was a bad move. It had sounded a novel idea at the time. Stuck inside his tiny tent listening to the wind howling like a banshee, he was beginning to have second thoughts.

Knowing it was the unpredictability of the weather that made K2 so deadly, most ascents were made during the months between June and August. At that time its mood swings were a little more predictable. Even then conditions could turn in the blink of an eye. In hindsight, attempting it in December was considered tantamount to cutting your throat with a blunt razor.

The list of those who had failed was long. For Chuck, two stood out. The first was in 1986, when thirteen climbers were snuffed out in a storm which swept in from nowhere. The other was in August 2008. In this instance, eleven climbers from South Korea, Pakistan, Ireland, Norway, Serbia and the Netherlands had died on the upper slopes after an avalanche caused by falling ice. One of the more sobering statistics was its fatality rate. Presently it stood at 27 per cent, meaning Chuck and his party had a one in four chance of survival. Amazingly, the same statistics indicated that you were three times more likely to die attempting to climb K2 than the mighty Everest. One of K2's odd features is that it is rocky up to 6,000 metres, after that it becomes an ocean of snow for the final 2,000 metres.

Snuggling into his thermal sleeping bag, Chuck pondered the irony that for the first few days the 'savage mountain' had been deceptively benign. It hadn't lasted. He awoke the following morning to find that conditions had improved. Not wanting to push the others, who he knew were exhausted, he suggested that they set off down to base camp. Brokering no argument, he made it perfectly clear that he was going on.

By now the others had come to realise that such was Chuck's determination, he would either make the summit or die in the attempt. Breaking camp, Chuck said goodbye to his companions before he and his friend Santos made their way upwards. Knowing that traditionally American parties fared worse than other nationalities in conquering the peak only fuelled his determination. An adrenaline junkie, it was times like this he lived for. It was at camp 8 at around 7,772 metres that the old mountain finally showed her teeth. The blizzard lasted several days. When it was over, despite being in fairly bad shape, they pushed forward and made it to the top. Resting a short while only, they took advantage of a window in the weather and made their descent. Apart from one particular hairy moment at the bottleneck, a steep funnel some 1,300 feet from the peak they made their way down slowly. Days later they reached base camp.

Expecting to be greeted by their colleagues, they were a little put out when no one seemed to be around. Opening the first tent, Chuck stepped back in horror. Kyoto was dead, and had been for some time by the look of her. What was most worrying was how she had died. Her face was black, while all around lay pools of dried blood. The inside of the tent was covered with it. He searched every tent and with the same result. Every single one of his party was dead. What the hell was going on?

Despite being dog tired, the two decided to get the hell out of there as quickly as they could. Like the speleologists before them, none of the climbers had been given the vaccine. Once again, however, it wouldn't have made the slightest difference if they had. Long before they reached civilisation, both Chuck and Santos were dead.

The virus was remorseless. Cutting a swathe through civilisation, it was ruthlessly hunting down everything in its path.

In a quiet moment of self-contemplation, Wolfe knew that there would be no seventh cavalry riding over the hill at the eleventh hour. Medusa had planned everything meticulously. The armed forces, police and every other essential service would have been given the vaccine first, little realising that priority one in this case meant that they had merely been given the privilege of dying first.

His schematic for disaster would have been adhered to worldwide. Such was the rate of infection, virtually no one would survive. In the light of what he had just heard, the fragile belief that there might be a way out for the world had been shown to be a worthless sham. It was then he was reminded of the old saying, 'Abandon hope, all ye who enter here.'

After supper, Kathy and Samantha made their way back to the lab. To date, they had accomplished very little. Most of the time had been spent familiarising themselves with the mass of equipment on display. Medusa's fortune ensured that what was available was the cutting edge of technology. Most of the deadly cultures were kept in containers that looked remarkably like thermos flasks. The insides, containing liquid nitrogen served as coolants. The virus, however, was stored in a clear glass container. Sitting smugly on its podium, it radiated pure evil.

There was something hypnotic about it. And Jared had been right, thought Kathy, it did look remarkably like a lime green slush puppy. Slipping into professional mode, she suited up. Despite the fact that she was unused to dealing with such deadly cultures, Samantha's basic training had instilled in her a healthy respect for what she was looking at. And Kathy's warning had been explicit: at no time was she to forget what she was handling. Placing a drop of the fluid onto a glass slide, Kathy positioned it under the microscope. Switching on the illuminator, it took several seconds to adjust to the magnification. Once satisfied, she peered through the eyepiece.

"Fuck," she said, jumping back in horror. "This can't be right. Nothing acts this quickly."

Working on her breathing, she gradually gained control of her emotions. Turning the microscope to a higher setting, she double-checked her findings. At this magnification the thing was even more terrifying.

Closing her eyes for a moment, she attempted to blot out the horrors. Fear sharpened the mind, or so it was said. Acting as a stimulant, it enhances the senses; from her perspective that theory was a load of shit. Instead, her legs had turned to jelly. As for her brain, for a brief moment it had simply refused to function.

With an enormous effort of will she re-gathered her scattered thoughts, opened her eyes and continued studying the contents of the slide. A faint memory rippled across her mind. Tenuous, it was there one moment, gone the next. Her subconscious was trying to tell her that there was something disturbingly familiar about the virus. She had come across it before in some obscure medical journal. And if she wasn't mistaken, it had been fairly recently. The main problem was in the rapidity with which it was multiplying. Beyond anything she had ever heard of, it defied logic. Her mental gears clicked into place. Yes, she thought, she was right – she was sure of it. Using the modem, she accessed the network, knowing that somewhere among the huge amount of data stored in the computer's memory she would find what she was looking for.

Narrowing the mass of information down to manageable proportions, she decided on a certain date. Punching in the instructions for a printout of her request, she waited patiently. Shortly after, the laser printer clicked into life. Finally, with a faint buzz several loose pages emptied into the returning tray. Scanning them quickly, what she was looking for was on the second page. She had been right. It was remarkably like the plague – the Black Death. From past research she knew people who had died of the plague had certain characteristics in common. Invariably their bodies were covered by small purple haemorrhagic spots on the skin. In extreme cases, these spots became almost black in appearance. Even now she doubted the evidence of her eyes. Yet, all the signs were there. And if that was the case, the thing was a product of Medusa's evil mind.

Slumping back into her chair, she stared at the wall. From the safety of his hermetically sealed Plexiglas prison, Jared was breathing nothing but purified air. As an added precaution, the air pumped out of the room was treated by intense heat, the heat acting as a double safety feature. And the reason was simple. There was nothing better than intense heat to destroy germs. Listening to the conversation between the two women, had he not heard what had been said, one look at Kathy's face would have been sufficient. There would be no cure.

Explaining her findings to the others over a late supper, they listened in stunned disbelief.

"I was wrong in my estimation of how many will survive. There will be far fewer. Those that refused the inoculation are in for a surprise. Rather than being saved, it's simply a case of delaying the inevitable. Only later, when the so-called survivors start to display the same symptoms will they become aware of the true horror facing them. There's no escaping the virus. Even those who look for somewhere to hide will eventually become contaminated. Unless like us, they're lucky enough to find a facility like this, the plague will follow them. Like a blanket it will reach everywhere, settle over everything. Some will take longer to die than others, but believe me eventually the thing will hunt everyone down. Those with the knowledge of air-borne viruses might put two and two together and look for somewhere safe. Sadly, I doubt many will have time."

"What about the ones who manage to survive the initial few weeks?" asked Tina.

"Then they'll be staring at 'Satan's Alternative'. Having witnessed the deaths of their loved ones, they'll know exactly what's in store for them. With their families dead, they'll be forced to make the decision as to whether they want to be part of a world without them. I suspect under those circumstances most will choose to take their own lives."

"And the symptoms?" enquired Wolfe.

"As the virus is unique, I can't list them all. Some of the indicators would include multiple organ failure, bursting blood vessels, breathing problems and so on. Other telltale signs would include vomiting, diarrhoea and, of course, uncontrollable muscle spasms. In the main, death will arrive quickly. You'll literally drown in your own blood."

Seeing they were having difficulty getting their heads around what she was trying to say, Kathy chose an example close to home.

"Think of being bitten by a snake. You die of poisoning, right? Wrong. Different venoms have different side effects. The Russell's viper found in Asia is a case in point. Its venom dissolves the artery walls causing bleeding from the eyes, ears and every possible orifice. Unless treated, death occurs in two hours. The symptoms of the virus are remarkably similar, with one major difference – there is no cure for the virus."

FORTY-TWO

Thursday, 20 December 2012
Jerusalem, Israel

THE SLEEK GULFSTREAM G450 came to rest on a strip of concrete in the far corner of the airfield. According to instructions his limousine would be waiting. And it was. Tel Aviv turned out to be a modern city. Architecturally, the sprawling metropolis was a disappointment. The houses were simple concrete structures, box like and monotonous. One or two were impressive, but they were the exception. The one constant was the large cylindrical hot-water tanks that dominated the skyline like some monstrous birds of prey.

Leaving the city, they headed for highway 1. Continuing into the West Bank, they swept past the Israeli settlement of Ma'ale Adumim towards route 90, south of Jericho. From the tinted windows of the limousine, the scars of a troubled past were in evidence everywhere. At one point a cafe slid into focus. Outside, masquerading as chairs and tables were an assortment of barrels and wooden crates. An old man recognising the vehicle as transporting someone of note, raised his glass in silent greeting.

Arriving at The David Citadel, the concierge had been all smiles, as had the bell boy who had shown them to their palatial suite. Hoping for generous tips, neither had been disappointed. While the family unpacked, Solomon thought about the disturbing scenes he had witnessed earlier. Heathrow airport had been a nightmare. It had all started with the PM's announcement. His face grave and lined with concern, the picture he had painted was so bleak, that if his words were to be believed, the odds on there being a tomorrow were slim. The official word was that a mysterious illness was threatening to sweep the globe. Labelled a possible pandemic, the figures talked about were staggering. According to the mysterious 'they' the first symptoms appeared in forty-eight hours. For the following twenty-eight days it was lethal. And, seemingly, there was no cure. But he had thought that that was what the inoculation programme had been all about. So what was the government now saying, that the vaccine was useless? Despite the severity of the warning, many of his colleagues had played down the threat. Their take was that it was nothing but scaremongering. Things like that couldn't happen in this day and age.

But it was an attitude that had not been mirrored by the masses. Since the announcement, a good many of the inhabitants of London had decided to flee the city. The fact that it was a global problem had somehow escaped them.

From the safety of the VIP balcony at Heathrow he had seen how the mob had become more restless by the minute. In no time reasoned argument had given way to finger pointing and threatening.

Sensing the mood of the crowd, armed guards had suddenly appeared from nowhere. Fingering their snub-nosed machine pistols, they looked distinctly nervous. Worryingly, things seemed to be spiralling out of control. He had breathed a sigh of relief when he'd heard his flight being called.

The following morning, bright and early, Jacob Levi started his preparations. He had been looking forward to this moment for months. Until now, his parents had been responsible for his actions. Come tomorrow, in the eyes of both God and the community he would be a man. His studies had taught him that since the time of the Middle Ages there had been a ceremony to mark the occasion. Known as bar mitzvah, it was normally held in the local synagogue on the first Sabbath after your thirteenth birthday. His father being wealthy meant that he was able to celebrate his in the shadow of the sacred Wailing Wall.

Sensing someone watching, he caught his father's reflection in the mirror. His expression made him want to hug him tightly, to thank him for everything. But he controlled the impulse. He was a man now, and grown-ups didn't do that kind of thing.

Like Jacob, Ruth had looked forward to the trip for months. To date what she had seen hadn't disappointed her. At this time of year the weather, though hot, was comfortable. Staring from beneath a cloudless sky, the sun was relatively benign. Despite this she wore sun glasses. Behind the protection of the dark lenses, she gazed at her surroundings in wonder. Enthralled, she wound her way through the labyrinth of alleyways. The narrow cobblestone streets were replete with sights and sounds the likes of which she had never experienced before. The smell of frankincense was heavy in the air and for a fleeting instant she was transported back to another time, another place.

The medley of human activity fell broadly into two separate categories. The first group scurried about like headless chickens. The second set a more leisurely pace. Intent on savouring every moment, they peered into shop windows, windows filled with all manner of sacred relics, most of which she knew were nothing but cleverly produced replicas.

Her husband had been right. It was one thing to study the Holy City in glossy magazines; it was another thing entirely to experience it at first hand. Here, the sights and sounds were real, the legends alive. Acutely aware of its troubled history, she marvelled at how followers of such diverse faiths could mingle freely, seemingly without a care in the world.

Continuing along the maze of narrow streets, time ceased to

have meaning. The headscarf covering her lustrous raven hair was worn as a mark of respect. Like most Western women, she was forced to endure the endless stares of passers-by. Fending off the advances of the myriads of street vendors, she squeezed her daughter's hand tightly. Responding to the intimate gesture, the little girl looked up, her eyes fixing her mother with a look of trust and love. Solomon caught the moment and smiled.

Suddenly they were there. Knowing that the area that he and Jacob were about to enter was restricted to males only, Solomon lifted Naomi into his arms and kissed her tenderly on the forehead. Touching his wife's shoulder, he mouthed the words, 'I love you', before turning and walking away. Watching them disappear, Ruth was filled with an aching sense of loss, one which she was unable to explain. Fortunately, she had no time to ponder her feelings. Minutes later from her vantage point overlooking the Wailing Wall, she gazed down at the throng of worshippers. Picking them out from the milling crowd was difficult but, finally, she spotted them. Worryingly, the feeling of unease returned.

Despite arriving early, the area was fairly crowded. Jacob noticed that several, like him, were celebrating their bar mitzvahs. Dancing and clapping their hands, one or two were holding the Torah aloft. The men, especially those belonging to the stricter sects of Judaism, were praying earnestly. Heads bobbing up and down, they recited the Shema in the direction of the wall. Dozens of others were placing bits of paper containing prayers into cracks. The scene was a mixture of happiness and religious devotion.

And then it happened. Several figures dressed in camouflage fatigues strolled into the sacred enclosure. While the worshippers looked on in stunned disbelief the terrorists opened fire. The combination of AK-47s and M16s decimated the onlookers. Many died where they stood, cut in half by the blanket of spraying lead. In several instances bullets ploughed clean through the bodies of worshippers.

In seconds it was all over. After the deafening noise of the weapons, the ensuing silence was eerie. The only sound was the cries of the pitiful few survivors. One looked at his clothes in disbelief. Attempting to brush away the gore, the bright red of the blood contrasted sharply with the pristine blue and white of his prayer shawl. Such was the ferocity of the attack that arterial sprays had somehow managed to climb the wall to a height of several feet.

Jacob and his father had died instantly, mown down in the first volley. Unable to accept the evidence of her own eyes, Ruth slid to the floor silently. Naomi, too young to take in what had happened simply stared.

Usef Ahmed was kneeling in prayer. Situated a stone's throw from the Wailing Wall, the Dome of the Rock was full to capacity. Like many Muslim children, he had been taught how to pray from an early age. In a moment of quiet contemplation, he pondered the vagaries of his fellow countrymen. His holy book, the Qur'an, had shown him all he wanted to know about Allah. As the creator of the universe, he had lifted up the heavens, set up the mountains and made all things. And so he was at a loss to explain why so many of his fellow believers acted in such blasphemous ways.

In a flash of inspiration, he realised what was happening. It was Allah's will. He had singled out those who had not honoured the orphan, had not fed the poor, but in particular those who had loved wealth to excess. As one of the faithful, he would be spared the coming apocalypse.

At roughly the same moment as Usef was savouring his burst of enlightenment, a lone Israeli F-151 Ra'am took off from Palmachim air base south of Tel Aviv. In minutes it was in range. Its laser guidance system locked onto the target and with a flick of the switch, the pilot released the bunker buster from beneath the wing. Designed to penetrate the reinforced layers of concrete that sheath nuclear or biological weapon sites, the Dome of the Rock was an easy kill. Very few countries in the world had access to such high-tech weapons. Israel was one.

Hitting the golden dome exactly where it was supposed to, the missile cut through the outer shell like a knife through butter. Moments later it exploded. In a single heartbeat, the third most sacred site in Islam was reduced to a huge crater and a smouldering pile of rubble. A direct reprisal for what had taken place earlier: thousands of Muslim faithful were taken out in an act of mindless retribution.

When the dust finally settled there was an awful silence, an unearthly silence, the silence of the dead.

FORTY-THREE

Thursday, 20 December 2012
Sanctuary

A CREATURE OF habit, old Daniel clung to the trappings of normality for a few moments longer. Taking a final deep breath, he pulled himself together, opened the door and made his way into the main body of the church.

Danny had kept his promise. No indication had been given as to why the vicar had called the meeting, only it was imperative every single member of the community attend. The old church was roofed. Though he had been expecting as much, it still came as a surprise, prompting Daniel to ruminate on how long it had been since God's house had been this full.

On hearing the news every single person listened in stunned disbelief. Then the place erupted. Instantly the crowd turned hostile, looking for something, or someone, to vent their anger on. Slowly, order was restored. When sanity prevailed, different people reacted in different ways.

Some directed their hatred towards God, suggesting if he could abandon his people in such a manner they wanted no part of him. Others, refusing to believe the evidence of their own ears elected to carry on as if nothing had happened. The vast majority saw the afterlife as their only hope. Rediscovering their faith, they embraced the almighty with open arms.

Standing outside, Daniel noticed it was still dark, but not for much longer.

Soon dawn would break, bringing with it the promise of a new day, a new beginning. Rubbing the tiredness from his eyes, he was nearing the end of his tether. Despite the encouraging noises made for the benefit of his parishioners, he knew that the world was doomed.

Making his way along the gravel path towards the lychgate, he stopped. A shiver ran down his spine. It was as if someone had walked over his grave. With a sense of finality, he knew this would be the last time he would have the opportunity to see the sun rise over his beloved valley.

Lifting his head skywards, he waited. In a short while his patience was rewarded as the first stirrings of dawn appeared on the distant horizon. Hesitant at first, then with ever greater confidence, the sun, nothing more than a pale orb seconds ago began to assert itself. Moments later it rose majestically like a phoenix from the ashes.

Beginning at the tips of the distant mountain peaks, the first beams of sunlight gradually inched their way down the sides of the mountains, before flowing like molten lava across the wide expanse of the forest. Finally, they reached the perimeter of the small church grounds. Seconds later, the little building was bathed in a deep rich glow.

A thought popped into his head concerning dusk. He hated it, always had. The analogy it brought to mind was of a thief. Intent on sucking the life out of nature, it left behind darkness and the legacy of fear. Dawn, however, had the opposite effect. For him it bore the subtle message of hope. But not this time, this time there was no way out. With that, despair like the coils of a giant serpent settled around him.

Kathy needed a break. But she couldn't stop. Jared's life hung in the balance. The forty-eight-hour window when the virus would suddenly become infectious was approaching rapidly and so, for the safety of the others, he was now in quarantine. Fortunately, the hermetically sealed facility was located next to the laboratory she was working in. Dog tired, she willed herself to find the energy to carry on. Glancing at her watch, there was less than six hours before the virus would take hold.

What he was going through was anyone's guess. A strange man, he was a complicated amalgam of strengths and emotions. Confidence was usually a fragile thing; more importantly, it was something that could be gained either by experience or by imitation. For some reason, Jared was different. Somehow, he seemed to have broken the mould, to have re-written the rules.

One thing kept her going when her body screamed out that it couldn't go on. Jodie had lost one parent – she was not about to lose the other. But she was so tired. Snapping on her face mask and re-adjusting her goggles, she willed herself into a positive frame of mind. The breaking of glass snapped her out of her mood of defeatism. Looking for the source of the problem, she noticed Jodie in the next room. She was holding her hand. Moments later, Kathy reached her side. Relieved, Kathy saw the cut wasn't deep. A tiny sliver of glass had lodged in her finger. Instead of crying, she was trying to remove it.

"Come here, sweetie," said Kathy. In response she got an annoyed look, one that suggested she was being patronised. Leading her to the sink, Kathy picked up a pair of tweezers and removed the splinter. A few drops of blood appeared.

"Why is the disease so deadly, Kathy?" asked Jodie.

Struggling to explain in simple terms, she settled on, "Many viruses have the ability to change their genetic make-up."

"To reinvent themselves, you mean?"

Kathy was amazed how in a few concise words, a 10-year-old had described perfectly what she had hoped to get across. Yes, there was definitely something very special about Jodie. One thing she was sure of, she would have to start treating her more like an adult if she was ever going to gain her trust.

"So existing vaccines are useless," continued Jodie.

This time, Kathy camouflaged her feelings. "Precisely," she said.

Cleaning the wound, Kathy added a smidgen of disinfectant. Throughout the whole of the undertaking Jodie had not uttered a single cry of discomfort. Suddenly, the little girl hiding behind a woman's intellect rushed to the surface.

"You will find a cure for Daddy, won't you?"

Searching for a way to answer the question, Kathy accidentally spilt a drop of Jodie's blood onto the glass slide she had been studying earlier. Seconds later she returned to her work. Blinking, she rubbed her eyes. For some reason, the sample looked different. Placing it under the microscope she studied it carefully. Thinking her eyes were deceiving her, she blinked rapidly. The virus was attempting to replicate itself. Yet, as quickly as it was doing so, a mysterious substance was fighting it. In moments the battle was over. Somehow the intruder had produced a reaction that had nullified the virus. More than that, it had done so with incredible speed and efficiency.

Trawling her memory to think of any outside agency that might have produced such a result, the truth hit her. There was only one possible answer. Somehow, she must have spilt a drop of Jodie's blood onto the glass slide while she was removing the splinter. Unable to contain her excitement, she hurried next door. Beckoning Jared close, she spoke to him through the build-in microphones sited around the room.

"Jodie," she shouted in excitement, "the answer to beating the virus is in her blood."

Seeing Jared's face, she stopped, her mouth open. "But you knew Jodie was special, didn't you. How? Why? I don't understand?"

"It's a long story, Kathy, but take my word for it: Jodie is a very special little girl. I can give you the abbreviated version; whether you'll believe the story is another thing."

Seeing the nod, he continued, "It goes back to the time of Christ, to something known as the Lazarus Project." Gathering his thoughts he said, "You see, Jesus never died on the cross. He was administered a powerful drug, and it gave the appearance of death. Sure, it raised a few eyebrows that Christ had died so quickly. Even Pilate was taken by surprise but Joseph of Arimathea had done his homework. He knew exactly what he was doing. Smuggled from the tomb, Jesus was eventually nursed back to health."

"But how do you know all this?" she said in stunned amazement.

"Because my mother was a descendant of a sect known as the Guardians – a group of people sworn to protect the secret that not only was Jesus married but he had a child by Mary Magdalene, a boy. So, you see, Jodie and I are able to trace our bloodline back to Christ. It's why she's so special."

Holding up his hand to ward off further questions, he said, "Not now, there isn't time. But I have proof. In a secret room in my mansion. Hermetically sealed, it contains a library of documents unknown to the outside world. They bear witness to my claim. There's even a document written by Joseph himself explaining how and why he instigated the Lazarus Project. Much of the proof is on my computer. This evening, if things turn out as I expect, I'll download the evidence. Danny and the team, along with Edna and Eric, were part of the original adventure, so they know the score. The rest of you will find it an interesting read. It's time Jodie knew the truth. But, for now, accept the gift of my daughter's blood for what it is: a miracle."

After a brief pause, Jared said, "I know why she's special, what I don't understand is how she's able to do the things she can. As a scientist can you explain it?"

"Can't give you an immediate answer. It must be something to do with her DNA. I'll have to analyse it before coming up with any definitive answers, but let me tell you something about DNA. Contrary to popular belief, it's not fixed. It does alter over time. Extremely rare, the same person can even have two sets. Your daughter is something else. For want of a better word, she appears to be unique."

Carried away by the excitement of her discovery, she failed to see the grin on Jared's face.

Retracing her steps, Kathy was halted mid-stride. "Does this mean we can use Jodie's blood to save other people?"

Shaking her head, she answered, "Not going to happen. The amount of serum we'd have to manufacture would take months. Besides, your daughter has only so much blood. For people outside the complex it's already too late."

An hour later, Kathy found out just how special Jodie was. Preparing a trial sample of serum with which to inject Jared, she had a sudden thought. If Jodie had a unique DNA pattern, the odds were Jared had it too. Suiting up again, she took a sample of blood from Jared and ran the same tests she had done previously on his daughter. Predictably, the results were the same. There was one slight difference, Jodie had two extra genes, ones that she had never come across before. Knowing Jodie was able to cure birds and animals her guess was that one of them was some kind of healing gene. As for the other, she didn't have a clue.

When Kathy returned a short while later, Jared's face told her one thing, he had pre-empted the result.

Holding up his hands, he said, "I guessed."

Although he didn't allow himself the luxury of a cartwheel across the floor, even a whoop of joy, he was unable to stop the smile that began to tweak the corners of his mouth.

FORTY-FOUR

Friday, 21 December 2012

THAT EVENING, JARED made good on his promise to Kathy. Before he had downloaded the information, he had spoken to Jodie in private and prepared her for what was to come. In particular, he'd briefed her as to the origins of why she was special, why she was able to do the things she did. As usual she took the information in her stride.

Before he began he paused a moment, his mind sifting through the information flooding his brain. Those involved in the Judas Codex incident already knew the truth concerning the death and resurrection of Jesus. He remembered the profound impact hearing the words of Joseph of Arimathea had on him, and he wondered how Wolfe, Kinsey, Samantha and Kathy would react to the revelation.

"Earlier today Kathy asked me why Jodie is such a special young girl and I promised should I pull through I'd explain why. As you can see," he said smiling, "I have pulled through, so it's time to come clean. The last few years since Emma's death haven't been easy for Jodie. Several incidents of spontaneous healing involving birds and animals raised a few eyebrows in her previous school, as you can imagine. Things became decidedly more problematical when she healed the broken wrist of a friend hurt in a playground accident. When asked what had happened, the young boy explained that Jodie had rushed over, rubbed his arm a few times and his wrist got better. Pushed for a few details he said he'd felt a tingling sensation creep along his whole arm and then he was cured. It was as simple as that. Knowing it would be impossible to keep something like this from the local press, I took her out of school. Since then she's been receiving home tuition."

Glancing at his daughter, Jared said, "The bottom line is, it's worked well. The downside of the arrangement is that she misses playing with children of her own age."

Serious again, he said, "What you're about to hear are the actual words of Joseph of Arimathea. Yes, the Joseph of Arimathea spoken of in the New Testament." Sucking in his cheeks, he said, "The truth of what you're about to hear is beyond question; it's what you do with that truth that's the problem."

Turning the screen of the laptop towards him, he took a deep breath and started reading:

> From the beginning it must be made clear that Jesus had no knowledge of the Lazarus Project. In fact when the truth was made known to him he was in despair, feeling that he was a charlatan. His only crime, if indeed it can be viewed as a crime, was in believing he was the Messiah.
>
> It was apparent from day one that the carpenter's son was far different to other prophets who had gone before him. The problem was his charismatic personality ensured that he became a victim of his own success. In a very short time everyone became convinced that he was the long awaited saviour, the one spoken of in the scriptures. So convinced was he of the validity of his claim that he was prepared to die and rise again three days later to prove it.
>
> What was I to do?
>
> Was I the only one who could see the disastrous consequences of his being wrong, of his failure to return to life as promised?
>
> Imagine my consternation. Suddenly a germ of an idea blossomed. It would have to be a closely guarded secret, the

number kept to an absolute minimum. There were so many people that would have to be deceived: the Roman authorities, including Pilate, and then of course there would be the eyewitnesses crowding the cross like bloodthirsty vultures. In particular though, the Apostles would have to be convinced. As a result, I decided on four people. Besides myself, there would be Mary, the mother of Jesus, Nicodemus, and finally Mary Magdalene, who as his wife and the mother of his child, had to be included.

At first, the logistics of the project seemed insurmountable. Yet, from my perspective there was no alternative, the consequences of failure didn't bear thinking about. From what Jesus and Judas had arranged between them, the expected crucifixion was to take place on the Friday, the eve of the Sabbath. I calculated roughly how long it would take for Pilate to pass sentence, how Jesus would react to the questioning, but in particular the answers that he would give.

It wasn't difficult because Jesus wanted to die. According to his reasoning it was his destiny. I knew that he wouldn't defend himself against the accusations levelled at him, and that the verdict would be treason. He would be scourged and crucified. Following the Jewish custom, he would have to be taken down before the beginning of Sabbath, which would allow a maximum of four hours. And I knew well that people had survived for far longer than that. The rest was relatively easy.

I already owned a property near Golgotha, close to where the crucifixion would take place, and so the tomb was made ready. Private, away from prying eyes, it was perfect for the next stage of the operation.

One of the most crucial parts of the plan was to make it look as if Jesus had really died on the cross, while at the same time ensuring Jesus himself knew nothing about it. He would have to be drugged. The whole thing would be staged managed to appear as if Jesus had died prematurely. It wasn't unusual for a refreshing drink to be administered to a dying man, and so things went perfectly.

The following part of the scheme was the trickiest. As soon as he had lapsed into unconsciousness, his head dropped onto his chest in the classic posture of death.

And then I made my move.

As an important member of the Sanhedrin, the Jewish council, gaining an audience with Pilate wasn't difficult. It was the next part that was problematical. As I'd envisioned, Pilate was suspicious when I asked for the body. He was astonished to hear that Jesus had died so quickly, but I'd already pre-empted that. Making a great deal of the intensity of the scourging, it was then I produced my ace. As a precaution I paid a soldier handsomely to drive a spear into the side of Jesus. He had orders to make it look authentic; a flesh wound only, it was one that should produce plenty of blood. Still unconvinced, Pilate sent one of his soldiers to check on my story with the centurion in charge. When he returned shortly afterwards with the confirmation, he grudgingly gave his consent.

From here on the women's task was vital. The body had to be transported to the tomb post haste, and Jesus patched up in readiness for moving him that night. It involved a certain amount of risk, since we might have been spotted, but more importantly from the point of view of Jesus' health, it had to be done. The spices and linen bandages, along with everything else required for a speedy recovery, were already in place. For a while I was worried that someone would notice that the spices placed in the tomb were those associated with healing rather than the normal ones used for preparing a body for burial. Again I took a chance.

That night, we smuggled him away, giving credence to the idea that he had risen from the grave. We took him to a property which I owned on the outskirts of Jerusalem, where for the next few days he received the best possible care and attention. Even so, it was touch and go for a while, and it was several more days before he was fit to walk.

The most difficult part of the Lazarus Project was convincing Jesus that everything had been done with his best interests in mind. After much soul searching he agreed to go along with the plan. Once that was taken care of there was one more problem to overcome. In order to perpetuate the myth that he had risen from the dead, he would have to make several personal appearances, in particular to the disciples. His conscience greatly troubled, he eventually consented to my request.

Sometime later, when it appeared everyone was satisfied and that the fledgling religion was going from strength to strength, I smuggled Jesus, Mary and the boy child overseas. After a short stay in France, I moved them to Glastonbury, a safe place in my estimation as no one had the slightest idea of who they were.

It was several moments before anyway said a word. And then everyone spoke at once. Stilling the storm, Jared pointing to Eric, said, "Think I'll let you finish the story."

Taking it up Eric said, "Jared's tale is a bizarre one. He grew up never realising his biological father was someone he'd come to regard as his uncle: Edwin. Edwin's mother was a quite brilliant woman; it's where Jared gets his intellectual ability from. Shortly after Edwin was born, she began to get the feeling the Brotherhood, a collection of ancient assassins intent on wiping out the guardians, were closing in on her. Resorting to a desperate ploy to safeguard her newborn infant, she abandoned him along with another orphan child on the steps of a local nursing home. The idea was that no one would ever think of looking for an adopted infant. And it worked. But the child was never alone. The last of the guardians whose cover still remained intact kept a constant eye on things. Shortly afterwards her instincts proved to be correct, as she and her husband were murdered by the Brotherhood."

"And where does the bloodline of Jesus fit into all this?" asked Wolfe.

"Each guardian was a direct descendant; it was why there were so few," replied Eric. "From the moment Edwin was born he was special. It was his mother who noticed the mark and remembered the prophecy. No one but a select few ever knew about the prophecy, and once the codex disappeared, it was left to the senior guardian in every generation to ensure its secret was handed on. And so for almost 2,000 years it was regarded as a myth, a sacred tale without real substance. When Edwin was born everything changed. Bearing the mark, he had to be protected at all costs. It was why his mother concocted the elaborate charade. But the prophecy is complicated, for it to come to fruition three members of the same family must bear the mark of Le Serpent Rouge, or the Red Serpent. The choice of title is deliberately symbolic, and when you accept that everything else falls into place. The serpent uncoiling across centuries describes the family tree of Jesus. And of course the colour red symbolises his blood, the blood he shed on the cross."

"And its relevance?" asked Samantha.

"The Red Serpent is the mark of the chosen ones. The first to bear it was Edwin, the bringer of life. The second, his son Jared, was the destroyer, while the third was to be the chosen one. Unfortunately the prophecy was doomed to failure. Jared not being married and without a child meant that the prophecy had come to a dead end."

"But Jared did have a child: Jodie," said Samantha.

"True, but he was unaware of that. Until Emma's revelation, he had no idea. And he was still unaware that Jodie was the final piece of the jigsaw until he noticed the birthmark on her neck at Emma's funeral. After the tragedy I gave it some thought. But like everyone else involved in the Judas Codex incident, for the life of me I could make no sense of the prophecy."

"And now you can?" said Jared sitting bolt upright.

"Until Kathy stumbled on Jodie's unique gene pattern I couldn't. Now it's blindingly obvious. The prophecy says that the third member of the family would be the chosen one. Another name for chosen one is Messiah, the literal translation of which means 'saviour'. And that was the title given to Jesus. Regardless of whether his rising from the dead was stage-managed by Joseph or not, one thing is certain, he had healing powers. Put two and two together and the solution's before your very eyes."

It was Tina who cleared up the riddle. "Of course, Edwin was the creator who gave birth to Jared. Jared became the destroyer, and where the Brotherhood was concerned he made a good job of it. Thirdly, Jodie became the saviour."

"And so?" said Gareth still very much in the dark.

"As a direct descendant of Christ, Jodie is in receipt of a unique DNA blueprint. Until Medusa culled the world's population Jodie was nothing more than a bit part player. Now, however, with global population down to almost zero, her healing powers offer hope to a dead world."

Seeing the look of amazement on Wolfe's and Kathy's faces Jared interrupted. "Take it from me, when it was first explained to me, I was as sceptical as you. Once Edwin showed me the hidden room and the wealth of precious manuscripts it held I was sold. A background in Semitic languages has its uses. It meant I was able to read the contents of some of the manuscripts. I've only scratched the surface so far but what I've discovered is incredible."

Knowing that they were still trying to get their heads around what they had just heard Jared changed tack.

"Several of the more obscure manuscripts dealt with a list of doomsday prophecies, a topic which until the arrival of the virus was in vogue."

Scrunching his eyes in an effort to remember what they had said, he suddenly had it. Not all of it, there were still gaps in his memory. What he did recall, however, made some kind of weird sense of everything.

"The manuscripts weren't written in the form of one long narrative. They seemed to be chunks of unrelated material stuck together. In places they shot from one thing to another. Still, I'll give you the gist of what they said. According to various ancient cultures, the end of the world is supposed to arrive in the year 2012. One of the manuscripts spoke about melting glaciers, rising sea levels, the sun becoming unbearably hot, typhoons, massive hurricanes, polar shift, tsunamis, etc. My first impression was, here we go again. Nearly put the thing down, but one particular reference caught my eye. It involved the Mayans."

"Aren't they the people who developed incredibly accurate calendars?" said Samantha.

"Yes, they were so precise they could predict eclipses thousands of years in advance. According to their philosophy, the world is divided into five cycles, the first four of which have already come and gone. In each of these cycles, God created man from something found in nature – mud and wood are two examples. After a certain period of time, a trial run if you like, God decided he wasn't happy. As a result he wiped everything out and started again. The final cycle is due to begin this year. As with the first four, before that happens, mankind will have to be destroyed. Fresh start, new beginning – the phrase crops up time and again."

Shifting emphasis, he moved onto the topic of seers and oracles.

"Seers claim to be able to look into the future and predict forthcoming events. One of the most famous was the Sybil. She foresaw all manner of things; one of her more impressive feats was predicting the rise of Constantine. And that was some 800 years before his birth. She also prophesied the birth of Jesus."

"Impressive track record," said Kathy.

"Impressive enough for Michelangelo to give her a spot on the ceiling of the Sistine Chapel," said Jared.

Pausing briefly, he posed a question, "Anyone know anything about Merlin?"

"The magician, you mean?" chipped in Gareth.

"One and the same," said Jared. "There's fairly compelling evidence both he and King Arthur were Welsh. Merlin, or Myrddin as he's called in the Welsh language, isn't a name, it's a title. These days he's looked on as a wise sage or wizard. Historically speaking he was a very different animal. Known as a Celtic shaman, he was regarded as half man, half demon. Ancient writings describe him as a seer of doom. Believe it or not, he predicted the coming of the first American colony, and by name. And this was 1,000 years before they arrived. Among some of his more famous oracles were the ones pertaining to our century. And believe me, they were spectacular. I won't bore you with details, but he suggested the world would end with a devastating apocalypse. Those who've studied his words say they point to a polar shift. Albert Einstein predicted much the same in 1955."

By now, the others were intrigued.

"Then we have the Bible. Pound for pound, it's probably the greatest doomsday predictor of all time. Armageddon, the final battle between the armies of good and evil, the anti-Christ, the Apocalypse, the revelation of St John the divine, need I go on?"

"Where's all this leading?" Kathy queried.

"To the prediction of the end of the world," said Jared.

"But we've heard it all before. As someone with a scientific background, global destruction to me is Mother Nature's way of fighting back. She doesn't take kindly to being upstaged."

"That's precisely my point," said Jared. "What if the experts got it wrong and the ancients got it right? The Hopi Indians, the Chinese, Merlin and Mayans are adamant in their conviction that the world will end. And of course one day it will: nothing lasts forever. The scientific establishment tell us eventually our sun will implode. Without its light and warmth all life will be snuffed out, and virtually overnight. I'm not arguing against the world coming to an end, only when. Black Elk was one of the greatest seers amongst the American Indians. He had a series of visions or apocalyptic dreams and he predicted the next apocalypse would affect the whole world. The inhabitants would die wailing and screaming, is how he put it. As opposed to others, he emphasised the signs must be right before it happens. And here's the funny thing. Near the end of days, as he called it, the earth would be criss-crossed by a spider's web. Till recently no one had a clue what he was referring to. Since the late 1990s the world has indeed become criss-crossed with a spider's web: one of a technological kind called the WebBot. Take it you're familiar with the term?"

Getting a negative response, even from Gareth, Jared explained.

"The WebBot was a project developed in the 1990s. Created to assist in making stock market predictions, the technology was relatively simple. Using a system of spiders, it 'crawled', rather than 'trawled' the internet in an attempt to search for keywords. When these keywords were located, it provided people with a 'snapshot' of what was happening in society."

"So it was an attempt to tap into the 'collective unconscious' of the universe and its populace then?" said Wolfe.

"Exactly," said Jared, impressed. "Shortly after it came into existence, some very bright people started to grasp its potential. Scanning the language, they quickly got a feel for what was happening around the globe. In no time they were able to detect a series of patterns. By tapping into the subconscious minds of the populace, they got a feel for the mood of society. To their astonishment they found they were able to predict the outcome of certain key issues. To cut a long story short, the people behind the programme came to the startling conclusion that its influence would reach its climax in 2012. True prophecy or random choice, take your pick. It's uncanny, nevertheless."

Seeing they still hadn't managed to work out where it was leading, he elaborated.

"As you pointed out earlier, the Mayans were obsessed with time keeping, right? And the accuracy of that time keeping was astonishing. They could nail down an event such as the alignment of a specific celestial body, one which occurred only once in 250,800 years. The chilling thing is, the Mayan calendar, accepted as the most accurate in history, mysteriously comes to an end in the year 2012. Not only that, it also gives a specific date for the end of the world."

"Which is?" said Samantha.

"December 21st," replied Jared.

The implications hit the little band of survivors like a thunderbolt.

"And so," said Jared, speaking to a hushed audience, "according to that reasoning, once the virus has completed its deadly work, it can justifiably be said to be the end of the world as we know it."

FORTY-FIVE

WATCHING A REPLAY of a live-feed broadcast the following morning, the survivors were afforded their first glimpse of how the nation would react under pressure. The departure lounge of Heathrow's terminal three was packed with people attempting to flee the country. Little realising that the problem was worldwide, they had stormed the building hours ago. The scene was one of utter chaos. There was nothing on sale, the kiosks and booths dotted around the airport fringes were closed, their fronts shuttered and locked down.

In an effort to buy time, the authorities had announced that there would be no more flights until further notice. During the last few minutes the crowd had turned ugly. Tempers frayed and stretched to busting point, something had to give. And it did.

A single fight broke out, and then several more followed in quick succession. In no time the whole lounge erupted. Three guards dressed in Kevlar jackets and carrying snub-nosed machine pistols moved forward hesitantly. Unsure of what to do, the youngest whispered, "Don't like the look of this shit, sarge, what do you suggest?"

"Only one answer," said the sergeant firing a few rounds into the air. Cutting through the false ceiling like a knife through butter, plaster drifted to the floor from above. Settling on the sergeant's shoulders, it looked remarkably like a bad case of dandruff. The shots had the desired effect. The rioting stopped and an eerie silence descended.

Confused and frightened, the rioters turned in unison. Spotting the guards, a transformation came over them. Seen as the symbol of airport authority, an authority that had seemingly cold bloodedly abandoned them, they advanced menacingly, a foot at a time. Gone was the bitterness of moments ago, their rage now had a focus. Knowing they would be surrounded unless they did something, the sergeant panicked and opened fire several feet in front of the advancing mob. The crowd stopped in their tracks. It didn't last.

Faces contorted into masks of fury, the mob rushed forward baying for blood. The guards did the only thing they could. The sound of the weapons opening fire was startlingly loud in the confined space of the airport lounge. From the safety of the balcony above, several VIPs watched in stunned disbelief as the first twenty or thirty people disintegrated in a burst of bright red arterial blood. The guards kept their fingers on the triggers until every single bullet was spent.

Magazines empty, they turned on their heels and rushed for the emergency exit.

FORTY-SIX

WRACKING HIS BRAIN to put together some kind of strategy, Paul Hudson ran through the conversation he'd had with Wolfe. Though his mind refused to accept what Wolfe had told him, deep down, he knew that he had been listening to the truth. It all fit. He didn't doubt that some would have ignored the warning given in the broadcast. Unwilling to accept the evidence of their own ears, they would blithely carry on as normal. And then there was the other type, those that in blind panic would… the consequences of that was already in evidence.

The stupid thing was that the nation had never seen it coming. Switching on the television, the street riots seemed to be escalating. Everything had an almost post-apocalyptic feel to it. The bonfires, the gutted carcasses of vehicles, the noise, the looting, it was all there. But things had deteriorated so quickly it beggared belief.

Refocusing, he thought about the PM's words. The symptoms – how long had he said they took to appear? Forty-eight hours? Rushing to the bathroom he studied his face. It was blemish free. And he felt fine. Perhaps he was one of the lucky ones. Maybe he was special, someone who for some unknown reason was immune to the virus. Who was he kidding? Things like that happened in fiction only. The reality was always different.

Wolfe had made it perfectly clear: those who had been given the inoculation were doomed. So what the hell was he going to do? From what he had seen on the box, outside was a no-go area. He could stay here, he supposed, the office was warm and comfortable. Mulling over his options, he came to a firm decision: riots or not, he was heading home.

Making his way downstairs, his footsteps echoed off the marbled stone floor. Eerily quiet, the whole thing had about it a sepulchral feel. Approaching evening, he appeared to be the only one left in the building. And that was odd. Despite the late hour there should have been at least a dozen others. To satisfy his curiosity, he tried several offices.

The empty rooms told their own story: the others had decided to abandon ship hours ago. The first sign of trouble was waiting for him at the front entrance. From behind the safety of the massive wooden door he saw dozens of people milling around. Several were carrying lengths of copper piping honed to razor sharpness. Alarmingly the number seemed to be growing steadily. For a moment, he was puzzled. Why target the Palace of Westminster? And then it struck him. The public had decided to vent their feelings on those who they saw as having brought about their demise.

In a heartbeat, politicians had become fair game. According to that reasoning, the building, the seat of power for the nation, had become a physical manifestation for their hatred. Lying on the north bank of the river Thames, the Palace of Westminster, also known as the Houses of Parliament, is the seat of the House of Lords and House of Commons. An emblem of parliamentary democracy, it hadn't taken long to become the focus of the mob's rage.

The first brick arrived shortly afterwards, followed by several bottles. Landing against the door they immediately burst into flames. Home-made Molotov cocktails was Paul's guess. There didn't seem to be any weapons in evidence, and overall the whole affair seemed uncoordinated. But that would soon change.

Escaping this way was out of the question. There was only

one answer. Unknown to the public, the powers that be had made contingency plans. Foreseeing such a scenario decades ago, they had built a hidden passageway. Running several hundreds of yards underground, it lead to the back of a small gun shop about a mile or so on the other side of the river. A gun shop, thought Paul ironically, there was nothing like being prepared, was there? The door was unmarked. Set amongst a row of other doors, it was innocuous. A cursory glance indicated that it was no different from its counterparts. A more careful study would have shown that it was the only one that required a digital code to gain access. Punching in the numbers from memory, he pushed open the door and hit the light switch. Lit by low-energy bulbs placed at precise six foot intervals, the tunnel seemed to go on for miles. About three or four feet wide, one side was covered with scores of cardboard boxes. Unmarked, the contents were a mystery. Having come to the conclusion that it would never be needed, the hierarchy had seen it as somewhere else to store unwanted junk.

Twenty minutes later he reached the end of the passageway. Fingering the same digits, he entered the shop. Pitch black, he wondered why it should be so dark. Hitting the light switch to his right the reason became obvious: the length of the store was protected by a metal shutter. Using a different code, he opened the front door and risked a quick glance. It was quiet. Exiting the shop, he stepped between mounds of casually thrown rubbish and headed for the main road.

Glancing at his watch, it was 8.00 p.m. The night air was strangely warm. Under more pleasant circumstances it would have been a perfect evening for a stroll. But these were far from normal circumstances. Reaching his destination he scanned the area before taking the plunge. Setting off at a brisk pace, he stalked the shadows. Looking nervously over his shoulder every few yards, the tension was almost unbearable. Up ahead, the bright orange glow of several street bonfires lit the skyline. Almost every corner appeared to be crowded with youths. Wearing baseball caps, the majority acted as if they were pissed out of their skulls, or high on drugs. Hooking the next right, he stopped in his tracks. Pressed tightly against the wall, he watched invisible as a gang of youngsters, some no older than twelve or thirteen, stood around a makeshift pyre of scrap wood. Helped initially by a generous dousing of petrol, the whole thing was burning fiercely. The flames fanned by the evening breeze reached a height of ten to twelve feet. Several held their hands in front of their faces to protect their eyes. One stood out in particular. A head taller than the rest, he was issuing instructions. His hands moving in all directions it was clear he was the alpha male of the pack. The remainder were handing out crates of booze from the shattered remains of an off-licence. The shutters had failed to work and so the store had become an easy target. Everything was taking place to the background of a thudding base sound from the open window of a large white van. There was no way around them. Backtracking he had a thought, what he had just witnessed was eerily reminiscent of some zombie film. And the fun hadn't started yet.

Yards from making his escape, he heard a plaintive cry for help. Peering around the opening of a small alley, two youngsters dressed in hoodies were in the process of raping a young girl. Seemingly no more than seventeen or eighteen, she was fighting a losing battle. The taller of the youths oblivious to Paul's presence was hastily trying to shed his jeans. For a moment, Paul was rooted to the spot. It was only for an instant. Before he had time to rationalise his hasty action, he stepped into the alley. Searching for some kind of weapon, his eyes fell on a selection of empty bottles balanced on a refuse bin. Selecting the two largest, he closed on his quarry. Yards from his intended targets, one looked up. Jeans around his ankles, penis in hand he was unable to move. Smashing the bottle in his right hand against the thug's head, the blow shattered his cheekbone and he slid to the floor unconscious. His accomplice, deciding discretion was the better part of valour, took to his heels. Grabbing the young girl's hand, Paul dragged her out of the alley.

"Not that way," she spluttered, "it's a dead end."

Taking an immediate right, she led the way. A short distance further on, they found themselves back on the main road. About to step out, he pushed the girl behind him. The looting of the off-licence was still in full flow. There was one difference. In the short time he had been away several other stores on either side of the street had been broken into. The evidence was everywhere. Several beds and three-piece suites were on display. Trashed, they lay on their sides, springs poking through gaping holes in the material. Several other objects in various states of disrepair littered the pavements on either side.

Suddenly a group of camouflaged-clad youngsters strode around the corner. Things were about to turn ugly. Lifting automatic weapons to their shoulders, they opened fire indiscriminately. Muzzle flashes lit up the gloom and carnage ensued. Taken by surprise, the face of a nearby looter exploded in a shower of blood and brain tissue. Meanwhile, the sound of high-calibre bullets could be heard hitting defenceless bodies with dull smacking sounds.

In moments it was over, the air replete with the smell of cordite and acrid smoke.

"One of the fuckers is still alive," shouted someone.

"Finish the bastard," came the reply.

Lifting the weapon he took aim and pulled the trigger. Two shots rang out and the spasmodic twitching of the youngster ceased abruptly. Putting his hand over the girl's mouth, Paul shook his head. Gazing at the carnage in terrified fascination, Paul knew that the reason for the slaughter might have been something as simple as simmering rivalry between small town gangs, or even groups out to settle old scores. It made no difference. The outcome was that a whole new level of meaning had been introduced to the word fear.

Removing his hand, Paul mouthed, "Time to go."

A short while later, they stopped for a breather.

"What's your name?" Paul asked.

"Georgina," she replied, hands on knees, "but everyone calls me Georgie." "Mine's Paul," he said, before setting off again at a slow jog. Lulled into a false sense of security they almost stumbled headlong into another angry mob. Putting their heads down, he and Georgie ran for their lives. In seconds they were hundreds of yards ahead. Not to be denied, the crowd raced after them. Gasping for breath, Georgie spluttered. "We're not going to make my flat, any suggestions?"

"This way," he shouted in desperation.

Though they made good headway, disturbingly the shouting of their pursuers seemed to be getting louder. And there seemed to be more of them. As if drawn by some animal instinct, another gang had decided to join in the hunt. Listening to some frequency only thugs and murderers could tune into, they had decided that they too wanted a piece of the action.

Coming across yet another dead end, Paul's veins flooded with despair. There was no escape. But what did it matter? They were going to die shortly anyway. Be it tomorrow, the day after, or the day after that. So why not give in, get it over with. Once the mob caught up with them, it would be a quick death. Painful no doubt, but no more than the virus would be. He had almost made the decision to stop when a little voice told him life was precious. Giving in was the easy way out. He picked up his pace.

Running hard, he headed for a towering brick wall directly in front of him. Taking off, he grasped the top with both hands. Drawing himself up an inch at a time, he finally managed to throw one leg over the top. Using it as leverage, he hefted himself up. Tottering on the brink for a moment, he swivelled his arms like a human windmill. God, he hated heights, he thought.

Righting himself, he took a second to marshal his courage. Recovered, he leaned over beckoning Georgie to follow. For a moment she hesitated. Hearing noises behind, she reached up. Grabbing both her wrists, Paul lifted her to safety. Dropping onto the other side, in no time they were running through a series of small gardens protected by low wooden fences. Risking a glance over his shoulder, he was in time to see the head of the first pursuer appear over the wall. Spotting his prey, he shouted encouragement to the others. They had won a brief respite, yet unless they could find somewhere more permanent to hide it would be a temporary reprieve only. It was then that the idea came to him. It took a while, but eventually he located the little cul-de-sac. Guessing he was about to lead them into a trap, Georgie shouted, "There's no way out of there."

"But there is," came the reply. "The problem is we have to get inside quickly."

Reaching the door, he put his hands on his knees, took several deep breaths and started punching in the code. His hands were shaking so badly he failed twice. By now the mob had almost reached the opening to the alley. He could almost smell the fetid stench of their breath, the testosterone coming off them in waves.

Forty-seven

THE PARTY TO celebrate Jared's escape from the virus turned out to be a huge success. Raiding the stores, an ample supply of alcohol was found. Over the last few days several detailed searches had been made for Lucifer. Every nook and cranny had been turned over but there was no sign of him. Everyone was of the opinion that he had fled the complex; all except Jared, that is. Knowing how resourceful the bastard was, he wasn't convinced. Unlike him, most had given up carrying weapons.

For the occasion the room overlooking the expanse of lawns fronting the complex was chosen. Over the coming months it was to become a favourite spot for many of the survivors. The view from the window afforded a spectacular view across the mountains.

Several comfortable loungers were moved into place and a make-shift bar was set up. The floor, covered with sheepskin rugs ensured the overall picture was one of warmth and comfort. Overhead, tungsten bulbs strategically placed in the ceiling cleverly gave the impression of natural daylight.

Sitting down, with her knees tucked under her chin, Jodie had chosen to sit near her father. The only person missing was Kathy. Researching Jodie's gene pool, she had thrown herself into her work at the expense of everything else.

Levering himself from the sofa, Wolfe said, "Back in a minute."

Making his way towards the lab, he stuck his head around the door. "All work and no play makes Kathy a dull girl, remember."

"One second," she replied chuckling.

Opening a draw to her right, it slid open smoothly on runners made up of ball bearings. Checking her findings, she replaced the folder, closed the draw and returned her attention to the laptop. Punching a few digits on the keyboard, she waited a few seconds and logged off.

"Right," she said, spinning around and exiting the chair, "All yours."

While Kathy had been finishing up, Wolfe had taken a peek at her notebook. In amusement, he saw her calculations were punctured here and there with doodles. Many of the complicated formulae, meaningless to him, had been written over several times. Thickened, they stood out with crystal clarity. Several entries had been interwoven with carefully constructed cartoon figures.

Shortly after, they joined the others.

Danny wasn't amused. "All this booze and there's no beer. Plenty of lager, even cases of canned bloody Guinness, which I hate by the way. Didn't expect there would be any Brains or Buckleys, but not to have any beer at all, that's crazy."

Wolfe made a suggestion. "Try the wine. Not your three-for-ten pounds stuff, believe me. And before you ask, yes, I've found a corkscrew."

Taking the first sip Danny grimaced, "How come the first mouthful always tastes like dishwater? Even an expensive one?"

"Give it a few mouthfuls. It'll get better," said Wolfe.

"Christ, your right," said Danny moments later. "It's a bloody miracle."

Halfway through the bottle, Danny came to a conclusion. Turning to the others, he declared. "There's nothing wrong with wine. Truth is, the more of it you shove down your neck, the better it gets."

"And why should that be?" asked Jared deadpan.

"Might the alcohol be dulling his senses?" quipped Gareth.

Two bottles later and Danny had completely forgotten how bad the stuff really was. It took the combined efforts of Jared and Gareth to see him to his dormitory. Sometime later, the others, many in no better shape, headed towards their beds.

Alone in her bed, Kathy recognised that she desperately needed to be comforted. Swallowing her pride, she dressed hurriedly before tip-toeing her way down the hall. Wolfe was woken by a knock.

Stepping out of bed, he made his way over to the door. Bleary eyed, he was surprised to see Kathy standing in the corridor.

"Can I come in?" she enquired shyly. "I don't want to be alone. Because I've been struggling to find a cure for the virus, I didn't have time to dwell on what was happening, but now..."

When the tears came, there was no holding back. Stroking Kathy's head tenderly, the whorl of stray hairs covering the nape of her neck brought back feelings Wolfe had long since buried. He longed to kiss them. The impulse was so strong, so overpowering, it took all of his considerable will power to hold back.

He wondered at how fate had thrown them together. Shaped by their personal tragedies they were helping to fill the hollowness, the emptiness in each other. If so, perhaps they had a fighting chance of making each other whole again. As if reading his mind, Kathy looked into his eyes. Lifting her hand, she stroked the outline of his cheek with the tips of her fingers. Standing on tip toe, she pulled his face down and kissed him. Tenderly at first, in seconds she was kissing him with a desperation she had never felt before. Wolfe's breathing was coming in short ragged gasps, while his body was pushing against her fiercely. In moments she felt him harden against her stomach. Instantly, her tongue was in his mouth, sliding between his teeth, probing. Wolfe broke away and Kathy had a moment's panic. Had she done something wrong?

Holding her at arm's length, he whispered, "Are you sure this is what you want?"

Afraid to spoil the moment with words, she nodded. Undressing slowly, his eyes devoured every inch of her body. And it excited her. Glancing at her breasts hungrily, Wolfe saw her nipples were dark, suffused with blood. In seconds he was on his knees in front of her. Pressing his face into her bushy mound, he breathed in the delicious aroma of her arousal. And then his tongue was buried deep inside, licking and nibbling her clitoris. Kathy's vagina flooded with warm sticky juices and her thighs became wet with anticipation. Moments later, he lifted her and threw her onto the bed. And then he was inside her, filling every centimetre.

Despite fighting the urge, she was unable to stifle the gasps of pleasure as they escaped her lips. Pushing deeper and deeper inside, he thrust hard. Oh God, her insides had started to tighten involuntarily, her climax was approaching. There was nothing she could do to stop it. Fighting hard to stave off the inevitable, she was oblivious to the fact that Wolfe sensing it had increased his rhythm. Moments later, Wolfe came. The first time had been fast and frenetic, the second was more leisurely, each of them taking time to get to know each other's bodies. An hour later, spent, they rolled over.

Afterwards, Wolfe unburdened himself. He admitted to Kathy that he often spoke to his family in the still of the night. He spoke to them about his fears. Although he knew they couldn't hear him, it made him feel better.

Kathy was overjoyed: allowing her a glimpse of his private thoughts showed he felt deeply for her too. When Wolfe dropped off, it was with an image of Kathy in his mind.

Glancing at the clock, Sean Maloney saw that it was nearly 1.00 p.m. In the good old days, they would be queuing outside the door. A cursory peek showed that there were barely a dozen waiting. During the last few years, a combination of factors had made small chip shops like his a dying breed. Having owned the place for decades, he had seen it all. First there had been the potato shortage of the mid-1970s. It was too hot the farmers had complained, and so the things had become scarce. The result had been easy to predict, the prices had gone through the roof. Fine, he could understand that, but the following year had produced a bumper crop. According to his reasoning the prices should have been reduced, but had they? Had they bollocks.

Now there was another excuse. Thanks to what scientists labelled global warming, they'd had so much rain the potatoes had rotted in the ground, leading of course to another price hike. At this rate he would be out of business in a year. Not that he cared anymore. Approaching his sixty-fifth birthday, he was ready to finish. It was the youngsters he was worried about. What would the future hold for them?

Giving the chips a final shake, he lifted out the first pan-full and tried one. Just right, he declared. Then he began to dip the fish into his secret batter recipe. And that set him off again. Thanks to overfishing, the price of cod had skyrocketed. As for hake, he couldn't get that for love or money. He had tried alternatives, but no one had bought the bloody things. He was tired of explaining to his customers why he had to keep putting up the prices. Most of them understood, but there was always the odd awkward individual. On top of everything else there appeared to be some kind of super flu doing the rounds. At least he'd had the foresight to get the inoculation. It had been a bugger, his arm was still inflamed. Scratching it irritably, he looked up at the tiny portable sitting on the shelf. Once again the focus of attention was the bug. Why the big fuss, he thought? No one around here had come down with it.

"Hey Sean," said one of his regulars, "turn the thing up, mate."

Seconds later, they caught the voice of the news reporter. "I'll repeat the warning. It appears that despite the inoculation programme, the flu is spreading at an alarming rate. The early symptoms are respiratory problems, dysentery and then bleeding, especially from the nose and ears. This is followed by suppurating sores, in particular the area of the face."

For a second or two he was unable to continue. Finally summoning the courage, he added in barely a whisper. "Once that stage is reached, death occurs in a matter of hours. According to medical evidence, the mortality rate is staggering. And there seems to be no cure."

"Bloody scaremongers," said Sean, switching off the set. "No bloody flu bug around here, so what the hell are they on about?"

Ladling the first few portions of chips into greaseproof bags, he looked up.

"Salt and vinegar?" he asked the first customer. Seeing the nod, he added both. As he did so, he noticed something dripping onto the chips.

"Christ Sean, your nose is bleeding," said Hannah Dowling.

"And it's all over my chips, Mum," shouted her little daughter, leaning over the counter. "Yuk, I don't want them now."

About to say something else, the little girl lifted her hand to her nose. To her mother's surprise, she too was bleeding. Instantly, several more customers started displaying the same symptoms. Sean put his hands to his face. The first of the boils had made an appearance. The largest burst open with a sickly squelching sound. In the panic to get out of the shop, no one witnessed what happened next.

He was clutching his throat: for some inexplicable reason Sean was unable to breathe. Shortly after, he felt a searing burst of pain inside his head. One of the main arteries leading to the brain burst and he toppled head first into the deep fat fryer. In a millisecond, his face turned into a mass of bubbling hot grease, while his hair burst into flames. Fortunately, he was dead before the boiling contents had time to finish their grizzly task.

Forty-Eight

"GIVE ME THE bloody code," shouted Georgie after the third failure. Seconds before they were discovered, he blurted out: 761390. Her youthful fingers danced over the key pad and a green light appeared in the tiny display panel. Instantly it was followed by an audible click.

Throwing himself inside, Paul snaked out a hand and dragged Georgie after him.

"Are we safe?" she whispered breathlessly.

"For the moment," he replied.

Pressing their ears against the steel shutter, the mob could be heard outside sniffing around like rabid animals. At a loss to understand how their prey had escaped they were livid.

"Where are we?" asked Georgie.

"A small gun shop. Can't stay long, though, there's no food or water. Don't worry, I've got something more permanent in mind. What you're about to see is known only to those of us who work for the PM."

"Some sort of office boy, are you?" asked Georgie.

"I'm the prime minister's private secretary."

"You're almost royalty, then." Despite the carefree banter she was secretly impressed.

"So why aren't you with the PM? Sitting it out in some private bolt-hole, I mean?"

"It's a long story," was the reply.

The cupboards containing the guns were locked. It didn't take long to force them open. Removing a Glock G36, it was expensive, but money didn't matter anymore. As an afterthought, he slipped several spare clips of ammo into his pocket. Selecting a Glock 19 from the top shelf, he handed it to Georgie, "Made for someone with small hands, should be perfect. Know how to handle a gun?"

Shaking her head, she replied, "Appears you do."

"Belonged to a club at one time, but I've never fired a shot in anger. Shooting at paper targets is easy, they don't fire back. After what we've been through today, though, I think I could kill someone if I had to."

It was something in the eyes, but Georgie knew it was no idle boast. And somehow it made her feel a whole lot better. As for her, she doubted she would have the courage. Sliding a few bullets into the chamber, the weapon felt good in Paul's hand. Dormant as long as the safety catch was on, armed and ready it was a different beast.

Raising his head, Paul sniffed the air. "Smell something?"

Before Georgie could answer, currents of acrid smoke rushed to meet them from beneath the door.

The fire took hold far more quickly than Paul had expected. Coughing and spluttering, his eyes streaming, he tried desperately to drag some air into his tortured lungs. He knew that in the case of fire, most of the damage was caused by smoke inhalation. Suddenly he had an idea. Tearing one of the sleeves from his shirt, he wrapped it around his mouth and nose. Fighting his growing panic, he gradually began to feel better. Arms outstretched, he worked his way painstakingly towards the rear of the store. Unable to see the keys of the combination pad, he ran his fingers across the digits and punched in the code. This time, Lady Luck was on his side and it opened immediately. Tumbling through the opening, he tripped on the first step. Spreadeagled on the hard concrete floor, he fought to control his panic. A few mouthfuls of clean air worked wonders. Shortly, he had recovered enough to dash back into the shop. Grasping Georgie by the ankles, he dragged the inert figure to the safety of the narrow passageway. The outer door, self-sealing, meant they were now safe.

Clean air worked wonders for Georgie too. In moments, she was able to push forward under her own steam. Some twenty minutes later, they reached the end of the tunnel. Securing the door, Paul headed for the front entrance. Amazingly, it was still intact. Daunted by the thickness of the wood, it appeared the crowd had decided to look for easier pickings.

"Never been here before," said Georgie. "Bigger than I expected, though."

"Fools a lot of people, the size, I mean," said Paul. "The Palace of Westminster is a huge complex. Made up of over 1,100 rooms, 100 staircases and 4.8 kilometres of passageways, the building includes four floors. The ground floor is made up of offices, dining rooms and some nineteen bars and restaurants. The first, known in the trade as the principal floor, houses the main rooms. Should the mob return, it's here they'll target."

Thinking for a moment, he decided that their best bet would be the fourth floor. It took them a while to reach their destination. Entering the lounge, Samantha sank into the leather sofa with weary resignation.

"Back in a minute," said Paul.

Scrambling to her feet, Georgie ran after him. "Don't leave me," she said grabbing his arm. "I don't want to be left on my own."

Touching her cheek with his fingertips, Paul whispered, "I've no intention of leaving you, I'm not that kind of guy."

Burying her head in his shoulder, she began to sob quietly.

Stroking her hair tenderly, he said, "We need something to

eat and drink. Can't promise a gourmet meal, but I know where to get something to keep us going till tomorrow."

Seeing the confusion in her eyes, he explained.

"There's a vending machine in the next corridor."

Delving into her pocket for change, Paul chuckled. "No need for that."

Suddenly the tension of the last few hours was broken and they burst out laughing.

Moments later, the sound of breaking glass was followed by the sound of Paul's return. Throwing her a bottle of coke and a few chocolate bars, he said, "Get stuck in."

Deciding she would rather sit on the floor than the chair, Georgie slid to her backside. Munching the chocolate, she washed down every mouthful with gulps of coke.

Afraid to switch on the lights, they ate beneath the muted glow of a candle that Paul had found in a side drawer. The snack eaten, Geordie said, "Thank you for saving me."

Shuffling wearily to one of the couches in the far corner, Georgie kicked off her shoes and dropped onto it fully clothed. She was asleep instantly. Watching her still figure, he wondered yet again how women looked so vulnerable when they were sleeping. Feeling the efforts of the last few hours catching up with him too, it wasn't long before he joined her in the land of nod.

Paul's dreams were disturbed, frightening. Waking, the room felt hot and stuffy. Running his fingers inside his shirt, the perspiration was trickling down his back. Astonished to find that he had lost one sleeve, memories of the previous night came flooding back.

With a huge force of will, he refocused. Rising, he made his way to the bathroom at the end of the hall. The hot bath did wonders in easing away most of the aches and pains. Sponging the worst of the bruises from his body, he noticed that several had already turned an angry yellow, the edges tinged with dark purple. Eventually they would turn a greenish hue; it was a sign of recovery. As his body was fit and healthy, it would happen quickly. He cut his train of thought – it didn't fucking matter how quickly his body recovered. Long before the bruises had disappeared he would be dead.

Like most of his colleagues, he had often been forced to spend the night in the building. As a result, he had several changes of clothing at his disposal. Georgie would need fresh clothes too. There were plenty hanging around, the problem was in finding ones that fit.

Standing at the fourth floor window, he allowed his gaze to wander. Much of the city, charred and battered, was reminiscent of a war zone. Occasionally, the stillness of the morning air was disturbed by the wail of sirens. On the whole though, the streets appeared calmer than last night.

Not for the first time he wondered why thugs and cowards were more at home in the dark. It was almost as if they were creatures of the night. Window open, a subtle smell hung on the breeze. It was a curious mixture. The stench of burning rubber was clearly discernible, that and something else, something he couldn't quite put his finger on. Then it clicked, it was the odour of decaying flesh.

He had learned early on that when people's backs were against the wall the invisible line between classes blurred. At times like this, they disappeared completely. In a few brutal days, the upper classes had learned that instead of blue blood running through their veins, it was red. Just like their lower-class cousins.

Sitting up slowly, Georgie tried to make sense of her surroundings. Her head hurt and her throat was painfully dry.

Sliding her feet to the floor, it felt hard. Staying in the same position for several minutes, she gathered her scattered thoughts. Then, like Paul earlier, her memory returned.

She remembered the chase, the nearness of death, the fire, everything. Panicked, she looked around for her saviour. The couch was empty. Had he deserted her? And then she spotted him. Standing near the window she was sure that he had changed his clothes.

Aware of her scrutiny, he said, "The bloody place is falling apart."

"What did you expect?" said Georgie.

"But it's unravelled so quickly."

"It's what occurs when humans descend to the gutter," replied Georgie.

Looking at some spot in the far distance, she continued, "Animals act on instinct, they do whatever it takes to survive. Humans are different. They often do horrific things to each other, yet instead of feeling guilty, they look for some excuse to justify their actions. Some of us know when we've done wrong. In those cases we hold our hands up in the 'it's a fair cop, governor', syndrome. Called conscience, the problem comes when people have none. That's when the shit hits the fan. Without that safeguard, it's possible to justify any misdemeanour, however evil. What's happening down there is another ball game entirely. It's what takes place when you've nothing left to live for. When the rules society has made for itself are thrown out of the window, the law of the jungle takes over. And that's what we're seeing now."

Looking at her in astonishment, Paul asked, "How old are you?"

"Older than I look. I won't see twenty again. I'm a second-year university student. And, before you ask, it's psychology," she said smiling.

Though the streets seemed deserted, Paul knew it was an illusion. Those left alive, curious, but terrified, would be peeking out from behind closed curtains. Barricaded in their homes, they were under the mistaken impression that they were safe. He knew differently.

Parts of the city seemed to have power, while others had none. Strangely, there seemed to be no pattern to any of it. The situation with the water was more of a problem. Shortly, most of the purifying plants would close down. The looters would commandeer most of the bottled water, and so the genuine survivors would be forced to drink anything they could get their hands on. All this was to come.

Technically, Paul should have lasted forty-eight hours before the virus took hold. For some unknown reason he managed to survive for longer. Whether it was because he was fit and young he never knew. Despite his seeming good fortune, by the fourth day he woke feeling dreadful.

"This is it, Georgie," he said, his voice full of resignation. "End of the line, I'm afraid. From what the PM said, the next step will be severe bleeding, followed by sores and God knows what else. Been thinking about this moment for days. I had hoped I was immune, or perhaps someone would find a last-minute cure. Not going to happen though."

Taking the gun from the coffee table, he placed it against his temple.

Knocking the weapon sideways, Georgie pleaded. "Don't, Paul. I can't handle this alone."

"Couldn't have done it anyway," he said shaking his head. "I'm a coward."

An hour later, the boils made an appearance. Shortly after, blood began seeping from his eyes and ears.

Sensing she was about to approach, he shouted. "Stay back, don't come near. Close the door and get yourself to another part of the building. It's a long shot, but it might buy you some time. And take the gun. When the time comes, perhaps you'll have more guts than me."

Picking up the weapon, she made for the door. Hesitating a moment, she took one last lingering look at the grotesque figure. Unable to hold back the tears, she began sobbing uncontrollably. Pulling herself together, she blew him a kiss and ran.

A day later, Georgie noticed the spots. She, too, was doomed. She made an instant decision. Retrieving the gun from the drawer, she slipped the safety catch, placed the muzzle in her mouth and pulled the trigger.

Forty-nine

Kimberly and her brother listened to the noises coming from their parents' bedroom. It was almost as if they were in agony. Kimberly knew better than to disturb them. The first time she had heard the commotion she had opened the door to find her parents fighting. Her mother was biting her father. Then they had noticed her, and she had been beaten black and blue. Weeks later, while talking to one of the older girls in school she found out they were having sex. One of her classmates had explained in graphic detail what they had been up to. Kimberly still didn't really understand. If it was supposed to be so enjoyable why did they sound as if they were in pain?

Abused since an early age, the children didn't understand. Unaware that parents were supposed to love their children, to comfort and care for them, they had come to accept their daily dose of beatings as normal.

It was 8.00 a.m.; by now Kimberley would normally be getting her brother ready for school. But it was the Christmas holidays. Slipping into her clothes, she made her way to the kitchen. There would be no food. Every penny her parents had was spent on fags, booze and drugs. Over the last few weeks her grandmother had given her a little money. Returning to the bedroom, she retrieved a tin hidden under her bed. Counting its contents, there was nearly four pounds. Pulling back the shabby duvet, she shook her little brother awake. Bleary eyed he looked up. "Get dressed, going to treat you to breakfast at Greasy Sam's."

Unable to believe his ears, he jumped out of bed and hurried to put on his clothes. Sam's was a burger stall and the food was awful, but at least there was plenty of it. Besides, it was all she could afford. Closing the door quietly, she held Tommy's hand.

"Why's it so quiet, Kim?" he asked.

Normally the estate was full of sound, but this morning it was as quiet as the grave. Not even a bird could be heard, and that was strange. Leaning over the balcony, Kimberly gazed at the courtyard some thirty floors below. There seemed to be no one around. Everything appeared deserted. What was going on?

One corner of the filthy quadrangle was filled with garbage of all descriptions, while on the opposite side stood several gutted and abandoned cars. The remaining refuse was of a generic nature. Overall, the scene was more reminiscent of war-torn Iraq than an estate situated on the outskirts of London. Making their way downstairs, they stepped carefully over mounds of dog shit and pools of stinking urine. Here and there were dirty needles. Thanks to her parents, she knew exactly what they were for. They could have taken the lift had it been working. The smell was so overpowering it made her want to throw up. Skirting the burnt-out husks of the cars, Kimberly found it unsettling that they hadn't come across anyone else.

"Why ain't we seen anyone, Kim?" asked Tommy. "Something's wrong, ain't it?"

Clutching his sister's hand like a vice, he added, "I'm scared."

And then they found the first of the bodies.

For some strange reason they were everywhere. Tommy noticed the grotesque figures had one thing in common, underneath each corpse was a pool of black blood. And the faces were covered with boils.

Too young to understand the implications of what he was

seeing, Tommy tugged at Kimberly's hand. "Are they dead, Kim? Are they all dead?"

"No, some are only sleeping," she answered, trying to allay his fears.

"But the blood, Kim, there's so much blood. And their faces, what's on their faces?"

Unable to explain, Kimberly simply stared at her brother.

Five minutes later they reached Sam's, having passed dozens more bodies along the way. Fat Sam, as he was affectionately called, was leaning across the counter of his stall. Death must have been sudden, thought Kimberly: he still had his apron on. Sprawled along the grass verge in various poses were three other bodies. Knowing that she and Tommy needed food, Kimberly blocked the horrors from her mind. To Sam's right sat a selection of hot dogs, while to his left was a giant hamburger covered in mustard. The food was cold, but hadn't one of her teachers told her beggars couldn't be choosers?

Handing the burger to her little brother, she wolfed down the hot dogs greedily. Retracing their steps, they passed one or two people clinging to life by their fingernails. Turning the corner, they stopped in their tracks. Standing directly in front of them was an elderly couple. They appeared desperately ill. The woman had a kind face and so Kimberley approached her.

"Please, missus, can you tell me what's happening?"

The old lady's heart reached out to them.

"Haven't you been watching TV, love?"

"Haven't got a TV, missus. Not even a radio," Kimberly replied.

With a rush of understanding the old dear knew where the kids were from, and it explained everything. She had a thought. "Did you and your little brother have it? The jab I mean?"

Shaking her head, Kimberley said, "No, my Mum and Dad did, day before yesterday."

The old woman continued, "It's the flu, seems to be a special kind of strain. The strange thing is, those of us who were given the vaccine ended up worse off. And it wasn't supposed to be like that. It was supposed to help. Anyway, it's too late for us, love, like everyone else around here we're going to die. Get yourselves home to your parents, see if they're alright. If not, move further into the city. Find somewhere safe."

With that, the old couple shuffled away. Searching for her brother's hand, she headed for the safety of their flat. Knocking on the bedroom door, she waited. She knocked again, but there was still no answer. Plucking up her courage, she opened the door with one hand, while holding her brother behind her back with the other. The sight was beyond comprehension. Slack jawed and covered in blood, both parents lay on their backs staring at the ceiling.

Sobbing quietly, Kimberly levered the dirty bedclothes over their bodies. Despite everything they had been her parents. And in a funny little place, deep inside, she had loved them. No doubt a psychologist might have attempted to rationalise it as a special type of love, the kind a child unconditionally bestows on a parent. At that moment, she wondered whether perhaps they had loved her just a little bit too. She doubted it.

Mouthing a prayer, one she had learned at school, she dried her eyes, wiped her hands on the side of her tattered jeans and closed the door. Stuffing their few meagre possessions into a worn kit bag, they exited the flat and left the estate. Their clothes old and worn were the result of castoffs and charity shop bargains. Kimberly washed them regularly so they were always clean. As for fitting, that was another matter. Hers always seemed too small, his too big. Hours later, bone weary and starving, Kimberly made the decision to find somewhere to spend the night. In all that time they hadn't seen anyone else and so she guessed that they must be the only ones left alive in this part of the world. Streetwise, the little girl was astute enough to recognise that if that was the case they could choose any house that they wanted.

A hundred yards further on she came across what she was looking for. Set back from the main road, it was a bungalow with a huge lawn. Seemingly deserted, she grasped the handle of the front door tentatively. It was locked. Undaunted, she made her way around the gravel path to the back door. This time she had more luck, it was open an inch or two. Tapping the glass firmly, she shouted, "Anyone home?" There was no answer. Pushing the door with her foot, it was a while before she plucked up the courage to venture over the threshold. The kitchen was huge and so clean, she thought. Letting go of Tommy's hand, she opened one cupboard after another and gasped in amazement. They were packed with food of all descriptions. There were several tins of ham, corned beef, soups and much, much more. Some of the things she had never heard of, while others she had never seen outside a shop. The inside of her mouth flooded with juices. Even then, she stopped for a second, knowing that stealing was wrong. It was her little brother who made the decision for her.

"I'm starving, Kim. Can we have something to eat?" he pleaded.

A thought struck her, if the owners were dead it wasn't stealing, was it? It took her a while to figure out how to work the cooker, but eventually she managed. Some twenty minutes or so later, she and her brother sat down to the finest meal that they had ever eaten. Tommy couldn't believe it. Besides chips, they had a large tin of corned beef all to themselves, plus baked beans and bread with real butter. Watching her little brother mop up every trace of the juice from his plate, she smiled.

Full to bursting point, they decided to explore the remainder of the house. The lounge was the first port of call. The television was the biggest they had ever seen, but there was also a DVD and a computer. Though she knew how to work a computer from school, Kimberly decided not to tamper. Despite the luxury goods that almost filled one whole side of the lounge, it was not these which caught the attention of the children. Instead, it was the Christmas tree. Standing in the far corner, it almost touched the roof. And it looked real.

She had seen lots of fake ones, some of her school friends had them. Of course, she and Tommy had never been given one, or presents. They had come to accept early in life that Christmas was something that happened to other families. Intrigued, she touched the tree gingerly and her suspicions were confirmed – it was real. Underneath were dozens of boxes of what she guessed were presents. Covered with brightly coloured wrapping paper, the designs were incredible. Father Christmas himself was displayed on one. Resplendent in a bright red coat, black boots and a wide black belt, he was being pulled along in his sleigh by several reindeer. The largest of which must be Rudolph, she reasoned.

Gazing around the room in wonder, one look at the decorations was enough to set her mind reeling. Lost in her own little world, she had a thought: this was what it must be like for normal families at Christmas.

A cursory examination of the rest of the house showed it had two bathrooms and three bedrooms, one of which was huge. The bedclothes were so clean they sparkled. Making a few mental calculations, she knew it must be Christmas Eve. Looking at Tommy, he too was mesmerised by what he was looking at. It was then she made a decision. If by tomorrow the owners hadn't returned, they would celebrate a real Christmas. She would cook them a proper meal and open the presents under the tree. For a moment she wondered if she should leave a note, explain things just in case. Deep down she knew that there was no need. From what they had encountered on their exodus, no one was ever coming back. It she wasn't mistaken, they were probably the only two people left in the whole world.

When the owners didn't return, Kimberly made good on her promise. Cooking was one thing she was good at. She had learned from a very young age that unless she utilised the scraps of food littered around the house, she and her little brother would starve. Most of the presents contained toys of all descriptions, prompting Kimberly to question whether the owners had been a young family. Opening them, Tommy's eyes got bigger and bigger. By the third parcel, his hands were trembling so badly that Kimberly had to complete the task. They had deliberately kept the biggest box until last. Inside was a huge teddy bear. Hugging it tightly to his little chest, it seemed to Kimberly that Tommy would never let it go. As it turned out she was right. For the next few days, wherever Tommy went, so did the bear. At night it was tucked tightly under one arm, while Kimberly lay beneath the other.

They stayed in the house for several days and for both it was undoubtedly the happiest time of their short lives. During the afternoons they would search the surrounding area in the vain hope of finding someone else alive. But there was no one.

On the third day, Tommy complained of feeling unwell. An hour later, his nose began to bleed. Kimberly knew the signs only too well, in a few hours he would be dead. And she was right. She was still fine; more importantly, she was displaying no signs of the mysterious disease. But her health was irrelevant.

Her baby brother was the only one who had ever cared about her. His was the only love she had ever known. Life without him was unthinkable, meaningless. And so she made a decision.

Knowing what to do, she left the house. An hour later she returned. First she made herself a cup of hot chocolate, then she removed the lid of the container. Tipping the contents into the palm of her hand, she began to take the pills one at a time. She took two dozen in all. By this time, she was feeling drowsy and so she made her way towards the back bedroom. Earlier in the day, despite knowing Tommy was dead she had run a hot bath and washed him thoroughly. By the time she had finished, no trace of the stinking black blood remained. Unlike most of the other bodies she had come across, his little face was free of the suppurating boils which had become the trade mark of the filthy disease. The only thing that marred his almost flawless skin was the odd black lesion. In particular, they had appeared under his armpits and the tips of his fingers.

Finally, she had dressed him in a pair of brand new Mickey Mouse pyjamas taken from one of the shops nearby. To complete the picture, she had put on a pair of light blue socks decorated with the same motif. Against the sparkling white sheets of the clean bedclothes, he looked like an angel.

Climbing into bed, she reached down. Tucking the teddy bear tightly under Tommy's arm, she pulled the duvet over them both and pulled him close. Kissing him tenderly on the forehead, she realised that this was the only time in her brother's desperately short life that he had ever owned anything new.

FIFTY

THE SPECTRE OF the grim reaper had forged a strong bond between the survivors. Several things occurred in the next few days that highlighted their privileged position inside the complex. For a while they were both fascinated and horrified by what they saw. The plasma-screen TV, fitted with HD specifications, brought home in gory detail the true impact of the virus on society. The once great cities of the world now had one thing in common: they were rapidly turning into charnel houses. In a cruel twist of fate, the media, statistically, seemed to be less affected than other institutions. Jared had a thought: it appeared that once again the Devil was looking after its own.

By the following week the scenario had altered. Those same cities had been turned into morgues. To make matters worse, almost every clip included a glimpse of Christmas preparations. Supposed to be the festive season, it had quickly turned into a nightmare. Though each of the sights had been horrific, some had been more harrowing than others. Places of worship worldwide were full of the dead and dying. It was clear that since science had failed to find a cure for the disease, the majority of the population had decided to take a chance on religion. They had flocked to God's houses in the vain hope that the Almighty would grant them a last minute stay of execution.

The scene from the Vatican had been an all too familiar one. The square full of people, hands held towards heaven, had begged help from a deity who it seemed had callously abandoned them.

Hospitals were struggling to cope. The pitiful few doctors that had survived were unable to keep up with the ever increasing flow of patients. Exhausted, they moved around like automatons.

One in particular had been singled out for attention. The harrowing pictures showed blackened corpses lying in corridors. Other bodies, bloated and covered with sores were sprawled across gurneys, drips hanging from lifeless arms. Several patients bent double, spewed out gouts of fresh black blood.

Gazing in horrified fascination, the survivors followed the crew as it pushed through a set of double doors leading into an antiseptic room containing several stainless steel tables. Instantly Jared's imagination conjured up the odours normally associated with such places. Regardless of the elaborate precautions taken to mask the smell, he knew the stench of sick and diseased humans would be overpowering. He had once heard it described in the trade as the 'death smell'.

Seconds later, the shoulder camera zoomed in on one table garishly highlighted by the overhead fluorescents. To the side of the surgeon, clothed in a green gown, his face covered by a white mask, was a small portable trolley holding myriads of instruments. Some would not have looked out of place in a butcher's shop, thought Danny in horror. Leaning over the body, which was twitching spasmodically, the surgeon's latex gloves were covered in blood.

A hideous sight, it was beyond Wolfe how anyone could contemplate earning a living doing that kind of thing. Looking closely, he noticed that body fluids and something he didn't really want to think about were seeping from the patient's nose and ears. The eyes had haemorrhaged. Staring lifelessly at the camera, they were a dark crimson.

As the lens swivelled through a 180° arc, the party were afforded a view of someone hosing stinking black blood from a gurney into runnels situated on either side of the table. Swirling down a large hole in the floor, pieces of flesh were discernible amongst the thick cloying goo.

Wolfe hated hospitals, ever since the death of his parents. The sight of so many people desperately ill pierced his facade of invincibility.

He had witnessed at first-hand the death of his mother, his father having passed away peacefully years before. It had happened in a matter of minutes. She had slipped away before his very eyes. The first indication anything was wrong had been the altered tone of the ECG machine. The luminous tracing of the electrocardiograph skipping a beat had been enough to trigger the alarm. Instantly, the room had flooded with nurses and doctors. Ushered out, he had watched through the window as they desperately tried to resuscitate her. First by the use of a portable defibrillator, and when that hadn't worked, a syringe full of epinephrine. It had been to no avail, his mother had never recovered.

Staring at her lifeless form, an empty feeling had settled deep inside him. At that moment he'd realised one thing: the body was nothing but an empty shell. Her real self, her soul, or whatever it was believers labelled it, had long since departed. Since that day, he'd often wondered about the afterlife. Was there really anything waiting on the other side?

In the US, those with live feed capabilities such as CNN, NBC, ABC and CBS were falling over themselves to gain a piece of the action. Crowding around targets, they reminded Jared of sharks in a feeding frenzy; unaware that within a few days, they too would be showing symptoms of the virus. As nothing of this magnitude had happened for centuries, they were determined to make hay while the sun shone.

In one or two cities, audiences were afforded a glimpse of just how low humanity could descend. Though blindingly obvious that material goods were no longer of any value, the dregs of society were roaming the streets looting and burning everything in their paths. More sickeningly, some individuals had gone on killing sprees. Just for the hell of it. In many instances the police had become a target for mindless retribution. Overturned and burnt out patrol cars bore mute testimony to the sad fact.

Interspersed among the scenes of horror, the nation was afforded glimpses of violence on a global scale. It had finally sunk in that everyone had but a few days to live. And so religious zealots, those whose fanaticism had been simmering beneath the surface for decades, had decided it was now time for action.

FIFTY-ONE

WHILE THE METHOD of delivery may have differed in those countries deemed 'third world', the effect of the plague was equally as devastating. The infected food and bottled water had done their work exceptionally well. Isolated villages were afforded a brief respite only. Days later, either carried on the wind or by personal contact from those already infected, they too eventually succumbed.

Covering thousands of miles daily, helicopters rented on behalf of the larger media corporations roamed the outskirts of several African countries. Their remit was to film close-ups of dead bodies. Heartbreakingly, the vast majority seemed to be little children. In a vain attempt to escape the killer disease, many parents had simply abandoned them as unwanted baggage.

Some villages had stockpiled corpses before setting fire to them. The flames of the funeral pyres could be seen for miles. The thick black smoke acted like beacons to the helicopters as they swooped in for a closer look. Begging for help, survivors lifted their hands to the helicopters in gestures of supplication.

The only winners were the vultures and other predators. Watching the huge birds tearing the flesh from the corpses, Danny was reminded of the film *Ice Age: The Meltdown*, in particular the scene where the vultures contemplating a terrible disaster were singing, 'Food Glorious Food'. To his mind it was one of the funniest clips in the film. In this instance, however, what he was witnessing was fact, not fantasy. The disaster was on such an unprecedented scale that for several months afterwards all manner of predators, both winged and four legged, would have sufficient supplies of fresh meat to satisfy even their voracious appetites.

Most of the stations showed much the same shots. By now, those of the media who had survived had decided to relocate to more central areas. In some cases, fewer than a dozen or so people found themselves in charge of what had once been huge television channels and the way in which the disaster had been portrayed underwent a shift in emphasis. As if those left behind had finally had their fill of blood and gore, the human interest angle came more to the fore. Pathos became the byword, rather than cheap sensationalism.

A few of the smaller news stations in Britain provided evidence of just how serious the situation had become. Close-ups showed scores of figures wearing anti-plague suits loading body bags into a convoy of lorries. Nearby was a school yard. Shockingly, hundreds and hundreds of bodies sewn into cheap cotton sacks had been laid out side by side. And there didn't seem to be room for any more.

Breaking across their thoughts, Kathy explained that the suits were specially designed. Comprising socks, underwear, hoods, smocks, respirators, goggles, boots and safety glasses, they afforded the collectors some kind of protection. Whether it would be enough to fend off the effects of Genesis was another matter, thought Kathy. Personally, she doubted it.

Sadly, it was a sight that was to become all too familiar. During one clip, one reporter had posed the question, "What happens when the bodies outnumber the collectors?" The next seventy-two hours provided the answer. By then there was no one left alive to do the collecting.

On the fourth day, the first of the major stations stopped

reporting. One moment they were on air, the next they had disappeared in a burst of static. Gradually, each of the others closed down. Depending on where they stood in relation to the international time line, some stayed on air longer than others. Overall, however, it happened quickly. For a while the survivors had been puzzled, until eventually it struck home: there were no more pictures because there was no one left alive to do the broadcasting.

And so Christmas Day arrived. It was a low-key affair. Edna, helped by Kathy and Samantha, had prepared what they could. Fresh produce such as eggs and milk had run out, so they had been forced to improvise. For obvious reasons their hearts were not in the festivities. Yet, for the sake of their sanity more than anything else they had made the effort. In the lead up to the festivities, hours of rummaging through cupboards had eventually turned up what they had hoped for, a massive boxed tree. Kinsey, who had spent a good deal of time in the days leading up to Christmas exploring every nook and cranny, had unearthed several large cardboard boxes full of decorations. Amazingly, he had even found some crackers. And so, for a brief while, the day had all the trappings of normality. Dinner over, several hours were spent wishing the people in the other facilities yuletide greetings and swapping the odd story. Apart from that, it was a day like any other.

That evening, as if deciding mankind had been punished enough, winter decided to throw the survivors a lifeline. Clouds rushed in from nowhere and the temperature plummeted. The sky became a dull grey, covering the whole valley with a gunmetal sheen. In no time, light powdery snow looking remarkably like cotton buds began to fall. Lightly at first, the flakes steadily grew in intensity until in minutes they were falling in earnest. Within the hour the whole thing had turned into a blizzard.

The following morning, staring out of the huge glass window of the lounge Danny gazed at the results of last night's snowstorm.

"Jesus, it looks bloody cold," he said, turning to Jared.

"Colder the better," was the reply.

Puzzled, Danny said, "Why would you say that?"

"Keep the germs at bay. Though we've escaped the effects of the virus, the millions of rotting corpses dotted around the country will provide their own health hazard. Survivors left rummaging through that little lot will have several infectious diseases to contend with. The cold will help nullify the effects."

"Point taken," said Danny.

A mug of steaming coffee in hand, Jared took a deep swig before placing it on the table. Following Danny's gaze, he saw the evidence of winter's heavy hand everywhere. In several places along the perimeter, the drifts were several feet thick. Here and there, snow was trapped in the eaves of trees. A sudden gust of wind whistling through the branches of the conifers disturbed a flurry. As he watched, they feathered to the floor with the grace and elegance of a butterfly.

FIFTY-TWO

AROUND THE FIRE in Medusa's office, questions were raised. Confused by the fact that Anna Heche had been working on two projects simultaneously the others tackled Kathy.

"The best way of dealing with your queries might be to look at the issues separately. Take the virus, how Medusa pulled if off was a case of the Trojan Horse Syndrome."

"Beware of Greeks bearing gifts," said Jared.

"Exactly, the TV programme on bird flu was a master stroke. Painting the worst-case scenario as it did, it not only scared the living daylights out of people, it made them realise how important the inoculation programme was."

"Still can't get my head round the fact our scientists failed to spot what was going on. We gave the bloody stuff our seal of approval, for God's sake. Surely they couldn't have all been in on the act?" asked a bemused Wolfe.

"They weren't," said Jared, "it was Stanford."

"Of course," said Wolfe, "only someone with his influence could have pulled the wool over the eyes of so many important people."

Tina was next up. "You mentioned genetics when you were trying to find a cure for Jared. What exactly do you mean by the term?"

"Genetics is used to treat illnesses such as AIDS and cancer. And believe me it hasn't all been plain sailing. The research involves replacing defective genes with working copies, ones that won't be rejected. The main problem has always been in finding a method of transposing the healthy genes into the diseased ones so the process of healing can begin. Eventually a way was found."

"Retroviruses!" exclaimed Samantha.

"Correct," said Kathy. "Retroviruses use genes that aren't able to reproduce. The body not recognising them as a threat leaves them alone. More importantly, once they've carried out their pre-programmed task they die. Or that's the theory anyway. Unfortunately it doesn't always work like that. In some cases impurities occur, like inflammation for instance. When this happens we're left with an immune system problem."

"And the solution?" asked Jared.

"Retrotransposers," said Kathy. "It's the way we try to fool the body's defences. We modify retroviruses in order to make them appear like bits of your own DNA."

"Let me see if I've got this right," said Tina. "Retroviruses are used to transport genes into the patient's own cells, yes? If that's the case, I suspect Anna Heche's retroviruses mutated, didn't they?"

"Yes, they remade themselves. But they not only mutated, they did so far more quickly and aggressively than she ever envisaged."

"What do you think Anna was trying to achieve, Kath?" asked Danny.

"It's difficult to say, but her first priority was to complete her father's project."

"Which was?"

"Create a world free of impurities. Course to do that, he had to produce a generation of 'genetic perfects'. He knew it wouldn't happen overnight. Instead, it would be the children of the present survivors, those who now inhabit the arks that would be the benefactors. These would be the first of the 'specials', if you want to put it that way."

"In what way would they be special?" queried Eric.

"Again, I can't give you an exact answer. My guess is they would be born with enhanced immune systems for a start."

"That's why she needed so many young children, isn't it?" said Danny with a burst of enlightenment. "She needed a constant supply of young healthy bodies to carry out her research."

"Precisely. Part of what she was doing involved the use of embryonic stem cell research, which is highly controversial or, should I say, was. On the one hand, using human embryos infringed the human rights' bill, while on the other it opened the door for all kinds of protests from religious institutions."

"So what went wrong?" queried Danny.

"Nothing went wrong, it's just that being as mad as a hatter she decided that creating the 'specials' for her father wasn't enough of a challenge. Instead, she began conducting some research of her own. What it was we'll probably never know. If only I could have managed to get hold of her notes," she said wistfully. "The one person who knew the location of her hidden laboratory was Mark. Course the secret died with him."

"What about the animals?" asked Tina. "What happened to them?"

"By now the poor devils will have starved to death," was the reply. "To get back to your original question, about what Anna was attempting to create, the answer is I don't know. She was such a genius it could have been anything. Many revolutionary ideas look good on paper," she added. "When put into practice it's a different matter. Yet, in this case it might be the opposite was true."

"Care to hazard a guess?" said Tina.

"Based on what Mark told us in the pub that day, I can make an educated stab. In my opinion she was working on something that until now has been regarded as nothing more than a working hypothesis. Several papers have been written on the subject; achieving it was thought to be years away. The clue is in the disappearance of so many adults. Unlike the children, these vanished in a precise spot in and around the complex, and in a short time span."

"You believe she was tampering with nature?"

"If theoretical genetics is tampering with nature, then the answer's yes. It's an idea that's been around for quite a while. It means the transferring of genetic material from one species to another. If you insert human genes directly into something like animal embryos, then you create a transgenic animal."

"This was way beyond that though, wasn't it?" said Samantha.

"If my guess is right she managed to create something even she didn't understand."

"An accident?" asked Jared.

"Possibly. Yet, she was such a twisted genius she may have deliberately set out to create a new species. Either way it seems clear she produced something that transcended human boundaries."

"What's it got to do with the missing tourists?" asked Gareth.

"I believe one of Anna's little experiments managed to escape the complex, and has been living in the forest ever since. It's the only explanation."

Jared broke into the conversation. Over the course of the next few moments, he filled the others in on what he had discovered. The caves, the skulls neatly arranged as trophies in the clearing, the strange footprints, finally the feeling of being watched. Completing his story, he asked, "Make any kind of sense, Kathy?"

"Ticks all the right boxes," she answered. "But let's get one thing straight, whatever she created is nothing remotely human. I'd lay odds it's completely unique. The only consolation is that it will either fall prey to the virus, or be killed off during the winter."

"Amen to that," said Danny. "God knows what it might have been capable of had it survived. And Anna, what about her?"

"Depends. One of three things might have happened. She could have been killed by the creature, she might have succumbed to the plague or, thirdly, she might have frozen to death. Either way we shan't be hearing from her again."

"Same applies to Lucifer, I suppose," added Wolfe.

Before Kathy had an opportunity to agree, Jared interrupted. "I hope so, but knowing his animal cunning I wouldn't put it beyond the bounds of possibility he survived somehow."

Jared's hunch was right. Lucifer was far from dead. In fact he was in better shape than he had ever been. After a rigorous workout, he stepped out of the shower and towelled himself down. His humiliating defeat at the hands of Jared burned inside him like a furnace, and he vowed that the next time their paths crossed he would be ready. At one point he had thought about picking off the survivors one by one, but had decided against it. At present they had no idea he was alive and he wanted to keep it that way. There would be ample opportunity to make his move later.

Knowing the location of Anna's secret laboratory had turned out to be a bonus. Delivering the children at night had required knowledge of both the location and access codes to the flat behind the laboratory. As a result he had more than enough food and water to survive for several months. Surprisingly, Anna hadn't returned, forcing him to the conclusion that she was either dead or had decided to look for another bolt-hole.

New Year's Eve, like Christmas, was another festive occasion that, if the survivors were honest, made its way under the radar unannounced. It was tolerated rather than celebrated by the odd drink and a good deal of melancholy.

The one positive outcome was that Danny, having learned from past mistakes, had limited himself to a single bottle of red wine. Much to the amusement of the others, he had stated that knowing how strong the stuff was he had decided to treat it with the respect it deserved. As a result he had woken up the following day feeling, in his own words, "almost human".

And so, 2013 arrived with a whimper rather than a bang.

During the months of enforced solitude, the survivors found different ways of amusing themselves. The extensive library proved popular, as did the gymnasium. Surprisingly, the kitchen provided the main focus of attention. Tired of the constant diet of frozen meals it became the vogue to experiment. Several turned out to be surprisingly proficient in terms of culinary skills. Chinese and Indian dishes were the most popular. Having spent so much time overseas, Jared and Ian were almost addicted to spicy food. Despite the incredible amount of alcohol on offer, none of them were big drinkers.

In the first few weeks, Wolfe and Kathy became an item. While Kathy reverted to her maiden name of Melrose, Wolfe decided that Michael Conrad should be laid to rest along with his family. As for Jared and Samantha, at present Jared was still trying to get his head around that.

The enforced leisure time produced a few bizarre results. The most surprising was the way in which Danny chose to spend his. For the last five years he had been promising to take up some kind of exercise. Like all his good intentions, after the first few days, the tedium of trying to keep to a rigid timetable had ensured that he had given up. The fact was he lacked the mental discipline to make a go of it. It had been the same with the cigarettes. But, of course, he had a ready-made excuse. The pressures of work and the fact that the job was far from being nine to five had helped soothe his guilty conscience.

Some two months ago, to the amazement of the others, Danny had not only given up the cigarettes but he had followed a strict training regime. And the results had been incredible. With the help of Jared and Ian, he had lost over a stone in weight and shed inches from his waist. On the wrong end of many a ribbing from the others, especially Gareth and Tina, secretly everyone had been pleased for him.

Towards the end of December, each knew that the time was approaching when a decision would need to be made about leaving. After much discussion, it was decided that Jared and Kinsey should conduct an aerial survey of the countryside, to test the lay of the land. As things turned out, they covered far more ground than expected.

FIFTY-THREE

8 April 2013
10.00 a.m.
Sanctuary, Wales

THE HELICOPTER USED to transport Kathy and Wolfe to the complex all those months ago was now to prove its worth in other ways. As it gained height, Jared felt the familiar sensation of weightlessness. Many hated the feeling: it made them feel nauseous and dizzy. In battle, choppers were forced to hug the ground to avoid radar detection. Without that problem, it lifted vertically, hovered for a moment fifty or so feet above the watching survivors, pivoted to the right and headed into the distance.

Minutes into the flight their worst fears were confirmed. Gazing at an alien landscape, not a single person appeared to be left alive. The further they went, the worse things became. The motorways were packed with traffic of all descriptions. Yet every single vehicle had a common denominator, none of them would ever move again.

Wherever they looked the scene was the same, one of utter devastation. On close inspection several large buildings appeared to have sustained substantial damage to their infrastructure. The odd one was nothing but a charred and mangled shell.

"Gas explosions," explained Jared. "Death came knocking so swiftly many household utilities were left on. Afraid that kind of thing would have been commonplace for the first few months. There's no guarantee that the same thing won't happen again. Spontaneously, I mean. The rest of what we're seeing is no doubt the result of mindless violence. During that forty-eight-hour window, when people knew they were going to die, the shit would have hit the fan big time."

Reaching the first of the large cities, Bristol, Kinsey witnessed at first hand what Jared had been alluding to earlier. An animal lover, Kinsey decided to take a look at the zoo. The odd one or two animals, especially the larger creatures trapped in their cages, had died of starvation. To his relief, it appeared that the majority had been released. Why so selective, he wondered? A germ of an idea took root. Dipping low, his hunch was confirmed. Two uniformed figures lay some fifty feet apart. In the process of opening the doors of the cages, it was obvious that the virus had struck from nowhere.

Being a Manchester United supporter, Kinsey decided to take a look at Old Trafford. The scenes were heart wrenching – thousands of bodies littered the pitch, many of them were young children. In some instances whole families lay tightly packed. Beneath winter coats, many could be seen wearing their kits proudly. Several, following the fashion trend of the day had tied their scarves to their wrists. Having seen enough, they headed for Liverpool. Hovering above the cathedral, Kinsey and Jared stared in amazement at the sight which greeted them. The network of small roads converging onto the cathedral was crammed with thousands of dead bodies, while the steps leading to God's house were littered with corpses. With a flash of cruel humour, Jared realised that, when the chips had been down many had rediscovered their faith. Yet, it had been a futile gesture. In the end the virus had been indiscriminate, killing the faithful as well as the unbeliever.

Flying over a particularly grim housing estate brought back unwelcome memories. On many an occasion Jared had been drawn into a discussion regarding the merits of such places. The government's philosophy had been simple: create something self-contained and efficient. From that respect he supposed the architect had been successful. However, aesthetic beauty had been a phrase millions of years removed from the project. In his mind they all looked exactly the same, chicken coops. It was an impression further heightened by the inevitable wire meshing decorating most of the windows. Averting his eyes, he banished the thought from his mind.

Sometime later, nudging the helicopter to his right, Kinsey pointed downwards: it was an area that Kinsey was familiar with. Playing off a handicap of four, he was an accomplished golfer. He had once had the pleasure of a round on the course he was circling. On that occasion, finding the club house amidst the maze of winding country lanes had been a nightmare. He had almost missed his tee-off time. The trouble had been well worth it in the end.

Regaining his focus, he pointed downwards. "The Isle of Purbeck. At one time those houses were some of the most sought after real estate in the country. Now they're empty, they look kind of sad."

Unknown to Kinsey, Jared was thinking along the same lines. A thought snagged his mind. Homes without the happy laughter of children and the hustle and bustle of everyday life became nothing but empty shells. And that's exactly what was on display here. All that remained was the painful memory of how things had once been.

Intent on giving Jared a tour, Kinsey dropped even lower. To Jared's right was a small car ferry. Almost full, most of the occupants had died in their vehicles. Those that had managed to disembark hadn't got very far. A cursory glance showed that the majority of passengers had been Christmas shopping. Brightly decorated parcels were strewn around like confetti at a wedding.

There was even the odd tree, though by now most of the pine needles had withered and died.

At this altitude, Jared could make out individual bodies strewn all over the beach. Looking at the pitiful remains, one in particular caught his attention. Partially covered with seaweed, the fish and crabs had stripped the carcase to the bone. Lifting the chopper, Kinsey flew over the small harbour. Few boats had made the decision to remain behind. Those that had were scattered across the tiny estuary in various states of disrepair. His eyes came to rest on a small wooden jetty. One of the owners had died while in the process of losing the moorings. Amongst the debris lapping against the wooden pilings were a few lifeless corpses. Resplendent in bright yellow life jackets, they were easily identifiable. Having seen enough, Kinsey banked sharply and headed for Bournemouth, a short distance along the coast.

Disappointingly, the looting that they had glimpsed sporadically on television was in evidence here also. Shop windows had been broken, while furniture and household goods littered the narrow winding streets. Out of the corner of his eye, Kinsey spotted a lone bus. Lying on its side, the windows had been smashed; the carcass gutted and scorched.

Forced to stop for fuel a second time, they selected Gatwick airport. While Kinsey fuelled the chopper, Jared studied the surrounding area. The whole thing had a surreal feel to it.

To his immediate left was a private jet. Small and sleek, it looked oddly out of place against the towering hulks of the other aircraft. The image it brought to mind was of a toy plane.

Wreckage lay strewn around in scattered clumps, further confirmation that the plague had struck so swiftly some aircraft had either crashed on take-off or landing. Taking to the air once more, they skimmed low over rural areas. Several abandoned cars lay on their sides in ditches, while in one instance, the headless torso of a driver could be seen spread-eagled across the bonnet. The force of the impact had thrown him through the windscreen. As for the head, it was nowhere to be seen.

One of the most popular places people had been drawn to during their last few hours on earth were supermarkets. The car parks were littered with corpses. Many had died where they stood, while others were scattered about in haphazard fashion. In one instance a body had been jammed into a trolley. Its feet and hands hanging out, it was strangely reminiscent of an adult Guy Fawkes. It might have appeared comical had not the situation been so serious.

An hour or so later, checking his gauge, Kinsey looked across, "We're down to 25 per cent fuel. About thirty-five minutes tops. If you want my advice it's time we turned for home."

"Suits me," said Jared, "I've seen enough for one day."

Heading out to sea, Kinsey looked at the sky. What he saw worried him. Ahead, the way was blocked by a layer of massive clouds, which had sprung up from nowhere. Dark and angry, they spelled trouble. Making a snap decision, he decided to take the long way home. Looking through the side window of the cockpit, Jared had a view of what had spooked Kinsey. The sky was ominously dark, while beneath the chopper, the sea had taken on a marbled appearance. From past experience Jared knew it was the harbinger of something nasty.

To date they hadn't sighted a single ship and it got him wondering. After all this time would there be any? Unlike aircraft, which simply dropped from the sky when there was no longer anyone to pilot them, ships were different. Large or small, they had to be navigated. So what happened when everyone on board was dead? In particular cruise vessels and tankers. Did they carry on roaming the seas until their fuel gave out or did they come to a halt only when they hit land, literally?

What did fate have in store for those vessels powered by nothing but the vagaries of the wind? At the mercy of the elements, would they flounder in the first hurricane force storm? With their crews long since dead, were they doomed to sail around the world for evermore? Rendered nothing but ghost ships, was their fate to keep on going until they eventually slid off the end of the earth? These were questions Jared wasn't sure he wanted answered.

Suddenly, the storm that had been threatening erupted with a savage fury. The angry purple clouds blacked out every last vestige of an already weakened sun. Beneath the little helicopter, the mountainous waves were far higher than anything Jared had seen in previous storms. Whipped into a mad frenzy by the hurricane force winds, the massive white caps seemed frighteningly close.

Lightening streaked overhead, the remnants of the forks looking remarkably like fingers pointing downwards in an accusatory gesture. A glance behind showed that the coastline, until now just about visible, had disappeared completely, hidden by a blanket of thick fog which had rolled in unannounced. Both Kinsey and Jared were grateful that they were heading away from the storm.

FIFTY-FOUR

15 April 2013
Sanctuary, Wales

AND, SO, THE time had finally arrived to abandon the safety of the complex. The last week had been a nightmare of indecision. Several of the group, despite being sick of their enforced imprisonment, were fearful of what might be waiting on the outside. Having been in contact with the Russian, German, French and American arks, they found that they, too, were suffering similar misgivings. Several had used the phrase, 'better the Devil you know'. In the end, common sense had prevailed. In the case of those holed up in the London underground, they were given instructions to stay put. Jared had explained that, during the course of the next few days, he and the other survivors of the complex would make the effort to join them.

Deciding to take the Winnebago, it had been stripped of everything that Jared had deemed surplus to requirements. As such, only the bare essentials remained. Should they need to they could always visit one of the larger car marts and commandeer two large SUVs, they had reasoned. It was doubtful that they would ever return to the complex but it was comforting to know that should they need to the old place would be there.

The first smells of spring had long since come and gone. Due to freak winter conditions, most of the tiny buds had woken later than normal. Nevertheless, by now most had decided to make an appearance. Dotted across the foothills of the valley, those flowers more courageous than the others had already bloomed.

Entering the village, Jared had something to take care of before heading for the open road. Guessing Samantha's intentions, he put a hand on her shoulder.

"I know you want to find out what happened to your father. I'm not sure it's a good idea. Me, I'd want to remember him as he was."

Sensing the battle raging inside, he allowed her space to come to her own decision. After a slight pause, she lifted her head and nodded. Heading for the church, no one had taken up his offer to accompany him. Even Ian had remained tight-lipped. He was soon there. Playing the scene in his mind, everything came back to him in neat, precise detail. The lychgate, the layout of the interior, including the rough wooden pews, the commemorative plaques, even the hymn numbers, the ones Daniel had altered the day they had visited Sam Parsons's cottage. He was willing to bet that they were still the same.

Though it had been just over four months, in reality it seemed a lifetime away. The day both he and Daniel had accepted Sam was dead he'd felt a wave of sympathy for the old poacher. Now he wasn't sure whether he'd been the lucky one. At least for him death had been swift.

Facing the large wooden door, he felt a stab of indecision. Steeling himself, he pushed it open and stepped inside. It was exactly as he had imagined it, except for one thing, it was dark. Staring into the gloom, he made out the solitary brass crucifix sitting serenely astride the plain altar in the distance. Allowing time for his eyes to adjust to the lack of light, he made his way forward. On one side of the little building stood the tiny organ, complete with steel pipes; on the other was the board holding the hymn numbers. And he was right, they hadn't been altered.

Every single pew was full of black emaciated corpses. No evidence of any last-minute panic was in evidence. Those who had chosen to remain had accepted their fate with calm dignity.

At the base of the altar, kneeling and looking up at the cross was Daniel. It seemed fitting somehow. Studying the vicar at close quarters, his hair once immaculate hung over his shrunken forehead in a straggly heap. The virus had reduced him to a sick parody of what he had once been.

Retracing his steps, he had a sudden thought. Through the centuries, prayers had been successful in gaining the attention of God. In this instance, it appeared that the Devil had been listening too. Jumping into the passenger seat, not a word was said. Risking a glance at Samantha, he was reassured to see she was holding up. Dry eyed, it appeared something had given her life new focus. With a flash of insight, he wondered whether he and Jodie might be a part of it.

The nearer they got to civilisation, the more the reality of the situation hit home. Jared and Kinsey had witnessed the devastation from the air. Then, everything had been rendered cold and impersonal. Distance did that. Here, in close proximity to the carnage it was a different matter.

By-passing the city of Cardiff, they headed for the outskirts of London. The going was far more difficult than anticipated. The M4 motorway was a minefield. Vehicles of all shapes and sizes, many nothing but gutted shells, lay everywhere. It was as if the whole of civilisation had somehow been abducted, and transported to another world. Had it not been for the bodies it might have been an accurate assessment. The initial plan had been to follow the M4 to the outskirts of the city, before using one of the smaller arterial roads from there in. A few miles further on, they drove off a slip road and pulled in. Checking his bearings, Danny declared, "It's that way."

Almost immediately they came to the remains of a small petrol station. The scene was one of devastation.

"Looters," said Jared.

The small shops lining the road proved Jared's thinking to be correct. Jagged splinters of wood jutting from doors bore evidence of forced entry, while every single window had been smashed.

Some thirty-odd miles from their destination, Jared was forced into a decision. Bulky and cumbersome, it was becoming more and more difficult to thread the Winnebago through the abandoned carcasses of vehicles which littered the motorway as far as the eye could see. Taking only what they would need for a day or so, they made their way forward to what they were now convinced was a dead city.

Wanting to distance his little party from what was waiting for them, realistically Jared knew that it was impossible. The side streets were full of dozens of cars. Parked at all kinds of crazy angles, several bodies were slumped behind steering wheels. Inadvertently, Kathy's eyes were drawn to a people carrier immediately to her right. All that remained was a pair of jeans and a quilted parka, inside of which were bones and scraps of flesh.

The spectre of Christmas hung everywhere. Whole communities in some instances had gathered together in an effort to make their street look better than their neighbours'. The further they went, the more the bodies began to pile up. Yet the whole thing seemed so peaceful. The analogy of a wicked magician sprang to Kathy's mind. With a single wave of his wand he had frozen everyone in time. If that was the case, all it needed was a reversal of the process and everything would return to normal.

A gust of wind caught the party by surprise. Springing up from nowhere, it was powerful enough to disturb litter scattered on either side of the pavement. In several places, mini tornadoes brushed passed the group. Had it been a scene from a western, they would have been accompanied by tumbleweeds.

And then it was over. As quickly as the strange phenomena had developed, it petered out, leaving them alone with their thoughts. Pushing further into the city, they advanced slowly and in single file. Turning a corner, they stumbled onto a small square. Stopping in amazement, their immediate thought was that the object was too grand for such a humble setting. Standing before them was an incredibly ornate fountain. Boasting a complicated centrepiece, the sculpture was made up of a mixture of nymphs and satyrs. Every square inch of space had been utilised to display some mystical or allegorical rendering, one which was beyond the little party. Towering over everything was the resplendent figure of some unknown water god.

Speaking for them all, Eric said, "What's it doing here? Rather than hidden away, it should be on display in some more elegant setting."

"Somewhere like Venice, or Rome you mean?" said Kathy.

"My thinking precisely," said Eric.

Its waters reduced to a trickle, Jared peered into the bowl. What little remained was dark and stagnant. A sudden ray of sunlight afforded him a glimpse of the bottom which was covered in bright green slime. Standing beneath the magnificent sculpture, the grandiose circular bowl had provided a perfect trap for unwary insects. The remains of which were floating on top. Once they had ventured in, there had been no way out. Unless of course they'd had wings or had been afforded divine intervention. An image flashed into Jared's mind, that of a cenote. A sacred Mayan well, it was a place notorious for the sacrificing of men, women and children. Yet, those sacrifices paled into insignificance compared to the one made willingly by Medusa for his god.

Snapping out of it, Jared noticed a bird of prey circling overhead. Shielding his eyes from the sun, he squinted, trying to make out what kind of bird it was. But it was too high up to make an accurate assessment.

The further they went, the more dead birds they came across, especially pigeons.

The only thing that seemed to be thriving was rats. And if he wasn't mistaken, they seemed to be much larger than the ones he had grown accustomed to.

At times, the silence was so unnerving that even simple things like the displacement of everyday objects seemed preternaturally loud. Gradually, however, they came to terms with it.

Several toilet stops were made and in each instance, Jared and Ian checked out the buildings before allowing anyone inside. Some ten minutes or so after making the latest, they came to an abrupt halt. A group of born-again Christians lay scattered at various angles across the road. Holding placards which quoted the New Testament, they declared that as long as people turned to Jesus there was hope for them. But Jesus hadn't seemed to have done much to help his own. Instead, the virus had been impartial in its choice of victims. A question tugged at Jared's mind. When they knew death was inevitable, had they pleaded with God? Had they begged to know why he'd allowed such an appalling fate to wipe out mankind?

Studying the pitiful husks lying in crumpled heaps, Jared knew one thing: despite the fact that Medusa had died before witnessing the success of Genesis, it appeared he had been the only winner. Thanks to his meticulous planning, his vision had become a terrifying reality.

On the other side of the road was a lone figure. He, too, was holding a placard. In this instance, he was lying face down. Approaching cautiously, Jared flipped the placard over with his foot. Rather than conveying a biblical message, it carried a stark warning: 'Repent, for the end of the world is nigh.' And he had been right. The only thing the carrier hadn't foreseen was just how quickly the prophecy would be fulfilled.

FIFTY-FIVE

STEPPING INTO PROFESSIONAL mode, the easy, carefree Jared, the one they had known in the complex, was gone. He'd made no excuses. Getting the party safely to the ark was his main priority. Except for Jodie and Edna, everyone was carrying a weapon. To date they hadn't come across any wild animals, nevertheless each person was on high alert. Knowing that the virus might affect different species in different ways, they didn't know what to expect.

Stumbling across a mini shopping mall, the maze of units sitting silently on either side seemed to stare in mute appreciation at the little band of survivors.

Without warning Samantha's hand flew to her mouth. Jared saw instantly what had caused the reaction. Lying against a refuse bin on the opposite side of the street was the body of what he assumed had once been a man. It was difficult to tell with any certainty, his eyes had long since disappeared. Eaten away by rats or dogs, was his guess. Horrifyingly, although the skin had rotted away, in several places there was still evidence of muscle tissue. His face wore a vindictive grin; almost as if he was the recipient of some hidden secret, thought Jared. Unable to tear her eyes from the sight, Samantha watched in fascination as a beetle made its way leisurely out of one of the bleached eye sockets. Gagging, she turned away quickly.

Sometime later, Jared's attention was snagged by a weather-beaten sign hanging above a narrow alley to his left. Making his way towards it, he stopped and looked up. Meant to depict some famous snooker player, very little remained of the face. Putting two and two together, Jared reasoned that in his heyday, the character was probably well known. By now, however, the sign was so badly rusted, Jared felt even his own mother would have had difficulty in recognising him.

"Some kind of community centre by the look of it," said Ian standing behind.

Intrigued, they made their way into the alley. Finally, they found the entrance. Barely wider than the door of a single storey house, in comparison the windows to either side were substantial. Despite the gloom, Jared was able to make out coloured letters engraved on the window to his right. A cursory glance told him that the letters indicated the centre's hours of opening. Or had, for most of the digits had long since peeled away.

Beckoning Ian to follow, Jared went inside. The first room they entered turned out to be some kind of office. Standing against the furthest wall stood a bank of large filing cabinets. One glance was enough to establish that several of the drawers had been forced open. Loose sheets were hanging out of other drawers while on the floor the remaining paperwork was scattered around the room. The carpet, at one time a bright crimson, was filthy and decorated in places with scores of cigarette burns. The window blinds were nicotine stained, as was the ceiling. It was obvious that the smoking ban had never been enforced here.

The slats of the venetian blinds were completely shut. Allowing very little light to penetrate, it was almost as if the room was home to a nest of vampires. More in hope than expectation, Jared pressed the light switch. He was surprised when the overhead fluorescent flickered into life.

"Business was no doubt booming," said Ian, glancing over.

Further into the building, they pushed through a set of double doors and found themselves in a small bar. The room was dark and smelled fetid. Sitting around a circular table were several bodies. Though the corpses were long since dead, the pair eyed them warily, as if expecting them to suddenly spring to life.

One corpse held a whiskey glass. Long strands of white hair hung from his yellowish coloured head, indicating that he must have been an old man. Sitting opposite him were the remains of someone much younger. Wearing one of the loudest Hawaiian shirts Ian had ever seen; it was so bright it should have carried a health warning. A quick survey of the room showed that most of the other bodies were wearing faded denims. In almost every case, they were filthy with grime. T-shirts sporting all kinds of stains, none of which bore thinking about, seemed to be the order of the day. On the other side of the room, the words 'male shithouse' had been spray-painted on the wall above a split level saloon door. No female toilet was in evidence.

Catching Ian's eye, Jared joked. "Bet it was full on Thursdays."

Seeing the look he explained, "When the benefit checks arrived."

Having seen enough, they made their exit.

Everywhere they looked, the little party was greeted by death and decay. Despite what he and Kinsey had seen from the helicopter, Jared had still harboured a futile hope that, somewhere amongst the ruins of the big city, some enclave of humanity had survived Medusa's cull.

Having once been a man of the cloth, even though he had long since renounced his faith, a residue still lingered. And, because of it, the sights hit old Eric particularly hard.

Fifty-six

It was Ian who spotted them. For the last mile or so, they had been tailed by a pack of hungry-looking dogs. Keeping to the shadows, it had been difficult to make out what they were exactly, until one more careless than the rest had given their position away. Not wanting to alarm the others, Ian had simply monitored their movement. Then as quickly as they had appeared, they vanished.

Ian hated dogs, had done so since he was attacked as a child. The wound had been deep: he had needed twelve stitches. The pain had been so intense that the incident was still fresh in his memory. The tetanus shot he had been forced to endure afterwards had hurt even bloody more.

Dogs were so unpredictable. Some breeds more so than others. Four in all, the clever bastards had somehow managed to outflank them. It didn't take a rocket scientist to work out that they were roaming the streets looking for their next meal. The way they were blocking the path and the aggressive nature of their postures led Ian to believe that the leader, a huge black Dobermann, was convinced that they had found it. A thick drool of coloured saliva hung from its mouth and what few teeth remained were yellow and blackened stumps. Here and there, gums ravaged by some kind of disease displayed huge gaping holes.

One look was enough to establish that they were sick. A diet of rotting human flesh had rendered them half mad. The eyes of the Dobermann confirmed Ian's belief. There was something in the pupils that he hadn't seen in any other animal that he had ever come across before. A single bite from one of those rotten stumps could spell death. Either way, he knew that ignoring them would be to put the lives of the others in jeopardy. Risking a glance in Jared's direction, it was apparent that he, too, had seen them.

A slight inclination of the head was enough. Slipping the safety catches off their weapons, Jared and Ian lifted the muzzles of their guns. Four shots rang out in quick succession. In the stillness of the afternoon the sound was unnaturally loud. Startled, all the others saw were four disease-riddled bodies hitting the floor in rapid succession. Without another word, the party turned on its heels and headed into the distance.

Apart from the dogs, it seemed as a result of the holocaust that most animals had become wary of humans. Oddly they had seen no cats, which meant that either the virus had wiped them out or they were hiding. Perhaps they sensed that mankind had caused the demise of its own species. And if so, they should be left well alone.

Having spent so much time in the complex, the group were unused to the bright sunlight. By mid-afternoon it was surprisingly warm. Soon, perspiration was streaming down the backs of everyone. Those who had decided on two layers of clothing had shed their outer garments long ago.

For the next few minutes, each lost in their own private hell, no one said a word. The comment when it came arrived from a completely unexpected source.

"I don't know about you, Dad," said Jodie, "but seeing all this makes me wonder if there really is a God."

Taken aback, Jared said, "Why would you say that, princess?"

For a moment, Jodie was thrown. "Did you know that was Mam's favourite expression for me?"

"Of course I did, she used it often enough."

Smiling, Jodie said, "There can't really be a God. But if there is, he's either turned his back on us, or become so fed up with our quarrelling, he's left us to fend for ourselves." Pensive for a moment, she added, "There might be another answer though. Perhaps God was testing us. If so, his plan backfired, didn't it?"

Watching the expressions of the others, he saw that they were as shocked as he was. In a few concise sentences, Jodie had managed to summarise an extremely complicated situation. Terminating the conversation, Jodie wandered over to a little stream in the distance. Plucking a stem of grass from the ground, she popped it into her mouth and chewed on it furiously. Jared felt as if someone had gripped his heart and squeezed. It was exactly the kind of thing her mother used to do. A habit she never grew out of. She was so like Emma at times that it took his breath away. Satisfied there was no moisture remaining, Jodie took the grass from her mouth and tossed it into the water. The blade landed on the surface as gently as a feather. Stuck in an eddy, it appeared to be going nowhere until, unexpectedly, released by the current, it began to pick up speed.

Spellbound, she watched as it gathered momentum. In her mind, it seemed as if the little stalk was making a desperate dash for freedom. Willing it on, in the space of a few short yards it had dwindled in size. Seconds later, it was nothing but a speck. In the blink of an eye it had disappeared altogether.

After it was gone, Jodie felt a profound sense of sadness. She stood staring into the distance for what seemed an age. Finally, deciding it was time to go, she gave a tired sigh and made her way back to her father.

Knowing what horrors lay in store, Jared had steered away from certain buildings. It was Danny who said, “You’ve avoided hospitals to protect us, but what about doctors, those with quarantine facilities? Might some of those have survived?”

“It’s a possibility,” answered Kathy, “but I hate to state the obvious. There’s only so long you can go without food and water. It’s not unheard of for people to survive for a week without food, as long as they have access to water. That’s in very exceptional cases, though. To cut a long story short, if somehow they managed to gain access to a supply of both, they’d have stood a fighting chance.”

Danny fired off another question, “What kind of world can we expect when only a handful of us are expected to survive?”

“There’s no hard and fast answer,” replied Kathy. “I can take a stab at what might happen in certain countries like America. Take those cities situated in mainly desert regions.”

“Like Phoenix in Arizona?” chipped in Wolfe.

“Precisely, in areas like that, artificial lakes and reservoirs would eventually dry up. Shortly afterwards, it would be the turn of the small rivers and streams fed by those water supplies. Many of the surrounding areas once green and fertile would quickly wither and die. And of course the whole thing is accumulative. Birds and animals would be doomed. Without the benefit of life giving water, the desert would move in to reclaim its former territories. In no time the whole area would become nothing but a giant graveyard.”

“And you say all this would take place in as little as six months?” asked Jared.

“Yes. By now, many American states will be feeling the first effects.”

“What about five or ten years down the line?” Samantha asked.

"Most countries will be subjected to huge dust storms. Many on a scale never envisaged. The quantity of dust will be such that it will infiltrate every nook and cranny. High-rise buildings in particular will be vulnerable. The windows will shatter over time and provide no defence against its remorseless invasion. Eventually the floors will be covered in deposits several feet deep."

"But there's worse to come, isn't there?" said Wolfe.

"Heat rising from the sun-baked earth will create its own mini climate. Storms will sweep across the surface of the earth and the dust will turn to mud. The weight of the mud will bring buildings crashing to earth."

She added, "Those areas that rely on man-made canals and irrigation ditches to protect the low-lying land will become overrun. Millions of square miles will be turned into nothing but vast swamps."

"Plant life, will it take a stranglehold?" asked Tina.

"Undoubtedly, in the absence of mankind and its pesticides, aggressive plants, those invasive species such as rushes and vines will take hold. Within say fifty years or so, many of the major cities will be unrecognisable. It'll be a whole lot worse in equatorial countries. By that time civilisation will have disappeared completely."

"In much the same way the ancient Mayan empire did," said Jared. "The jungle didn't take long to hide almost every trace of its existence, did it?"

Nodding her head, Kathy said, "As difficult as it is to accept, the same thing will happen here. Only it will take longer. Even the mightiest structures ever built will eventually come crashing down. Without constant maintenance the vagaries of the weather will undermine their infrastructures. Wood rots, iron rusts, it's a simple fact. There's no escaping the inevitable."

FIFTY-SEVEN

TO DATE THE journey had required more walking than Jared had envisaged and it was beginning to take its toll on some of the party. But there was something else. For the last few miles Jared's sixth sense had gone into overdrive. For a while now he'd the distinct impression that someone or something was stalking them. On several occasions, without alarming the others, he had dropped behind looking for signs of pursuit. Yet, try as he might, he could find no evidence of any tracks, either human or animal. He had scanned the area thoroughly, in particular high-rise buildings, for a glint of metal in the off chance that someone might be scoping them through the lens of a sniper rifle. But he couldn't see anything. Not that it would have done any good, as Jared well knew, if there really was someone following them, and he was a pro, he would have taken every necessary precaution to avoid detection. After one final sweep, Jared reluctantly dismissed the thought from his mind and hurried to catch up with the others.

Reaching them, he studied the little group. Eric was holding up reasonably well. His grandmother was a different matter. A few rough mental calculations told him that they'd travelled at least fifteen miles. According to Kinsey, they had at least that left before reaching the ark. The further they'd ventured towards the centre of the capital, the more Edna had become withdrawn. And she didn't look well. Unknown to the others, she was consumed by guilt. The euphoria of knowing that she had survived when so many had perished had quickly faded, to be replaced by a feeling of disquiet. During the last hour she had embarked on a journey of self-analysis. She had begun to question why someone like her, someone who in her own eyes was well past her sell by date, had been spared, when so many young lives had been callously snuffed out.

The majority of the bodies they'd encountered hadn't smelled as badly as they had envisaged. The stench in the streets, sometimes unpleasant, hadn't been noxious or foul. It meant one thing: the corruption had run its course.

Kathy knew that in the first few weeks, the body's internal organs would have putrefied, before disintegrating shortly afterwards. During that time, contamination levels would have been at their most dangerous. What was left of the victims had by now rotted, leaving nothing more than skeletal remains.

Attempting to clarify the dangers, she explained. "Once a person dies, it takes only a few minutes for the process of decomposition to begin. In no time, the body becomes a veritable gourmet meal for organisms such as bacteria. Soon afterwards it becomes the turn of the insects. Once they've satisfied their hunger, they pack their bags and desert the host. In short, heat and humidity speed up the process of decomposition, animals and insects accelerate it."

"Sounds like some kind of primitive pecking order," commented Gareth.

"As a matter of fact, that's a fairly accurate analogy," replied Kathy. Continuing, she said, "Unless outside agencies are brought into play, physical decomposition works to a specific timetable. That's why this year's severe winter was so beneficial. It not only slowed down the rate of decomposition, it stopped typhoid and other contagions from taking hold. Not that it mattered to the poor devils lying around here," she added as an afterthought.

Shortly after, they came across a nest of pavement cafes resting snugly on the side of the road. On the one side, sitting beneath a substantial wooden bench, was a huge mound of leaves. For some strange reason they were dark and brittle, the legacy of the strong winds that had swept through the area earlier.

On the opposite side stood the cafes themselves. At first glance it seemed each one of the owners had attempted to outdo each other in terms of producing the most brightly decorated tablecloths. Though the battered aluminium tables were rudimentary, they were pleasing to the eye in a rustic way. Flanked by several massive oak trees, the bright colours added to the overall appeal of the location.

Before the advent of the virus, the branches were no doubt trimmed regularly. Yet, despite the fact it was still mid-April, many were growing at an alarming rate. At their present rate of growth Jared was convinced that it wouldn't be long before they would be running wild.

Several of the smaller twigs looked like hands, hands wrapped in brown paper. In Kathy's imagination the ends became fingers, the nails sharp and yellow. A few more daring than the rest seemed to be making their way remorselessly across the fabric of the tablecloths. To what purpose she hadn't a clue.

Fanned metal sheets protected the roots of the huge trees. The trunks were reminiscent of columns supporting a Gothic church. Matt black, they looked oddly out of place in relation to the rest of the surroundings. Wooden boxes painted a bright red and filled with sand were placed strategically at the foot of various tables to capture any stray cigarette ends. Baskets filled with flowers of all varieties hung from upstairs windows. Once a riot of colour, without the care and attention of their owners, they had long since withered and died.

The only other things of note were the by now familiar

bodies, either sitting or slumped across tables. Their rotting clothes had long since become their burial shrouds. Edna, who until now hadn't uttered a word, voiced what was on most of their minds, "It's hard to believe these desiccated husks were once living, breathing people."

It was Jodie who noticed the graveyard and drew the others' attention to it. The cemetery had once been tended to lovingly, but now, with no one left to care for it, the weeds and grass had run amok. It looked a sorry sight. Most of the headstones were covered by ivy and thick rushes. Here and there a few names could still be made out. Peering closely, Eric read a few. Shaking his head, he knew that in most cases these people had been forgotten by most and remembered by few. It was a phrase he had once heard someone use to describe war heroes. He had been so impressed with it that it had stuck in his mind ever since. A more morbid thought struck him. Who would be left to remember the dead after their days? Who would be left to grieve for them?

In a world of her own, Edna began to pray quietly for the sound of other voices. Even for the sound of a car. Even a television would do, she told herself. Anything to destroy the knowledge that apart from their little band, and the survivors left in the arks, they might be the only people left on earth. Unknown to her, the same thoughts were going through the minds of the others.

A mile or so further on and traffic lights began to appear. Perched on top of the nearest were several large crows. At least they looked like crows, reasoned Wolfe. Not being an expert on birds, he wasn't sure. Perhaps they were ravens. Something clicked in his head. He recalled the legend that maintained if ever they deserted the tower, London would fall. Should that be the case, for once an old wives' tale had turned out to be true.

As if reading his mind, Kathy said, "Forget it. They're not the ravens that used to guard the Tower of London."

"How can you be so sure?"

"Each one had a wing clipped. Unable to fly far, they couldn't escape, get it?"

"Appears someone took the legend seriously anyway," quipped Danny.

"It was more to do with finance than romance, I'm afraid. Attracting the tourists as they did, they became a source of much needed revenue. Contrary to popular belief, that they'd lived in the tower for centuries, most experts became convinced early on that the legend was nothing but a typical piece of Victorian romance. Historians scoured the records and found no hard evidence to suggest that they were ever there before the late nineteenth century. Either way, the tower was definitely raven-less by the Second World War. Some were killed off in the bombing raids, while others simply died of shock. When the tower was reopened to the public on January the 1st, 1946, the ravens were back in place. Who obtained them and how is a mystery. But it shows one thing, by then the legend was so entrenched it had to be kept going."

Gazing down menacingly, it was as almost as if the birds could understand what Kathy was saying. Watching from beneath hooded eyes, their hate-filled expressions seemed to span the centuries. Lost in thought, Wolf wondered how many people had lived in the vicinity during the good old days. Unaware he was thinking aloud, Kathy interrupted.

"Did you say something?"

"Miles away, sorry," replied Wolfe in embarrassment. "Just running a few facts and figures in my head, that's all."

"And what conclusions did you come to?"

"Before all this happened London had a thriving multicultural society. This particular area," he said, gesturing with an outstretched arm, "is a classic case in point. At the last count, the city had an estimated population of 8 million, all of which were squashed into an area roughly 95,000 square miles in diameter. The population of the UK stood at somewhere in the region of 60 million. And now most, if not all, are dead. Just can't get my brain around it."

With darkness approaching Jared made a decision, "Time we looked for somewhere to hole up for the night." Pointing to several substantial-looking hotels skirting the side of a tree-lined avenue, he added, "Least we have plenty of choice."

The weather, until now excellent, was due to change. During the last few minutes the clear blue sky had taken on a disturbingly unhealthy sheen. As if heavy with unshed tears, Jared thought. Hurrying towards his chosen hotel, the mood lightened. Access to the impressive lobby was gained through an equally impressive set of revolving doors. To the right-hand side were two small lounges, both tastefully furnished. Opposite was the reception desk.

Until now, all the buildings they had entered had seemed to carry the same musty smell. The smell places acquire when no one has been living in them for quite some time. Fortunately this one was different. The larger of the two lounges displayed a high ceiling and boasted a huge glass chandelier. Unexpectedly, a certain episode from the TV comedy hit *Only Fools and Horses* popped into his mind; in particular, the one concerning the restoration of priceless chandeliers in an upper-class family mansion. Backing out, Jared stumbled on a sign pointing to the dining room. Next to it was a list of floors.

"What do you suggest?" enquired Jared. "Want to sleep in the lounge, or would you prefer a bed?"

Exhausted, Kathy mumbled, "I'd like a bed."

Seeing the others were in agreement, he quipped, "Your wish is my command. If you would be so kind as to follow me, madam, I'll lead the way. Leave your cases, I'll instruct the bell boy to bring them up later."

The carefree banter had the effect of taking their minds off things for a while. Reasoning that it would be wise to stay close to each other, Jared decided on the top floor. Pushing through a set of large double doors, weapon in hand, he led the way. Ascending the graceful old staircase the party made their way ever upwards. Pausing every so often, Jared listened for any strange sounds. But there weren't any. The only thing discernible was the wind, by now strong enough to be heard soughing through the gables of the old building.

Moments later they were there. Reaching the first of the doors, Jared breathed a sigh of relief: it wasn't one that required a fancy magnetic swipe-card to open. And for that he was grateful. Had that been the case, he would have had to retrace his steps and rummage through reception for the cards. There was another reason, too: his record with those things was dismal. Unlike others, who seemed to open their rooms in seconds, it always seemed to take him an age.

Turning the handle cautiously, it was unlocked. Using his foot, he pushed it open. The room was empty. There were no rotting corpses sitting in chairs, no bodies stretched out on the bed waiting to embrace him. Fortunately, all the others room were free of mummified husks too.

Each of the others reacted differently. Most crept exhausted to their beds, knowing wearily that in a few short hours it would be the start of another difficult day. Entering his chosen room, Jared saw that it was large and neat, perfect for their needs. Knowing instinctively that Samantha wouldn't want to be alone, he had invited her to stay with Jodie and him. There were two beds. Selecting the single for himself, he left the huge double for Jodie and Samantha. Sitting on the sofa on the far side of the room, ankles tucked beneath her legs, her skin-tight jeans displayed her shapely figure to perfection. Watching her father casting his eyes over Samantha, Jodie allowed herself a sly grin.

Eric and his grandmother had decided to share a room together for the sake of company. Both of them had aged, though after what they had been through, it was hardly surprising. Their features, especially Edna's, had sunk inwards, and her hair was now completely white. The horrors of what she had witnessed recently were indelibly etched into her face.

Thinking about his grandmother, Jared had a flash of insight: she and Eric were probably the last old people alive, or perhaps the last of the 'old world' might be a better way to put it.

The wind had picked up alarmingly in a short space of time. Despite the fact the room boasted double glazing, it still seemed inordinately loud. Suddenly, everything was illuminated in white as a bolt of lightning streaked across the sky. It was followed in seconds by a clap of thunder, indicating that the storm which had been threatening for the last half-hour had finally arrived. Amazingly, the electricity was still working. For the moment, at least, Jared mused. Curiously it seemed to be functioning in some parts of the city and not others. Terrified of the lightening, Jodie and Samantha looked across the room in expectation. Moments later, Jared joined them in the double bed. Legs stretched out before him he wrapped one arm around Jodie, while the other snaked around Samantha. Content, they burrowed closer.

Listening to the rhythmic staccato of the rain on the window pane was strangely hypnotic. In a short space of time Jodie nodded off. Shortly after, Samantha totally spent, followed suit.

From his vantage point on the top floor, Wolfe was staring through the curtains at the skyline of the sprawling metropolis. Not a single light apart from theirs was visible, bringing to mind the analogy of a ghost city. Lost in his own little world, his mind began to dwell on happier times.

"A penny for them," said Kathy.

Smiling, he told her what was on his mind. "Should the world ever recover, the present generation will become a glaring example of mankind's greed and stupidity. There's an old saying, 'you reap what you sow'. According to that homespun philosophy we contributed to our own downfall. We can't say we weren't warned. The signs had been there for decades but, intent on making as much money as possible, we chose to ignore the fact that the country was heading towards the abyss. In the end everyone was too busy to care. Blinded by the need for material wealth, we sat back and watched as the world stripped of its moral guidelines was turned on its head."

"That was before your time," said Kathy in his defence.

"But I could have, should have gone on air earlier. At least then people might have had a fighting chance."

"How would that have made a difference? You made the announcement as soon as you were aware of the situation," said Kathy. "It wasn't your fault it was already too late, that the vast majority of the population had already been inoculated. Besides, I'm not sure the broadcast was of any benefit," she continued.

"The revelation led to confusion, disbelief and eventually widespread panic. No, David, as things turned out, most died so swiftly they were blissfully unaware of the true horror waiting in the wings."

"I could have phoned Paul sooner. And there were others in the cabinet I should have contacted. All of those and their families might have survived had I been more decisive."

"Same thing applies. By the time we knew what was going on it was too late. Remember, you as PM were supposed to receive the first shot. But for the fact that you and I were busy investigating Medusa Industries we too, would be dead. It's a miracle we're alive. All those of importance, and that includes the cabinet and their families, the opposition and so many more had already been vaccinated. By the time we had evidence, the virus was already in the bloodstream of most of the population. And remember one thing: it's exactly what medusa had counted on."

FIFTY-EIGHT

EASING HIS WAY out of bed so as not to disturb the others, Jared drew the curtains a few inches and peeked out. It was going to be a fine day. Leaving Jodie and Samantha to catch up on their sleep, he dressed and made his way downstairs. Standing in the street, he looked around. Gloomy, in a few minutes dawn would break, dispelling the last few lingering vestiges of night. As a result of yesterday's deluge, the landscape would be washed clean. Sparkling, it would be bursting with new found energy.

Cupping his hands to his eyes, he watched spellbound as slowly the scene was transformed. Spreading like ghostly fingers, the sun's rays crawled across a landscape fronted by high buildings and waste land. Over the rise, the towering office blocks stood out starkly against the first flush of dawn. His spirits lifted, he made his way back inside.

Breakfast was a hurried affair: the remnants of what they had brought with them. To Jared's mind everyone looked a little better this morning, especially his grandmother. Last night's sleep appeared to have done her the world of good. He didn't get too carried away as he knew there was still some way to go. Worryingly, the nagging feeling that they were being followed was still with him.

About two hours into the journey, he turned to Kinsey, "How much further?"

Doing the mental calculations in his head, he replied. "About another two hours by my reckoning. Can anyone spot the Thames?" he asked.

Jodie's young eyes saw it first. "There it is, Kinsey, to your right."

"Then it's that way," he declared.

Following the direction of her outstretched arm, the others suddenly saw it. Coiling smoothly into the distance, it looked like some monstrous grey eel. Sometime later, prompted by the need for a break, Jared asked if anyone wanted a drink.

Dropping her pack and unzipping the back pocket, Samantha removed her water bottle.

"Not from the ration packs, from a real bar. That one over there," he said pointing to the opposite side of the road. Following his gaze, the others saw what he was looking at.

Stepping inside, they had a pleasant surprise. The whole thing had a distinctly 1960s or 1970s feel to it. Almost every inch of available space was filled with posters of various rock bands, bands that had been big some forty odd years ago. The bar itself was decorated with signed photographs. Standing proudly in one corner was a huge juke box. In remarkably good condition, many of the songs were familiar to Jared; others were way before his time.

"Reminds me of the day I left you and Jodie near Trafalgar Square," said Danny addressing Jared. "Soon as you'd disappeared I went for a stroll."

"You never go for a stroll, Danny, what were you looking for?"

"A pub," came the answer.

"Should have known," said Gareth and Tina in unison.

Holding up his hand, Danny countered, "Not just any pub, the Harp was the first in the capital to be named national pub of the year."

"How did you get to know about it?" asked Gareth.

"CAMRA. For the uninitiated that stands for The Campaign for Real Ale. Described as a small friendly independent house, the article went on to say it had rapidly become a haven for beer drinkers. Note the word beer, real beer, not this chemical crap they serve up these days." As soon as the swear word had left his mouth, he looked for Jodie and Edna. Fortunately they were out of earshot.

"And inside?" asked Jared.

"Brilliant."

"Brilliant in what way?" asked Wolfe.

"No bloody intrusive music, not even a TV."

"Odd." said Gareth turning to Jared and winking. "What kind of pub is that?"

"One that caters for people who enjoy their drinking," came the reply. "Nothing is allowed to detract from the serious business. Yards from Trafalgar Square, it boasts eight different varieties of real ales and a generous selection of ciders. A real gem it is."

Listening to the banter in amusement, Ian eased himself into one of several chrome chairs. Letting his eyes wander around the room, he took in the gaudy linoleum floor, the art deco salt and pepper shakers and the almost antique napkin holders. Each of the tables housed a bottle of ketchup. Though Heinz was emblazoned on the sides, he would have bet a month's wages that they contained something less expensive. He felt as if he had stepped into the Twilight Zone.

Thankfully, the place was free of any bodies and so they spent a pleasant half-hour browsing through the posters and helping themselves to whatever took their fancy.

Unwittingly, the little bar had become a port in a storm. Somewhere for a brief while where they could forget the horrors of the past. Sadly, the illusion was to prove all too fleeting.

Crossing a section of waste ground, Samantha looked nervous. The grass was almost waist high, bringing to mind images of creepy crawlies. Still, she reasoned, as long as there were no snakes she would manage. Please let there be no snakes, she chanted soundlessly. She had read somewhere that adders, the only poisonous reptiles in Britain, are more afraid of us than we are of them. At this particular moment, though, she wasn't sure if she wanted to put that theory to the test. As a matter of fact, she told herself, she was sure she wasn't.

To repress her fear, she bit down hard on her lip. Seconds later she was back in control. But there were no snakes. In a determined effort not to lose sight of the others, she pushed forward hurriedly: the thick stalks of the tall reeds whipping at her legs made her thankful she was wearing jeans. Shortly after, they reached the other side. It was then that she spotted the tiny park. Making her way over, she was halted in her tracks. In the far corner were three empty swings. Disturbed by a sudden gust of wind, they began moving soundlessly. It was almost as if they were being pushed by some invisible entity. To her left, she noticed a small merry-go-round. And then she saw the bodies. In one instance, a young child and her mother lay half in and half out of the brightly decorated carousel. Gripping her daughter's hand tightly, the mother had died leaning backwards, her head brushing the floor. On the other side, a mother and child clutched each other in a final loving embrace. The scene was so peaceful it looked almost as if they had simply fallen asleep. Near the bodies, a doll lay in a sitting position, its bright yellow hair platted in pig tails at each side of its head. The eyes, a deep sapphire blue seemed to bore into Samantha's with an accusatory stare. It was the final straw.

Sliding to her knees in a gesture of abject submission, she pummelled the floor with her fists in fury. Tortured sounds escaped her throat and she was unaware of anyone besides herself. Her dull lifeless eyes looked through Jared and into a void only she could see. A short while later, sobbed out, she lifted her head to the sky. For the first time in her life she now understood, really understood, that there was a thin dividing line between sanity and madness.

Desperately wanting to hold her, Jared sensed that she needed space. Instead of intruding on her grief, he allowed her time to marshal her thoughts. And it worked. Moments later, dry eyed, she joined the others.

Several miles distant from their destination, Kinsey beckoned Jared over. "Before we reach Green Park and Down Street, we should give the others a taste of what's in store. The underground, I mean. People react strangely when confronted with confined places and darkness, so a trial run might be a sensible precaution. What do you think?"

Seeing the sense of Kinsey's reasoning Jared agreed. Calling them into a huddle, Jared explained the situation. Surprisingly, there were no dissenting voices. Heading for the nearest tube station, the fact that Edna had fallen behind had escaped their attention. Lost in her own little world, she suddenly snapped out of it. Looking up she thought, it couldn't be. Rubbing her rheumy old eyes with the heels of her hands, she refocused. She hadn't imagined it. Standing mere yards away was some kind of huge cat. Knowing nothing about wild animals, she hadn't a clue what it was, only that whatever the species, it looked distinctly dangerous.

The adult leopard, a magnificent specimen simply glared at her. By now the others had seen it too. Soundlessly, Jared and Ian lifted their weapons. Guessing their intentions, Jodie stopped them. In a whisper, she said, "Don't shoot, Dad. It's as frightened of us as we are of it. I couldn't do anything to save the dogs, they were dying. She's fit and healthy."

Talking from the corner of his mouth, Jared asked, "How do you know it's a she?"

"Because she's pregnant, silly," was the reply.

Embarrassed, it was then he noticed the distended belly. Inching her way towards her grandmother cautiously, Jodie began talking in soothing tones to the leopard. With a start, Jared realised what his daughter was about to do. He knew that she had a special way with animals, he had seen it first-hand. And her teachers had informed him she'd done much the same thing with all kinds of pets. But this was a fully grown leopard, for Christ's sake. Frozen to the spot, he felt as if his insides had turned to ice. As Jodie was between him and the animal, even had he wanted to he would have been unable to get a clear shot. Looking at Ian, he knew that he was facing the same dilemma. And so he watched the whole thing pan out in slow motion. Once her grandmother was safe, Jodie inched her way forward. At first, the beast was spooked. Lifting its head, it snarled a warning. The nearer Jodie got, the more it became perplexed. Ten yards turned into five, five became two; suddenly, she was within touching distance. Sensing the little girl meant no harm, the beast turned its head from side to side. Talking quietly to the leopard, the others were too far away to hear what was being said. As they gazed in stunned disbelief, the animal suddenly dropped its head and allowed Jodie to stroke it. Within moments it seemed to have accepted her completely, allowing her to cradle its head in her arms. Whispering something in its ear, the leopard stepped back. Taking one last lingering look at the others, it growled menacingly, before turning smartly on its heels and heading into the distance.

Wolfe broke the silence. "Dear God, did I just see what I thought I saw?"

"I knew exactly what she was going to do," said Jared. "By then it was too late. Believe me, she's just taken ten years off my life."

Bending down and tousling Jodie's hair, he surprised her by asking, "Is her mate around?"

"Watching from the shadow of that building over there," she said pointing to the other side of the road. "But he's gone now."

"Where the hell did it come from?" asked Ian in bewilderment.

"London Zoo probably," replied Jared.

"But wouldn't the animals have died of starvation – seeing as they were locked in their cages?"

"Solution's simple," said Jared, before explaining what he and Kinsey had witnessed in Bristol Zoo. "So I suppose the same thing happened here. Many of the animals were released before the virus took a firm hold."

"If she gives birth, it means there's a glimmer of hope for some of the animal kingdom at least," said Kathy breaking into the conversation.

FIFTY-NINE

THE ROAD LEADING to the entrance of the subway was narrow and long, the street chocked with vehicles of every description. Surprisingly, the area was relatively free of bodies. Outside the tube station was a flower stall. A cursory examination showed that the exhibits, like the owner, had long since withered and died.

Scanning the surrounding area in a wide arc, Jared and Ian gave the place the once over. Try as he may, Jared could not rid himself of the feeling that he was being studied. Once again forcing the thought into the back of his mind, he took the lead, while Ian, weapon at the ready, brought up the rear. Ian's eyes were never still for a minute as the incident with the leopard, though amusing in hindsight, might well have ended very differently. Since then his alertness had intensified.

Unknown to Jared, his sixth sense had been right all along. There had been someone stalking them. Adjusting the focus of the telescopic sight, Lucifer allowed himself a chuckle. The hairs of the scope were fixed directly on Jared's forehead. And it felt good. Easing his finger from the trigger of the Dragunov sniper rifle took all of his considerable will power. He wanted Jared so badly it hurt. But it was too easy. For the whole of yesterday he had stalked the party, and now the moment had finally arrived. First, he would take out the two oldest and then he would take his time with the others; turn it into a game. Never spontaneous, his sadism was always premeditated. It was why he had chosen to wait until the survivors were in sight of their destination before taking action.

A single shot rang out. The sound took everyone by surprise. Birds erupted from trees, while nearby a huge rat rummaging through one of the large rubbish bins at the side of the road made a dash for freedom. Such was the velocity of the high-powered round that Eric was spun around like a top. Hitting the ground amidst a spray of blood and gore, he jerked spasmodically several times before death claimed him. Jared was already moving when the second shot arrived. This time it was Edna who fell, half her head missing. Thanks to Jared's lightening reactions, the others had already been bundled into the underground. Struggling to overcome his surprise, Jared forced himself to concentrate. There would be time for grief and recriminations later, at present his main priority was the safety of the others. Whoever the bastard was had them dead to rights. Had he wanted to the sniper could have taken out at least two more of them. But he hadn't, so it begged the question why? And then the answer hit him. He was playing with them as a cat would a mouse, which could mean only one thing, the killer was Lucifer.

The oldest of the group had deliberately been culled first: they posed no threat. Knowing Lucifer as he did, Jared guessed that he would target the remainder according to his own primitive pecking order. He, Jared, would be left until last, and for obvious reasons.

Hidden in the shadows, Jared took stock. Despite all his precautions he had been caught unprepared. He had backtracked several times, but the search hadn't been extensive enough. For the first time in his life he'd ignored his sixth sense, the one which warned him of impending danger. And because of it two people were dead, one his own grandmother, the other someone he had come to love like a father.

"Lucifer didn't die of the virus," said Wolfe breaking into Jared's thoughts. "You were right."

"Must have hidden away in the complex," said Ian. "Once we made our move he decided to follow. And of course he didn't have to rush: he knew exactly where we were heading. One thing's for sure: as long as he's on the loose we'll never be safe."

"The bodies," said Samantha, her voice barely a whisper. "What about the bodies?"

"Have to be left," said Jared. Holding up his hand to ward off the storm of protests, he added, "Goes against everything I hold sacred, but there's no alternative. It's what Lucifer wants. Anyone foolish enough to stick their heads out would be committing suicide."

Gradually the rumblings of discontent died away. The initial few steps into the maw of the underground were empty. Turning the corner, the first of the corpses came into view. Decorating a wall once antiseptic white was a piece of graffiti written in black blood. Standing several feet above the ground someone had written the letters RIP. Underneath was a street musician. Legs splayed, guitar slung around his neck, a battered sombrero covered his face. A cursory glance showed the cheap vinyl cover of his instrument still held a collection of assorted coins. It amounted to very little. Hurrying to and from the station on that particular day, the passengers must have had more pressing things on their minds. Apart from the sick bastard who had decorated the wall, thought Jared. With a savage sense of irony he wondered how long he had lasted before the virus claimed him. To his right-hand side were several other figures. Twenty yards further on and they came to the barriers. They were closed. Climbing over, they walked the short distance to the lift. It had come to a standstill months ago. Descending, each of them glanced at the posters lining the walls. On display were a variety of luxury items which until recently had been in vogue. It was another stark reminder of a time in the not-so-distant past when everything had been normal.

Reaching the platform, there were several more corpses on display, though fewer than Jared had expected. On the downside, there were plenty of rats. Kicking out at one of the larger ones who had become a little too inquisitive for his liking, the party pressed forward. Two of the bodies blocking their path stood out. The first slumped against the wall was a beggar. The cap lying by his side was empty. Unlike the musician, he must have been having a bad day. To his right was a dog, or what remained of one. Most of the body had been eaten. The rats had feasted well.

The other corpse was wearing a pinstripe suit. Inside, all that remained was a skeleton. The bones bleached white, one hand was holding a large black umbrella, the other was clutching a briefcase. An expensive one by the look of it, thought Wolfe.

Stepping over the inert figure, Ian dropped over the side of the platform onto the line. Holding out his hand he guided the others down one by one. Once they were safe, Jared turned to Ian, "Look after them till I get back."

"What are you going to do?" stammered Jodie.

"It's time to end this."

Unable to bear the fear and apprehension in Jodie's eyes, he hurried away before his resolve faltered. Retracing his steps he eventually arrived at his destination. Removing the sombrero from the corpse lying at his feet, he dragged the body further along the platform. Taking its place at the foot of the stairs, Jared stilled his breathing. Pulling the sombrero over his face so that he was unrecognisable, he played dead. For his ruse to be successful he had to remain perfectly motionless. It was then the first of the rats made an appearance. Using every last ounce of will power he possessed, he fought the urge to brush them off. If he had guessed correctly Lucifer would soon make an appearance.

Within moments he heard the sound of feet. Stopping every few yards it was obvious his adversary was taking nothing for granted. Once again his admiration for Lucifer notched up a gear. By now he was sure the bastard was looking directly at him. Had he seen through his ploy, Jared wondered? If so, he was finished.

But his fear was groundless. After a brief pause the footsteps moved away. Counting to three, Jared eased the sombrero from his head and looked up. Lucifer was ten yards away, scanning the shadows on either side of the platform. Getting to his feet slowly, he eased the twin throwing knives from the leather holder at the base of his neck. Hearing the faintest of noises, Lucifer stopped in his tracks.

"Time to finish the game," whispered Jared.

Remembering his adversary's mocking tone when he had got the better of him in the forest, Jared turned the screw. "Surprised someone of your reputation allowed yourself to be fooled so easily."

With the swiftness of a striking cobra, Lucifer turned and fired. Knowing the man's incredible reactions, Jared had anticipated the move. From that moment on everything appeared to take place in slow motion.

The knives were in the air and heading for their target as Lucifer managed to bring his weapon to bear. His finger on the trigger, the first knife took him in the throat. A millisecond later the other pierced his heart.

A look of stunned surprise appeared on Lucifer's face, it wasn't supposed to happen like this, he thought. He was Lucifer; he was invincible. Clutching his throat, he tugged the knife free.

A gurgling wheezing noise escaped his throat before a spray of bright red blood shot outwards from the gaping wound. Pitching forward, he was dead before he hit the floor. Removing his weapon from the waistband of his trousers, Jared moved forward cautiously. Lucifer was finally dead. Not prepared to take the slightest risk, however, he fired two rounds into his head at point blank range. He had one more task to perform.

Returning to the entrance of the underground; mercifully the bodies of Eric and his grandmother had not been desecrated by scavengers. Knowing there would be no time to bury them properly, he did the best he could. Forcing his way into a building on the opposite side of the road, he found what he was looking for. Placing the bodies on leather couches, he was filled with remorse. Their last resting place was far from perfect, but it was the best Jared could manage. Glancing at the pitiful remains for a final time, he mouthed a silent prayer before hurrying to rejoin the others.

Jared's face told those waiting all they needed to know. The spectre of Lucifer had finally been removed. Giving in to their emotions, both Jodie and Samantha allowed the tears to flow. Clutching Jodie to him fiercely, she whispered, "I knew you'd come back."

A firm handshake from Wolfe and Kinsey, a knowing nod from Ian and it was business as usual.

Heading into the impenetrable gloom of the tunnel, Jared paused for a moment to remove a torch from the mesh holder of his backpack. Shaking it several times, he switched it on. Instantly, the beam cut a swath through the almost Stygian darkness. There had been several groans of protest when he had ordered the others to bring them because they were heavy. Seeing what lay ahead, they could now see the sense of his argument.

Two hundred yards further on and an unpleasant smell began to drift towards them. Cloying more than overpowering, it told Jared one thing. What he had been secretly dreading was waiting up ahead. The two trains must have been travelling at incredible speeds. Such was the impact, both were pointing to the roof. The concertina effect had caused so much damage that it was difficult to tell one carriage from another. All that remained was mangled wreckage and twisted steel. The windows were shattered and bodies lay strewn along the lines like life-size puppets. Several headless torsos were on display, hanging out of windows at distorted angles. And everywhere, they heard the sights and sounds of rats. From the safety of the darkness, their eyes, tiny red pinpricks of light, gleamed at them malevolently.

By now the creatures would have eaten every scrap of flesh from the bodies and so worryingly from Jared's point of view, they would be on the lookout for an alternative source of nutrition. Urging the others on, he traversed his snub-nosed machine pistol in a wide sweep. Forsaking his beloved Sig Sauer P228, Jared had opted for something he knew could do a lot more damage. The rapid rate of fire produced by a machine pistol would be far more effective against a horde of hungry rats than a few well-placed bullets.

Playing his torch over the final carriage, he froze. Staring at him was a bright orange disk. It took him a few seconds to recognise that what he was seeing was the reflection of his own torch beam. Feeling foolish, he turned on his heels.

SIXTY

THE CONTRAST FROM pitch blackness to sunlight caught the party unawares. Shielding his eyes against the glare, Kinsey swivelled his head, "And now for the real thing."

"More difficult than what we just encountered?" asked Jared.

"No, but there's less room and the going is more tricky. It's why I wanted a trial run."

"Where the hell are we?" asked Danny.

Pointing to his right, Kinsey said, "Over there's Green Park. One of only four London parks referred to as royal. More peaceful than its neighbour, St James's Park, it's bounded on the north by Piccadilly, the east by Queen's Walk and the south by Constitution Hill. Open all year round, the paths are normally full of joggers; can be a pain sometimes." Suddenly he fell silent; unintentionally he had slipped into the trap of speaking in the present tense.

"Park's said to have been a swampy burial ground for lepers originally."

Samantha suppressed a shudder.

"Government offices and corridors linking the nearby Royal Palace run beneath the east side of Green Park and continue to the south. The glass roofs can be seen just below ground level. The rooms are thought to be conversions of some of the tunnels built as part of the cabinet war rooms from the Second World War. And that's the way we're heading."

Without the happy sounds of tourists and children the park seemed strangely uninviting. It was as if the little party didn't belong. Noticing certain areas had been sectioned off, Tina said, "Why all the works?"

"Part of an underground upgrading scheme," said Kinsey. "Due to be completed in the spring of 2012, everything was way behind schedule."

"One thing's certain," said Gareth. "It'll never be finished now."

"In terms of conversation that was a real show stopper," added Tina.

What seemed like ages later, the little party skirted the impressive Royal Thai Embassy and turned the corner into Down Street. Facing them was the ox-blood facade of Green Station.

"See what you mean about distinctive," said Jared.

"And the ground floor newsagent's is just as you described," said Tina.

Hoping to replenish their supply of bottled water they were disappointed. The door was hanging from its hinges, the windows smashed. Inside it was much the same. Everything of value had been looted. To the right stood what looked like the opening to an alleyway. Seeing Ian's confusion, Kinsey shook his head. "You've passed the entrance."

Finding the door unlocked was a bonus. Descending a narrow flight of steps, they arrived at the top of a staircase.

"Aluminium," said Kinsey, tapping the surface with his hand. "They replaced the old one in the 1970s. The original had deteriorated so badly it was dangerous." Indicating the centre of the spiral staircase, he said, "That space used to be occupied by a small two persons' lift. Installed for Churchill. Legend has it he got stuck in it on one occasion."

"Why build a spiral staircase in a disused station?" enquired Kathy.

"Down Street is a designated emergency point for the Piccadilly line. It's why unlike most other stations round here the staircase and corridors are reasonably well lit. Emergency generators must be working otherwise we'd have needed our torches by now. One thing's sure we'll need them from here on in."

Typical of so many stations built in the 1900s the walls were decorated with maroon and white tiles. Three-quarters of the way down Kinsey shone his beam at a fire door. Seemingly new, it was locked.

"An alternative route to the office complex we're aiming for," explained Kinsey.

At the bottom of the staircase, Kinsey called a breather.

"A hundred and three steps altogether," declared Jodie, "twenty-three for the staircase and eighty in the spiral shaft."

Smiling, Kinsey said, "Smells musty, but believe it or not this complex was one of the first air-conditioned places in Britain. It operated on the basis of positive air pressure."

Along the walls of the passageways several signs were in evidence. The one indicating the 'Enquiries and Committee Room' used during the Second World War was in plain sight.

"Used to be partition walls running down the centre of the corridor," said Kinsey. "They were removed in the 1960s to enable workers installing a new signalling system access; came in handy for Medusa's crew when he decided to commandeer the complex no doubt."

Turning yet another corner, the survivors came face to face with the site of the actual committee room. A little further on, they negotiated a bridge that spanned the east bound Piccadilly line. Making their way down a short staircase, they arrived at the original platform area. Standing on a small T-junction, the way ahead was bricked off. A sign to their right informed them that they were almost exactly half way between Green Park and Hyde Park Corner.

Seeing a few pensive expressions, Kinsey explained, "The maze of tunnels around here is so confusing; the line workers need something to use as a focal point."

Directly ahead was a cast iron door with meshing to either side. Emblazoned with the word Danger, Jared made short work of the lock. Seconds later they were standing on what had once been the original east bound platform. Since the 1930s it had been bricked up for almost its entire length, except for a few small grills.

"If my guess is correct," said Kinsey standing in front of a huge steel door, "this is the entrance to Medusa's London ark."

Approaching, the pulses of the group began to quicken at the prospect of meeting up with other survivors.

"How do we get in? The lock's a state-of-the-art digital thing," said Samantha.

"Don't think we need to worry about that somehow," said Jared pointing to a CCTV camera above his head. "They know we're here."

About to say something else, he never had the opportunity. The door flew open and several figures came rushing out to meet them. Hugging them tightly, it was obvious that meeting fellow human beings was a joyous occasion.

Ushering Wolfe and the others inside, they were taken aback. Never in their wildest dreams had they expected anything on such a grand scale. In a bizarre twist of fate, the spot on which the two groups were now standing was the one on which Dan Dempsey, one of the first victims of Genesis, had been killed. Though the blood had since been removed, a cursory examination would have shown that a small area, roughly circular in diameter still remained.

After the introductions, they were given a conducted tour of the shelter. As expected, a natural hierarchy had been established, one which at first glance seemed to be working. Wolfe was spared one unpleasant task. Having accessed the old man's files, the occupants of the London ark had discovered his plans for the future. Horrified initially, they had eventually come to terms with the fact that their offspring would be the first of the 'specials', as Medusa had termed the children.

As for pairing off, Mother Nature had taken care of that side of things. By now several had been living with each other for months, becoming 'couples' in every sense of the word. As had he and Kathy, thought Wolfe wryly. If the other arks had reacted in such a positive manner, there was yet hope for mankind.

During that first hour, Jared had time to reflect on how Medusa's plan had worked out perfectly. Used as incubators for the virus, mankind had been turned into a biological version of a dirty bomb. Genetically engineered, the plague had been so successful that it had instantly paved the way for phase two, to repopulate the world with people of his own choosing. His biological perfects, as they had been labelled. And on the evidence of what he had just witnessed, that was a matter of years away.

Unknown to anyone, both Anna Heche and the creature had defied the odds. In fact, Anna had lasted for more than three months. By the time she finally succumbed, she had served her purpose. A few days before her death, she had given birth to something that looked remarkably like a litter of pups. Over the course of the next few weeks the things grew at an astonishing rate. By the time Jared and the others had decided to leave the complex they had become totally self-sufficient.

The book of Genesis claims that man was created in the

image of God. What Anna had sired had nothing remotely to do with the Almighty. Her experiment had one curious side effect. From this day forward mankind would have to compete with others for dominion of her father's new world. And so, deep in the forest of Sanctuary, beyond the periphery of the light, they waited, content in the knowledge that their time would come.

Satan's Alternative is just one of a whole range of publications from Y Lolfa. For a full list of books currently in print, send now for your free copy of our new full-colour catalogue. Or simply surf into our website

www.ylolfa.com

for secure on-line ordering.

TALYBONT CEREDIGION CYMRU SY24 5HE
e-mail ylolfa@ylolfa.com
website www.ylolfa.com
phone (01970) 832 304
fax 832 782